House

of

Stone

A MAGIC CITY STORY

T.K. THORNE

CAMEL PRESS

Kenmore, WA

A Camel Press book published by Epicenter Press

Epicenter Press
6524 NE 181st St.
Suite 2
Kenmore, WA 98028

For more information go to:
www.Camelpress.com
www.Coffeetownpress.com
www.Epicenterpress.com
www.TKThorne.com

This is a work of fiction. Names, characters, places, brands, media, and incidents are either the product of the author's imagination or are used fictitiously.

Cover design by Scott Book
Design by Melissa Vail Coffman

House of Stone

ISBN: 978-1-60381-789-9 (Trade Paper)
ISBN: 978-1-60381-790-5 (eBook)

Printed in the United States of America

*This book is dedicated to my
beloved and brilliant brother Dan Katz,
who is always there when I need him.*

Acknowledgements

The first person to read my work is always my husband, Roger. I'm grateful to him for his patience and keen eye as an editor and for his constant support. He is my rock. My family has always given the priceless gifts of their support and belief in me, especially my sister, Laura, who is my cheerleader and the queen of my Super Fan Club.

Thanks also to my literary agent and friend, Kimberley Cameron, and to everyone at Camel Press, especially Jennifer McCord. Both Kimberly and Jennifer have kept me going with their belief and enthusiasm in the Magic City Stories, not to mention their wisdom and advice.

Appreciation to my beta readers and to the professionals who offered technical assistance—Birmingham Deputy Chief Henry Irby; Dan Katz, communications engineer at Johns Hopkins Applied Physics Lab; Pat Curry, retired homicide detective and medical examiner investigator; Dr. D.P. Lyle, medical forensics expert; Sally Reilly, Esq., and David Brody, Esq., and former Jefferson County District Attorney, Brandon Falls.

Finally, I want to thank all the readers who love the story and the characters. I love Rose, Becca, and Aunt Alice, as well, and am grateful that they allow me to write their adventures.

Chapter One

Witches and warlocks abide in Birmingham, Alabama in three ancient Houses—Rose, Iron and Stone. They arrived over two centuries ago to draw their powers from the abundant ores beneath and around Red Mountain. I'm the only living witch with the blood of two Houses and that makes me possibly the most dangerous thing since the atom bomb.

I'm also a police officer, a detective.

Before I discovered magic was real, I assumed I was a normal person, not knowing there was a possibility of being anything else. Unsure what to do with a psychology major and art minor, I pondered my next move after college, but the concept of a career in law enforcement never entered my mind. After graduation, I moved to Birmingham, drawn, I thought, by the desire to come home after living as a military foster child all over the map.

But it was magic that drew me back. The red diamond pendant, the rose-stone I wear under my blouse, is an heirloom of my House, the family I knew nothing about until I met my Great Aunt Alice. According to her, the rose-stone is the real reason I returned to this city—to claim it.

Whatever the reason, I found myself here and needed a job, and the police department was hiring. Entry level for all officers is a mandatory twenty weeks of police academy training and an additional sixteen weeks in the Patrol Bureau as a street officer paired with an FTO, a Field Training Officer. After that, the norm is several years duty in Patrol. You have to pay your dues with time on the street. It was interesting, challenging, sometimes boring, sometimes intense, often frustrating, and occasionally rewarding. Earning the respect of police officers did not come easily.

I loved it all.

I also loved being outside, wandering the nearby woods on Red Mountain, but for the past four months, since I came back from the hospital, I have not set a foot outside the door I am staring at—the front door of Aunt Alice's house.

"Rose, dear," Alice says from the kitchen in her native British accent. "You look very nice. It's good to see you in something besides a tee shirt and jeans. I know it's hard, the first day back to your job after a long—" Her mouth twists in sympathy at my expression. "I'm sure everything will work itself out."

"Of course it will," I reply automatically. One hand goes to my throat to contain the unpredictable panic that begins with an erratic pulse. I eye the short distance to the door. I'm not supposed to be afraid to walk out a door. I'm supposed to be the one who charges *into* danger. But four months ago, my world changed. Being kidnapped and tortured by a madman can alter a girl's perspective. I learned to be afraid. Now I don't trust myself to do my job.

On the far side of that door, I will walk into the light of a spring morning on the city's Southside, a residential area built between the 1880s and 1920s sandwiched between Red Mountain on its south and to its north, the sprawling red brick university and medical complex of the University of Alabama at Birmingham, known simply as UAB. The houses on Southside sit close together like gossiping widows, the residents a diverse mix of classes, races, and professions. Out there on its narrow streets and aging, cracked sidewalks is normal life—people going to work or getting kids ready for school. Magic is something they read in books. Not part of real life.

I'm a rookie in both worlds—a rookie cop and a rookie witch, struggling to understand the power within me. Not that I have everything figured out about being a cop. I thought I became one because I needed a job, but now I understand that what I really wanted was to be a hero, to make up for being a coward when a man killed my family. When I crawled out my bedroom window to escape him, I was only five years old. But survivor's guilt is not rational. Deep down, I believe I abandoned my family.

The bane of studying psychology is that I'm the subject of my own psyche dissection. My name is Rose, Rose Brighton, but my personality reflects the thorny part of that name. It's not a giant leap of analysis to realize I avoided close relationships all my life to keep from being in a position of letting down people I cared about. No people to care about, no letting them down.

That didn't work out so well. . . .

That failure—my best friend, Becca—thanks to me, now lies on her stomach, hands under her chin, on the living room floor before the TV. Though we are both twenty-two, Becca follows the colors and movements of the cartoon characters with the avid attention of a young child.

Will she fall apart when I step through that door and leave her behind?

Helping to care for her is the reason I moved into my Great Aunt Alice's house, along with her three cats and an assortment of potted plants from around the world. I ache for solitude, but I want Becca back.

Four months ago, she followed me into a mining tunnel and cave beneath Red Mountain, whose slope I can see from the kitchen window, and into hell at the hands of the head of House of Iron, a hell I call the Ordeal. I came out a wreck, physically and mentally. A four-year-old boy came out with life-threatening burns. Becca came out stripped of memory and personality. My partner did not come out.

Becca's natural ash-white brows knit in concentration as she follows the cartoon. My friend is trapped inside her damaged mind. Somewhere she is screaming. Or maybe it's my mind that is screaming . . .

Catching sight of me, she scrambles to her feet and grabs my hand. With a huge crescent smile, as if she has discovered a secret, she drags me to Alice's bedroom to stand before the old-fashioned oval mirror, the kind in a carved wooden frame that tilts.

Still grasping my hand, she points to me and says, "Rose-Red." Then she turns her forefinger on herself. "Snow-White."

"What?"

It's the first time she has spoken since the Ordeal.

I stare at her, hardly daring to believe it. Weeks ago in the basement of this house, I held her head in my lap, and she opened her eyes to see me for the first time since the Ordeal. Not that her eyes had been closed, but they hadn't "seen" anything since Theophalus Blackwell, head of House of Iron and the warlock who killed my family seventeen years ago, wiped her mind with a touch.

Since that awakening in the basement, Becca has taken tiny steps, learning something new about the world she has forgotten, but her attention span is extremely short. She can't focus on anything for more than a few seconds. Until this moment, she hasn't spoken a word.

I don't cry, but my nose starts to run.

She repeats the designations. "Snow-White. Rose-Red."

Only on her third try can I force my mind from the fact that she has spoken words and try to figure out what she's actually saying. Then it hits me: the Brothers Grimm fairy tale. Not the one with the dwarfs, something older. I can't remember the whole story, but it's one my adoptive mother read to me—two beautiful sisters, one dark and one light, and magic bushes that grew red and white roses.

Becca is beaming into the mirror. Other than the fact that we are both too thin, she is right that we are opposites. Her snowy eyebrows lift in delight with herself. She doesn't need the words she can't find. I can read those brows. Before the Ordeal, she penciled them a yellow-brown, and I called them her "golden arches." She never changed her white hair, but she wore contacts in addition to coloring her eyebrows to keep people from staring at her albino eyes that can shine red in a certain angle of light and freak out people who don't know her.

At the sound of her favorite cartoon in the living room, she drops my hand and trots off in that direction. I stare at the hand and realize it's shaking, and I'm light-headed. Maybe I'm not as ready to go back to work as I think I am. Among other things, I've had a serious head injury and those are unpredictable. That saved me from having to describe exactly what happened. The police department had to explain unexplainable things—my melted handcuffs and burnt hands; the charred remains of my kidnapper; the burns that nearly killed a little child and did kill my partner; and a young woman who was pretty much catatonic. Becca's condition was attributed to a severe case of traumatic stress syndrome. There wasn't enough left of Blackwell to reach any hard conclusions. It's still an open homicide case. Their best theory about what happened was that my kidnapper's (now-melted) electric cattle prod set off an explosion. They decided that a spark from the prod ignited with some kind of gas—possibly acetylene—that burns at extremely high temperatures, though no gas container was found at the scene. One of Blackwell's henchmen had fled, so it was assumed he took that evidence with him.

But it was none of those things.

It was me.

In me, the blood of two Houses flows. It is a deadly magical combo, two separate powers that I smashed together to stop Theophalus

Blackwell and have no idea how to control. But no handcuff-and-flesh-melting inferno has erupted from me since the Ordeal, so maybe I'm safe to be around.

Reluctantly, I lift my gaze to meet Rose-Red's in the mirror, eyes the same deep green as my Great Aunt Alice's, the telltale sign of a witch of House of Rose.

"You can't hide in this house anymore, Rose," I whisper.

I have been hiding, ignoring phone calls from Detective Tracey Lohan, my only other friend beside Becca. He finally gave up and just sent a text saying he'd been promoted to the Homicide Unit and to call him when I was ready. The doctor and department psychologist have now cleared me, and I have to come out of this turtle shell that is my aunt's house—the shell that I'm both afraid to leave and desperate to escape.

I take a breath and turn from the merciless sheen of the mirror. Today, I break out of the shell. Today, I will report to the Burglary Unit in navy pants, a white blouse and navy blazer, an outfit the old Becca helped me pick out when she was . . . herself . . . because my sense of fashion involves which tee shirt to wear with jeans. As a patrol officer, I never had to worry about clothes, because I wore a uniform. But detectives don't wear a uniform.

Back in the living room, Aunt Alice gives me a questioning look.

"Becca said something," I tell her. "She *spoke.*"

A sparkle wakes in Alice's eyes. "That's a big step."

Alice did her best to heal Becca with her own magic, but the damage to Becca's mind was too deep. Alice had to stop, hoping nature would do the rest.

Becca has resumed her position on the floor, a foot from the TV screen, this time with her legs folded under her, as limber as a child.

Alice watches me watch Becca. "It is not your fault."

Becca mimics the expressions of the cartoon characters as if she's trying to figure out how to "do" emotions.

I want to smash something.

"Rose, look at me."

There's nothing to smash except Alice's potted plants. I drag my gaze from Becca to my diminutive aunt. I have to look down because we are standing, and her head comes to the bottom of my chin. She looks about half of her 100-plus years. Even inside her own home, she wears a red wig and contacts that change her green eyes to brown. She's right to be cautious. Not only are we the last witches of the House of Rose—she is supposed to be dead.

As if she senses my distress, my little gray cat, Angel, removes herself from the company of Alice's three cats and weaves a figure eight between my legs, rubbing her head and the ragged piece of her left ear against my ankles, marking me with her scent as her property, according to Alice. Why Angel wants to claim me is beyond comprehension. I am cat illiterate.

"What happened to Becca is not your fault," Alice repeats stubbornly. "You did what you had to."

Her words are ants scampering across the surface of my brain. I hear them, but they have no meaning. This has not stopped her from saying them at least once a day.

I change the subject. "Are you sure I can leave?"

Alice glances at Becca. She knows I'm not talking about my own health. My body has healed of its injuries—a head wound, shocks from a cattle prod, and severe dehydration. The cadre of doctors at UAB have had to admit no signs of damage remain visible.

Under the skin is a different matter.

"I think it will be a good thing for you to return to work. And you worrying about Becca is not going to change anything. It will work itself out one way or another. But perhaps you should have a cup of tea first."

Aunt Alice's answer to all of life's problems is a cup of tea.

"I don't have time."

"Well, don't worry about anything here. Becca and I will be fine."

I nod, my insides a churning mixture of guilt, frustration, and—*admit it*—fear. In addition to the Ordeal, I've been shot at, bludgeoned with a car, and remain a target of an unidentified enemy within House of Iron. With a deep breath, I check that my gun is indeed in its special compartment in my purse, along with my badge case, and head toward the door. I know it's best not to say goodbye to Becca and upset her. But it feels cowardly to slip out.

Nothing I can do here, I tell myself, shifting the purse over my shoulder. I've already killed the man who broke Becca's mind. I just have to live with the consequences.

Firmly, I twist the knob and pull the door open, only to find two more of those consequences standing on Alice's front porch.

One of them is a child—the same boy kidnapped by Theophalus Blackwell, the same boy who suffered severe burns in the wake of my mixing magics. His hand is patched with grafted pink-white skin that matches the swath on his face. With it, he grasps his mother's pant leg. The other hand is rolled into a fist and stuffed into his mouth in a familiar gesture.

For a moment I can't breathe.

"Can we come in?" the woman asks.

Flummoxed, I have no answer and just step back, allowing them inside.

From over my shoulder, Alice says, "Well, hello, Daniel. Hello, Mrs. Pate."

Replying around the hand still in his mouth, the child says, "Lo,"—a shortened form of "hello," I assume. Then his gaze darts to the cartoons. Releasing his mother's leg, he heads for the TV—or telly, as Alice calls it—plopping onto the floor beside Becca.

I'm rooted in shock.

"Cup of tea?" Alice asks.

Chapter Two

I walk into the Burglary Unit office thinking my life can't get more complicated. I'm wrong, of course. My lieutenant is not happy. That is evident, even from my position at the doorway.

On my last day of training in Patrol, I shot a man in the back. That was also the day magic awoke in me. I kept my mouth shut about that part. The homicide was ruled justifiable, or, in cop terms, a "good" shooting—I did it to protect my partner, but the nuances of that were lost on the public. The chief decided to hustle me out of sight by reassigning me to the Detective Bureau, a move that didn't go over very well with my fellows. An assignment as a detective—working day hours in plain clothes—is considered an earned perk, not a position normally given to a rookie, unless the administration really wants to keep that rookie out of trouble and out of the public eye.

"What the crap are they thinking?" the Burglary lieutenant rails at no one in particular.

The two detectives in the office busy themselves in paperwork with far more concentration than is called for.

Only the lieutenant has an office, more a cubicle. The rest of the space is open with desks and computers. Lieutenant Jake Fisher—"Fish" behind his back—has thick black eyebrows, now scrunched close to his eyes, a jutting jaw and belly, and a grumpy attitude. He stands in the doorway to his office, glowering, and spots me before I can melt into the chair at my desk.

"*Detective* Brighton, glad you could make it to work."

His sarcastic emphasis on my title is meant to draw attention to the fact that I have no business being in the Detective Bureau, despite the fact that I have been assigned here for several months. Granted, the last four I was not actually working. Some of my time off from work was to heal from my injuries and some of it was on administrative leave while the incident—the Ordeal, which involved a couple of bodies—was all being investigated.

Fish does not have to verbalize that he is not happy that one of his detectives got herself held hostage by a deranged man who "somehow" spontaneously combusted. It was all over the news, including the fact that I was the same officer who only a few months before had shot a man in the back. All this did not sit well with the Department's plan to keep me out of sight and let things quiet down.

"Do you think you can just sashay in here any old time you feel like it?" Fish demands.

I know it's a rhetorical question, but I want to say—*Sorry, sir, but as I was about to leave for the office, a woman and her child showed up on my front porch, and I couldn't leave because I was responsible for the magical fire that burned the boy's face, hand, and back, and nearly killed him. Okay?* Instead, I tighten my lips and find my desk, wishing Tracey Lohan was here to fill me in on what's bugging Fish. The lieutenant was obviously worked up before I showed my face in the doorway. Tracey, however, has been whisked away to Homicide to fill the vacancy left by another of my victims.

My life is really complicated.

As quietly as I can, I slip into my chair. A stack of paperwork halfway to my shoulder sits there. Apparently, no one decided to help with my caseload while I was recovering, at least with the routine stuff. Somewhere outside, a car backfires and I flinch. For a second, I'm paralyzed with fear. My pulse beats a fitful rhythm in my throat. Looking down, I realize my fingers are clutching the edges of my desk. Thankfully, I don't dive under it. With luck, no one saw my reaction to the *pop* of the backfire. Dark curls hide the sweat beads on my forehead, and I manage to wipe them surreptitiously as I pluck a report from the stack.

"In my office, Brighton!" Fish says before I can read it.

No one looks up or gives me a clue what is going on. He has already chewed me out for being late. How could I possibly be in more trouble already? I've been back at work less than five minutes.

Scowling, Fish plops into his chair, which barely contains him. I stand at the doorway to the cubicle, because there is only room for his desk and one empty chair that he has not invited me to sit in.

"I don't like this one bit," Fish says.

"What, sir?"

"Do they think they're the only ones having to work with no people? Do they think they have the only crimes going on in this city?"

I have no idea who "they" are and decide the best response is to wait until he elects to tell me.

With a yank, he snatches open the top drawer to his desk and pulls out a round can, spitting a wad of brown tobacco into the trash basket.

My nose wrinkles in distaste.

"Homicide is short-handed and wants one of my people." He glares up at me as if it's my idea.

"Why?"

"They don't teach you what short-handed means in college?"

I bite my tongue. No point in rising to the bait.

When I don't answer, he says, "They got too many dead bodies lying around and not enough living bodies to count the corpses." He leans back in his chair, which creaks at his weight and looks like it might tip over if he goes an inch further.

"They *say* the gang problem is responsible for a slew of homicides, and all their experienced detectives are working cases. They *say* they need somebody to work the routine homicides and the other stuff. That's what they say."

I remain silent.

"What *I* say," he mutters, his face flushing red, "is that they are using the gang stuff as an excuse to grab one of my people."

All the departments play this manpower game. All claiming to be short-handed. Actually, all of them *are* short-handed, and they each have to make a case as to why they need people. Patrol wants the Detective Bureau to give up bodies; Robbery cries they need people from Vice/Narcotics; and Vice/Narcotics plucks people out of Patrol. The Burglary Unit probably has the hardest time keeping people, as it is on the lowest rung in the Detective Bureau in terms of priorities and internal status.

"If they think I'm sending my best detective, they are smoking grass, because they already got him."

"Lohan?"

He grunts. "Damn straight."

I have no idea why Fish is telling me this. There is no way he is going to send me to the elite Homicide Unit.

"I'm sending you to Homicide," he says, cramming a wad of fresh tobacco into the other side of his mouth.

My mouth opens.

"Don't just stand there gawking. They'll throw you back soon enough. Report to Homicide. It's right down the hall."

Chapter Three

The Homicide office is down the hall from the Burglary Unit in the Administration Building. The only person I know there is Tracey Lohan. A few months ago, I would have said I had no friends and didn't want any. Now I have two, and Tracey is one of them. If he knew that Becca was in the shape she was in because of me, he might not want that status.

Enough with the guilt trip.

When I walk into the Homicide office, I feel the attention of everyone. I'm used to that in a roomful of men. Becca once told me, "Honestly, Rose, you'd think you don't like being gorgeous."

"I don't," I said.

She'd squinted her eyes at me the way she did when I told her I didn't like to shop. When she finally believed me, she declared me genetically defective. Maybe I am. I pushed boys away as a teenager and even in college, only going on a few dates. It wasn't hard there because there was no lack of beautiful girls on the University of Alabama campus, and I refused to do the sorority thing. I dressed down and let my overly curly hair live in its natural, wild state. Even so, I'm used to drawing men's gazes, but this is different. Hostility clots the air. My mouth flattens in a grim line, and I tilt up my chin. *Screw them.*

"Rose!" Tracey Lohan's voice is a haven. He is difficult to miss, especially when he stands. Brown hair and a square jaw remind me of Paul, my deceased former partner. That's the only resemblance. Paul had been short and square, intense, while Tracey is a big-boned, clumsy bear with an open smile.

I step closer and ask quietly, "Who's the lieutenant here?"

"Faraday." He points at the glass cubicle similar to Fish's.

I give him a quick nod of thanks and report to the lieutenant.

Lieutenant Faraday is a block of a woman with coffee skin, a strong nose, and a haughty bearing that makes me think of African nobility. She wears her dark hair cut short in natural tight curls. Dark-framed glasses magnify her piercing eyes. I stand in her doorway a good minute before she looks up over the glasses.

"Brighton?"

"Yes ma'am."

She sighs. "How long have you been in Burglary?"

"Um, almost seven months, but I've been on leave the last four of them."

"Well, I guess I asked for a warm body."

I don't know what to say.

"Are you sure you're together enough to do this? A lot of dead people to look at, and they're not pretty."

"I saw dead people in Patrol."

"I don't guess I need to warn you that your reception won't be overly warm by some of my detectives."

My back stiffens. "I didn't ask to be assigned here." *Any more than you asked to have me.*

"I'm putting you with Detective Lohan for a while and we'll see."

Her attention drops back to the report she was reading, and I take that as a dismissal. Returning to Tracey, I sit in the empty desk next to him.

"Looks like you are the lucky guy assigned to babysit me."

His gray eyes scan my face. "You okay?"

Tracey came to see me while I was in the hospital, but I made it clear I didn't want any visitors after that. That was rude on my part, especially given the fact that he saved my life by finding me in a cave under Red Mountain and getting me to the hospital.

"I'm fine."

"You're one tough cookie."

I sniff. "I could use a cookie. Are you packing?"

He grins and opens the drawer to his desk, pulling out a pack of cookies and offering one to me. Even though I don't cry, I want to because they are chocolate chip, my favorite, and because it makes me remember Paul with a milk mustache and a purloined cookie standing in the hallway of my house. That was the night my now dead partner became my lover, at least for a while.

"Welcome to Homicide," Tracey says.

My first homicide case awaits us the next day. Tracey and I ride together to a red brick administrative office in the sprawling UAB campus and medical complex. Two uniformed officers, one from Birmingham and one from the UAB Police Department, await us. We step under the crime scene tape to get to the room beyond.

A body sprawls face up on the floor behind a rich mahogany desk. My response to Lieutenant Faraday that I have seen dead men before was not a lie. In Patrol, where I worked for four months, that was the first informal test my peers imposed—how would I react to a gruesome death? I did okay and managed not to do anything "girly" like faint or vomit. But seeing dead bodies is not the same as "working" the homicide—finding out what happened and who was responsible. Other than a class at the police academy, my total preparation for this is that last night I read the first three chapters of a homicide investigation book I borrowed from Tracey yesterday.

Fortunately, there is nothing particularly gruesome here, other than the stark pallor of the man on the floor and his glazed eyes staring at nothing. Above him, rich oil paintings hang on the walls. Thick, crimson carpeting swallows our footsteps. Framed certificates cover the entire opposite wall. A credenza holds a few glass and acrylic awards, a silver-framed photo of a woman with luxurious red hair, and a small mini refrigerator.

According to the name on his door, the victim is Benjamin M. Crompton, head of the School of Public Health.

So far, no signs of foul play. Patrol called it in as an apparent natural death, most likely a heart attack. Hence, the two Homicide rookies—Tracey and I—were assigned the case. Normally, detectives work by themselves with a "team" to call on when needed, but I'm not ready to go solo for a while, as Lieutenant Faraday quickly let me know.

No evidence tech has been called yet, although the first patrol officers to arrive sealed off and guarded the room as soon as the paramedics declared a DOS—dead on the scene. Those officers will remain stationed in the hall, protecting the scene until we make a determination that all the evidence has been collected.

It's obvious from the size and decor of the office that the victim was a "somebody" at the medical center. Tracey kneels beside the body and his sudden stillness catches my attention. His face is almost the pallor of the corpse's.

"What is it, Lohan?"

For a moment, he doesn't respond. Slowly, his gaze shifts to me, as if he's forgotten I'm there. He shakes his head.

"What?" I demand.

"I know him."

That stops me. "How well do you know him?"

His mouth twitches.

"We should get someone else here," I say. "You can't work a case on someone you know."

With another small shake of his head, he says, "No, I can do it. He was a . . . professor in one of my classes here. I'm just surprised, that's all."

I study the man on the floor again. He doesn't look like he should have had a heart attack, but people in their fifties and sixties die from one every day. I stand back, near the mini fridge that rests on a counter, my gaze traveling around the room. Maybe he had a stressful job. Maybe he had a lot of drama in his home life.

Without warning, the witch part of myself engages. Unbidden, a sudden golden warmth of energy flushes over me from my toes to my head, suspending me in the color-leached, unfocused world of a time flow. This is my particular "gift," to see the past or the future related to a place. I can't control when or what I see, even though I can draw energy at will from the living-green. That is the term House of Rose witches use for the source of their magic—underground deposits of coal. Although it is no longer "living," coal contains the essence and energy of plant life condensed eons ago by the weight of earth and stone.

On the floor in the office, black and gray shadow-figures of paramedics huddle around Crompton's body and move backward, indicating that I'm seeing the recent past, a vision I know only I am privy to. The scene ripples, as if I were looking through a bad reception. They lift him from the floor to the chair, where they leave him with his upper half sprawled on the desk. Then the paramedics back out of the door. Crompton's body animates, lifting off the desk into a sitting position in a slow-motion reversal. I'm stuck in time and can only watch as he sits at his desk, picks up an empty syringe on the desk, moves it into a fold of pinched skin on his stomach, withdraws liquid from his injection into a syringe, releases the skin of his stomach, pulls his shirt together, and gives a full syringe to a petite young woman. The woman with the syringe backs up across the room and turns to face a drawer next to the mini fridge, which is an arm's length from me. I imagine if I were in her path, she would just go through me.

She opens the drawer, then pulls an empty vial from her pocket and places the syringe needle into the vial, pushing on the plunger and forcing liquid from the syringe into the vial. After she pulls the needle out, a cap and plastic wrapper float through the air from a nearby trashcan into her hand, and she places them onto the needle, putting the full vial into her pocket. Then she opens and closes the refrigerator with one hand, the other holding the wrapped needle, which she puts into the drawer and closes.

The world snaps back to full color and reality. My head aches as if it's been forced apart, then crammed with something larger than the space available inside.

Tracey is still kneeling by the body, which is now back on the floor in the present, but I scan the desk for the syringe I saw in the shadow world. Nothing on the desk.

When he passed out, Crompton fell forward on the desk on top of the syringe. The paramedics would have been in a hurry to get him into a position where they could try to resuscitate him. In the process of moving him, several papers apparently were dragged off the desk onto the floor. Kneeling, I gingerly move them aside with a pen to keep from contaminating anything with my fingerprints. Beneath one, I find what I'm looking for—an empty syringe.

"Got something here," I say.

Tracey looks up. His eyes are shiny, and I suspect tears are a blink away, despite his claim at detachment. He clears his throat and stands.

"What?" he asks.

"An empty syringe."

With a frown, he joins me. Our hips touch in the close quarters.

He stares at the needle as if it's a poisonous snake. Returning to Crompton's body, he rolls up the corpse's shirtsleeves.

"There aren't any tracks on his arms," he says.

I can't reveal that the victim injected himself in the abdomen because there is no "normal" way I could know that. Until a few months ago, I would have sworn all this magic stuff was the product of my disturbed mind, but I know better now. It's real. And protecting the secrets of the Houses is critical, even if one faction, the House of Iron, tried to eradicate mine. If society knew there were certain people with powers beyond theirs, all hell would break out. History is filled with that lesson.

"Did you touch anything?" Tracey asks.

I hold up my pen. "Only with this to move aside the papers."

He looks down again at the syringe, his face tight. "Guess we better call in the evidence technicians and see if we can find some people to interview."

I nod. I know one person I particularly want to interview—the woman who handed this man a syringe.

Chapter Four

That evening, when I return to Alice's, I find to my dismay that Nora Pate and her five-year-old son Daniel have taken the spare bedroom. The house is already crowded with three people and four cats. Nora is an alcoholic. Children make me nervous.

Moving in with Alice and giving up my own living space was tough, but I didn't have a choice because it took both Alice and me to handle Becca's needs when she was, for all intents and purposes, catatonic. She still requires a lot of attention. The upside of the arrangement is having a real dinner every night, and Alice has given me the basement. When I go to my room, I have privacy. Angel is the only cat allowed there.

I confront Alice in the kitchen where plants sprout on every available space that gets even a modicum of light, as they do in the living room, the side porch, and the bathrooms with windows. I should list them as additional occupants.

"Why?" I demand when we are alone in the kitchen.

"Why what, dear?" she replies, her accent going heavily British, as it tends to with any hint of confrontation. It's the only thing she allows to slip in her disguise while in her own home. Otherwise, she does a good Southern drawl.

I glare at her.

She gives me a cheery smile and offers the teapot.

"You know perfectly well what I'm asking," I say, ignoring the pot.

"Would you have me throw them out on the street?"

"They have a house, Alice, only a block away from here."

"Apparently, not anymore. When Nora went to hospital to be with Daniel 24/7, she lost her job and couldn't make the rent. There is no father present and no family."

"Shit."

Alice frowns at what she calls my vulgarity, but I ignore her. She has been around a long time, over a century, and I'm sure has seen and heard things that would make me blush, even after the raw months I spent in a patrol car.

She knows I feel guilty about Daniel's burns.

"It is only temporary," Alice adds. "Go take a gander in the living room."

Fuming, I do, expecting to see Nora vegged out on the couch, which is, indeed, the first thing I see. Her thin brown hair is almost plastered to her head, her skin pale from the many days at her son's bedside. Red-rimmed eyes are fixed on a commercial, but I'm not sure she's really seeing it. Her hands, resting lightly on her knees, tremble.

No money for alcohol. I have no sympathy.

In patrol work, I stepped inside many dysfunctional, sad lives, but at the end of the call, I left. My part was over. I didn't have to take anyone home with me. This one has followed me home. My gaze slides to the floor where Becca sits cross-legged opposite Daniel. Playing cards are laid out between them.

"That's a queen," Daniel says, pointing to the face card.

"Queen," Becca repeats, head bent down to study the card, her face hidden behind the fall of fine white hair.

I draw a breath, watching without moving as he puts down the next card, a six of diamonds.

Becca wrinkles her forehead. "Nine?"

"Nope." Daniel shakes his head. "Six. Nine is upside down six."

She nods solemnly, her attention remaining on him, waiting for the next card. This is something two neurologists, a psychologist, and a counselor have been unable to achieve. I'm trembling as badly as Nora's hands, and I sit on the other end of the couch, as far away from Nora as possible, unable to look elsewhere than the miracle taking place on the floor.

When the doorbell rings, I'm loath to pull away from watching Daniel and Becca, but Alice never answers the door. The less contact she has with the world, the better. She doesn't exist anymore after faking her own death, a feat she carried off thanks to some exotic herbal extracts, a little magic, and an "in" with the medical examiner's office. Her persona is now a short, hunched woman with flaming red hair. It's a clever disguise, as her hair draws attention and the hunched position keeps anyone from having a good look at her.

As always, I check out the window before opening the door, a caution I practice since I learned that someone from the House of Iron wants me dead. I thought I had killed that someone and the problem, until I found a black rose on my doorstep, a message that the hunt is not over, and I'm the prey.

The man on the porch is the last person I ever thought I would see there—Jason Blackwell, a warlock of House of Iron. There is no good thing that could come from opening the door.

I open the door.

Jason is a beautiful man. Thick gold hair and electric blue eyes, but the effect he has on me goes beyond hormonal attraction. It exists on an elemental magical level. I believe it's a rare phenomenon between Houses. My grandmother experienced it with the former head of House of Iron, a man I know nothing about except that he was named Adam, died before my birth, and was not directly related to Jason. Adam and my grandmother had an affair. My mother was the end product of that disaster, making a quarter of my blood Iron. There is a third House, House of Stone, but I have never met a member of it and know little about it.

Jason and I stare at one another. I hope he is not aware of the reaction my body has to his presence.

"Hello, Rose," he says, shattering the silence between us like a glass dropped onto a stone floor. "May I come in?"

My warning systems register high alert, but my mouth doesn't seem able to make a noise. My heart is making plenty of noise. I shake my head.

He frowns. "I realize this is awkward."

"What are you doing here?" The words come out in a rush of breath that leaves me fearful I might have a dizzy spell right here in front of him. He would scoop me up in his arms and carry me inside—*Stop! This is not me. It's the magic.*

His gaze has not wavered from me. "I cannot stop thinking about you." I've always had trouble placing his accent—Italian?

I snort. "Not a very original line."

The smallest quiver of his mouth. "Agreed, but it is the truth." He spreads his hands, palms up, as if to say he's helpless to feel otherwise.

"May I come in?" he asks again.

I ignore the jagged rhythm of my pulse and glare at him. "If House of Iron wants to hurt me or mine, you will have to kill me first."

"I take it that is a 'no.'"

"That is a definite 'no.'" I stand in the doorway, blocking him from entering.

"If I wanted to hurt you or your friends, I would hardly knock on your door."

I narrow my eyes. "Perhaps not." He did have a point. As a male of House of Iron, Jason Blackwell could temporarily "enslave" anyone not of the Houses to his will with a touch and a suggestion. He could make the postman walk up on the porch and shoot me.

I reach for the familiar reassurance of the living-green beneath the ground. The warm gold hum of energy fills me. Expecting it to be a comfort and bulwark, I'm stunned to find it heightens the magnetic pull to Jason. Beads of sweat pop out on my forehead, and I dump the magic as fast as I can.

Scanning the porch, Jason moves to one of Alice's wicker rocking chairs and sits.

"I am prepared to wait to talk with you," he says. "As long as it takes."

This could be more than awkward. He cannot learn that Alice is alive, and I will not expose Becca to anything threatening. She is fragile, and this connection with Daniel . . . maybe— I stomp on the hope. Alice says to focus on and be grateful for each tiny step she can make. She's right. I can't expect more or push her.

With a deep breath, I sit in the other chair facing him, glad for the little wicker table with a blooming orchid on it between us. Alice's orchids seem to always be in bloom. My back is to the rust-colored stone facade of the Southside house. Over the concrete ledges, crowded with more pots of plants, and between the rock columns of the porch, I can see a gleaming black car parked at the curb and, inside, the vague shape of a waiting driver.

"Okay," I say. "Talk."

He leans forward, and I press back against the wicker of my chair, trying to keep distance between us, arms crossed over my chest.

"I am not your enemy," Jason says. "I did not know my uncle kidnapped you."

My heart races, but this time not because of him. Memories from the Ordeal reel out: *I strain against the cuffs that fasten me to a chair of iron, deep in the heart of Red Mountain. Beside me, Jason's uncle, Theophalus*

Blackwell, lowers an electric prod to my neck. Oblivious of the urine soaking my pants or the pain of my bloody wrists, I am lost in agony.

"Rose?"

I realize I have been staring through Jason and, amazingly, momentarily unaware of the pull between us. I focus back on the now and him. He was the one who first told me that genetic mixing between the Houses was forbidden, that the offspring would be an abomination. I have not and do not plan to tell him I am that abomination. I haven't even told Alice. Having the blood and powers of House of Rose and House of Iron terrifies me. Mixing those magics caused the wildfire that killed Theophalus Blackwell and my partner, Paul, and burned little Daniel.

I speak slowly, keeping my arms across my chest, clammy hands knotted into fists under my armpits. "Your uncle shot my family and set our house on fire when I was a child. He kidnapped and tortured me. I don't know why."

Strangely, it's not easy to lie to him. I do know why Theophalus Blackwell tortured me. He wanted the rose-stone—to destroy, I presume—as only House of Rose can use it. But I have no choice. I can't tell him that. It's not just my own life that is at stake. I have to protect Alice. I don't know if Jason is part of the plot to eliminate House of Rose, but I can't take any chances. No one from House of Iron can know she is alive.

"I apologize that I did not believe you when you tried to tell me," he says. "I am also deeply sorry for what you and your friends went through at the hands of my Family, but no one is trying to kill you now. Theophalus is dead.

"I hope you do not blame me," he adds after a moment. "I want to see more of you."

His gaze is burning into mine, saying a lot more than "see more of you."

My mouth is dry as bone. "I . . . I don't think that's a good idea."

A quick, wry smile. "Maybe not, but I am giving you fair warning." The smile warms into charming territory. "I do not plan to take a 'no' forever."

Chapter Five

The petite young woman from my vision at the homicide scene is Laurie Stokes, Dr. Benjamin Crompton's assistant—straight blond hair, lots of eye makeup. Tanned. I can't tell if it's from the sun or a bottle. Tracey is handling the questions in a cramped interview room at Homicide, and I'm taking notes. Only notes, per Tracey's instructions. I get it. I'm in training. He doesn't want me to screw things up.

"And you prepared his insulin shot as you normally do?" Tracey asks her.

"Yes, the same," Stokes says, her hands flittering on the table, but her brimming eyes meeting ours. A tear breaks loose and rolls down her cheek.

"You used a vial from the refrigerator?" I ask. So much for just being a note taker.

She nods.

"Say it aloud, please," Tracey says, indicating the running tape recorder. I can't tell if he is annoyed or amused at my interruption.

"Yes, I always use the vial from the refrigerator. He takes 50 units of Lantus."

Lie. You took the vial from your pocket. Because I saw this in the vision, I can't say it. The only reason I can think of is that the vial in her pocket contained something else besides insulin, something deadly. I start to push her, but it hits me that I don't actually know what it is I see in the black and gray world. On more than one occasion, my action has changed the future, which means it's not set. Suppose what I saw in Crompton's office was just a possibility or something that actually happened on another timeline? Alice is the one with the quantum physics theories. I only have a BS in psychology and a minor in art. I realize I'm chewing on my pen.

"That's interesting that he lets you prepare his medicine," Tracey says. "Are you a medical student or a nurse?"

She flushes. "I work with him as his assistant. I'm a first-year med student."

"He must trust you a lot."

She studies her fingernails, which are polished green.

"Were you . . . close?" he asks.

A sniff. Her teeth find her upper lip, and she doesn't respond for a moment. Then finally, she puts her hand over her mouth, and her shoulders shake. The tears flow freely. I hand her a tissue from the side table, unwilling to feel sorry for the woman who murdered a man so coldly, but in admiration of her acting ability. Despite my questions about the nature of my visions, until I learn they are *not* real, that is what I'm going with.

"Yes, we were close." She glares defiantly at Tracey. Her nose, as petite as she, is red. "Closer than he was to his batty wife."

"I'm not trying to bring trouble to you or to his family." Tracey's voice is gentle, his gray eyes kind and concerned.

Frustrated, I ask, "What kind of project were you assisting Dr. Crompton with?" I remember the papers scattered on the floor were some kind of lab reports.

Tracey frowns at me. This time I've changed the subject. I imagine he's not amused anymore.

Stokes brightens, wiping her tears. "He's . . . he was reviewing the study status on a new drug. Well, it's not a new drug, zahablan—it's been around for a long time for blood pressure, but it's new as a diabetes treatment, and it's very promising."

"What stage is it?" Tracey asks, to my surprise not trying to get back on his previous track of their relationship, but following my train, despite any annoyance at my failure to follow instructions.

"Human testing. We're almost finished with a triple-blind study. We won't be able to say for sure until the data is all in, but it looked really good on the cell and animal studies, and the cases we tried it on, and it's UAB's project. It would be a breakthrough if this works."

"What happens now?" I ask.

"What do you mean?"

"I mean what happens to the research now that he's dead?"

She shrugs. "I'm sure they'll give what he was doing to someone else. There are lots of people involved."

"Would that delay things moving forward?" I ask.

She stares at me.

"Are you suggesting he—that someone *killed* him?"

He is dead, honey. I bite my tongue to keep from saying it aloud.

"We're just looking at all the angles," Tracey says. "But please answer, if you can."

She considers, blotting the bottom of her eyes to keep eyeliner from running, a lost cause. "No, I don't think it will delay any of the research or the trials."

"What happened after you gave him the insulin?" Tracey asks.

She spreads her hands. "I left. I had classes."

"Did you go to them?"

"Yes, I did."

"There will be teachers and other students who saw you during that time." He says it more as a statement than a question.

"Of course."

"Has he ever had any kind of reaction to the insulin before?"

"No, not that I know of. I mean I've only been . . . with him for six months. He never mentioned any problems, and he only started asking me to prepare his shots in the last few weeks when he got really busy."

"How long have you had an affair?" I ask, leaning forward.

She bites her lower lip again. "Just the last two months. He was lonely. His wife is nuts."

"Have you met her?" Tracey asks.

"No."

"Then how do you know she's mentally unstable?"

"Benjamin told me. He says she is agoraphobic and thinks he's been taken over by aliens."

Chapter Six

"I think she's lying," I say, sipping my cup of hot tea and downing a ham-and-egg biscuit at my desk.

"The pre-med student, Stokes?" Tracey leans back in his chair, which squeaks in protest. He's a big guy, but not like Fish. There's no fat on Tracey Lohan that I can see.

The office is quiet, most of the detectives having received their cases and hightailed it out. Lieutenant Faraday is on the phone in her cubicle, a slightly larger space than the one Fish is allotted, though he has more detectives than Homicide has—another reason the higher-ups probably acquiesced to Faraday's squawk about needing manpower.

Tracey and I have interviewed several people, including two other women in the administration section of Crompton's office, but I note that Tracey immediately assumed I meant Stokes was the one lying. Was that because he has suspicions too?

"Yes, Laurie Stokes." I watch his face carefully.

"Why do you think she's lying?"

"Well to start with, she minored in theater as an undergrad."

"Interesting, but that doesn't mean she's lying."

Uncomfortable, I take a bite to give me a moment to think, something I probably should have done before I spoke. The weird thing is that if I didn't know she was lying, I would have believed her. But I *saw* her take that bottle from her pocket. She has to be lying. I've gone over every instance where I had a vision. Visions of the past have always been true, though visions of the future are changeable. I wish someone in House of Rose with my ability were alive to help me understand it. According to Aunt Alice, my mother had it to some degree. Obviously it didn't help her avoid being murdered, which blows the hell out of Alice's theory that a vision appears when needed. Alice knows about using the "living-green" for healing, and she has premonitions, not visions—advance warnings about little things, like a feeling that a visitor is coming—but her advice about scrying wasn't terribly helpful.

I finally respond about why I think Stokes is lying. "I don't know. A hunch."

"There's no evidence it was anything but an accident."

"Why are you defending her?"

He scratches his chin. "I'm just following the facts. We don't have a report in hand yet, but I talked to the medical examiner's office."

"That's pretty speedy results, isn't it?"

"Yeah, but since we wanted to check for insulin overdose, they had to draw the sample quickly. According to my contact there, post mortem blood glucose values are negligible for everyone and pretty unreliable, and insulin is metabolized very fast. The samples have to be taken quickly or frozen ASAP to preserve it."

"So what did they say?"

"No poison involved or other suspicious substances in his body. Basically, the results are inconclusive, but they don't rule out an overdose. Apparently a very tricky determination when the victim has Type 1 diabetes, which he had."

I take a moment to absorb this. "How do we know Miss Stokes didn't give him too much insulin? That can kill someone, can't it?"

"It can and she might have." He pauses. "But what makes you think it wasn't accidental?"

That damn trap again. I can't explain it without admitting that I "saw" Stokes take an insulin bottle from her pocket. No way I'm telling Tracey that. Even though I didn't grow up with the constant admonition of secrecy like other children of the Houses, I'm not a complete idiot. To start with, I'd be considered a nut and fired. If I "proved" I had the ability to see into time, people would freak. More so if they knew there were others with "powers." The path of logic wends inextricably on: All the Houses would be ostracized, maybe targeted by hate groups—see the X-Men movies. The government could decide to quarantine us or "study" us. If they determined we weren't "human," we wouldn't even have constitutional rights. As conspiracy-theory as it sounds, it's not a path to go down, and I certainly don't have the right to put Alice or members of House of Iron or House of Stone at risk.

"I know it's your first homicide case—" Tracey says.

"Don't patronize me, Lohan."

"I'm not. It's just you aren't easy to read, you know."

"What do you mean?"

"It's hard to figure out what's going on in there." He points to my head.

If only he knew what a mess it was in there.

"You mean I'm not being rational?"

"No, that's not what I mean. You've been through a lot. I'm just saying if you need somebody to talk to—"

"Thanks. I'm fine."

"Right."

"Lohan, they sent me to a shrink. I wouldn't be back here if I hadn't been cleared."

"I'm not talking about psychoanalyzing you. Just saying if you need a friend, I'm available."

I've never been good at friends. I told Becca it was because growing up in a military family, we moved around too much to really make them. That did make it challenging, but it wasn't the whole truth. Kids make friends quickly. When I was eight, my father was stationed at Merritt Field in Beaufort, South Carolina. I made a friend, a boy my age who didn't mind that I was a tomboy. In the sticky summer heat, we climbed gray-bearded oaks near the briny rivers that wound through base housing, throwing rocks at floating sticks we pretended were alligators or enemy subs. We decided we would be together forever, even cut our fingers and mingled our blood, but six months later, his father was reassigned, and I never saw him again. Since then, with the exception of Becca, friendships have been scarce and surface things. Tracey's offer feels genuine. I just don't know what to do with it.

"Thanks," I say. "But right now, I need to talk about Crompton's murderer."

"Rose, you can't make a murder out of an accidental insulin overdose."

I STAYED AT MY COMPUTER when everyone else went to lunch, checking the Web for clues. Assuming I'm not unbalanced or misunderstanding my gift, Dr. Benjamin Crompton was murdered. Why?

No criminal record. Married. No children. An affair with his assistant who wielded the murder weapon. Could be a big life insurance policy involved. Could wife and lover be in league?

Before going to UAB, Crompton was a researcher at Johns Hopkins. He's been at UAB as head of Public Health for the past ten years and was in charge of something called The Edge of Chaos. According to the Internet, The Edge of Chaos is a "project of the School of Public Health that brings together academia, business, and the community to find real and workable solutions to wicked problems."

Hmm. Diabetes is certainly a wicked problem. The disease makes the top ten list for causes of death in the U.S. But why would a grad student want to kill someone helping to solve it? Or maybe I'm barking up the wrong tree. Maybe Laurie Stokes is an actress, and those tears weren't real. Maybe Crompton dumped her and was going back to his wife. *If I can't have you, no one else can.*

"Hey, what are you doing?" Tracey asks as he plops in a chair next to mine.

"Just looking around."

"Are we over our spat?"

"Are you going to respect my intuition?"

He grins. "Nope. I'm a fact man."

"Well, I'm a gut girl. Sometimes."

"A fairly stubborn gut girl."

I sniff, reminding myself of Alice. "Ever hear of the Edge of Chaos?"

"Sure. That's the threshold of my house on laundry day."

"Seriously."

He frowns. "It's someplace on UAB campus, I think. I've never seen it."

"It's a collaborative space, and Crompton was in charge of it."

Both of Tracey's eyebrows lift, reminding me of Becca and sending a spear of guilt into my chest about being away from her so long. *She's got Daniel now*, I remind myself. That's the flip side of the claustrophobic crowding in Alice's house.

"A collaborative space?" Tracey asks.

"They have a lot of meetings."

"They could come here for that," he says, his arm arcing to embrace the entire admin building.

"Be serious."

"Yes, ma'am."

"And what are or were you studying anyway?" I ask.

"What?"

"I couldn't find where Dr. Crompton teaches any classes. You said he was one of your professors."

Tracey nods at the computer screen. "You're pretty good with that thing."

"Since I was transferred to Burglary with no experience or training and transferred to Homicide with no experience or training, I'm doing the best I can. How did you say Crompton was your professor?"

"Wait a minute. Sounds like you're interrogating *me*."

I hold his gaze. "Just a question."

"Not this semester, a couple of years ago. He taught biochemistry."

My nose wrinkles. Anything with the word "chemistry" is not in my vocabulary.

"A brief sojourn into my father's field of study."

"It's hard to imagine you in a white coat and glasses."

He chuckles. "Now on to more important matters. Have you eaten lunch?"

"Haven't you eaten?"

"Nope. Went to visit my father. Want to grab some food at Taj India?"

Glad to have the mystery of Tracey's class with Crompton solved, I snap closed my notebook. "Now you're talking my subject."

Chapter Seven

That night after supper, Alice and I remain at the kitchen table. The kitchen is the heart of her house, and Alice has refused to modernize, other than replacing the cracked Formica counter tops. By now, the cozy room is a familiar comfort—the yellowing wallpaper with small pink flowers, pots brimming with herbs on the windowsill, and a beautiful oak table she brought from England. The chairs, however, are early American, or so Becca (before the Ordeal) informed me.

Meals and tea are served with delicate china plates and cups. I think I own a few plates in my house, which is only a block down the street, but mostly I used paper plates at home, when I bothered with plates. A paper towel usually sufficed.

The braided rope rug in Alice's kitchen covers the entrance to the basement room where Alice hid after she "died," now my room. At night, when I'm ready to retire, we pull it back so I can exit if I need to, but once I'm upstairs in the morning, the rug goes down, the table over it. The secretive design of the hidden room makes me wonder if it was used to hide liquor during Prohibition.

Angel leaps into my lap and settles into a comforting ball. It's just the cats and Alice and me in the kitchen. Nora has retreated to the living room to watch television. Daniel and Becca play a board game on the floor—or, at least, Becca is trying to play. I think Daniel is adjusting the "rules" and simplifying it to help her out.

A parade of long tails—black, black with white tip, and one dark seal—caress my knees, accompanied by occasional, plaintive *meows*. These three cats belong to Alice. I think they are unhappy that Angel is in my lap, especially Charlie, the Siamese, who is sort of head cat and usually asserts his right to first choice. Alexander, solid black as a proper witch's cat, watches from an empty chair, and Boo Boo is rubbing Alice's leg, his white-tipped tail flipping with approval when she leans over to pet him.

Talking softly—though Nora seems totally absorbed in one of the sit-coms she watches continuously but never laughs at—I tell Alice about the homicide and the vision. "I need to know how to control the visions."

She sighs, wrapping her small hands around the warm comfort of an after-dinner cup of tea. "The conscious mind can't control it, any more than it controls the pumping of your heart or the release of enzymes in your body. It works on a subconscious level."

I frown. "Then how can you heal people at will and how can warlocks from House of Iron make people do whatever they put in their minds?"

"The same way you can override the autonomic mechanisms that keep you breathing. You learned somehow to hold your breath or slow it down or speed it up. Your brain has to find the connection."

"I thought we just needed to pull on the living-green."

"Magic is something we *do* with the energy from the living-green."

"What do you mean something we do? I thought the magic *was* the living-green?"

"No, coal is an element that we draw on for energy. We use it, transform it into magic or what appears to be magic. As I've said before, I think that on the quantum level—"

My great aunt is a scientist—she's not only been a medical doctor in her long life, she was also a physics professor and is just as likely to launch into an explanation about quantum theory as she is to comment on the weather. Sometimes I have no idea what she is talking about.

"Alice," I say quickly to keep her from jumping down the quantum rabbit hole, "I appreciate the fact that magic might just be something we don't understand, but what I need to know right now is how you use it."

"Our House uses it to heal."

I flinch. Healing is what witches do, but I can't heal a mosquito bite.

"I know that, but how do you make it work . . . in non-physics terms?"

"As I said, I don't know, any more than I know exactly how my body works to pick up this cup of tea."

I must look perplexed at the interjection of tea, because she elaborates—"I don't consciously know how to send the message to my muscles and control just how much they contract. I just think it, and my brain and body does the rest on an unconscious level. But, I can tell you that I believe I use the energy to accelerate the body's own healing powers, which are quite amazing."

As if aware of my disappointment in not being able to use the living-green to heal, she adds, "Healing isn't the only power of our House. As you know, I get occasional premonitions and, in more rare cases, a witch can have the gift of seeing into time, as you do."

But my mind is whirring with what she said about the ability to speed up the body's own healing processes. It suddenly occurs to me that there might be a common element involved between healing and my ability with visions—time. Maybe I have been thinking about it all wrong. Could healing be a matter of altering time? And is that what I do, too?

Alice has told me her theories about how time may actually flow in two directions from the Big Bang. I've also been privy to hear how there are possibly multiverses where time flows a little differently in each and how I may be peering into that.

I share my thought about time and how it might be related to healing.

"Oh, that is fascinating. I have never looked at it that way," Alice says, excitement in her voice. "But House of Iron draws on the energy in iron ore to manipulate minds, alter a normal person's thoughts. I don't see how that could be related to time." She frowns, either at the concept or the canned audience laughter from the living room.

Whatever it is, the nature of our magics is complex. Other than the inferno resulting from combining magics, it's a fortunate limitation that the powers of witches and warlocks cannot be used directly on other members of a House. They also don't work in water or when a significant volume of empty air—a high-rise building or an airplane—separates us from the earth.

"What about being in an airplane?" I ask. "Isn't there something about that and how time flows differently for that person?"

"Yes, Einstein's theory of special relativity, but it's related to movement, to speed, not to heights."

"Maybe time moves differently through different mediums, the way water and gravity slow down and bend light."

"That is a novel idea," she says. "The theory of general relativity says gravity can bend space/time and gravity decreases with distance from the Earth."

"Maybe water affects gravity. I'm certainly lighter in water."

"That is the effect of the water's thrust, at least as far as we know. I'll have to give it some thought."

"What about House of Stone?" I ask. "You've barely ever mentioned them."

"Actually, I don't even know who they are. They are the most secretive of the Houses and guard their members' identities obsessively. All I know is Family lore—that they use the energy from limestone to augment their strength."

It is no coincidence the three Houses moved from Britain to Birmingham, Alabama. Uniquely, perhaps in the world, in this city is the presence in close proximity of coal, iron ore, and limestone—the three elements needed to make steel. It catapulted the area from a cornfield to a boomtown so quickly, it seemed like magic was involved and earned the new town the moniker of "The Magic City." Normal people have no idea of the irony.

"Then it's not the living-green, the coal itself, that produces magic," I muse aloud. "It's me." I can feel my brow furrow in frustration. "I need to learn how to control it."

"How did you learn to hold your breath?"

"I have no idea."

"And I have no idea how to teach you to do it. I know that focusing is part of it, but sometimes it is like looking at a distant star at night."

"What does that mean?"

"If you look at the star directly, it disappears, but if you look to the side of it, you can see it."

Great, that is so *not* helpful. Focus, but don't look directly. I sigh in frustration. "What about the rose-stone? Is there anything you can tell me about using it?"

"I thought you had used it to reach the living-green," she says. "Remember, the first time, sitting in your backyard?"

I do remember, of course. It's not something I'm likely to ever forget—that first rush of golden warmth, the connection that made me feel as if, before that moment, I had never truly been alive.

"I just used it to focus," I say. "You told me I didn't need it to access the living-green, and you were right. I don't."

"And—?"

I'm getting even more frustrated and stand, pacing the length of the kitchen. "I guess I've learned how to pull the energy, but the visions seem random. The rose-stone has never seemed to be directly involved in that. I know from my mother's letter that it can hold power somehow."

I don't mention the reason I'm desperate to know more about that. I need to know how to contain the inferno that results when the powers of two Houses come together. What if I do that accidentally or under emotional duress? The only time it happened, I mixed a minuscule amount of the living-green, all that was available to me at the time, with the magic of Iron. If the inferno that roared out of me is magnified based on the amount of power I can normally pull—I don't even want to think about what I'm capable of.

"I don't know how to use the rose-stone, dear." Alice says. "I am not keeping secrets from you. If your mother hadn't died, she would have explained more."

I shut my eyes, but it doesn't help because I can smell the burning house, the burning flesh.

"The secrets of the rose-stone are only passed down through the eldest daughters." Alice pats my hand. "I was not in that line. I hoped the letter your mother left you would give you more explanation about your responsibility and what to tell your own daughter one day."

I don't plan on having a daughter or a son, for that matter. I'm simply not mother material, but that is beside the point.

"Don't you know what was in the letter?" I challenge. "You left it for me with a note in the bank lock-box after you 'died.'"

"I didn't read your mother's letter. It was sealed, wasn't it?"

Opening a sealed letter doesn't take magic, and I'm not sure I believe her, but it doesn't matter now.

She settles her cup carefully on the matching china saucer. "Besides, I remained in England for much of the time after the family moved here. But I am fairly sure no one has 'used' the rose-stone, whatever that means, in my lifetime or the several generations before that, at the least."

"You're implying someone did at some time."

"It always belonged to House of Rose, but it wasn't supposed to be worn except by someone of the three bloods, the *Y Tair*. At least, that is how the stories go."

I have read my mother's letter many times, trying to cull as much information from it as I can, and I pretty much have it memorized. In it, she referred to the powers of the Houses as "talents." I presume this was in case the letter fell into the wrong hands. Still standing, I recite the pertinent part for Alice:

The heirloom has a very long history in our "Families." It possesses the ability to contain the "talents" of all the Houses without the disasters that can occur if those are otherwise mixed. The rightful possessor of the heirloom is the Y Tair, who has the blood of all three Houses and can call upon those talents wherever she is, or—the Universe forbid the need— combine them. This ability ultimately protects everyone from the horrors that can unfold, both from fear of those different or from those who need restraint in using their power over others. Until the last century, the Y Tair was considered head of all the Families, and her word was law.

She looks thoughtful. "That is quite interesting, especially the part about the rose-stone holding power. I've never heard that."

"Alice, you know how you mentioned to me once that there were rumors about my grandmother and a man from House of Iron conceiving my mother?"

"Of course. But that was never proven."

I plop back into my chair. "It was true. I have the blood of two Houses, Rose and Iron.

"Oh my." She exhales. "My poor sister. She would never talk about it."

"I'm not the *Y Tair*, but I'm—"

"I know what you're thinking." Alice interrupts, her attention now on me, and her mouth set in a stern line. "It's hard to know which stories are true, but you are *not* an abomination."

My fists knot, remembering the roaring flames leaping from me and consuming a human being.

"No," I say through tight lips, "those stories are true."

Before Alice can respond, Becca appears in the doorway. She is wearing a pink nightgown, and it's not on backward or inside out.

"Rose, will you read us a story?" she asks.

Another perfect sentence. I'm speechless and look from Becca to Alice, who is grinning like the Cheshire cat in her namesake's story.

What can I do? Prying information from Alice will have to wait.

"Of course," I say, my throat thick, and follow her back to her room. Daniel is on her bed with a copy of a worn children's book from Alice's library. I crawl onto the bed between them and open the ragged pages of *The Glob*, reading about how the formless glob went "to and fro" in the early sea, consumed with the desire to get to land. He tried over and over, but kept getting smashed by waves. Eventually, he grew a pair of feet and then toes, which he learned to wiggle, and stared at in fascination for a long time, eons I imagine, until he figured out how to walk on them.

Chapter Eight

The next day, I report to the office early, fighting the anxiety that arises unbidden from the mundane act of walking across the police parking lot. I have no idea why this didn't happen yesterday. Maybe because the lot is empty now.

Certain I am in the crosshairs of an unseen weapon, I head straight to the bathroom and stand over the sink, clinching its edges until the attack passes. Then I wipe a wet paper towel over my face, concentrating on breathing slowly. There is medicine that can help me deal with this, but if the department discovers I'm having panic attacks, that would be enough excuse to fire me. I'm still on probation.

Even with the ladies room delay, I'm the first person at work, other than Lieutenant Faraday. I guess arriving early gives her a chance to go over the new reports.

Faraday tosses an incident report on my desk. Tracey is at the firing range all day, qualifying with his duty weapon. I'm on my own.

"Kidnapping," Faraday says. The lieutenant looks down at me through her dark framed glasses. She hasn't said two words to me since I first walked into her unit. I pick up the report and skim it.

Every detective in here is carrying a heavy caseload. That's why Faraday isn't complaining about a gift horse from Burglary (me) even though I'm a rookie. That said, I have the strong feeling this case is a test.

According to the report, a man claimed his wife went for a walk and never returned. He was certain someone had taken her. It happened in Avondale, an up-and-coming mixed neighborhood to the east of downtown. A lot of new restaurants and nightspots have sprouted near the renovated Avondale Park. Young energy pulses there, a happening place. But occasional robberies freak everyone out, threatening the mojo. A kidnapping was definitely not good for business.

"See what you can do with this," she says.

"Yes, ma'am."

I study the piece of paper that might predict my future. If I screw this up, I might find myself back in Fish's claws in the Burglary Unit. That wouldn't be so awful, but failing would be. I'm not going to let that happen.

"The patrol officers found her scarf in Avondale Park," Faraday says. "Otherwise it would just have been a 'Missing Person.'"

I nod. Missing Person cases are a dime a dozen. Unless foul play exists, or it's a child missing, they aren't investigated. Foul play, however, elevates the issue to the Homicide Unit.

Faraday pauses, giving me an appraising look. "Let me know if you need any assistance."

Surprised, I look up at her.

"Thanks. I will."

I won't, I promise myself quietly.

When she leaves, I read the case again. As I'm studying it, one of the other detectives saunters over and stops at my desk. He's an older man with a tic in his left cheek, his face a mottled red from either a Scotch-Irish heritage or a bottle. His hands are thick, workman's hands, but his nails have been professionally trimmed. I know who he is. I know them all, though none of them has said word one to me. His name is Frank Finkman, and he has been in Homicide since dirt.

"Hey, rookie," he says when the lieutenant is out of earshot.

"My name is Rose," I say. "Or Brighton."

"I know your name, *rookie.*"

I feel the scarlet rise to my cheeks and earlobes, but I put a tight governor on my mouth.

"You know you don't belong here," he says. "You're a patrol screw up, and another damn woman trying to do a man's job."

I meet his gaze. In my short stint in the Burglary Unit, I caught unfriendly glances from one of the detectives, but he never said anything directly to me. This is crossing the line.

"I didn't know there were still chauvinistic pigs in the PD."

So much for controlling my mouth. But I'm angry. Rookies often have to endure ritual put-downs that let them know where they stand on the status ladder. But no one has ever been in my face with one like that. My hands clench my knees under the table, and I quash my instinct to call on the living-green. *What good is being a witch, if you can't even put a hex on someone?* Maybe I could do a bad palm reading on him.

He laughs. "Got some spunk, anyway." He runs his tongue along the inside of his upper lip. "You going to go running to the lieutenant with a sexual harassment complaint?"

I could. He was out of line. I feel everyone's attention like needle pricks in my back. They are listening, even if they don't look like they are. Acceptance is earned here, not given. Same as in Patrol. A complaint to the lieutenant would seal my fate and open me up for either unwanted harassment or permanent ostracism.

"I can handle my own problems," I say.

"This ain't a detail for wussies." His gaze runs suggestively from my toes up to my breasts and his cheek twitches. "Just try not to get knocked up."

That is the least of my worries.

I change tactics and give him a bright smile. "If I do, it sure as hell won't be by you."

It's not until an hour later that I realize I could have used magic on Finkman and shut him up. Iron magic. I could, in fact, have made him do or say anything I wanted. Only once have I used the power of Iron to manipulate others—to get a nurse to allow Alice and me into Daniel's hospital room after the Ordeal. Alice's power to heal couldn't keep Daniel from being scarred, but she saved his life.

My perception of the living-green is a golden fire I feel more than actually "see." The presence of the power from iron ore feels like a black, oily liquid. When I touched the nurse who was stonewalling us and let it trickle into her, suggesting that she take us to Daniel's cubicle in ICU, she complied immediately. It was easy. But if I had made the tiniest mistake and let the two powers mix, I could have incinerated the entire hospital floor and everyone on it. I swore I would never risk using that power.

I can't.

Closing my eyes and taking several deep breaths brings my focus back to the task at hand. I have enough to deal with without worrying about Finkman.

Before I arrange a meeting with Mr. Hatcher, the man who reported his wife missing under fishy circumstances, I review the report again. According to it, the scarf was a worn one with a little tear in it that made him recognize it as hers. Hatcher was the one who had found it, not the police. He said his wife often walked in the park when she was upset. He had gone looking for her and found the scarf. I should find out why she had been upset.

But first, I have some digging to do.

An hour later, I walk back into Lieutenant Faraday's office.

She's busy reading reports, but looks up after a moment and frowns. "Need help already?"

"No ma'am."

She waits.

"I know where Mrs. Hatcher is."

"You do?"

I nod.

She jerks her head toward a chair and I sit.

"Where is she?" she asks.

"In Nashville."

"On her own steam?"

"Yup."

"Tell me how you know."

"Her social media posts. She apparently has a fantasy about becoming a country singer and making it big in Nashville."

"And you've confirmed that's where she is?"

"She has a Facebook friend who lives in Nashville. I tracked her down and called her, and she admitted Mrs. Hatcher was staying with her. She also volunteered that Mr. Hatcher was a jerk."

Faraday leans back in her chair and considers me. "What made you think it wasn't a kidnapping?"

I smile. "The scarf." What I don't tell her is that without having known Becca, it would never have occurred to me to be a clue.

Faraday tilts her head inquisitively.

"It was 'worn and had a hole in it,'" I say.

"And?"

"All the photos of her on Facebook show her dressed to the nines. A woman who cares about that would not have gone out with an old, torn scarf . . . unless she was going to leave it hanging on a bush. Besides that, it's not cold enough for a scarf."

That earns a grudging smile.

"Good work, Brighton. Now go tell Mr. Hatcher his wife has run away."

Chapter Nine

I feel terribly guilty as I push open the door to the UAB administrative office that says "Human Resources Department." But I spent the last two hours in the Homicide office after solving my "kidnapping" case, checking everything I could find on the Internet, and I hit a wall. So here I am. Lieutenant Faraday gave me the nod to get out and do some investigating on our case, but she has no idea I'm investigating my partner.

The weather reflects my dark mood, the sky overcast. I have to walk several blocks and, naturally, it starts to rain before I reach my destination. I jog, but my hair is a mass of wet curls by the time I get inside the sterile offices. A woman with her hair pulled into a tight bun and her mouth pulled even tighter into a scowl sits at the front desk.

"Can I help you?" she asks. Her eyes, thick with mascara and green eyeshadow, flick up to assess me and back down at whatever she is reading.

"I want to look at a personnel file."

"Is it your own?" This time she doesn't even bother to look up.

"No, it's a professor's."

"I'm sorry, we can't share that."

I take out my badge and stick it under her nose. "Detective Brighton. I'm working on a case."

She stiffens. "I'll have to get my supervisor." Standing, she gives two downward jerks to her skirt, a move that does nothing to its length, but asserts her authority. "Wait here." She directs me to a chair, and I cross the room obediently, hating that I'm doing this. Maybe I should leave. Just walk out the door and down the hall and forget about this. I would . . . if I didn't have to know.

Paul, my ex-training officer and ex-lover, once said I would make a good detective. "To be worth a damn, you have to ask questions, and that's something you're good at." He'd held his mouth perfectly still under that red mustache when he said it, but he couldn't hide the amused glint in his eyes.

I miss him.

He died of burns I inflicted on him. He died saving little Daniel.

Stop, I order my mind.

Looking for a diversion, I snatch up a National Geographic magazine. It falls open to a double-page photo spread of stars, haloed clusters of gleaming ovals and discs in shades of cream, gold, red and a few hues of blue against the blackness of space. Behind them, almost filling the pages are more, smaller and smaller, until they are dots fading into the distance. There are, according to the article, 100 billion of them. It's hard to wrap my mind around that. Then I realize I'm not looking at stars. Each object I thought was a star is actually a galaxy, each one containing billions of stars. And the two-page spread represents just a tiny area of space, a few inches worth of sky.

Stunned, I sit in silence for several moments. It's not that I didn't know the numbers, but numbers are one thing, seeing it like this is jolting—it's the difference between understanding the concept of an ocean's size and actually seeing the sweep of the sea and the endless stretch of horizon, *feeling*, if only for a moment, how tiny we are in the vastness of everything.

And Alice says this universe may be only one out of an infinity of universes. That, she says, is what I may be seeing when I have a vision, when I open a crack in time—another universe, like this one, but where different things happen, or possibly another universe just like ours but where time flows the other way. Either one sounds incredible, but the immensity of just this tiny piece of our beautiful universe in my lap is equally as incredible. Who am I to say what is possible or impossible?

I'm still staring at the photo when the woman with the bun comes back to escort me to her supervisor.

It takes yet another rung of supervisors and my assertion that I can come back with a subpoena if I have to—a bluff at this point— before someone with enough authority hands me the file I want. But I'm in the right. After all, how much expectation of privacy can a dead man expect?

I'm given a room and a desk to peruse the file. It's thick. Dr. Benjamin Crompton has done a lot just in his time at UAB. And he has taught classes periodically over the years. Different ones, but none were bio-chemistry. I check it all twice to make sure I haven't missed anything.

I leave the building in a daze that is not about universes. *My partner is lying to me.*

I would like to believe that Tracey was just mixed up about what class he took from Dr. Crompton, but Crompton's death hit him too hard for that to be the case. The man made an impression on him. Tracey was holding back tears when he recognized him. He is lying. But why? What does he know about this that he's not telling me? Why does he want me to stop pushing, to leave it alone as an accident? The only reason he would want me to do that is . . . not something I want to believe.

But there it is. *I asked the questions, Paul, and I don't like the answers.* Now what? I take a deep breath, duck out into the rain and answer my own question:

Now I'm doing this on my own.

A VOICE IN MY HEAD is calling me an idiot as I walk through the Burglary Unit office and tap on the wall of Fish's cubicle. Lieutenant Fisher has the role of "grumpy" down to an art.

He looks up and predictably scowls. "Is this a social call, Brighton? Or are you wanting out of Homicide?"

"Neither, sir."

He grunts. "Well, don't just stand there. Close the door behind you."

The door is glass. It's not exactly privacy, but at least other people can't hear us.

"Sit."

I do.

For a long moment, he regards me. I'm silent, waiting. Finally, he grunts. "Well, what is it?"

"I'd like your advice."

"That would be a novelty around here. On what subject?"

"Investigation."

He leans back and knits his stubby fingers together over the pouch of his belly. "About?"

"A case. I'd rather not get specific."

"Okay, then get general. I can't give advice about nothing, and I've got a stack of reports to go through as thick as—never mind."

"I have a homicide victim and a possible suspect, and I'm looking for a way tie them together." I add quickly, "I've already tried social media. What would you do?"

"And the reason you came to me and not Lieutenant Faraday?"

I glance down at my own hands, long fingers laced on my lap, and lie. "I don't want to give her the impression that I don't know what I'm doing."

"Which you don't."

I stay silent.

He sighs. "Not your fault the idiots upstairs swept you off the street before you had any experience."

Four months of experience is not enough to count in his book, I know. I continue to keep my mouth shut against its natural tendency to open at the wrong time.

To my disgust, but not surprise, he pulls out a can of tobacco and stuffs a piece in his mouth. I quietly hope that he will dispense any knowledge before it's time to spit.

"You got a dead person and you need info on who his or her connections are?"

"Yes sir."

"Well, you can get a search warrant on phone records, emails, etc., pretty easily on the victim. I'm assuming, however, you don't have probable cause to get that for the suspect."

I nod. "Probable cause" is the standard level of evidence required for arrests and search warrants. It is based on a reasonable person's conclusions given the totality of circumstances. Like pornography, it is difficult to define, but in law enforcement, you know it when you see it. In terms of certainty, it resides between "reasonable suspicion," which can justify a stop and questioning, and "beyond a reasonable doubt," which is the standard for conviction in a court. A search warrant requires articulable probable cause.

"Until you do, then, you'll have to make do with what connections you can find with the victim, whether he made any calls to your suspect—that's the easiest way to start."

"Umm, how do I go about getting the phone records?"

"Used to be a lot easier, but unless you have exigent circumstances, an emergency, you need a warrant for that." He squints at me. "I heard they paired you up with Lohan. He'll have the forms for that and you need to write up an affidavit with it explaining your probable cause."

"Lohan is qualifying at the firing range. I'd like to have it done when he gets back." I give him my best attempt at a respectful-request smile. "Any way you could get me a copy of the form I need?"

Chapter Ten

At my knock, a woman dressed in a kimono with large pink chrysanthemums on dark blue silk opens the door. Wrinkles map her mouth and filmy blue-gray eyes. After an inch, the dark roots of her hair abruptly transform into a bright orange-red halo.

"Hello," she says. "How can I help you?"

"Mrs. Crompton?"

"Yes. Valinda Crompton."

I show her my badge. "Detective Brighton with Birmingham Police. I'm investigating your husband's death." Just saying those words makes me feel guilty, like I'm the one betraying Tracey. *But he's the one hiding something.* He takes some kind of martial arts class on Mondays and Thursdays. I don't expect him to pop back in the office or be looking for me after he's finished at the firing range.

Her hand goes to her throat. "Oh."

"May I come in?"

"Of course, but don't mind the house. Since Ben died, I haven't felt like cleaning up, and the maid doesn't come until Thursday."

"I understand."

"How about some peppermint tea?" she says. "I made it fresh."

"That would be nice."

"Well, you sit down in the living room. Move anything in your way aside, okay?"

It's a large house in the adjacent over-the-mountain city of Mountain Brook, the destination on the southern flank of Red Mountain for wealthy white flight from Birmingham. If a driver doesn't know his way or have GPS, he is likely to get lost on the winding maze of streets flanked by towering trees and perfectly manicured lawns now dotted with blooming white dogwoods and early azaleas. I'm not surprised that a professor of Benjamin Crompton's stature lives here.

She serves the tea in glasses of ice with a sprig of mint. Of course. I've been drinking Alice's hot tea, and it slipped my mind that for most of the Southern world, "tea" means over ice with lots of sugar.

"Thank you," I say, taking my glass and sipping the sweet drink. "It's good."

She takes the other glass. "Now before business, come and see my garden."

"Sorry?"

"My garden."

I follow her out the kitchen door and down some steps.

"Wow," I say and mean it. We walk through an archway into a beautiful garden of tulips, dogwoods, rhododendrons, azaleas and ferns of every description.

"Do you do this yourself?"

"Oh, no. I don't dig the holes, if that's what you mean, but I plan it. I'm the maestro. Benjamin never cared anything about it. He was selfish with his time."

I imagine some of his time, other than that devoted to a mistress, was spent trying to find a cure for an awful disease, but I try to look compassionate.

"I'm sorry for your loss. Did he . . . leave you vulnerable?" I ask.

"What do you mean?"

"I mean financially. Are you going to be able to keep the house and this wonderful garden?"

"Oh yes. I imagine so."

"He left you life insurance?" I make it a question.

She narrows her eyes. "That seems a personal question. But I suppose it's legitimate, given you are a police detective, and he is dead."

I wait.

"No, he didn't leave any life insurance. We discussed it with our financial planner—I can give you his name if you'd like—and decided that it wasn't necessary at our ages. Ben was working out of choice."

That takes care of one obvious motivation, unless he left some money to his lover. But Mrs. Crompton doesn't seem too broken up about his death, more resentful that he spent time away from her. Or perhaps that he didn't appreciate her gardening efforts.

I follow her back inside, and she sits in a flower-patterned chair, directing me to the matching couch. "Now, what do you want to talk about?"

I set my iced tea on a coaster obviously placed there for this purpose. I have to laugh inwardly at what she calls bad housekeeping. Not a thing I can see is out of place, and I bet it would pass a white glove test.

"What do you know about your husband's work?" I ask.

She waves her hands as if the breeze they stir will push me back. "Little to nothing. He never talked to me about it. Something to do with diabetes, I think. He had diabetes, you know. Type 1."

"I know."

"Had to take insulin regularly. But he gave himself the shots. I can't do needles. It's a good thing he was the one with it because he would have had to give me shots, and he wasn't home enough to do that." Her gaze drifts. "He won't have to worry about doing that anymore, will he?"

"No, I guess not."

"Are you really a policeman?" she says suddenly and before I answer, amends, "Oh, I mean a police lady, of course."

"Yes, ma'am."

"I mean you are quite pretty. You could be a model. Have you ever shot anyone?"

I freeze.

She waits for my answer, her face merely polite and curious, and I realize she doesn't know that I have, indeed, shot someone. Not to mention frying someone alive with magic.

"I need to ask you some questions, if that's alright," I say.

"Of course. Never mind me. You go right ahead."

"Do you know if your husband knew a policeman named Tracey Lohan?"

She shakes her head. "Not that I can recall."

Dead end there. "What about a Laurie Stokes, Mr. Crompton's . . . assistant?" I didn't mean to hesitate at the word, but it just happened, and her face tightens.

"The little blonde?"

I clear my throat. "She is blond."

"If you're going to tell me she was having an affair with my husband, save your breath. I know about it. I knew about all of them."

"All of them?"

"Oh, not at the same time. But over the years. He's a handsome man, you know. All the aliens are."

I blink. "I beg your pardon?"

"I said they're all handsome." She enunciates the words carefully.

"I thought you said 'aliens.'" I laugh and try to make it a cough.

"I did."

"You're saying that your husband was an alien? Like from another country?"

"No, like from another planet."

"Another planet," I repeat.

"Absolutely. No one believes me, of course." She leans forward, a gleam in her eyes. "But I know. I've been watching him for forty years."

Chapter Eleven

It's Saturday morning. Alice and I are the only ones awake. Still groggy from one of my familiar nightmares—a dark room, the looming threat of an electric prod at my neck—I join her in the kitchen, side-stepping a toy dinosaur and a dump truck.

"I fixed you tea," Alice says as she sets a delicate china cup on the kitchen table. Alice does not believe in mugs. "We'll have breakfast when Daniel and Becca wake up. Nora doesn't like breakfast."

I look at the steaming tea apprehensively. As always, she made it with fresh mint from her garden and lemon or cream, depending on her mood. But it's not the tea that worries me. Alice seems to be in an especially cheery mood, and that is a warning she wants "a talk."

Alexander, Alice's solid black cat, sniffs my leg. He has been the least friendly, which is fine with me. I give him his space, and he gives me mine.

"What do you want to know?" I ask, continuing to stand.

Alice sits at the table's end with her own steaming cup. "Everything, of course. Tell me."

"You mean about my case?" I told her previously about the vision, but not what's worrying me about my partner.

"No, you already told me about that."

"Then what specifically?"

She purses her lips. "Rose, you know perfectly well what I want to know. I didn't bring it up before because you were so upset about that dead man."

"I wasn't upset about the dead man. That's my job. I was upset about seeing him animate and relive his last moments backward."

She frowns and ignores my sarcasm. "That man on the porch the other day was House of Iron, wasn't he?"

"Oh. That."

It isn't easy to hide anything from Alice. I don't know if she had a premonition or looked out the window. She believes every warlock of House of Iron is as evil as Theophalus Blackwell was. That is one death on my shoulders I do not regret.

"Yes," I say, "the man on the porch was Jason Blackwell of House of Iron."

"What did he want?"

I sit and take a sip of the tea she put at my usual place—the chair with the back to the kitchen cabinets. No police officer is comfortable with his or her back to the door, and the kitchen opens up into the living room and front door. I decide to answer her honestly.

"Justin Blackwell wants me."

Her eyes narrow. "To do what?"

"To be his lover." I blow on the tea and try another sip, though it's very hot.

Her spine snaps straight. "How impertinent!"

She catches me mid-swallow. I can't help a sputtering laugh. "I guess, but there's more to it."

"What do you mean?"

I have dreaded this conversation, put it off. Suddenly, there is nothing funny about anything. I put my hand to my forehead.

Immediately, her expression changes. "Are you all right?"

"I'm fine."

She reaches for my head, but I pull back. "I'm fine, Alice. The doctors released me, and you checked me out, remember?"

Alice's healing powers don't work on me, but she can scan me in some way and diagnose what she "sees" or "feels" is wrong. I guess that makes her a kind of walking MRI machine. In addition, for part of her long past, she was a doctor.

"Rose, I know you've had more dizzy spells than you have admitted."

I sigh. Like I said, it's hard to keep anything from my great aunt. But my dizzy spells are a symptom of the panic attacks. They're nothing physical that can be detected by medical scans or probably even a witch. They're "in my head."

"I have a checkup scheduled in a few days. They won't find anything."

The doctor's appointment is scheduled during my lunch hour. I can't take sick time for my first year. Fortunately, since I was technically responding to a felony in progress (kidnapping) during the Ordeal, I was considered "on duty," so recovering from my injuries was handled through workman's comp. The doctors and shrinks have cleared me. The less people who know about the panic attacks, the better, even Alice. She might start pushing me to get counseling, and that might reignite the whole competency issue.

Alice purses her lips, not happy about my refusal to let her check me out. "You seem to have something else to say about that Iron man."

"Jason. His name is Jason."

She sniffs.

"It's not just a regular kind of attraction between us."

"Between you?" Her silver brows lift. "You have . . . feelings for him?"

"Yes. No, not exactly. I—" This is as difficult as I thought it would be. I try a different starting place. "Alice, when Theophalus Blackwell thought he was going to kill me, he told me some things."

"About?"

I clear my throat. "About your sister, my grandmother."

"You already told me you thought she had an affair with an Iron man. Is there more?"

Her index finger wrapped around the teacup goes white. This is clearly a subject she would rather avoid.

"I'm pretty sure my grandmother and a man from House of Iron felt the same thing that Jason and I feel. Our magics pull us together. It's amazingly intense."

"Oh my."

"I'm sorry."

"You know who it was?" She hesitates. "The man my sister—?"

"I do."

Her face is suddenly vulnerable. "It wasn't Theophalus Blackwell, was it?" she asks. She almost chokes on the name.

"No, it was the former head of House of Iron. A man named Adam. I think they loved each other."

"Do you love this man, Jason Blackwell?"

I swallow. "No, I don't think so. I don't know. It's crazy. It's hard to say what I feel. Everything is overwhelming when I'm near him."

"Maybe," she says quietly, "maybe you shouldn't say no."

"What?"

"It was House of Iron that forbade the mixing of bloods, not House of Rose."

"What are you telling me?"

"It's not an easy thing to say. It's such a burden and unfair to you."

Somehow, everything has flipped. I thought I was the one who had to tell her something she didn't want to hear.

"What are you talking about?"

"We are the last of our House."

"I know that."

"But it is more than that."

"I wish you would make sense."

"I'm trying, dear. I just wish I didn't have to put this on you."

"Alice, please! Just spit it out."

"No, I think I need to back up a bit."

"How far?" I ask with suspicion.

"The beginning would be good."

"You mean like a Genesis beginning?"

She chuckles, an uncomfortable laughter. "Possibly. I've often wondered if our people could have been the half-angel, half-human creatures in that story. But, regardless, the history of our people *is* a long one, probably as old as mankind. We evolved additional ways to obtain the energy that feeds our abilities in order to help us survive. Physical strength, the ability to see the immediate future in an emergency, healing, and manipulating other creatures are all survival tools that developed along with the cerebral cortex." She takes a breath. "Which, in turn, evolved on top of our reptilian flight-or-fight brain to help us imagine and plan."

I fidget, but I know to let her work her way around to wherever she is going.

She drums her fingers on the table. "The important thing is that those abilities existed, as they do now, in various degrees and combinations. Based on the ancient stories and what we know of evolution, we can hypothesize that eventually we recognized each other and came together as tribes, with all the multiple abilities that made them suspect or possibly outcasts from other human tribes."

"Before there were Houses?"

"Yes, the tribes were just clusters of people who had additional different abilities. They would have been the forerunners of Houses. Being in tribes obviously had advantages, but the flip side was that the children came into pubescence with their extra abilities later than normal. Also, the adults weren't able to reproduce as quickly or in the same numbers as the rest of the human population who feared our people's abilities and hunted us. Eventually numbers won out, and the tribes were forced into hiding, so to speak, to blend into society. For hundreds of years, our ancestors thrived that way, keeping our Family groups secret and held together by an acknowledged ruler."

"The *Y Tair* my mother mentioned in her letter?"

"Yes, the *Y Tair*, 'The Three,' a queen of all three bloodlines—assuming, of course, this is fact and not myth. For various reasons, the families began to cluster into Houses by their abilities. Iron became the most affluent and powerful, in terms of politics and wealth. Intermarriage became a social class issue and eventually an outright taboo, fed by stories of abominations. I believe there is some truth to the tale that mixing the magics is dangerous, but House of Iron capitalized on that fear."

I press my lips together. I know there is truth to that tale, but I don't want to distract her, so I say nothing.

"Probably," she continues, "because a witch with more than one type of magic was the only power that could challenge them—especially a *Y Tair*—Iron decided being led by a queen interfered with their influence."

"And they began killing off House of Rose," I finish for her. House of Rose is dying out because of greed, because House of Iron fears we will produce a *Y Tair*.

"Okay," I say, "I get it that the House of Iron is threatened by us because the *Y Tair* must be a woman. Right?"

"Yes."

"But it doesn't have to be a woman of House of Rose. What about Iron and Stone? Why can't they produce a daughter?"

She shakes her head. "They can produce daughters, but the *Y Tair*, at least according to legend, must carry not just the bloodlines of all three Houses, but the magic of all three. This much is fact—the powers of Iron and Stone only manifest in the males. If a daughter of Stone parents and a son of Iron produced a boy, he would be Iron. Same the other way around. Females can be born to warlocks, but they don't inherit the powers. It's only House of Rose that can inherit both the blood and the magic and only in the female line. Sons of House of Rose are normals."

She lets that sink in.

"What you're saying is that since I'm the only child-producer in the House of Rose, any bearing of a *Y Tair* is on my shoulders or my daughter's or granddaughter's, assuming I have a child some day." Children, like friends, have never been on my to-do list.

"Yes, that is correct. But it is a great deal more than just producing a *Y Tair*." Her eyes crinkle in worry. "Rose, it is not just House of Rose that is dying."

"What do you mean?"

"All the Houses are dying."

"What? Why?"

She watches me closely. "Our ability to have children has declined over the years."

I recall something Stephanie, Jason's cousin, once told me—*Children are so rare.*

A knot of dread in my stomach begins to form. There is something I'm missing. Something critical.

"Do we know why?" I ask.

She knits her fingers, her gaze intent on me. "Some of us do. There is a geneticist in House of Stone who has studied it for many years. I don't know him personally or even his name. Stone protects their identities fiercely, but he sent me copies of his research. His work strongly supports his hypothesis that genetic switches in the male lines determine powers in the warlock Houses, at least in the House he studied, but one would assume that applied in House of Iron."

"That makes sense, but I don't get—"

"Yes, I know, that conclusion is evident. As I said, women in Iron and Stone do not inherit any of the Family abilities. Neither do sons in House of Rose. The important thing is that those same genetic switches also make childbirth rare. The more the inbreeding in a House, the more difficult it is."

I think about this. "Both warlock Houses will die out on their own."

"Yes, and House of Rose, as well—that is, if we could recover from having our members exterminated as if we were some kind of infestation. The fact that your mother had two children was looked upon as being a welcome, but very unusual, event." She plucks at a tealeaf stuck to the side of her cup. "If what you say about your grandmother having an affair with a man of Iron is true, that could explain your mother's fecundity."

"Well, how long did this geneticist think it would take for the Houses to be unable to have children?"

"He predicts this is the last generation."

The meaning of this reverberates like a struck tuning fork. My voice drops to a whisper.

"What you're saying is that all the Houses—we—are going extinct."

"Yes."

My mind whirls, trying to digest this. A whole people disappearing. No matter what kind of people some of them may be, it is wrong. Terribly wrong.

"Isn't there anything that can stop it?"

Her gaze drops to her cold cup of tea and then up to mine. "The only thing that can be done to restore genetic viability is to mix the blood of Iron or Stone with House of Rose."

It takes a moment to absorb what she is saying. "You mean the only way to save everyone is for me to have sex with a man from another House and have his baby?"

"That, I fear, is exactly what I am saying."

Chapter Twelve

The following afternoon, I head south through the cut in Red Mountain. It's Sunday and I'm off duty. But a police officer is never really off duty. Gun and badge are always present and, with them, the obligation to respond to any felony or emergency. Technically, I could claim overtime for doing actual detective work, but since I'm sneaking behind my partner's back, I will "forget" to claim it.

Alice's recent revelations bounce around in my head as I drive. Could she be wrong? Could she be lying? That seems highly unlikely, considering how much she hates House of Iron. She had to believe strongly every word, because it would take something on the level of annihilation of a race to get her to tell me to sleep with a man from Iron.

The bottom line is I'm a brood mare responsible for the survival of a race of beings that may or may not be fully human, depending on your definition. My knuckles whiten around the steering wheel. I force a deep breath. Getting angry isn't going to change anything. I need logic.

My first instinct stands—that extinction is wrong, akin to genocide—but what would actually happen if they . . . we . . . died out? Humanity would survive, wouldn't it? Witches can't heal the world. Iron manipulates people for its own purposes, and Stone is not out there doing anything as far as I can tell. Why not just let nature take its course? Let us go like the dodo birds or the woolly mammoth.

In the end, the world might be better off without the existence of the Houses. After all, some extinct creatures would pose a threat to humanity if they still existed—flesh-eating dinosaurs, giant crocodiles, rodents, and insects, not to mention my favorite horror, megalodon, a giant shark that ate whales for breakfast. Some things we are better off without. Personally, I could do fine in a world without mosquitoes.

It is not fair that this responsibility rests on my shoulders. The whole thing is too overwhelming to deal with. I tuck it away to ponder later. One thing at a time, and solving a homicide is at the top of my list.

Vestavia Hills is a small municipality just south of Birmingham's city limits. Named for Vesta, the Roman goddess of the hearth, home, and family, the city touts good schools and low crime. GPS guides me right to Laurie Stokes' apartment door. I knock, but nobody answers.

Just because the fate of a race of people depends on me, apparently doesn't mean the world has stopped and everyone is available when I want them to be. But Stokes shouldn't still be in church, if she goes, which a lot of people do. It's a well-worn joke that there's a church on every corner in the South. If that's not literally true, it's close enough.

Stepping to the curtained window, I try to see inside, but the day is too bright. I didn't call ahead, not wanting to leave a message or give her a callback number. I don't want her calling the office and inadvertently alerting Tracey that I'm investigating without him. Among my growing list of things I don't want to think about is how I'm going to handle it when he finds out I'm pursuing leads by myself. There's a shopping mall not far from here, and I have a story in mind about how I just happened to be in the neighborhood looking for a new pair of shoes and dropped by.

And the explanation I've worked out about why I went to interview Crompton's wife was that Lieutenant Faraday ran me out of the office the day he was qualifying at the firing range, and I didn't know what to do. But those tales are in my pocket, to be pulled out only if he confronts me. I'm not volunteering anything. He doesn't seem inclined to pursue the case. Maybe it won't come up, at least until I have a handle on what is going on. I need to understand why he lied to me about his connection with the homicide victim, Benjamin Crompton.

Just as I'm about to give up on anyone coming to the door, Stokes' next-door neighbor emerges, a man in his twenties. He's wearing white shorts and cradles a tennis racket in one arm. He closes his own door, starts toward the parking lot and sees me.

"You looking for Laurie?" he asks.

"Yes. Have a clue where she might be?"

He laughs and thumbs over his shoulder. "Try the pool in back. She's probably working on her tan."

"Thanks. How do I get there?"

This time he points at the sidewalk to my right. "Just follow that around. She can unlock the gate for you."

I nod and tread the concrete path around the building. The pool is a decent size, shaped with a stylish left crook to indicate the deep end. The sparkling blue water looks inviting, but it's not long enough to get in good laps. I promise myself an evening visit to the YMCA.

Surrounding the pool is a shoulder-high wooden fence. Woods ensure privacy on all sides, except from the windows in the back of the complex. It's a beautiful sunny day, but only a couple of people are at the pool. One is stretched out spread-legged on a recliner near the deep end, the top straps of her two-piece down, blonde hair spread in wet spikes from her head—Laurie.

Her eyes are closed. I find my way to the gate. It's a combo lock. I could jump over the fence, which is only intended to keep out wandering children, but that might be a bit too dramatic an entrance.

"Laurie?" I call.

Both occupants look my way. The other person is a middle-aged woman with two kids who are happily splashing in the shallow end.

Laurie sits up and shades her eyes. Without bothering to replace the straps on her suit, she gets up, holding her top to her chest and walks to the gate. I can see why she caught Crompton's eye. And, except for a little graying at his temples, I understand why she responded—an older man, secure in his position, her boss. Flattering.

Why did she kill him?

"Detective?" she asks quietly. "I didn't recognize you at first."

I'm wearing jeans and a tee shirt that says, "The Police Never Think It's As Funny As You Do."

"Can I come in?" I ask, pointing to the locked gate.

"Oh, sure." She opens it and stands aside.

"I love the sun," I say, "but maybe over there?" I gesture toward a table with a large umbrella. I want to be able to see her eyes.

She wriggles the straps of her top back over her shoulders and grabs a towel off the back of her lounge chair, wrapping it around her waist.

When we're seated, I ask, "How are you doing?" She has no idea I know she killed Crompton, so I try to put some compassion in my question.

She sighs. "I'm okay, or I'm getting there. Trying."

"Are you back at work?"

"Yeah, new boss."

"Already?"

"They just named him to the position, but he hasn't moved in. It's going to be weird having him there, and he may not keep me as his assistant."

"What happens if he doesn't?"

"I'll lose my job, unless they have something else for me. Just back to being a student on a student loan. I come from a rural farm family," she says. "Nobody believed I would ever make it through college, let alone get into medical school." Her lips spread in a wan smile. "They already call me 'Doctor Laurie' at home." She waves a hand to indicate the pool and apartment building behind us. "If he cans me, I'll probably have to find somewhere else to live."

"Crompton didn't leave you anything?"

She looks startled. "You mean like money?"

"Yeah, like money."

"No. I'm sure if he had a will, everything went to his wife."

"Were there any other family members he might have left something to?"

"Not that he ever mentioned. He told me once that he and his wife couldn't have children. They tried, but—" Her voices trails away.

"Have you talked to his wife?" she asks.

"I have. I agree she's a little unbalanced."

"Benjamin said she was crazy as a loon. I don't know if that was true or just a line he gave me. Funny, I never even questioned it until after he died. Isn't that weird?"

"Death makes us think about things we normally hide from ourselves," I say, thinking how Alice's "death" inflamed all my demon childhood memories.

"Guess so." She studies her chipped green fingernails. They were manicured and freshly painted the last time I saw her. Looks like she's been biting them.

I'm striking out in trying to identify a motive. She's apparently vulnerable financially. Could someone have enticed her to kill her boss in exchange for something?

"I'm trying to figure out who might gain from Dr. Crompton's death," I say. "Can you help me?"

"Why? It was an accident."

"How could it have been an accident?" I ask, watching her carefully.

"What do you mean? I thought he had a heart attack, but the rumor is he overdosed from too much insulin."

"Didn't you tell us you prepared his insulin syringe?"

Her tanned face pales.

"I do, I mean, I did."

"Did you put more insulin in the syringe than was called for?"

"No!"

"How do you know?"

"I'm always careful." Her thumb plays with the tops of her nails.

"Do you remember preparing it that morning?"

"Yes, I think. It's hard to remember, like parking your car in the same lot everyday but in a different place, you know? Sometimes I can't remember which spot I parked in because it all blurs together."

"Try to remember. Step through it, every detail."

"I always go to the drawer where he keeps the syringes and open a new one, go to the little refrigerator he has in his office and get out the insulin."

"You took the insulin from the refrigerator that morning?"

"Of course."

Lie.

"You wouldn't have had some in your pocket you used, accidentally?"

Her forehead wrinkles. "I don't carry insulin around with me. Why would I do that?"

When the autopsy report came back negative for poison, I looked up insulin doses. Stokes must have drawn from a bottle with a higher strength, the one in her pocket. Dr. Crompton was taking a U-40 strength, but the same amount in a U-500 strength could have been deadly.

"Go on," I say. "What do you do next?"

"I pull back the syringe and push it into the bottle to get out the air, then I measure his dosage and push a bit out the tip and take it to him. He injects himself." She looks lost. "I don't know what happened."

"Did he normally check the amount when you bring it to him?"

She looks down. "He used to, but no, not really. He trusted me." A tear leaks from her left eye and she brushes at it, automatically wiping under the lower lid to remove any smudged mascara.

"You think you made the mistake?" I ask.

"I . . . I don't know. Are you sure it wasn't a heart attack?" Her voice is hopeful.

"The autopsy results weren't clear, but we're pretty sure it was an overdose."

"Then it was my fault," she says. This time the tears run freely, and she makes no attempt to wipe them away.

I lean forward. This is my moment.

"Laurie, I can't help you unless you tell me the truth."

"I am," she sobs.

Either she is a damn good liar or actress or she's innocent and my visions are crap.

"I don't remember," she says. "I can't remember that morning. It was just like every morning, and I can't remember!"

I give her a moment to pull herself together. A child screams, catching my attention. The boy stands at the pool's edge, his toes hanging over, body bent at an angle as he works up the courage to jump in. Regardless of the tube around his waist and inflated wristbands, this daring move requires everything he's got. Other than his perfect skin, he reminds me of Daniel.

When I turn back to Laurie's tear-streaked face, she sobs, "How am I going to live with this?"

I know she wants me to say it was an accident, but I can't. I saw her pull a vial from her pocket.

"You can live with it if you tell me," I try again. "I want to hear your side of it."

"He said he was going to leave his wife, that she was unbalanced . . . and that he loved me."

"Did you find out he wasn't going to leave her?" I ask gently.

She sniffs and looks down. "I was beginning to wonder if he was telling the truth or leading me on. He's been married a long time. I was wondering if I was just being stupid and naive."

"And—?" My pulse picks up its tempo.

She sniffs again and looks at me. "But I decided it didn't matter because . . . I loved him."

"You would share him with her? With his wife?"

She nods. Her voice is barely a whisper. "If I had to." She pauses, studying her hands. "That makes me a slut, doesn't it?"

I lean back. Close, but no cigar. She didn't kill him out of jealousy or at least she isn't going to admit it. Back to ground zero.

"I'm not going to judge you," I say.

I give her a few minutes to make sure she's not going to change her mind. "Are you sure that's all?" I prompt.

She chews on a ragged nail. "Yes."

"Tell me more about the research project."

She sniffs. "What do you want to know?"

"You were working on verifying the effects of zahablan on Type 1 diabetes, right?"

"I didn't have anything to do with it directly. Benjamin. . . um, Dr. Crompton, was monitoring the research as part of the bigger project under the CDC."

"CDC?"

"Comprehensive Diabetes Center. Dr. Crompton actually volunteered to help on the data end. It wasn't part of his normal scope."

"He would have a personal interest in finding a cure, wouldn't he?" I say.

"Yeah, I think he would have volunteered for the human trials if he could have, but it wouldn't have been appropriate."

"Let me ask you something."

She looks up. Her eyes are red and despite her efforts, a black eyeliner streak runs from one corner across her cheekbone.

"Did you know my partner before we interviewed you?"

"The big guy?"

"Yeah."

"No."

"He never came in to visit Crompton?"

"Well, he might have, but I never saw him. I would have remembered. He's a hunk."

"Okay, one more thing. What would happen if the trials show this drug is able to treat or even cure diabetes?"

"That would be great. That's what we're all hoping for."

"It would be great for people with the disease."

She looks at me as if I have mentioned fish live in water. "Well, yeah."

"But what about all the billions of dollars invested in treating the disease?" I say.

"What do you mean?"

"The drugs, the testing strips, the insulin. Somebody has to make all that and profit by it."

"I guess." She shrugs. "Then they make something else."

"I'm not sure it's that simple, Laurie."

It obviously was for her. But the world doesn't work that way. Money is power and people or companies don't let go of power easily.

"What about the opposite?" I ask. "What if the results show that zahablan doesn't work?"

She sits up. "That would be disappointing. It looked really good in the lab and animal studies. But, animal results aren't human results. They pound that into our heads enough."

"And that's it?" I ask.

She frowns. "Actually, that would shift everything over to the private lab's work."

"What private lab's work?"

"UAB's research is funded by the government, so they can't market it. If something looks good, they partner with a private lab and drug companies to see if their research can be turned into something profitable."

"But if the drug doesn't work, wouldn't it be *less* likely that whatever a private lab came up with would work?"

"Not necessarily. The lab work on TXNIP was solid."

At my confused expression, she says, "It's a protein that can inhibit beta cells from producing insulin. The discovery that zahablan might help was actually kind of a side thing."

I decide not to go down the technical detour of whatever she is talking about. "The research will go on either way then," I say.

She nods. "Yeah, but that path with the private lab will take years. They'll be looking at different molecules and seeing what works on a cellular level first. Benjamin wanted to help people now."

Chapter Thirteen

ollow the money.

When I left Stokes, my mind was buzzing and the sight of the complex's swimming pool reminded me that I haven't been to the gym for the last four months. I've kept up my membership at the downtown YMCA, so I headed that way for a much-needed workout. Then I rewarded myself with a swim in the pool. While I stroked through the pristine water, those three words popped into my head—*follow the money.*

Physically drained, but feeling better than I have in a long time, I sit cross-legged on my bed in the basement of Alice's house, laptop in lap. Angel curls next to me, a paw on my arm.

Alice moved all of her plants back upstairs, and I have made the basement room mine in little ways, like clothes and books scattered about and one of my early attempts at a landscape that I like, which hangs on the wall. I keep my easel and paints at my own house because the sunroom light is perfect there. I miss the privacy of my house. I miss painting, and I miss windows. The front porch is a preferable hangout, but this time of day, the mosquitos hang there too.

My basement room is the best place for privacy, which I need if I'm going to have a chance at figuring out why Laurie Stokes killed Benjamin Crompton. Tracey is convinced there's no evidence Crompton was murdered, but I know better. There must be some motivation for Stokes to have killed a man she was supposed to be in love with. Maybe they had a big falling out.

Or maybe if I hunt from a different perspective, I'll stumble on something. A lot of what I want to know can be found on the Internet, including verification of what Laurie Stokes told me about the drug research Crompton was helping with.

Angel keeps her paw on my arm while I type in a few queries. "Aha!" I announce. UAB is indeed, as Stokes said, partnering with a private lab in a separate research effort to look at "more effective" drugs that might shut down TCIP cells, the little devils responsible for inhibiting insulin production.

"Fine," I say to Angel. "But why would they be going to all that trouble when they have a good drug at hand like zahablan that does the same thing? It costs millions of dollars to do scratch research like that."

Angel decides I have been at my toy long enough and crawls on top of the keyboard where she sprawls on her side, looking coyly up at me. I don't know if that's because the laptop is warm or she wants to be petted but, in any case, she's not going anywhere unless I stop and give her attention.

"Alright," I say. "I get it."

I set the laptop aside on my unmade bed and pull her into my lap. I don't know how Alice handles all the cats in the house on top of Daniel and Becca, but she never complains. I should do more helping with them.

Angel butts my hands, reminding me that my attention has wandered. I lift her to my chest, feeling the little power-motor of her contentment. How on earth did I become a cat person?

"Dinner is ready!" Daniel cries from the top of the basement stairs.

"Coming!" I shout back.

At the table, Alice has made fried chicken, green beans, black-eyed peas and cornbread. A Southern meal if ever I saw one.

"Looks great," I say, joining everyone.

"Looks great," Becca says, and my heart sinks. Not because I don't think she is enthusiastic about the meal, but because she is just echoing me, like she is trying to find her way in a strange world. Where is she—the Becca I knew? Is she in there somewhere?

Nora is picking at her food. I wrinkle my nose. I don't think she's had a shower for several days.

Alice catches the look on my face. She knows I'm sensitive to odors. "I'll handle it," she says under her breath.

After dinner, dishes are put up, and then Nora retreats to the couch and the TV.

"Go Fish?" Daniel asks.

"I have some work to do," I say.

"Go Fish!" Becca agrees and produces the stack of playing cards.

"Your turn," Alice says to me. "I want to read my book. I've been playing 'Go Fish' all day."

Resigned, I sit back down at the table. Daniel deals, careful to count every card, and Becca follows what he is doing with hungry eyes.

"Do you have a frog?" Daniel asks me, apparently not aware that the dealer never starts.

I consult my hand and nod at the stack of downturned cards in the center. "Nope, go fish."

Two hours later, after several games of "Go Fish," and reading two bedtime stories, I'm back in my basement hideaway. Angel is curled on my pillow, fast asleep as only a cat can sleep. Careful not to disturb her, I pluck my laptop from the bed and settle into the rocking chair.

During "Go Fish," a thought occurred to me, and I want to check it out—a possible reason why a drug company or a university would invest all that money in a separate research effort with a private lab when zahablan already exists. It doesn't take but a few minutes of searching to confirm my suspicion. It's all about asking the right question.

It seems the patent on zahablan-based brand drugs, which are used to treat blood pressure, has run out. Zahablan is now a generic drug, which means it's cheap, and the pharmaceutical company that owns it can't make any real money on it. Browsing the Web on that subject yields confirmation. In fact, researchers who had identified possible clinical uses for other generic drugs all gave up trying to find financial partners because there was no incentive in repurposing drugs. The head of one drug research company came right out and said that because of the high cost for FDA approval and the low return on a generic drug, no generic drug has ever been approved for a new use without modifying it. This means if the human trials on zahablan's effect on diabetes turn out well, nobody would make a profit by getting it approved for diabetes treatment.

To make it profitable, they have to tweak the same molecule, making it "different"—long-acting or combining it with aspirin or something. Then it's considered a "new" drug by the FDA, and a new patent can be issued for it. And then the cost will go up, and the money will roll in.

Over a million people have Type 1 diabetes, just in the United States. Having a "new" drug with a patent would be a lucrative endeavor for a pharmaceutical company, especially since university and government funding are being tapped to share the costs of development. And that's exactly what's happening at the private lab. If there is a drug company helping to fund that private lab research—to tweak the zahablan molecule and have, in effect, a "new" drug—that pharmaceutical company would have a vested interest in the failure of the University's generic zahablan drug trials failing.

But there's a big, gaping hole in that hypothesis—a lot of other companies would have an interest in zahablan failing. All the manufacturers of other drugs for diabetes, the makers of insulin and drug test strips would lose a lot of money if there were a cure.

And Benjamin Crompton wasn't exactly a linchpin in the research or the test results. According to Stokes, he wasn't even directly involved, just helping some with the data, along with many other people.

I'm not sure what I need to look for next. I need my partner. Unfortunately, my partner may be somehow involved. I feel like I'm picking at a thread in a giant, tangled ball of yarn.

Chapter Fourteen

The next morning, Lieutenant Faraday takes the gloves off and assigns us several cases. The Homicide Unit works serious assaults and kidnappings as well as homicides. Tracey and I agree to work the first one together, an assault victim at UAB Hospital, and then he'll drop me off back at the Administration building, and we'll split up to handle the rest.

On the way to the hospital, I ask Tracey about his martial arts class.

"Is it open to anyone?"

"Sure. But sensei doesn't advertise. It's word of mouth."

"Mind if I tag along?"

"Nope."

"Do I need a special uniform?"

He grins. "Why don't you try it out in sweats first? Sensei has some extra if you decide to stick with it."

My back stiffens. "You don't think I will?"

"It's not for everybody." He glances sideways at me. "But you're pretty stubborn."

"Is that supposed to be a compliment, Lohan?"

"Yep."

Parking is a hassle, and we finally use the deck. Once inside, we find our victim, whose condition meets the definition of "assault with a deadly weapon resulting in serious injury." That puts his case in our camp. In this case, it's a stabbing.

The assault happened last night, and patrol interviewed the victim in the ER. His name is Ferdinand Johnson. Today he is in a room. There are two beds, but the other one is empty. According to the patrol report,

Johnson is an African American male, twenty-four years of age with heavy sideburns and a short beard. A man fitting that description is lying in a bed. His left foot appears to have been amputated, the stub wrapped heavily in bandages, although blood is seeping through one side.

I check the report again. It says a stab wound to the abdomen.

"Are you Mr. Ferdinand Johnson?" Tracey asks.

He opens one eye. "I'm Ferd Johnson. Who the hell are you?" Then he catches sight of me and the other eye opens wide. "And hell-lo, sweetheart."

I'm not amused, but it's not worth the effort to be offended, especially by a man who has just had his foot removed. "I'm Detective Brighton," I say, flipping open my badge, "and this is Detective Lohan."

"Cops," he groans and rolls his eyes to the ceiling. "Here I am dying, and I gotta do twenty questions."

"Our report says you have a stab wound to your abdomen." Tracey looks pointedly at the abrupt end of his left leg. "It's been a while since I had anatomy, but that seems rather low for the abdomen."

"Yeah, ain't that sweet? I come in to get my guts stitched, and they take off my damn foot."

"Why?" I ask.

"It was rotten. Doc said if it didn't go, I would die. They were opening me up to stitch my guts anyway."

"Diabetes?" I ask.

"Yeah, had it since I was a kid. Poor circulation in my feet. It was always messing with my life. I could of run track. I was fast." He shifts in the bed and groans, clutching his belly and panting, his eyes shut tight. After a moment, he opens his eyes again, but sweat beads his forehead.

"I could of gone to college on a scholarship, but I got an infection that wouldn't go away. They kept chipping away pieces of my foot, and I couldn't feel nothing down there anymore."

"I'm sorry about your foot," Tracey says, "but tell us about how you got stabbed."

"Like I told the po-lice last night. My old lady done it."

"How come?"

He shrugs. "I was drunk. I think I may have whacked her a couple of times."

"She stabbed you?" I ask.

"Yeah, she grabbed up a kitchen knife and came at me. She don't like it when I drink in front of the kids. But she don't have a rotten foot."

I'm thinking what a train wreck this man's life is. Would it have been any different if he had been able to run track in school, if he'd gone to college? There was a time when he would have disgusted me. He made choices that put him where he was, but some of his choices were stolen from him. Zahablan, or something like it, might have made a difference in the trajectory of his life and his family's.

"What about your wife?" Tracey asks. "You said you whacked her."

"I said I may have. I don't remember. If I did, it didn't amount to nothin'. She ain't hurt."

According to the police report, the wife had no sign of injury and admitted to stabbing him with scissors, but Tracey is making sure.

"What?" Johnson fumbles in the sheets. "Where's that damn call button? I'm *hurting*, man."

I follow the cord under a tangle of sheets and press it for him.

He's sweating.

"Can I help you?" a female voice says over the intercom.

"Where's my pain meds? This is shit!"

"I'll check with your nurse," she says with a cheerful lilt.

"Mr. Johnson." Tracey leans over him to get his attention. "We'll leave you alone, but first tell me if you want to press charges on your wife for stabbing you."

"Put Shanna in jail? Who would take care of the kids? No man, don't do that to me. I got problems enough."

Chapter Fifteen

That evening I meet Tracey in Trussville, a small municipality just to the east of Birmingham. The Trussville Sports complex is a red brick building that holds a gym and several rooms set off from the road in a row, like a strip mall. I'm early.

Until Tracey pulls up, I stay in my car, staring at the paper with results of the phone records on Benjamin Crompton sent by the phone company in response to my warrant. I've starred two calls to a city hall number. More disturbing are the two outgoing calls Crompton made to Tracey's cell over the past three months. The relationship between Tracey and Crompton was ongoing when Crompton was killed. *Why is he hiding that from me?*

I've backed into the space, so I see Tracey's car when he pulls into the lot. Hastily, I fold the paper, put it into the depths of my purse and join him at the back of his car, scanning the area while he opens his trunk. He makes no comment about my nervous fidgeting. Cops are supposed to be aware of their environment and suspicious of everyone.

"Are you sure you want to do this?" he asks. "It's a little different from the police academy training."

I'm not sure, but I am sure I don't want to be afraid anymore. Not that martial arts can stop a bullet. It might be a waste of time, but at least I will be trying to get my self-confidence back.

Tracey hoists a gym bag and closes the trunk.

I follow him to a room in the complex that Tracey referred to as a "dojo." That's about the extent of my knowledge. Physical training in the police academy was squeezed into a crowded curriculum.

The dojo is a long rectangular room. Several mats pushed tightly together cover the majority of the floor. The inner mats are blue and the outer ones are green. A ballet bar runs the length of one wall.

A few people stand or sit on the mats, stretching. Tracey approaches a large man in a robin's-egg-blue gi, an outfit resembling shapeless, thick pajamas that would have appalled Becca, at least the fashion-conscious Becca-before-the-Ordeal. The end of the man's black belt is embroidered with crimson Japanese letters.

Beckoning me over, Tracey introduces me to his teacher, his sensei, Richard Worthington.

"Welcome," Richard says with a friendly smile. He is a big bear of a man, matching Tracey's size.

Tracey is already wearing white gi pants, but peels out of his shirt to put on his top. It's the first time I've seen him shirtless. I can hear Becca's gasp in my head. "Oh my!"

I silence her and try to follow the process when he ties his black belt, which is very long and has to be looped around twice and then knotted in front. For all the convolutions, it comes out looking neat.

At the mat's edge, Tracey gives a little bow to no one in particular and steps onto it with his left foot first. Feeling out of place in my gray sweats, I copy him. We do a few stretches.

At a barked Japanese word, we all line up before Mark, another sensei, who seems more taciturn than Sensei Richard. I'm relegated to the far end of the line. Tracey's position is at the other end with an assortment of black, white, blue, and brown belts between us in ranking order, I presume. Some wear a white gi, some blue. I'm the only one in just a t-shirt and sweat pants. I'm also the only female. Mark points to Tracey and, at Tracey's command, we all bow at the waist to Mark, then turn and bow to Richard.

So far, this is a piece of cake.

Mark leads us in a series of light warm up exercises. Then we follow him in what he calls a "walking *kata*," a series of steps, some with just footwork and then with sweeping arm moves that thoroughly confuse me, but I follow as best as I can. My assessment of Tracey as a "clumsy" bear crumbles. Despite his size, on the mat, every movement is agile and suggests constrained power.

Falling in various ways follows this exercise. Richard has me start from a squatting position for the back falls and then lie on my back and roll from side to side, practicing landing positions. I just watch when the rest line up and one by one take graceful forward rolls that look easy, but I suspect take practice, as I'm not allowed to attempt them. When that is done, we work on what is termed "the releases," where we take turns grabbing a partner's wrist and practice how to get out of it in several different ways. This seems strange, but I sense it fits into a larger pattern I haven't grasped. When Mark demonstrates variations of the releases and how they lead to wrist locks and throws, I'm pretty lost, although I recognize one move from police academy training.

For the rest of the evening, we work on turning someone's punch into a wristlock. I'm realizing that my suspicion of a wide gap in my hand fighting education was correct. Birmingham Police Academy PT, in retrospect, consisted of getting into shape, getting yelled at, practicing with a short baton, disarming people, handcuff techniques, ground fighting, and more getting into shape and getting yelled at.

My partner in the releases is a baby-faced man named Chris with sandy brown hair in a military buzz cut. He wears a brown belt and looks familiar.

"Do I know you?" I ask.

He smiles. "Chris Lane. I work West Precinct."

"You're a police officer?"

"Yeah." He grasps my wrist, and I try to mimic his smooth movements and end up where I'm supposed to, on the outside of his arm. With great patience, he corrects my posture. "It's about moving your hips," he says. "You don't want to be standing still when attacked. Move out of the way."

"Sounds simple."

"It is, but it's not that easy to do it. You have to overcome the reflex to stand your ground and flinch."

I get that and try to move the way he wants me too. He's really cute. If Becca weren't a mental five year old—

The hour passes way too fast and way before I have any feeling of having truly accomplished anything, except being aware of the difference between where I'm supposed to end up and where I do. The founder of this style is dead, but his students, our teachers, hold him in high esteem. From the way Richard speaks of him, I find myself wishing I could have met him.

We line up and repeat the bowing thing, including a reverse of what we did stepping onto the mat, this time stepping off with the right foot first.

Back in the parking lot, I'm strangely happy.

"Well?" Tracey asks.

"I like it. I want to come back."

He laughs. "Okay."

"What is it anyway? I mean I know it's a martial art, but which one?"

"It's called Akayama Ryu."

"Never heard of it."

"Means the Red Mountain style."

"Really? Like our Red Mountain, the one Vulcan stands on?" Vulcan was the Roman god of fire, metalworking, and the forge, but in Birmingham he is a huge iron statue and the city's icon, a source of pride and a reminder of the Magic City's roots in the iron and steel industry.

"The very one."

"Is that a coincidence?"

"Nope, it originated here. A short old man named Alex Marshall designed it. It's primarily Jujitsu, but contains a mixture of techniques from Jujitsu, Aikido, and Judo."

"Alex Marshall?" I wrinkle my forehead. "Sounds familiar for some reason."

"He taught at the Police Academy years ago. Somewhat of a legend."

"How long have you been at it?"

"I started as a child, actually. Not in this system. I did karate when I was younger and then studied Aikido and Judo. I've only been doing Akayama for five years."

I eye his big frame. "Why do you keep doing it?"

He shrugs. "Keeps me from hurting people."

My brows rise. "*Keeps* you from hurting people?"

"I have a temper."

I study his blunt features, but can't tell if he is being truthful or facetious.

Chapter Sixteen

Enduring a City Council meeting is on my list of not-fun things to do, ranking up there with shopping. Instead, I sit in vigilance in a hallway that doubles as a waiting area. Councilman Orson Hobart will have to pass me to get in his office.

I told Tracey and Lieutenant Faraday I had a doctor's appointment. True, but I'm skipping the going to it part.

The numbers to City Hall in Crompton's phone records were to Councilor Hobart's office. I pay no attention to politics, but I do know he is the council president. I casually quizzed his assistant, and she didn't know Crompton. She could be lying, but I don't think so.

In addition to investigating behind Tracey's back, I'm now putting my career, or at least my position in Homicide, in jeopardy. A city councilman isn't immune to investigation, of course, but even I know that protocol would be to give my lieutenant a heads-up before interviewing him. She would want to know details, however, and I can't give her any that would support me questioning Hobart, at least not anything that didn't involve Tracey lying or magic. I'm going to bluff my way. What's the worst thing that could happen—they send me back to be a patrol officer, something I repeatedly requested?

A well built, distinguished-looking man, maybe in his sixties, steel gray at his temples approaches the receptionist's counter. I recognize Hobart from his photo on the city website and restrain myself from jumping up and confronting him in the hallway. The receptionist knows I'm waiting, and that it's official police business. He stops at her desk, and she leans toward him over the counter. He glances at me.

The receptionist hands him a piece of paper, which he consults before turning to me.

"Detective Brighton?"

I stand and take the offered hand.

"Shall we go to my office?"

I follow him down a hall to an office that is smaller than I expected. Inside, I close the door behind me. The office is uncluttered—a desk, shelves of books and two chairs arranged to slightly face each other and the occupant of the desk. Several certificates hang on the wall. I can make out an "M.D." on one of them.

"Please sit down." He glances at his watch. "How can I help you?"

"I'm investigating the death of Benjamin Crompton."

His mouth tightens. "That was an accident, an overdose of insulin."

"How do you know that?"

He shrugs. "That's what roared through the halls of the University ten minutes after it happened. Is there something I don't know?"

"Did you know Dr. Crompton?"

"Yes, I did. Why do you ask?"

"I—we aren't completely convinced it was an accident."

"We aren't?" asks a voice behind me.

I twist in my chair. A large hunk of a man fills the doorway, a familiar hunk. "Lohan?"

He steps inside and shuts the door behind him. "What are you doing here, Rose?"

I stand and face him. "What are *you* doing here?"

He stares hard at me. "I'm visiting my father."

Confusion hits and then unravels. "Councilor Hobart is your father?"

"I am," Hobart says.

"Then that's how you know Benjamin Crompton?" I ask Tracey.

"Is that what this is about? You're going behind my back about that?" There is a creeping stain of red at his neck.

"Why did you lie about it?" I ask.

"That's not . . . your business."

"It is my business." My fists clench. "We're supposed to be partners."

"There's absolutely no evidence of foul play. If there was, I'd be the first person to insist on solving the case."

Guilt stabs me. I'm keeping the truth from him as much as he is from me. But that doesn't change the situation. My ear lobes burn, an annoying side effect of anger.

Hobart clears his throat.

My ears burn hotter, now in embarrassment.

"Maybe you kids need to take this outside," Hobart says in an even voice. "I have work to do."

Tracey and I continue to stare at each other. He reaches behind him and opens the door, motioning me ahead.

We don't speak until we exit the building and reach a small concrete walkway on the basement level connecting a side door of City Hall to the employee parking deck. Efforts have been made to turn the utilitarian space into a garden area, but I catch the faint odor of urine and suspect homeless folks camp here during the night. We stay on the concrete walkway and face each other.

"What was that all about?" Tracey asks.

"I'm just doing my job investigating a murder."

"There is no murder. Why are you being so stubborn?"

"Why did you hide your relationship with Crompton?"

"It's complicated, but I didn't kill him, if that's what you're implying.

There's no doubting the tension in him, and I recall the ease with which he threw people to the ground in the dojo and what he said about his temper. Tracey Lohan is a dangerous man. But I'm angry myself.

"I don't think you killed him, but you have totally ignored my . . . instincts about Laurie Stokes. Is it because I'm a rookie or a woman?"

"Whoa. Everything is not about that."

"Then what is it about?"

"I think you're wrong."

My hands settle on my hips. "Well, I think *you're* wrong.

We are reduced again to the staring thing.

For a moment I wonder if he is going to break one of my bones. Then, almost imperceptibly, a corner of his mouth twitches.

"You are stubborn, Rose."

I sniff. "We've already established that."

My adoptive father taught me to be stubborn. A Marine drill sergeant, he made me an obstacle course in the back yard of whatever base housing we ended up in, and when I got old enough, I went on his morning runs with him. He pushed me physically, like I was one of his recruits. Maybe he was trying to break me. I think he thought the world would eventually, and it would be better for me to see that when it happened, it wouldn't kill me. Maybe that's what got me through the Ordeal. Standing up to Lohan is nothing compared to my father.

"Where do we go from here?" Tracey asks.

"Well, I guess you can flunk me as a partner, and I'll go back to Burglary or Patrol."

"Or—?"

"Or we can discuss this and figure out a path forward."

"Which means do it your way?"

"That's the reasonable path."

He barks a laugh. "How so?"

"If I'm wrong and it's just an accidental overdose, nobody gets hurt if we do our job and ask a few questions. But if you're wrong, a murderer goes free."

For a moment, he's quiet. "I'll make you a deal."

I wait.

"We'll give your way a shot, but if we don't find anything, you let it go."

Chapter Seventeen

The Edge of Chaos is on the fourth floor of one of the red brick buildings that make up the multiple-block campus and medical center of UAB. Still part of Southside, it is only a handful of blocks from the residential neighborhood where Alice and I live.

Stepping off the elevator, Tracey and I emerge in a large corridor that arcs around a central core. The ceiling is composed of chunks of thick white geometric pieces spaced in concentric rings with black, drop-down lighting between the pieces. Abstract artwork in jagged colors wraps columns that help support the unusual architectural design. A large chalkboard displays what appear to be random graffiti and a few equations. The place screams "environment designed to promote freethinking and creativity."

It makes me nervous.

Our escort is Fred Enslen, the director. He leads us around the circular hall, into a large, open rectangular space. Comfortable chairs arranged to entice conversation are clustered at one end next to large windows, but the rest of the area contains traditional tables and plastic chairs, whiteboards, and a video screen.

"We had a presentation here earlier," Enslen says, "but we can rearrange the room for other purposes. The idea is to encourage cross-disciplinary conversations and hopefully, collusions."

"Is it working?" Tracey asks.

Enslen shrugs. "It's a difficult thing to measure. But it's a community space too, and we have an active schedule of events." He waves us back down the circular hallway. "My office is just to the right. Why don't we go in there and see how I can help you?"

His office is a traditional square cube with enough space for two or three visitors. Somehow, I expected it to be a weird shape or rainbow colors or something in keeping with the avant-garde design. On his desk are photos of two children. "My niece and nephew," he says, seeing my attention.

Tracey nods at a photograph of a young lieutenant in an Army uniform. "That you?"

"It is." Enslen says. "Did you serve?"

"I did. Marine Corps. Afghanistan."

I give Tracey a quick look at this new information. Not that I should be surprised. I know very little about him other than he looks like a linebacker, takes his coffee black, keeps chocolate chip cookies in his desk and likes Indian food.

"We're investigating the death of Dr. Benjamin Crompton," Tracey says.

Enslen glances down. "Terrible thing to lose Benjamin like that. Terrible. But I don't understand why it's a homicide case. I heard he had an accidental insulin overdose."

"Yeah, well, we're just checking all the possibilities," Tracey says. "We're interested in the diabetes project he was overseeing."

I'm grateful for what he didn't say—*My partner has this hunch based on no evidence whatsoever, but I'm humoring her.*

"Why is this place under the domain of Public Health?" I ask.

"To tell the truth, we had some space in the back, and they put a bunch of data people from Public Health there."

"Data people?"

"Research data people." His hands wave the air like an orchestra conductor readying his players. "Do you know why there is hype about how good almonds are for you?"

I stare at him.

"It's because there is lots of research on almonds." He points at me. "But what about pecans? They're good for you too, equally as good as almonds, but you never hear about pecans, do you?"

"Uh, never thought about it," Tracey says. "Do your data guys study pecans?"

Caught up in his teaching moment, Enslen doesn't miss a beat. "The reason there is research on almonds is because almond growers have deep pockets, or at least the companies selling them do."

"So they advertise," Tracey says with a shrug.

"Yes, but not just advertising," Enslen says. "They have to have data to tout almonds as being healthy."

"The almond people fund research on their own product?" I ask.

"You got it. And that's how everything works, except for the pure research that universities and nonprofits do, including the pharmaceutical companies. The drug companies fund the research into their own new drugs."

"That sounds a bit creepy." I say. "How can you trust the results?"

"Exactly. And that's what the university data people do on private research data—they do meta-analysis, studying the studies, correcting for biases in particular samples and measures or anything else that jumps out at them. A simpler way to put it is they go over the research that was funded by businesses that have a direct interest in the results."

"Glad to hear someone does," Tracey says. "I'd hate to think all those almonds I eat were a waste of nutrition."

I surreptitiously step on his toe.

"That's fascinating." I say. "Can we see the offices?"

"Sure."

"We're particularly interested in the ongoing study about diabetes."

"Which one? There are several."

"The one about the drug zahablan," I say.

"Well, lucky day for you." He consults his watch. "You've got fifteen minutes."

"What happens in fifteen minutes?" I ask.

"Deon Segal is out the door at noon, no matter what is happening."

"Maybe he doesn't like eating lunch at his desk," Tracey says.

"I don't ask his business. It's his lunch break."

Enslen leads us to a hallway and a row of cubicles, knocks, and opens a door. "Hi, Segal. Mind if we bother you for a minute?"

"No, not at all."

We step into the room behind Enslen. A fine-looking young black man sits at a computer console. His hair hangs in a single, thick braid of woven dreadlocks down his back.

"This is D. Segal," Enslen says, "probably our top data guy. I think he hacks into NSA on his lunch break."

"Now Mr. Enslen, you know I wouldn't do that."

Enslen chuckles at his own joke. "Segal, these folks are detectives from the Birmingham Police Department. Detective Lohan and Miss—?" He looks at me for help.

"Detective Brighton."

"Right, sorry." He turns back to Segal.

Enslen's cell phone rings, and he pulls it off the clip on his belt and answers it.

"Yeah, right. Sure." He looks up at us. "You need me for anything else? I have a meeting."

Tracey looks at me and I shrug.

"We have your number," Tracey says. "We'll call if we do."

Enslen waves at Segal. "He can answer any questions you might have. He's in charge of data collection management for the project you mentioned." He puts the phone back to his ear. "I'll be there in five."

Segal looks to us when Enslen is gone. He appears too young to even have to shave, with his long hair and eyebrows that seem perpetually quizzical behind half-inch-thick glasses.

"Deon Segal?" I say, writing his name in my notebook.

"Yeah, but everybody calls me Segal. What are you investigating?" he says. "If it's okay to ask."

"We're working on a homicide," Tracey says.

"Cool."

Tracey turns to me. "You're the computer geek. Ask away."

I'm pretty certain calling me a computer geek compared to Segal is like calling a donkey a thoroughbred, but I guess I'm the one with the questions.

"What do you do?" I ask and hastily add, "In general terms."

"Me? I mostly go over data, look for anomalies and biases in test reports, things that don't agree or raise a red flag. I dig into the nitty-gritty, you might say."

"What can you tell us about the testing on zahablan?"

"Yeah, that's my project. I mean, not *my* project. I'm only a data guy, but I can tell you about it. It's really exciting."

Tracey looks about as excited as a man watching cement set, but I nod. "Just talk about it, and we'll stop you if you go over my head."

"Sure." He pushes away from his computer. "We're trying to establish whether zahablan is a TXNIP inhibitor in human beta cells."

"Stop," Tracey says. "I'm drowning."

"Oh, sorry. Okay, let's start here—beta cells live inside the pancreas. They're critical to producing insulin. And I'm sure you know that the body's failure to produce insulin naturally is what Type 1 diabetes is all about. That's why people with the condition have to take artificial insulin."

I nod.

"There is a protein," he continues, "called TXNIP in beta cells and when there is too much of it, it kills the beta cells."

This is what Laurie Stokes told me, but I haven't told Tracey that I spoke with her after our initial interview or that I interviewed Crompton's wife.

"And the body can't produce insulin?" Tracey asks.

"Right. Am I going too slow?"

"No," Tracey says. "You're just right. Go on."

"Zahablan is a common blood pressure medication. It's been around for a long time, but a researcher discovered that it can lower TXNIP in mice models, and the beta cells recovered and produced insulin *on their own*." He looks up at us to see if we get the significance.

"If it works," he says, his voice hushed with awe, "it may not be just a treatment, it would be closer to a *cure*."

Chapter Eighteen

The next Saturday presses down on me, overcast and dreary as if the sky was sinking. The cats all seem to want attention at once, and Alexander has cut a nice groove in my arm that smarts. Becca and Daniel are playing hide-and-seek and screaming.

"Why don't you take them somewhere?" Alice asks. "It's not healthy for them to be cooped up in the house. Becca has not been out since her 'accident.'" That's what Alice calls the Ordeal.

"Not today," I need some time alone. *Selfish*. I promise myself I will take Becca and Daniel somewhere soon. Nora doesn't seem inclined to go anywhere other than the couch and the bedroom as far as I can see. Next year, if they are still at Alice's, Daniel will have to go to school.

I need some time to myself, but not in my room. I've spent enough time in my basement bedroom the past four months. There are no windows, and the door just leads to an unfinished portion of the basement. I'm naturally a bit claustrophobic anyway.

"And we won't tell anyone that we sleep with a light on, will we?" I say softly, grabbing a raincoat and scooping up Angel.

It's only a short walk along the cracked sidewalks in the rain to my own house, but I suddenly have to fight a bout of anxiety that rises unbidden and unwanted. Regardless of whether it is totally in my mind or not, I *feel* eyes on me and quicken my steps.

The wind buffets. This is the time of year when tornados are prone to form, when the mix of hot and cold temperature fronts collide in a whirl of death. The image, I think, is more an internal reflection than a weather prediction.

But I'm not more than a half a block away when my neck prickles, adding to the feeling of being watched. I tell myself it's because this is approximately where I was a few months ago—on the same route from Alice's house to mine—when a car barreled down the street that intersects here and tried to run over me. That was my first stay in the hospital.

Dizzy, I lean against a nearby light pole. I've read up on panic attacks. They're sudden episodes of intense fear with no apparent cause. Even so, I do a three-sixty, my body certain of imminent danger. No car lurks with the engine running and evil intent. A man is walking a black Labrador in the opposite direction. An elderly woman with a purple scarf is getting into her car. I press Angel closer to my chest. She *meows* in protest. My heart is thumping hard. My chest hurts. I make myself release the pressure on Angel. She would be well within her rights to add to Alexander's scratch on my arm.

Just a panic attack, I tell myself, fighting the lightheadedness. My free hand fumbles inside my purse, wrapping around the butt of my gun. I concentrate on that. If some bad guy is watching me, he is going to be surprised. I don't care who he is. Magic is not going to stop a bullet. It doesn't work that way.

Nothing happens. I take several shaky breaths, willing calmness, and start walking again, the need to be within the safety of my own house propelling me forward. Raindrops begin to fall.

Opening the door and entering my abandoned house calms the runaway, out-of-control storm that battered me on the street, but it isn't the psychological balm I had hoped for. It is opening Pandora's box, only the contents are not evil spirits, but my personal past. Maybe they are one and the same.

I pull Angel from the interior of my windbreaker where she has curled against my chest. As soon as I set her down, she begins exploring, tail aloft, as if it's a totally foreign environment. It feels a bit that way.

After being released from the hospital, I went on a cleaning jag before I moved in with Alice. The house is unrecognizable. Let's just say housekeeping is not my best trait, other than taking care of the bathroom. My adoptive father was Marine-strict about that, and I can clean a toilet. In fact, I once had to clean it with a toothbrush when I let my grades drop.

"I thought you could use a break, too," I tell Angel. "Now you have a whole house and me to yourself, at least for a while."

I haven't been back here since Angel and I moved in with Alice to help care for Becca, but this is my refuge, *my* house. I sit on the worn couch, and Angel immediately returns and jumps into my lap, purring happily. I stroke her, revving the amazing engine inside that tiny body.

Maybe coming here wasn't a stupid idea. Angel seems happy. Walking in the woods has always been a solace, but now being outside seems to trigger the panic attacks, and the woods around here have dark associations now. Besides, it's the kind of rain that settles in like a fat gray doom for the afternoon.

A fresh wave of guilt washes over me about leaving Alice alone again taking care of Becca and Daniel. Alice has to stay in that house with them all day. I don't know how she does it. But Alice has laid a lot on me. I want to think about what she told me about the Houses and the implications of an entire race going extinct, not about my past. Naturally—genius that I am—I came straight to the place where a bunch of that past was born.

The brown reclining chair opposite me is where Becca took out her contacts and confessed she was an albino. And six months ago, sitting alone on this faded couch, I downed an entire bottle of wine after Alice's "death," unaware that she had given herself some exotic drug that slowed her heartbeat to almost nothing. After only knowing me as an adult for a short while, she decided dramatic performance was not my *forte*. She feared if she gave me advance notice of her intentions, I wouldn't act shocked enough when I encountered her body.

I was plenty shocked. To my hermit self's surprise, I was also devastated. She was the last of my family. My real family.

Alice is alive. I have to remind myself, even now. It had seemed too real.

I was at her funeral!

I haven't forgiven her for that. I'd already lost my birth family to murder, my adoptive mother to a car accident and my father to an IED. I thought I was steeled against caring about anyone else, but losing Alice so soon after finding her was hard, much harder than I could have imagined.

Aside from watching her casket (not knowing it was empty) lowered into a grave, I had to look at the names of all my immediate family on gravestones in that cemetery . . . including my own.

Alice had faked my childhood death seventeen years ago. She'd arranged things so that the world, and more importantly, House of Iron, believed I had died in the fire that consumed my birth family.

Then she quietly sent me off to be fostered. I was adopted through an agency that kept everything anonymous. I didn't find out who I really was until I knocked on Alice's door as an adult.

I have to admit, faking our deaths did keep House of Iron from killing us for real. No sense in hunting down deceased persons. Of course, now they know I'm alive, but Alice remains "dead." I hope.

I lift Angel from my lap and put her down. Tail askew, she pads down the hall, straight to the bedroom where I'm sure she will jump onto my bed and curl into a ball in her "spot." I follow her and confirm her intentions. That is precisely where she went the first night she invited herself into my house and my bed.

That night she woke me. It took me a minute to remember why a cat was in my bed and realize that she was hissing at the window. It was convenient to keep my duty weapon in the holster on my utility belt. Easier to have all the equipment there when it was time to put on my uniform. But even before the Ordeal, I disliked the feeling of being trapped under sheets and kept an extra gun under my pillow. Something about Angel's arched back and fierce hissing that night raised every hair on the back of my own neck. I snatched the gun and held the window at bay until she let me know the threat was gone. Footprints in the muddy ground the next morning proved her worth as a guard kitty, and I named her Angel.

Angel is clearly suggesting a nap in "her" bed is called for, but I'm not ready to stop poking at memories. The worst place to look is not the bedroom or the hall where I encountered Paul and his milk-stained mustache and purloined cookie, but the kitchen.

Although she is actually asleep at the end of my bed, for a moment, I "see" Angel draped along the kitchen windowsill, which doubled as her scratching post and bears the scars of it. One gray paw is dangling, tail switching lazily in the morning sun. Paul is at the oven, opening it to proudly reveal homemade biscuits. The smell of bacon and eggs and the promise of a life with another human being scared the bejesus out of me.

I couldn't handle it. I told myself I was protecting him, but it was me doing the same push-people-away I had practiced into a fine art. As I've already determined, it's because I don't want to let them down. Maybe it's also so I don't have to lose them. I'm not good relationship material. Becca just wouldn't go when I pushed. Despite my well-honed skill at aloofness, she insisted on being my friend and pushed right back . . . and into my life.

I don't deserve her.

She doesn't deserve what happened.

To keep my mind from digging deeper into that dark mental groove, I focus on Angel, who has just realized I'm in the kitchen and has abandoned her nap plans. She paces back and forth along where her empty food dish sits. She knows there are cans of tuna fish in the cabinet. Why not? She has gotten a little thinner since the trauma of living in a house full of territorial cats and a little boy who bounces off the walls. I open a can for her. She catches the aroma instantly and stitches herself through my legs until I place the can on the floor, not bothering to dump it in her bowl. The electric can opener leaves smooth edges. No point in having to clean something.

There's another room I want to visit. The reason I came. My private room where no one, not even Paul, was allowed.

The wooden door has swollen and sticks. I have to shove it hard with my shoulder before it opens, revealing its secrets. I chose it for its great light. It was originally a sunroom with east and north windows. The play of dust motes reminded me of my younger sister, Amber. As children, we sat beneath a window in a house that was next to Alice's, a house that no longer exists, where we both were born. We would pretend the gleaming motes were dancing fairies. The warmth of that memory melts, as it always does, to the one of Amber under a blood-soaked Cinderella blanket, courtesy of Theophalus Blackwell. I jerk back to the here and now, forcing myself to answer the question of what to paint.

Most of the paintings, now stacked in the closet, are of fire parted by the vertical black streak representing my family's murderer before I had a name for him. I don't particularly want to look at them. I consider the easel, canvas, and my colors. What will I paint, now that my subconscious doesn't need to express demons I have laid to rest? I have laid them to rest, haven't I?

Do the mind's demons ever rest?

I put a fresh canvas on the easel and open the paints, dabbing bits of red, blue, and yellow on their places on the palette. The blank white canvas stares at me. I even dip my brush into a color, a blue. I won't paint flames anymore. Maybe water. The sea.

I start out with a restful blue, but my mind returns to the conversation with Alice, the burden that she placed on me—to bear a child, children. Unfair. This is my body, my life. I get to say whether I want children, and I don't.

The peaceful turquoise water becomes a storm-wracked blue-black. Waves cresting foam. Bloated, angry clouds.

After an hour, my cell plays the chorus from "Purple Rain." I look at it for several measures before answering.

"Hello, Jason."

"What are you doing?"

"I'm painting."

"A room?"

"No, a canvas."

"Ah, something I didn't know about you, *il mio amore*. Art is one of the great mysteries. Why do you suppose you do it?

"Because it relaxes me."

"Is that all? A glass of wine could accomplish that."

"Maybe so."

"I imagine the paints let you express yourself in a way that words cannot, no?"

"What do you want, Jason?"

"I have been thinking about you."

I'm silent. There is no magic forcing my heart into a gallop, but my breaths come short and shallow.

"I would like to see you," he says.

"I know."

"What about dinner? Tomorrow night?"

"No."

"Why not?"

"I'm not— Just 'no.'"

"You do know I am not giving up that easily."

"I know," I say quietly and end the call.

Chapter Nineteen

Losing my desire to paint after the conversation with Jason, I head home where I give in to the guilt and Alice's nudging and take Becca and Daniel out. A trip to the grocery store makes my list of things I avoid doing, ranking somewhere between clothes shopping and the dentist. But this, Alice has informed me, is therapy. I have a food item list and Becca and Daniel in tow. The therapy is for Becca, who has improved enough to take out in public, though she is chewing on her thumb.

My usual excuse about not taking them somewhere—besides the copout that I needed to be alone—is that I've been busy, but the truth is I've also been afraid of what might happen when Becca encounters the world. Will she have a meltdown?

"It's okay," Daniel says to Becca. He is sensitive to her emotional states. His head is the height of her hip, but he's taken on the big brother role. Her fingers curl tight, eclipsing his small hand.

She looks down at him and then at me.

"Yup," I agree. "It's okay. You're okay."

With the air of a deer checking an open pasture in hunting season, her gaze travels the expanse of the downtown Publix parking deck. She's not the only one nervous. The hairs on the back of my neck prickle, and I scan the parking deck too, looking for—an assassin.

I press the soft leather of my purse, where my gun lives, anchoring it against my hip with one hand and take Becca's free hand with the other, willing the anxiety down. Maybe it's because I'm not alone. This time I'm more successful at squelching it.

The three of us make our way slowly to the elevator. When the door slides open, Becca's eyes widen at the revealed close space, but she steps inside at Daniel's urging. I smile encouragingly at Becca, but she is not paying any attention, fascinated by the buttons, pushing them all.

Fortunately, the elevator was already going down, and there are only "2" and "1" options. On the first floor, we step out into the store. I grab a basket, which Becca immediately takes from me and starts up the pristine rows as if she is finally home and knows what to do. I scrounge in my purse for the list Alice made.

We are noticed. I have pulled my wayward hair into a long ponytail and wear my usual jeans and tee, but Becca—who wore red-heeled boots and a matching leather jacket to hike the woods of Red Mountain—is sporting a mixture from her closet, whatever attracted her eye. Mostly people blink at her or smile in tolerant amusement, but their gaze lingers on Daniel's pink-white skin grafts. He doesn't seem to notice, walking quietly beside Becca, protective of his charge. I let out a sigh, releasing the tension that had built from expectation of disaster. Becca is not freaking out—in fact, she seems curious about the people.

The first item on the list is milk. I gently guide her in that direction. When we reach the refrigerated section, I open a glass door and grab a two-percent carton.

"No," Becca says.

I freeze. "No milk?"

She shakes her head and points. "Green."

"Green?" I follow the direction of her finger and indeed, the organic milk has a green logo.

"Sure. Green." I exchange one carton for the other. It makes no difference to me, as long as there is milk to go with midnight cookies.

The rest of the items proceed in a similar manner, with Becca excitedly pointing to cans and boxes she seems to recognize. I buy whatever she wants, delighted with her delight. She hums along with the music piped over the store's system. Daniel scores chocolate sugar cereal, definitely not on the list. I try at least to include the things Alice asked for, although I'm not able to resist the beautiful sushi, second only to Indian on my list of favorite foods. I like to eat. It's cooking that's a challenge. My own refrigerator and pantry bear that out, stocked with chocolate chip cookies, milk, sliced cheese, peanut butter and tuna fish, hence Angel's addiction to tuna. She turns her little nose up at cat food of any type. With that reminder, I head to the canned meat section.

When I reach for the multiple small cans of tuna, a crawling sensation ripples the back of my arms. I don't know if it's part of being a witch of House of Rose or just a primordial human warning thing, but I know I'm being watched. Then my heart launches into a staccato dance.

"Hello," says a voice I would know anywhere.

With a jerk, I whirl to face Jason Blackwell. While I work on steadying my breathing, he reaches out to take Becca's hand.

"You must be Becca."

She tilts her head, her strangely clear eyes sparking momentarily red in the overhead fluorescent lights.

I grab her hand and snatch it away. "Don't touch her," I hiss. "Your House has hurt her enough!"

Jason seems undisturbed by my reaction. "All right." Then his gaze drifts to Daniel, and Jason goes still.

"This is the boy who was there," he says.

It's not a question, and I say nothing, knowing he means in the cave with his uncle . . . the Ordeal.

Jason looks at me again. I'm shaking, but this time it's not because of his proximity.

Hot white fire blooms from me, embracing Theophalus Blackwell and the child he holds, the child whose throat he was about to slice open. Paul snatches Daniel from Blackwell's grasp, covering him with his own body, his movements fast, instinctual, a policeman doing what he does . . . protecting. It's the last thing he will ever do.

I am breathing. Just breathing. *Don't faint.*

Jason steps forward and grabs my arms. My already erratic pulse thunders in response. *Damn this magic.*

He takes a ragged breath. "Rose, are you alright?"

"Yes," I whisper and step back, shaking loose and making my voice firm. "Yes."

He drops his hands and stares at them for a moment. Do they burn with a magical heat like the places he touched on my arms?

"Are you following me?" I demand.

"I want to make up for what happened." He meets my eyes.

"You can't."

"At least listen."

"No."

"I want to help." He looks first at Becca, who is staring at him, and then at Daniel, who is shuffling and swinging his arms, obviously bored.

This gives me pause. If there is something that might help Becca or Daniel, I will at least listen.

"What do you have in mind?"

"Any counseling or medical surgery that might help, I will pay for. Anything. No questions asked."

I consider. According to the UAB doctors, Daniel will need additional surgeries that would be considered "cosmetic," although the hospital wrote off most of the charges for what they did to save his life.

Their efforts were aided, unbeknownst to them, by Alice's healing intervention. Without her, I'm fairly certain Daniel would have died. The medical team considered it nothing short of miraculous that he didn't. Nora certainly couldn't pay for anything. My city insurance wouldn't. I only have single coverage, and even if I had family coverage, Daniel isn't family. I have no idea what Alice's financial situation is and don't want to ask her. I have a small inheritance from my parents. House of Iron, on the other hand, has deep pockets. Not surprising when you can influence anyone you touch.

"We've already sent Becca to an in-house program with a psychologist and a psychiatrist."

The latter gave her pills that made her sleep. Alice pronounced them worthless. Shock treatment was the next suggestion, but I refused to go there. We tried a counselor, but that didn't help either. Becca just curled up in a fetal position. Alice, who had done all she could directly, insisted we bring her home and let "nature take its course." And Becca is getting better, especially since Daniel has become her buddy. Much as I hate sharing the cramped space of Alice's house, I have to admit that.

"The boy then?" Jason asks.

I take a breath. I have no right to deny Daniel a chance, but I will not be beholding to Jason Blackwell. "What strings are attached to this magnanimous offer?" I ask.

"No strings."

"Then . . . I accept."

Regardless of his insistence of no strings, I feel like the first strands of a web have been draped across my shoulders.

"Good." He smiles. "Perhaps you would consider a short cruise in my yacht. I find being out on the water peaceful and therapeutic. And," he adds before I can refuse, "you would have no worries about influence. In addition to my word, we can't access our, um, abilities, on water, as I'm sure you know."

Alice has told me the same thing. And I remember sitting on the beach once and sensing that I couldn't pull any of the living-green from what had to be the sea's vast resources of carbon.

"Boat?" Becca says suddenly.

"Yes," Jason says, gracing her with his dazzling smile. "A boat."

She smiles and turns to me. "Yes?"

It's the first spoken request, other than the ones to read to her or direction for other items like the milk in the green carton, since Black's touch burned her mind. I open my mouth to say "no." But the hope and expectation of joy in her eyes slams me hard enough to make my chest hurt.

"I like to swim," Daniel says.

Another strand of web tangles.

"Then it's settled," Jason says. "What about this weekend? The weather will be beautiful, and I have a small plane. We'll be in Orange Beach before you can blink."

"I . . . can't promise anything without asking Daniel's mother."

What am I doing? Alice is not going to like this. *I* don't like this.

"We'll see," I hedge. Maybe Becca will forget about it. Her attention span is not long.

"Fair enough. I will call you." He hands me a card. "You have my number, but you can send any bills to this address."

I take the card numbly. He bows like some ancient courtier. Perhaps he was one. I have no idea how old he is.

"Boat?" Becca echoes plaintively as he leaves.

My mind whirls while we finish shopping, and I absently hand over my credit card to the cashier. Can I trust Jason? He is House of Iron. Alice insists they're all the enemy, but are they? Or was it just Theophalus Blackwell's warped personal vengeance for House of Rose? Isn't that all over now?

But four months ago, a black rose was left on the steps to Alice's house. A warning? I'm not sure. It's not over, but who issued the unspoken threat? There are three Houses. What about House of Stone? Alice said they were reclusive and secretive. I know so little. How do I even know the rose was a threat? One was left in my hospital room and members of Iron dropped red roses into Alice's grave at her "funeral." Maybe the message is not a threat at all. I'm ignorant, and ignorance can get me killed . . . or kill those I love.

Chapter Twenty

"You cannot be serious," Alice says, one hand brushing invisible crumbs from her apron as if they are spiders. Rolling pin in the other hand, she turns from the kitchen counter and the mound of raw dough dusted with flour.

"I know. It's—"

"Dangerous," she finishes for me and brandishes the rolling pin. "And reckless. Do I have to remind you that House of Iron was behind the death of your family, *our* family?"

"No, you do not have to remind me. But that was Jason's uncle. Jason was hurt badly trying to help me. He came to check on me in the hospital even though he was a patient himself and could barely stand."

"There are layers and layers in the game that Iron plays," Alice says. "Don't be taken in."

"I won't. I don't trust him."

"Then why put yourself, Becca, and Daniel in such a dangerous position?"

"Becca has not stopped talking about 'the boat.' She's still picking out what to wear."

To anyone else, this would seem an innocuous statement, but Alice understands what an enormous thing it is for Becca to care about clothes again. It was not too long ago that she was a zombie, relying on me to chop up her food and feed her.

"My friend is coming back," I say. "I'm not going to let anything stop that."

Alice locks eyes with me and, despite the fact that her gift is healing, I think she is going to try a real witch's hex on me, but she melts a bit and sniffs.

Angel jumps into my lap and kneads the tops of my thighs. She does this with her claws retracted, which is not something I can say of all the other cats in the house. What she wants is a bit of the cream Alice puts on the table for tea. When my great aunt isn't looking, I sometimes sneak a drop onto my finger for her, and she licks it with her small, rough tongue. But Alice is looking right at me. She is glaring, in fact.

"And Alice, not that I have any intention of fulfilling this, but weren't you the one who told me I needed to have a child by a man of one of the Houses?"

She practically sputters. "Is that why you're going?"

"Of course not. I told you. It's for Becca."

"There is this magical attraction thing though, isn't there?"

I sigh. "Yes, there is."

It's not difficult to imagine the war raging in her—the need to keep me away from Iron versus the need to get me pregnant.

"All right," she says. "But don't be completely foolish. Take that bobby with you."

"Bobby? Who are you talking about?"

"The rozzer, the detective you work with."

It takes me a moment to figure that one out. When stressed, Alice tends to slip into British slang. "Tracey? I can't—"

"House of Iron might think twice about doffing you and a policeman. I would go, but I'm afraid my wig would fly off, and I don't want House of Iron getting too good a look, in any case. Being dead is a terrible bother."

"It kept you safe."

"Hmm. Maybe, but it left you a target. I thought I could protect you better if House of Iron thought I was out of the picture, but—" She hesitates. "That might have been a miscalculation."

"We don't know that the entire House of Iron was behind it," I say reasonably. My mother's letter mentioned that there was a cabal intent on wiping out House of Rose.

"I don't trust any of House of Iron," Alice says. "Don't go."

I say nothing.

"I see that stubborn line to your mouth," she says. "It means you are going to do it anyway." She closes her eyes and sniffs dramatically. "Then at least take the bobby with you."

I start to say no, but can't think of a good reason. "I'll ask him, but I doubt he will."

She raises a silver eyebrow.

"What?" I ask.

"Is he married?"

"No."

"Gay?"

"No. I mean . . . I don't think—how would I know?" I hate it that I'm flustered. Alice often has that effect on me.

"Well, you will find out if he is or not," she says.

"Alice, what are you talking about?"

"Any red-blooded man will jump at the chance to go sailing with you. Have you never looked in a mirror, my dear?"

I find my mouth is open and snap it shut.

THAT EVENING AT JUJITSU CLASS, we concentrate on how to choke people and how to respond to someone trying to choke us. I learn how to scrape my foot down an attacker's shin and stomp his foot, then shift my weight to the side and under his arm. We're supposed to end up in a wristlock, but I can't seem to get that part right.

We switch partners periodically, but Chris is my favorite to work with. He's closer to my height and is cooperative, which helps me learn the moves. Others test me, which I don't think is fair, since I'm doing the scraping and stomping part with restraint. The sensei only step in to help when asked or when it is obvious they are needed. And Tracey deliberately works with other people.

Afterward, in the parking lot, I ask Tracey if he's eaten. "I could use a hamburger."

"You can eat after training?"

"I can always eat."

"It's pretty late."

"I know, but I want to ask you something. You don't have to eat anything."

"It's not about Crompton, is it?"

I still don't understand why Tracey lied to me about how he knew Crompton, but we've pretty much hit a wall with that and the investigation, for that matter.

"No, something personal."

"Fast food joint okay?"

"Fine."

Tracey lowers himself into the plastic chair, a cup of steaming coffee in his hand.

"How can you drink caffeine at this time of night?" I ask.

He shrugs and eyes the double cheeseburger I'm unwrapping. "It doesn't keep me awake. What's the big mystery?"

"I just wanted to ask you, that is, are you tied up this weekend?"

I have his attention. "Actually, no."

I clear my throat. *How do I say I want you to escort me on a boat ride because the boat's owner is a warlock from House of Iron and is very powerful, and I need a witness, even though he could burn out your mind with a touch? How do I even have the right to ask him to do this?*

"I have a potentially awkward situation and was wondering if you would help."

"How?"

"Well," I take a deep breath, "there is this man who has offered to take Becca and Daniel and me on his boat at Orange Beach, and Becca has grabbed onto the idea and is excited. She hasn't been excited about anything since—"

"And the problem is?"

"The problem is that I'm . . . uncomfortable around this man and don't want to be alone with him on a boat with just a child and—" I can't bring myself to say a *brain-damaged person.*

Thankfully, I don't have to. Tracey knows about Becca. He was the one who found us in the cave after the Ordeal.

"I see."

"I thought if you were there—"

He grins. "Sure."

"What?"

"Yeah, I'll go. I get it."

I let out a sigh of relief and give him a grateful smile. That wasn't so hard. Now what could possibly go wrong?

Chapter Twenty-One

We stand on a long pier behind The Wharf, a multi-building, multi-level shopping mecca in Orange Beach, Alabama, staring up at the sleek *Iron Fist*. She rocks in the gentle stir of the Intracoastal Waterway, a narrow band running north of, but roughly parallel with the Gulf of Mexico shoreline. It's only midmorning. I'd declined Jason's offer of a private plane. If I desire a quick exit, I want my car handy. Actually, it's Alice's car. I'm not supposed to drive my city vehicle beyond the city limits, unless it's for a case. Moving up to Homicide didn't merit me a better car, so I'm still driving the ragged-out one from Burglary. Not complaining; it has four wheels, though I've had to put it in the city shop on more than one occasion. Regardless of rules, I wouldn't trust it to drive the five hours to the coast. We left after work last evening, a Friday, and stayed at a cheap hotel to give us a full day.

The Iron Fist is the biggest yacht in sight. Daniel's mouth hangs open, and Becca's smile makes the five-hour drive already worthwhile. She wears a yellow, wide-brim straw hat tied with a white scarf, white Capri pants and a yellow-and-white striped shirt with long balloon sleeves. It took her days to pick out the outfit, something Becca-before-the-Ordeal would have thrown together without a thought. I made sure she had every inch of her fair albino skin covered in sunscreen. Daniel too. His pink skin grafts are very susceptible to burning.

I was surprised at Nora's quick acquiescence to my bringing Daniel. She showed no interest in coming herself, for which I'm grateful. Watching out for Becca and Daniel is more than enough on my plate. I don't trust Jason or his family, but Alice confirmed Jason's claim that water interferes with accessing power for members of any of the Houses.

Worried that the wooden pilings holding up the pier would provide a conduit that bypassed the water's anti-magic effect, I tried to access the living-green as soon as we stepped onto the pier, to no avail. If I could have pulled the smallest bit, we would all be piling back into the car and heading home, despite the disappointment for Becca. But I do feel a vague itch, as if the living-green is there, but out of reach.

A familiar figure striding down the long, narrow pier catches my attention, his hair tossed by a breeze and glinting in the sunshine. Designer glasses hide his eyes. Not that I can tell designer glasses from a drug store brand. I'm just assuming. The Blackwell family, Alice tells me, is worth more dollars than I could count in my lifetime.

A shorter man follows a step or two behind him, a darker presence to Jason's bright gold. Something about the way the man moves implies law enforcement or military. A bodyguard?

I spent most of my life as a military brat, and I know a military bearing when I see one. When he gets closer, I recognize him as the "bouncer" at the All Hallows Eve party Paul and I attended at the Blackwell mansion last year. The party where Aunt Alice "died" in the kitchen.

Even though we are on the pier, I position myself between Jason and Becca. She hasn't released Daniel's hand since we piled out of the car. Despite Alice's assertions and my own experimentation, I cringe when Jason shakes hands with Tracey, stepping close to make sure he doesn't whisper something. That's all it takes when a member of House of Iron touches a victim and draws on iron ore to fuel his power. A little whisper in a banker's ear, a stockbroker, a policeman—it doesn't take long to spin a web that touches government, finance, or politics. I realize I have no idea how far those webs extend. The only hitch is that normally Iron's influence wears off with time. Unless they blow out someone's mind, as Theophalus did with Becca.

Jason looks miffed when he sees Tracey. "I had not expected a fourth person."

I shrug. "We can go home if you'd like." I ignore Becca's stricken look. Tracey doesn't flinch.

"No, of course, it is fine," Jason recovers smoothly. "The chef will adjust."

But there is no doubt he resents Tracey's presence and would like to know what our relationship is.

"This is my driver, Angola," Jason says, introducing the man behind him. "And a good man on a boat."

"Angola?" Tracey says. "Like the country in Africa?"

"Yes, precisely," the man replies in an accent I can't quite identify. "My mother's homeland."

If his mother was African, the light coffee of his skin implies his father might have been Caucasian. His dark hair is bound at the nape of his neck into a short ponytail. Equally dark hairs stubble his cheeks. I suspect he is one of the unlucky men who need to shave more than once a day to keep a beard at bay. On another man it might be unkempt, but on him, it's a rugged, sexy look, if a bit effeminate.

Jason leads the way onto the *Iron Fist*. Tracey follows, extending his hand to Becca for balance. Daniel ignores the offer. "I can do it," he says.

I'm up after Daniel. Angola follows.

"Welcome aboard," Jason says.

Daniel gives him a salute, which he returns, not a hint of a smile on his sculptured face.

"Very pretty," Becca whispers in my ear, meaning Jason, and I can't help a smile and a surge of hope. She *is* getting better. Maybe I have not done something awful with this excursion.

On board, we meet two other crewmembers. The first is a man my age, deeply tanned with short brown hair, dressed in white slacks and a white sleeveless tee.

"This is Lawrence," Jason says. "Our pilot. Rest assured you are in good hands."

I can feel Lawrence's gaze giving me the once over as Jason introduces the others—Nate, an older man with a thick mustache, who is chef and bartender, and a young man in navy blue shorts whose name I don't catch, but I assume he is the one who handles things like ropes and anchors.

Jason gives us a tour, and I'm impressed in spite of my determination not to be. The top deck is less than a quarter of the boat's length and is crammed with equipment in what is obviously the pilot's domain. Huge antennae rise on either side of the exterior. The next level down contains a beautiful stateroom with seating around a fully stocked bar, a large table, and lounge area. Behind that, a modern kitchen gleams with stainless steel. Even I, who live from refrigerator takeout to microwave, can see that it's efficiently organized. Behind it is a narrow hall with two guest cabins that share a bathroom. Everything is spotless. Even the engine room gleams.

Last on the tour is the master bedroom, framed in rich oak paneling. It's twice the size of my room at Alice's house and dominated by a king-sized bed covered in a red satin spread. The bed looms in my perception. I'm grateful that the same water barrier that separates me from the living-green douses the electricity between Jason and me.

Sliding glass doors open from the bedroom onto a small private area of deck. We climb a short set of stairs, emerging onto a wider deck in the boat's stern to find the boy in shorts has untied us from the dock. Jason waves us into comfortable chairs, and the *Iron Fist* glides smoothly out into the channel. Behind us, the concrete bridge of the Foley Beach Expressway arcs across the waterway. We head into the morning sun, which is subdued enough to look at full on. On either side of the waterway, tall pine trees green the banks. The day is perfect. As we move forward at a stately pace into the first bay, the sun plays behind the clouds before emerging to sparkle the languid water with silver coins.

To my surprise, Angola appears with a tray of Bloody Marys and lemonade for Daniel. The drinks are works of art, sporting sprigs of celery, lime and pink boiled shrimp curved around the large glasses' edges. He offers one to me. I hesitate and glance at Tracey. "You driving, Lohan?"

"Only if he can make me a virgin one of those."

"Of course," Angola says.

I pluck the glass from the tray. It tastes as marvelous as it looks.

The day unwinds with the luxurious feeling of having cast off worries with the ropes that tied us to the dock. The waterway wends along, in no hurry to find the sea.

Jason turns to Becca. "Would you like to fish?"

Her eyes light and she nods.

"Do you know how?" he asks.

She curls her bottom lip under her front teeth, thinking. Trying to find memories? *Oh Becca, I'm so sorry. It's my fault. If I hadn't let you come with me that day when we found the entrance to a secret tunnel, you would not be like this.*

Jason waits, though I can see he is not used to being patient. Finally, Becca shakes her head, and Jason baits her hook. He has been respectful of his promise not to touch anyone. It's amusing to see him try to teach Becca to fish without brushing her. She doesn't notice, intent on holding the pole the way he shows her. He gives one to Daniel too and is rewarded with a wide grin. The two stand, Daniel's shoulder to Becca's hip, manning their poles, busy and happy doing, as far as I can tell, nothing.

The Iron Fist's sleek hull glides through water browned from recent rains as we slip through Wolf Bay. Houses pepper the southern bank on our right, but on our left, as far as we can see up into the bay, the land is green and pristine, with occasional strips of white sand. Then the waterway narrows again, and houses appear on both sides of the channel.

I bask happily in the intermittent sunshine, sipping my drink.

"How long have you known Rose?" Jason asks Tracey. His tone is casual, but everything about Jason is intense. This interrogation is no different. I'm grateful again for the muting of fireworks between us. Not something I want to endure or let Tracey see. Tracey Lohan sees a lot. That much is obvious, even in the short time we've worked together. He's also a liar, I remind myself.

"We met a few months ago," Tracey replies.

"In the police department?"

"Yep. We work together in the Homicide Unit."

Jason nods. I suspect he is not surprised. I have the feeling he knows a lot more about me than I'm comfortable with. Admittedly, the threshold for that bar is not very high.

The *Fist* moves into a curve of land that Jason informs us is Bay la Launch.

"There's something here I want to show you," he says.

Chapter Twenty-Two

Jason stands beside me at the side railing as the *Iron Fist* heads slowly toward the north shoreline. "Barber Marina," he says as we approach a couple of dozen yachts docked in parallel lines.

None of the boats are as large as the *Fist*. The lengths of pier extend out into the bay in a maze-like channel, forcing the boats to idle coming into or leaving the area. Just beyond the first bend, something I can't identify rises from the water. It's not quite big enough to be a yacht, but there are two pieces of it, one larger than the other.

Jason points at it. "Daniel, come look at this."

"What about my fish?" Daniel asks, looking at his pole.

I smile. There is no fish on his line, but he is certain there will be.

"Put it down," Jason says. "The fish won't mind. I want you to see the Lady in the Lake."

With a frown that reflects his reluctance to trade the possibility of catching a fish for looking at a woman, Daniel sets the pole down and joins us at the side rails. Becca, as always, follows him.

"Where?" Daniel says in a bored tone that quickly turns into a "Wow!"

As we get closer, the fuzzy objects in the water near the wharf resolve, and I laugh at the whimsy. It is indeed a lady in the water. "Lohan, come see this."

Tracey rises from his chair like a bear aroused from hibernation and lumbers to us. "What is it?"

I point.

"Well, bless my buttons," Tracey says.

"Bless your buttons?" I laugh again, this time at the incongruity of the expression coming from his mouth. "Where on earth did that come from?"

He smiles and shrugs. "A great aunt who grew up on a farm. She saved it for the real shockers."

The "lady" in the water is clearly visible now. A serene, dark-haired giant, she sits in the bay as if it is a bathtub. Only her head, the top of her chest, and her knees are visible.

Even Becca is entranced. "Who is she?"

I'm again surprised when a complete sentence comes out of her mouth. It's so unremarkable, no one else notices, but it's sweet music to my ears.

Jason is clearly pleased at his audience's reaction. "She's the Lady in the Lake." He tilts his chin to indicate the forest beyond the marina. "There are more wonders back there, if you care to get off for a while and find them." He looks at me and I know the unspoken question— *And if you trust me on land.*

"Yes!" Daniel shouts.

I hesitate. I do not trust him on land or myself with him on land.

"Yes," Becca echoes.

"I don't know," I say.

"Why not?" Tracey asks. "Why wouldn't we want to see more wonders?"

Trapped again. I narrow my eyes at Jason, demanding without words that he keep his agreement not to touch anyone. He gives a barely perceptible nod.

Lawrence negotiates the narrow channel skillfully. The boy in shorts appears and ties us off, and the six of us climb into a van, obviously left here for this purpose. Angola drives. I sit in the van's far back row, as far from Jason as possible. Our first stop is to view a huge black metal spider, which Daniel pronounces "cool." Becca shrinks against her seat in horror. We quickly move on.

Nothing but pine trees grow on either side of the road, tall trees planted in precise rows that allow an unhindered view into their depths. Normally, Alabama forests are invisible beyond the first layer of foliage, as plants crowd each other for every available drop of sunlight. The state is ranked in the top five in terms of plant diversity. But here, between the soldier rows of pine trees, years of needles have layered the ground, preventing other growth.

In their depths, we do find treasures, strange treasures. Jason has us leave the car and leads us to replicas of ancient Chinese warriors. At another stop, Daniel and Becca are delighted with a life-sized Stegosaurus and immediately clamber onto its back. Without being asked, Tracey, the tallest adult, moves into rescue range should either slip among the horned wedges of Steggie's back. Angola waits for us in the car. He is apparently one of those servants who believe in staying out of sight unless needed.

It's the first moment that Jason and I have the space to exchange a private word. The electricity between us resumes as soon as he moves within "range." The hum of it increases as he steps closer, careful not to touch me, even though, as members of the Houses, our powers don't affect each other. But our magic feeds what crackles between us, as if we are the negative and positive ends of an electromagnetic loop. "I want you to know," he whispers, "that I felt the same about you, even on the boat."

My mouth tightens. "In your dreams, Jason Blackwell. My life is complicated enough. You promised to leave me alone after this."

If anything, the blue ice of his gaze grows more intense. Maybe not being able to have something flames his interest.

"I got you!" Tracey says, snatching our attention. His big hands have scooped Daniel from a precarious position on the dinosaur's sloping back.

We pile back in the van and visit Tyrannosaurus rex, where Jason announces lunch. I look up at the intimidating colossus. This is another extinct creature the world can do without. I pull my hair up, twisting it into a long ponytail to let a breeze cool the back of my sticky neck. The fate of the Houses is something I have relegated to the back of my mind, but it emerges, full bloom, in the face of T-rex's giant head and gleaming jaws. If the dinosaurs had continued to dominate Earth, would humans have evolved and survived? The Houses have abilities—like this creature has enormous, razor teeth—that give them advantages over normal people. If the Houses persist, will humans survive them? What right do I have to determine the world's fate?

In the shadow of T-rex, Angola spreads a quilt and produces food from the back of the van. I'm expecting fried chicken or ham sandwiches, but it's fried shrimp and oyster po' boys with icy fruit punch. Daniel is too excited to eat more than a bite and keeps jumping up to touch the dinosaur, maybe reassuring himself it isn't real.

When we've finished, I try to help Angola clean up, but he waves me away. "It is faster if I do it myself," he says with a stiff smile. I notice he does not look at me, but shifts his eyes aside when I get close. I'm not used to this. Men look at me. It's subconscious. They just do. I don't normally notice, but Angola's lack of interest triggers my attention. I observe his precise motions and the way he watches Jason's every move. A servant's anticipation? Or something more?

I can't help an inner laugh at the way my mind flickers from the fate of the world to whether a man is gay. Minds are fickle things.

When everything is back in the van, we head toward the marina. A white gleam in the woods catches my attention.

"Saved this one for last," Jason says.

We must have passed it on the way to Tyrannosaurus rex, but I was sitting on the far side and didn't see it. Jason opens the door for me. Curious, I ask, "What is it?"

He only smiles. "I think you will recognize it when we get closer."

This time Angola accompanies us. After a walk of about 100 yards, the path spills out into a clearing, and I can't help a gasp. Before us, in an unmistakable pattern, is a ring of huge standing stones.

"Stonehenge," I say in an awed breath.

"Yes," Jason says. "Not real stones, but it's to scale. It's known around here as Bama Henge."

Becca and Daniel scamper into the structure. "Look how big!" Daniel says, craning his neck at the faux gray boulders. Drawn forward, I find myself in the center, pondering on the millennia of mysteries clinging to the mother structure in Britain. Tracey joins me, a silent presence, perhaps thinking the same.

Without warning, my vision clouds. A familiar rush of golden energy fills me. Color leaches from the scene before us, leaving only an out-of-focus, rippling gray shadow-world. In the sudden gloom, moonlight transforms the boulders into white teeth, rooted deep into the ground. Additional stones appear, some superimposed on the ones before me, a few others appearing beside them, some toppled over. Fog shifts among the solemn stones. My breath stops as time freezes. I have no control. I cannot move.

Before me, people in white robes materialize. They stand before the innermost stones, the oldest blue stones. I sense unseen energies crackling about us. In the circle's center, a young girl with red curls kneels, her head bowed. A woman, her features hidden by a cowl, steps forward holding something before her with both hands. She has moved between the girl and my position, and I can only see that she leans forward toward the kneeling girl, a delicate chain dangling from her hands.

The people and blue stones disappear as color floods the world, day replacing night. Sunlight dapples the clearing. In an echo of the girl's pose, I fall to my knees, my bones hollow.

I'm not certain if I lose consciousness or not, but slowly I become aware of Jason and Tracey on either side, holding me by my arms, worry in their clamoring voices. They help me stand. I feel Jason's touch as a muted electric shock. My head is throbbing.

"Are you alright?" Tracey asks. "Do you want me to carry you?"

"I'm okay," I say, brushing away his hand. "I can walk. I just got a little dizzy."

"It's not that long since you got out of the hospital," he says with a frown. "Or maybe too much sun."

"I'm fine, Lohan."

"You're stubborn," he says.

"I've noticed the same thing about her," Jason says. "Let's get back into the air-conditioned van. I'll round up Daniel and Becca."

Tracey insists on walking me back to the van.

I try to make sense of what happened. It's the first time I've ever seen any vision that was not the past or future of the place itself. Is this spot tied somehow to the real Stonehenge, thousands of miles away? Was it ancient past or present there or a future? It felt important, a key to some mystery, but I have no idea what I just saw or why I saw it.

Chapter Twenty-Three

Back in the *Iron Fist*, I'm ensconced in a comfortable deck chair. Tracey sits beside me. Becca stands along the railing, sandwiched between Jason and Daniel. They both are back at their posts with fishing poles trailing over the stern's edge. The wind picks up as we glide back into the bay, pass through a narrow bend into yet another wide bay, and head south. Houses cluster along both sides of the shore, their docks extending out toward us like fingers.

"We are not far from the Gulf," Jason says. He points to a long strip of land. "That's Ono Island, last bit of civilization before the open water."

Jason's cell phone rings, and he excuses himself into the cabin.

I turn to Tracey. On my second Bloody Mary, I'm feeling recovered from my dizzy spell and puzzling vision. I'm also feeling magnanimous. "Thank you for coming, Lohan."

"I wouldn't have missed it," he says. "It's not every day I get to see a Tyrannosaurus Rex and Stonehenge." He cocks his head, "But are you sure you're okay?"

"Okay-er now," I say, lifting my glass.

"Who is this guy?" he asks, nodding at Jason's retreating back.

"I . . . met him in a bookstore, and he's decided he can't live without me."

"Very pretty," Becca comments, her face happily turned into the wind.

Tracey waves to encompass the deck. "Maybe not a bad deal."

My face tightens. "I'm not interested in 'a deal.'"

"Really?" The question is a challenge.

"What makes you think that?" I hiss under my breath, not wanting Becca to hear.

"Why did you come, Rose?"

I cut my gaze toward Becca. "You know why."

He keeps his gaze steady on me. "Yeah, you told me she wanted to ride in a boat."

"And?"

"And there are plenty of boats down here. You could have rented one for the day."

I open my mouth for a retort, but can't think of one. My earlobes and cheeks tingle with a flush that has nothing to do with the bright sun or the drink. Why *didn't* I do that?

"I didn't . . . think of it."

Daniel leaves Becca's side to take a swallow of lemonade from his glass. Then he puts a small hand on my bare leg, peering up at me from under the hat I made him wear, and tugs at his life jacket. I have as much of a clue about being a mother as I do being a "best friend," a skill Becca had taken upon herself to teach me, but I'm not totally stupid. Life jackets are required on both Becca and Daniel at all times.

"You want a cookie or something?" I ask him.

He shakes his head. It's obvious, even to me, that he has something to say.

"What?" I ask. "Do you have to go potty?"

"No."

"Okay. What do you want to tell me?"

"I like it here," he says.

"You do?" I'm glad for a distraction from the tumble of thoughts that Tracey's observation has dislodged. "You like the water?"

"I like it *here*." He emphasizes the last word.

"What do you like about it?" Tracey asks.

"Nobody stares at me," Daniel says.

Tracey and I lock gazes. Something thickens in my throat.

Becca turns, searching for Daniel. She doesn't like him being more than a few feet away. I blink back tears. Must be the Bloody Mary. I don't cry.

"I think I need to powder my nose," I say, rising a bit unsteadily. How much vodka did Angola put in those things? Impossible to tell with all the spices.

Jason steps back out onto the deck, as I stand. He reaches out instinctively to steady me. "You okay?"

I stare at his fingers on my arm. It's weird not to feel that spark at his touch, but strangely my body doesn't seem to have completely gotten the message that we are unplugged. The feeling makes me think of Paul. *I miss him.* Not just as a lover, but as a friend. He was always there for me. Even though I broke it off, it's hard to remember that he's dead.

I bite my lip. I'm better off without relationships and commitments. Jason Blackwell is barking up the wrong tree.

Another voice intervenes. Aren't I being hard on him? It's not his fault his uncle tried to kill me. I don't believe in the sins of the fathers weighing on the son's back, or in this case the sins of the House. Maybe I should cut Jason a little slack.

Or maybe it's the Bloody Mary talking in my ear.

I give him a smile and an "I'm fine" and make my way down the steps into the cabin. The closest facilities are in the master bedroom, and I have to pass the red satin-covered bed. No doubt Jason has had plenty of women on that bed. Still, it would be pleasant to lie there at night and let the rock of the boat lull me to sleep. Maybe with someone's arms around me?

Stop it. I clamp down on my imagination—not hard to do, since I find I'm suddenly nauseous. I sit on the bed.

Angola appears in the hallway. His raven eyes assess me. "If you feel sick, you are better off on the deck."

I swallow. "Really?"

"We are out into the Gulf. Waves. Better on deck."

I nod. As soon as Angola disappears, I leave my heavy purse on the bed and stagger into the bathroom, where I offer back at least one of the Bloody Marys to the toilet god. Lesson learned about drinking on a boat.

When I emerge, there is no doubt we have transitioned to the sea. A vast, clean skyline has replaced the view of Ono Island, which now lies behind us. Indigo waves chop against the hull. Jason stands beside Becca, pointing out a shape in the water. I can't hear what he is saying, but "shape" automatically translates into "shark" in my mind. Too many late night reruns of *Jaws*.

Tracey sits between the two "fishermen" and me. Angola was right. Being on the deck settles my wayward stomach, even though we are rocking.

Lawrence engages the engine and we move forward slowly, dragging the fishing lines behind us. I have no idea what kind of fish Jason has set Becca and Daniel after, but the poles are anchored in holders.

There's no danger of a catch ripping the pole out of their hands or pulling them over.

Becca's pole suddenly bends, and she squeals.

"You got a fish!" Daniel cries. Before anyone can react, he is climbing the railing and reaching for her line. "I'll help."

A strong wave hits the *Fist's* side. The deck tilts and Daniel teeters. Everything slows down and happens at once. With a cry, Daniel loses his balance, disappearing over the railing.

Chapter Twenty-Four

As Daniel topples over the side of the boat, Becca screams hysterically and scrambles onto the railing after him. Jason grabs her, shouting over his shoulder, "Man overboard!"

Tracey vaults from his chair and over the railing in one swift move. Without thinking, I scramble around the chairs and tables on the deck and climb over the rail after him. As I fall, I realize the *Fist* has widened the gap between where I will land and where Daniel went in. Then the chill water swallows me. April is not enough time to warm up the sea even in the Gulf. Stunned and disoriented, it takes a moment to figure out where "up" is.

I break the surface only to have a wave slap me under. *Shit.* Salt stings my nose and sinuses. *Where is Daniel?* Adrenaline courses through me. Am I going to drown? Can't do that. If I drown, I can't help Daniel. *Where is he?*

My next break to the surface is in a trough. I tread water, unable to see Daniel or Tracey, but I follow the fading wake of the boat, swimming hard. Somehow the sky has turned a bloated gray. Weather happens fast down here.

Coughing, I stop and tread water again and try to think. Panic is not going to help. Tracey moved fast. He would closer to Daniel. The wind has picked up, sending spray into my eyes. I suck in a huge breath, trying to make myself more buoyant, and ride the next wave. It lifts me, and I get a quick glimpse of Daniel several yards away clinging to Tracey's head. Daniel must be terrified.

I abandon attempts to swim on top of the churning waves and dive underneath them, fear driving me forward. Below me, a dark shape glides by. It has a dorsal fin. My heart can't beat any harder, but nausea threatens again. I swallow hard to keep it down, but bile is sour in my mouth.

Twice more I have to bob up and locate them, relieved to see Lohan still with Daniel. I'm not in bad shape. Or at least I wasn't until the Ordeal. I used to swim regularly at the YMCA pool, but this is not a swimming pool. My limbs feel like they can barely move against the strong current. I'm a puny, laughable piece of flotsam against the sea's casual might.

Fortunately, the next rise to the surface brings me only a few feet away.

"Daniel," I sputter and swim to him. "Are you okay?"

He nods, but his eyes are wide and frightened, his long lashes clumped in wet spikes. That's when it hits me. Wildly, I look around. There's no sign of Lohan.

"Where's Tracey? Where's Mr. Lohan?"

Daniel's face contorts and he points down. *Down.*

I grasp the trailing end of strap on his life jacket and take a breath, looking under the surface. Nothing. The blotted sun only penetrates a few feet. Then the water world fades quickly into darkness. If I dive, I might lose Daniel, but the life jacket is keeping him afloat, and Tracey is down there somewhere. I have to find him. One more breath above water, then I release the strap and dive, assuming he went straight down. He's a big man, heavy. I have no idea how deep the water is here. Darkness swirls. My chest hurts.

Nothing.

I have to go up again and catch a breath. Daniel's eyes are wide, but his life jacket is keeping him up, bobbing on the waves. I dive again, deeper.

Something moves out the corner of my eye. Something big. I turn to face it, lungs aching, afraid it will be a torpedo shape with lots of teeth.

It's a man, pulling hard for the surface. His eyes are bulging. I reach for him, grasping his thick hair. He is unbelievably heavy, but he's kicking and pushing water with cupped hands, and I'm doing the same. Above us, the surface looks far away. Too far away. Bubbles escape from my mouth, an unstoppable trickle. I have to breathe. I want to stop, to drift downward and rest.

Don't stop.

Those are words from my Marine Master Sergeant father, running beside me when I was trying to get in shape to make the high school track team. I was tired. I wanted to collapse in a heap and give it all up, but he was in my ear. "Keep going, Rose. Find more to give. Dig. One foot and the other. Find it inside you. Pull it up!"

Pull it up. Dig. Kick. Kick!

My head breaks the surface. I suck blessed air. Tracey emerges beside me, gasping. I grab for Daniel's vest. A wave takes me up. I reach for Tracey.

He shakes his head, treading water desperately. "No. I'll pull you . . . both under."

"Lohan!"

"No," he sputters, moving away from us. His head dips below.

Daniel is crying.

Damn it. I swim forward and reach down, grasping a handful of Tracey's thick hair again. I try to keep us both up, but he is so damn heavy.

Something splashes beside me. The most beautiful thing I've ever seen. A simple round white ring, the innocuous adornment of every boat and swimming pool. I glance up and see Angola leaning over the rail.

With one hand, I grab the ring and haul upward with other that still grips Tracey. Both ring and I go under, but I'm kicking for all I'm worth. Tracey is kicking. Tracey is up again. Both my stretched arms cramp in pain.

"The ring!" I gasp.

Tracey reaches for it, and when he has it, I release it. It goes under with his weight, but his head stays above the water. On the deck, Angola pulls the lifesaver ring buoy. The life jacket supports Daniel and me.

Above us looms the *Iron Fist.*

Chapter Twenty-Five

Back at the dock, Jason insists we stay aboard while he sends his crew out to purchase dry clothes at The Wharf, where "on sale" means only twice as much as I can afford. While we wait, Tracey and Daniel use the bathroom in one of the yacht's guest rooms, and I take a hot shower in the elaborate master bathroom, washing seawater from my hair and skin and trying to get it out of my mind. It isn't the first time I've come close to dying, but experience doesn't really help. I take my time in the hot water.

When I step out of the bathroom, wrapped in a plush red towel, my new clothes are lying on the ruby satin bedspread. They fit. Even the pair of deck shoes. Someone has a good eye. Angola?

A knock on the door.

"Wait a sec." I hastily don the clothes and open the door, not wanting to be near the bed if Jason comes in.

Tracey's bulk fills the doorway. "Hi," he says. "You okay?"

"I wish everyone would stop asking that."

"I wanted to say I'm sorry."

"For what?"

"For almost drowning you."

"You almost drowned yourself."

"I know. That's what I mean. I didn't think. When I saw Daniel go over, I just—"

"If you hadn't, Daniel would have been all alone. A wave could have taken him under, anything could have happened."

I'm thinking about sharks again and shudder.

"It was my fault," I say. "I shouldn't have let him stand close to the edge. I shouldn't have had that second Bloody—"

"You don't understand," he interrupts. "I don't . . . swim well."

"Lohan, that makes you a stupid hero, but you're still a hero, so stop talking about it."

"I'm not a hero. I almost drowned you, and Daniel was fine with the vest on."

"Now who's being stubborn?"

"I—"

Jason is in the doorway and Tracey snaps his mouth closed.

"Everything fit?" Jason asks.

"Yes, thanks," I say.

"That was very considerate," Tracey says. "Can you send a bill?" He extends his hand with a wet business card. "I think you can read it."

Jason refuses the card. "Absolutely not. I take responsibility, and the clothes are the least I can do."

"Well . . . thanks." Tracey says, clearly uncomfortable with the arrangement, but not sure how to change it, I imagine, without insulting our host.

I observe Becca carefully on the way home, worried the trauma of the day's events might have affected her. Jason grabbed her to keep her from jumping off the ship after Daniel, but otherwise, I never saw him touch her. She was in my sight the entire time we were on land, except for the few seconds of my dizzy spell during the strange vision at Bama Henge, and Jason was nearer to me than her.

Becca seems the same as when we left, maybe even a bit better. She comments on various things she sees out the window, but she clings to Daniel even tighter. He doesn't seem to mind. By the time we get to Alice's, Daniel is bursting to tell his mother about his adventure.

This is a conversation I'm not eager to have.

When we arrive, Nora is sitting on the couch, watching TV, one of Alice's cats curled beside her. Another one drapes the back of the couch. Nora confines her smoking to the backyard, but I can smell it on her clothes.

Daniel climbs onto the sofa beside her, his exuberance disturbing Boo, the black-and-white cat, which Alice calls a "tuxedo." His ears flick back and forth and with a hiss of complaint, he jumps off the sofa, stalking away. Then he sits with his back to us and begins to lick his paws. Even I know he is sulking. But Daniel is oblivious.

"Mom, we went on a huge, ga-normous ship, and there was fishing, and Becca caught one, and I tried to help and I fell in, but everything

is okay because I had on a jacket, and Mr. Lohan jumped in too and—"
He pauses to take a breath.

Nora has turned her head toward him, but her gaze is unfixed.

I switch off the TV.

"Nora," I say. "Are you okay?"

She looks at me dully. "I'm fine."

"Are you hearing what Daniel is telling you?"

"I hear him. He fell?"

"Yes, he climbed over the rail and lost his balance. It's my fault."

"But he's okay?"

The thought that he might not be seems to stir her from her stupor, but I decide to search her room. I don't smell alcohol on her, but alcohol might just be her first drug of choice. It's really going to piss me off if Alice brought her into her home, and Nora has a cache of drugs here. Not to mention that I'm a rookie on probation. The last thing I need is for Internal Affairs to find out there are drugs in the house where I'm living. By the end of this train of thought, I'm angry.

Daniel has given up sharing his story and left the living room, dragging a willing Becca with him.

"Your son could have drowned," I say. "At least act like you care." I want to slap her.

"I care," she says. "Thank you for watching out for him."

Her voice is low. I barely hear what she says. But I do, and suddenly my anger drains. She has been through a lot. Her son was kidnapped while she lay in a drunken stupor, and he nearly died. She must feel pretty guilty about that.

I know something about guilt. It was my fault he was kidnapped in the first place. If I hadn't been stubborn about not telling Theophalus Blackwell where my stupid rose-stone necklace was, he wouldn't have tried to use Daniel to influence me, and Daniel would not have been there when hell erupted—from me—and almost killed him.

Nora is looking up at me. She sat with Daniel through the weeks he was in the hospital, never leaving his side. Her son has burn grafts on his face and hand and back that will scar him permanently. Life is hard enough to bear without a disfigurement like that. Ask Becca. She suffered throughout her childhood because of her albino eyes. Kids called her "devil" and even adults shunned her. Lots of "religious" people here in the South. Many believe in a real devil or witches—somebody like me.

"The important thing is that he is okay," I say, and, "I'm sorry."

"I know it wasn't your fault. You take good care of him, you and Alice. You're better mothers than me."

Chapter Twenty-Six

When Lieutenant Faraday hands us our daily allotment of cases, the boat, Stonehenge, and the trauma of Tracey and me almost drowning seem far away—another world. Perhaps I'm trying to anchor myself in this one by once again bringing up Benjamin Crompton.

"I don't think we've exhausted everything," I say to Tracey.

He lifts his hands in exasperation. "What is it that you think we're missing?"

"I'm not sure, but I think we need to go back to The Edge of Chaos and check out Deon Segal again. His boss said he disappears like clockwork every day. I want to know where he's going so compulsively."

Tracey rubs his temples. "We've got a stack of other cases to work, including some unsolved homicides, and you want to go see where this nerd guy goes to lunch?"

My cell plays "2001: A Space Odyssey." That's Alice. She rarely calls me at work.

"Hey," I answer. "Anything wrong?"

"You need to come home right away," Alice says.

"What is it?"

"It's Nora. She's locked herself in the bathroom for hours and will not open the door. Daniel is getting upset."

"Okay. I'm with my partner. We're on the way."

"Lohan, can you run me home for a minute? Got some family drama going on. I left my car in the shop this morning."

"Sure."

When we pull up at Alice's house, Alice is waiting on the front porch.

"Who's that?" Tracey asks.

"Irene, I hired her as a live-in to watch over Becca."

I gave Alice, AKA Irene, fair warning he was coming. The fewer people who know that she is alive, the better.

Alice, or rather, "Irene," meets us at the front door.

"I don't know what to do," she says. "Nora said she was taking a bath, but it has been two hours, and she won't open the door."

"That's strange. She's stayed in her room before, but she's never not responded," I say.

"I thought about calling the fire department to break down the door, but I called you first. Maybe she'll come out for you."

There are three bathrooms in the house, but only the master bedroom and this one, shared by the two guest rooms, has a full bath. I knock on the door. Everyone is crowded in the hall. If Nora wanted a production, she has it.

"Nora," I call. "It's Rose. Unlock the door."

Nothing.

I try again, louder.

Again nothing.

"How long did you say?" I ask Alice.

"Two hours."

"That's a long bath."

"I'm worried she may have fallen or something."

"Nora!" I ram my shoulder hard against the door. A burst of pain rewards that brilliant move. "Ouch!"

The pain makes me angry. I should be investigating a murder and trying to save lives, not busting my shoulder on the bathroom door because of an alcoholic—okay, Nora has stopped drinking, but she is still a wretched excuse for a mother.

"This is ridiculous," I mutter, holding my aching shoulder.

Tracey steps forward. "Can I help you with that door?"

"Just get it open, please," I whisper. "Don't pulverize it."

"It's all about where you put the pressure," he says. Instead of breaking open the door, he pulls a credit card out his wallet and works it between the doorframe and the latch. In seconds, the door pops open.

I glare at him, rubbing my shoulder where I'm certain I will have a bruise, and push the door wide.

Nora is in the tub, fully clothed. Her head lolls back, one hand draped over the edge, a pool of blood on the floor below it. The water is red.

"Mama!" Daniel cries and starts forward.

Tracey snatches him back.

"Oh my God," Alice mutters.

"Call 911," I say. "And get Daniel out of here." I take a step closer and realize there is nothing to do. Her eyes are closed, but the blood has stopped gushing from her pale wrist. Most people out to commit suicide cut their wrists horizontally, an inefficient method. Nora has slit hers vertically. It was probably one of the few things in her life she had done "right."

I stand in the bathroom, staring at her. There were signs I had ignored, not wanting to deal with her problems. She was not a model parent, but she had stayed at Daniel's side in the hospital when he recovered from his burns. She stopped drinking for him. But she couldn't stay alive for him.

I turn to walk out and stop. Tracey has Daniel away from the scene. Alice went to call rescue. But Becca is standing alone in the doorway, staring. She is almost as white as Nora. My heart stutters at her expression.

"Becca?" I ask softly.

Oh God, why did she have to see this?

I go to her, standing in front of her to block her view.

"Becca, please."

She doesn't look at me. She's not looking at anything.

Chapter Twenty-Seven

Becca, her body rigid, stares at Nora and the crimson water in the bathtub. I turn my friend gently. She offers no resistance. Not wanting to leave her alone, I walk her into the living room where Alice is comforting Daniel.

"Where is Tracey?" I ask, trying to keep my voice steady.

Alice rocks a sobbing Daniel. "He went out front to direct the paramedics in." Taking in Becca's state, the worry wrinkles deepen around her mouth. "Oh dear."

We are both thinking the same thing—what if Becca doesn't recover this time? What if this catatonia is permanent? I hold myself in "police mode," wrapped in the protective mindset that freezes emotions.

The paramedics arrive, followed by Tracey, and I point to the bathroom. "She's in there."

It doesn't take long before they return. "I'm sorry," one says to no one and everyone in general. "There's nothing we can do."

I nod at Becca. "Can you check her out?"

From long practice, I'm able to get Becca to sit in a chair while the paramedics bustle around her. She stares straight ahead, unblinking.

"Blood pressure is a little elevated," the tallest one says. "But that's not unexpected. How long has she been like this?"

"Just since she saw . . . the bathroom," I say.

"Shock then. If she doesn't snap out of it, you should take her to a hospital to get checked out."

I nod, knowing that will not help. Just more pills, more pushing for shock treatment, more psychiatrists.

A patrol car arrives. Tracey intervenes, letting them know who we are and what's happened. Once they are here and there's nothing for me to do, some of the focus and internal ice begins to melt. I sit beside Becca, holding her limp hand.

This is your fault, Rose, a voice in my head insists. *You're supposed to be a professional. If you had paid attention, if you had made some effort to help Nora—*

Daniel seems to have cried himself out, but remains nestled in Alice's arms, his face painted with dried tear trails. The paramedics leave. A patrol officer tapes crime scene tape across the bathroom entrance. A detective arrives from our own Homicide unit—fortunately not that ass, Finkman—and asks questions of everyone except Daniel. Becca doesn't reply to anything, and he gives up on her.

An evidence technician enters, not bothering to knock on the front door, and walks to the bathroom without speaking to anyone but the detective. The house is no longer our home, but a crime scene. I hear the snap of his camera. Tracey tells me a kitchen knife was found in the water. I'm sure it's now in a plastic bag in the evidence tech's possession, who will label it and turn it in to the property room with the details establishing a chain of who touched it and when.

An investigator from the medical examiner's office arrives to ask the same questions we have already been asked. Eventually, two funeral home people—the last of the parade of invading strangers— appear. At least they knock. We take Daniel and Becca to the back bedroom while they remove the body. Somebody unplugs the water in the tub. I hear it gurgling down the drain. I hope they are wiping up the blood.

And then everyone leaves, even Tracey, who promises to check in on me tomorrow and pick me up, so I won't have to worry about getting my car out of the shop today. I nod and thank him mechanically.

DANIEL IS ASLEEP IN ALICE'S BED. Becca lies alone on her own bed. Her eyes are open, focused on the ceiling. I think the worst is over, but there is a knock on the door. Alice gets up and goes with me to the door.

The young woman standing on the front porch introduces herself as Tanya Melbourne from Child Protective Services. I assume the detective called them in when he learned there was no next of kin for Daniel.

"You can't take him," I say.

He is all the hope Becca has.

"I'm sorry," Melbourne says, "but I have to while they search for family members."

"Where will he go?" Alice asks.

"A foster home."

"Can't he stay with us?" Alice's hands knit in a fierce knot and her voice breaks. "He knows us."

Is she thinking about when she sent me away as a child? She did it to protect me, but it must have been hard on her to give up her sister's grandchild, her only living family. Daniel calls her Gran-gran.

"No, I'm sorry," Melbourne says.

"For how long?" Alice says.

"There'll be a hearing scheduled in Family Court within seventy-two hours and a judge will decide."

"Can we ask to keep him?"

"Yes, but you have to be at the hearing."

Alice sniffs and looks pointedly at me. "We'll be there."

Gently, she wakes Daniel, and he starts crying again. She tries to explain to him what will happen.

"I don't want to go!" he screams. He runs to Becca's room and clings to her. She doesn't move, remaining prone in the bed, but her eyes widen in fright, the first sign of any emotional reaction since she saw Nora's body.

Alice turns to me. "Can't you do something?"

"Is there any way you can let him stay here, even temporarily?" I ask Melbourne.

"There's nothing I can do. The state has to step in. You can present a case to the judge asking for temporary custody."

All I have to do is reach out and touch Melbourne, just a trickle of Iron's power and a suggestion that she leave Daniel—the temptation is so strong, I'm trembling with the effort to restrain it. I used it before, but that was to save Daniel's life. What about his happiness? Is that any less important? To lose his mother and be ripped from the people who care about him? I know he loves Alice and Becca. And they love him.

But I swore I would not use Iron's power. I can feel the black, oily gush of it already in me. I can't stop drawing it, holding it at the ready, any more than I can stop breathing. But it's my choice whether to use it. If I do, I'm no better than House of Iron, manipulating whomever I want. Playing God. And how do I know what is best for Daniel? It may not be what he wants or what we want, but *what is best*? With a shaky breath, I cross my arms, pinning my hands under my armpits.

Custody. That is a word I have never considered. But something wrenches my gut when the woman marches Daniel out the door.

When it closes behind them, the unnatural quiet settles like a thick fog, making it difficult to breathe. The barrier that kept me going and functioning has dissolved. I make my way to the kitchen and sit in the chair I always sit in. Alice follows and without speaking begins to make tea.

Chapter Twenty-Eight

It's impossible to sleep. My mind bounces from one preoccupation to another—guilt about Nora; worry for Daniel; fear Becca is lost forever. For the moment, the fact that the fate of a race of people rests on my ovaries slips into the background.

Somewhere between two and three a.m., I give up and get out my laptop computer, propping up the pillows. I might as well try to work on one of my problems. Angel gives a meow of protest and resettles into her warm nest against my side.

A few hours later, I print out the results and stumble into the shower, making the water as hot as possible. Then I dress and check on Becca. When I open her door, I exhale in relief that she is asleep—at least, her eyes are closed. I was afraid she spent the night staring into nothingness.

I think longingly of falling back into bed, just closing my eyes and let go of all this worry. But I'd have to get up sometime or be AWOL, and I'd have to face Becca with her eyes open, staring into space. I don't want to have to feed her baby food and take her to the toilet. *I'm a coward.*

I make my way to the kitchen, suddenly craving a cold glass of orange juice. The house seems too quiet and wrong.

Since when do I like noise?

I try not to think about Daniel waking up in a strange place with strangers and having to deal with the memory of seeing his mother in a tub of bloody water. No one should have to see that.

No one should have to see blood-soaked sheets on their sister's body.

"Shut up."

"I beg your pardon?" Alice asks, stepping into the hallway. She ties the sash of a bathrobe with pink flowers that reminds me of Dr. Crompton's wife in her kimono.

"Nothing. I was talking to myself."

"What happens next?" she asks, running water for the teapot.

"About which particular crisis?"

"Daniel."

"I'm not sure. I'll check with someone in Youth Services and see what I can find out."

"Let me know, please. Maybe we can get Daniel back."

"I will." I pour a glass of orange juice. "You want one?"

"Yes."

I get a second glass down from the cupboard and pour it for her. My stomach won't tolerate anything else. I think I will forgo my cup of morning tea.

"I shouldn't leave you with Becca," I say.

"Why not?"

"It doesn't seem fair."

"Life is not fair, dear. It just is." She hasn't put her contacts in yet, the last touch of her disguise, and her eyes, undimmed by age, are the deep green of our House—meaning her and me.

"How do you feel?" she asks.

"Like hell."

She frowns. "You need to take care of yourself. Yesterday was hard, terrible. Poor Nora."

I clunk my juice glass on the table. "I think I'll wait on the porch until Tracey gets here."

At the door, I reach down to Angel, who is at my heels. Understanding I'm leaving, she puts a paw on my leg, rising upward to touch her nose to my outstretched finger—our goodbye-I'll-be-here-when-you-get-back routine. None of Alice's cats do anything like this. I guess it's just something Angel came up with. This time, however, after her ritual "goodbye," she slips out with me, as if she knows I'm going to sit on the porch, instead of leaving. She doesn't act surprised in the least when I do. Maybe animals have ways of drawing on magic that we haven't figured out yet. Or maybe there is some kind of cat rule that says never act surprised at anything.

The morning is a beautiful spring one with purple redbuds and white dogwoods blossoming in the yards of the Southside neighborhood.

Redbuds come out before the dogwoods. They are not red, but purple, which is confusing. The colors make me think of the April day last year when Becca visited in her yellow hat and matching purse. That was the same day I discovered how to reach into the earth, moving around the barriers of iron and stone to find seams of coal and pull on the living-green. I draw on it now, just to feel the comfort of golden warmth spreading through me.

The rocking chair is damp with dew, but I came armed with a dishtowel and dry it off before sitting in it to wait for Tracey. A small lizard with a startling blue tail emerges from a crevice in the rock half-wall of the porch. I watch Angel watching it with twitching tail as the lizard checks out the clutter of fallen Japanese maple blooms and debris deposited from the last rainstorm. Life goes on, no matter what dramas tornado through our lives. I briefly entertain the thought of sweeping off the porch while I wait, but that seems stupid. The wind will only blow more stuff onto the porch.

Chapter Twenty-Nine

During the day, I stop by the police department's Youth Services Unit and get an idea of what I need to do to try and get Daniel back. I don't have the courage to call Alice until after work.

She reports no change with Becca. My chest aches.

"Do you mind if I skip dinner and go to the Y?" I ask, feeling like a heel for not going home and supporting her, but I am too restless to be of any use.

"No dear, of course not. There's nothing you can do here, I'm afraid."

It's Tuesday, martial arts classes are Monday and Thursday, but I feel the need for physical exertion. My gym bag is in the trunk. The Academy gym is not far away, but it doesn't have a swimming pool. I head to the Y.

Inside, I check in and head to the women's locker room on the second floor. Then I climb the stairs to the fourth floor and the track, glad that there's no thumping basketball game going on in the gym below. The quiet suits me better. Only one man shares the track, walking on the inner circle, so I take the outer one. Running clears the cobwebs from my brain. Despite the fact that it's a mindless one-foot-in-front-of-the-other, or maybe because it is, everything else is driven out. I can't think about anything other than breathing in time to my feet, and that's a good thing when there's chaos inside.

Two miles later, I drop down to the second floor and hit the weights. Not a hard workout, one circuit, enough to let my muscles know they haven't been forgotten. Then a quick change in the locker room and down to the pool, my reward. It's an Olympic-sized pool in an isolated section of the gym and, as usual at this time, it's deserted.

I plunge in for a couple of leisurely laps. This water is smooth and still, friendly compared to the brutal sea. I feel cocooned, buffered from the world, and wonder if part of that feeling is being cut off from magic. I've never thought of it that way, but it's just the silk brush of the water against my skin. The last lap I do underwater. When I emerge at the deep end's edge, I encounter a pair of shoes at eye level.

The shoes are shiny black leather and occupied. Legs in black suit pants yield to a crisp white dress shirt, the top opened two buttons down to disclose a dark chest with curly black hair. I blink the chlorine water from my eyes and look up at a tawny face I recognize, this time closely shaved.

"Angola. What are you doing here?"

Jason's chauffeur takes a step back from the edge, and I hoist myself out with arms shaky from my workout. "Why are you here?"

"Mr. Blackwell would like to see you tomorrow night."

I wipe my face with the towel I left in a nearby chair and wrap it around my waist. "How did you know where I was?"

A slight shrug. "It is not important."

"It is to me. I don't like being followed around."

"I will relay your message," he says coolly. "But for the moment, I would like to relay mine."

"What is it?"

"Mr. Blackwell has important information for you and requests that you meet him to discuss it."

"Right. I already told him—no. We had a deal. If I went on the boat ride, he would leave me alone."

"He said you might have such a reaction. He instructed me to tell you it is about a possible way to help Becca, your friend."

The next day, I roll my only dress into my gym bag with a pair of heels. It's a black number Becca picked out before the Ordeal when we were supposed to be shopping for detective clothes. I stop at a fast food restaurant to change, not wanting to have to answer questions from Alice. I'll change back before I go home. The last time I had an invite to dinner from Jason Blackwell, it was at The Club, a private club on the top of Red Mountain. This time it's at Highlands Bar and Grill, a restaurant on a narrow street in Five Points South with an unassuming stone and stucco exterior, a dark green door, and matching awning. The owner-chef has won multiple national awards for his unique mix of French and Southern cuisine. Even I, Hamburger Queen, know this.

But right now I'm not in any mood for pride or fancy food. I'm angry at Jason for blackmailing me into having dinner with him. I can't decide if I'm angrier at having to wear heels or at having to endure sweating and panting at his presence. Not for a minute do I believe he has information about how to help Becca. But on the slim chance he might, I'm here.

I'm thankful it's not the weekend, but I wonder how Jason got a reservation so quickly. I have called Highlands before—curious to try the renowned restaurant—and couldn't get a reservation even a month out.

I'm grateful for the valet parking. I can't walk far on these damn heels. They are just two inches high, but I might as well be walking a tightrope. Becca, in her right mind, would have been horrified that I am carrying my brown leather work purse with a black dress, but she is not in her right mind, which is why I'm suffering and mad.

The truth is I'm using anger to get me through this.

I reach for the door, but it opens before I can touch it, held from the inside by Angola.

"Have you got a tracker on me or something?" I snap.

His head gives a slight bow, his gaze sliding from mine, ignoring my question, but once I step over the threshold, I stop dead at the quiet inside the popular restaurant. There is only one man seated at a table, his face lit by candlelight. It's a familiar and beautiful face.

Jason Blackwell stands with gentlemanly grace to greet me.

I had planned to lash him with my anger over him breaking our agreement. Instead, I look around, confused.

"Where is everyone?"

He smiles. "Don't worry, the chef and wait staff are all here. We are the only diners tonight."

"You . . . you bought the entire restaurant?"

"Only for tonight."

Chapter Thirty

I sit across from Jason at the table for two in the corner of the empty white table restaurant, trying to re-marshal my anger.

"You look amazing," he says.

Not the kind of comment that feeds a girl's ire. And I did dress for this, I admit to myself. Apparently, I don't know my own mind. *Saying yes to him might be saying yes to saving an entire race of people. A hero's move, right?* I take a deep breath to steady myself.

A waiter appears, almost as magically as Angola seems to, to take our wine order.

"May I order a bottle for us?" Jason asks.

"Sure. Why not?"

He nods at the waiter, who does not ask what he wants. Prearranged.

"I took the liberty of choosing what I thought you might enjoy," he says, noting my raised eyebrow.

"Are you surveiling my drinking preferences as well as my whereabouts?"

He smiles. "No. You are welcome to choose whatever you like from the menu."

"No, I trust you—for ordering food, anyway."

"Your trust does not come easily, Rose."

"That's what happens when your family tries to kill my family."

He raises a hand palm out in a "stop" gesture. "I thought we were beyond that."

"Hardly."

The waiter brings us chilled white wine, opens it and pours a sample for Jason, who sips and nods. Then he pours a glass for me. It's crisp and clean on my tongue. I'm not a wine connoisseur, but this is good stuff. Expensive, I'm sure. Good, I mean to cost him a pretty penny for making me meet him.

"Tell me what you think you know that might help Becca." I take another swallow, hoping the wine will help calm my elevated heart rate and provide an excuse for the flush in my cheeks. He makes me feel like a high school girl with a crush.

"Before the appetizer?" he asks.

"You know that is the only reason I met you."

"I do know and it breaks my heart."

"Please."

"I wish I knew how to convince you of my sincerity. I truly care about you, Rose."

"I'm going to be angry if this was a ruse," I say, trying to ignore the jump of my pulse at his words.

He sets his glass down and fixes me intently with his impossibly ice-blue eyes. "I would not do that. I know you think I am entirely self-serving. Perhaps I deserve that, but I do feel very badly about what happened to Becca. It occurred under my nose, so to speak, and I could not stop it."

"Couldn't or didn't?"

"What I reply does not matter. What do you truly think?"

"I . . . don't know." There is a lot I don't know. Too much.

The silent waiter slips two plates before us. Each contains a round construction of avocado, lump crabmeat, and red peppers topped with delicate raw tuna. A garnish of crab claws and greens pinwheel around it.

"Tuna Tartare Tower," the waiter announces proudly.

"Lovely," I smile at him. No point in taking out resentment at my forced attendance on the waiter. And, my mouth decides, no point in not eating either.

The dish is extraordinary, and I say so.

"It is," Jason agrees. "The view from The Club on top of Red Mountain is unmatched, but the food here is quite special. I travel a good bit, and this city has restaurants I would put up against any in the world." He uses his knife to cut into the tower, spearing his food with the fork, tines down in his left hand and holding on to the knife in his right. Very continental.

I know the quality of restaurants is not why House of Iron is in Birmingham. Alice says House of Rose came here first from England, but the other Houses followed, feeding their magic off the ores here.

When we finish the Tuna Tartare Towers, I put down the tiny fork across my plate. "Tell me what you meant about helping Becca."

Jason also places his fork on the appetizer plate but with the tines facing down. "Since we met in the grocery store, I have had an old friend doing research in England. The Family has a residence there and an extensive library. He's been searching for references to what happened to Becca and learned there is a name for it."

My belly tightens. Is that all he has to offer—a name?

"It is called a *tabula rasa* or a *rasa* state."

"*Tabula rasa*," I repeat, trying to remember my meager Latin. "A blank slate?"

"Exactly. It was originally a scraped tablet that could be written on again, but in this case, it means a mind wiped clean."

Becca staring into space with no idea how to eat or relieve herself, no words to speak, no idea of the concept of speaking.

"She was like that for weeks in the beginning," I say, shaking my head. "Then she began to speak a little and learn things again—an object, that it had a name. She was, and still is, like a child, as if the core of who she was is gone, and she had to start over." I don't mention the trauma of seeing Nora in a pool of blood has sent her back into a catatonic state.

"That is a very good way of describing a *tabula rasa*," Jason says. "The personality is wiped, and the entire brain suffers trauma, but then begins to reorganize itself."

"But how does knowing that help anything?"

"Be patient."

"I'm not good at that."

"I know." His lips twitch.

"This is not funny."

His smile fades, and he leans toward me, igniting a skip in my heartbeat. "I know that, too. And I know you care deeply about her. I do as well because, at the risk of repeating myself, I do care about you."

I lean back. "I'd like to believe that, but we are back to the 'trust' thing."

"It seems all roads lead to Rome or, at least, a roadblock. But let me continue. Once my friend had a name for the condition, his research began to yield information. This ability to create a *tabula rasa* is not something that just anyone in House of Iron can do."

"Your uncle did it."

"Theophalus was very powerful and experienced. He was apparently also able to manipulate your partner—Paul Nix."

I nod.

"Over a long period of time. That requires arranging to touch him on a regular basis, to keep the influence from fading. He was extraordinarily skillful—masterful, in fact."

A definite note of admiration has crept into his tone.

"What are you saying?"

"That normally, if one wishes to, say, change someone's mind or prompt them to do something, it has a temporary effect. Eventually, even when told to forget, they may remember that they weren't going to do something they were prompted to do or vice versa. They might even remember who was there when they decided differently. Wielding Iron's power is not a science. It's an art and a skill, and it is not infallible."

"I get that."

"There is also a very important difference between a *tabula rasa* and a *rasa*."

"What's the difference?"

"A *tabula rasa* is what my uncle did to Becca, a delicate procedure and theoretically reversible. A *rasa*, on the other hand, is the complete destruction of the personality, permanently. Any fool with enough power can do it."

My breath quickens and this time not from his presence. "Are you sure which one Theophalus did to Becca?"

"Since she has recovered somewhat, I believe it must be the former." He considers me for a long moment. "Strange to speak to a woman about House matters."

"You have women in House of Iron. I've met them."

"Of course, but they have no . . . abilities, and we do not discuss magic with them."

"I never imagined sitting at a restaurant with a man talking about magic of any kind."

He smiles. "I suppose not. I must keep reminding myself that you were not brought up in the Families."

Families. That's what my mother called the Houses.

Our waiter sets a beautifully presented plate of red snapper before me and lamb chops for Jason.

"Satisfactory?" Jason asks. "We can exchange if you prefer the chops."

"No, I'm fine." I wait until the waiter is out of earshot. "Why didn't you know this already?"

He frowns. "It is not common knowledge in the House. I imagine because it is so dangerous to perform. If one gets it wrong or uses too much power, an intended *tabula rasa* can become a *rasa* and you might as well have killed someone. So we are not taught that such a thing is even possible, although a few, including my uncle, apparently knew of it."

"How does any of this help Becca?"

Cutting into the lamb, Jason says, "It is thought that the way a *tabula rasa* works is to inhibit access to the brain's frontoparietal network, the area that compiles the elements of our personality."

I swallow. "Are you saying that somewhere in Becca, her personality might still be intact?"

"I do not want to give you false hope, but I think it is possible. I think Theophalus might have done it to prove, if even to himself, that he could. He had a massive ego. And, by the way, how did you manage to kill him?"

I haven't revealed to Jason that I have the blood of Iron, although he might suspect it. There were, no doubt, rumors in House of Iron as well as House of Rose about my grandmother's liaison. Let him continue to be curious. I ignore the question.

"Then what Becca is doing, the improvements she was making, were not really Becca coming back, but her brain trying to work around the blocks."

"Yes, and that is good evidence that it may be a *tabula rasa* and not simply a *rasa*. All the instances I could find of the latter imply there is no recovery of any degree."

What happened to Becca is a dark, cloying shadow that hovers over me every day, forcing itself into my nostrils and throat so I can never take a clean breath of air. I'm afraid to ask the next question, afraid the shadow will never dissipate. But I have been living with that. If there is a hope, I need to know.

"Did you find a way to fix it?" I ask, my voice a hoarse whisper.

Jason hesitates. "Again, theoretically."

"How?" My hand has a death grip on the fork.

"It could make things worse as well. There are reports of both occurring."

"How?" I repeat.

"It involves a similar procedure to what caused the *tabula rasa*."

I gasp. "You mean subjecting her to Iron's touch again?"

"Yes, it would require that."

"No," I say, crumpling my napkin and slapping it beside my plate. I stand to leave. "That is not going to happen again, *ever*."

Chapter Thirty-One

When I get notice of Daniel's hearing at Family Court, Alice and I decide it's better if I go and that she stays with Becca. Lieutenant Faraday allowed me some personal time when I explained the situation. Hopefully, she isn't docking me. I have no time off built up to take.

I sit on the courtroom's hard bench, crossing and uncrossing my legs while I wait for the administrative processes to wind its way through the labyrinths required to have Daniel's case come up. Daniel doesn't deserve losing his mother or seeing her like that, or being snatched away from the only people who care about him, though hopefully there is a relative somewhere who will come for him.

I was fortunate. My foster parents decided to adopt me, and they were good people. I have heard horror stories too. I can't remember much about the days before I went into foster care, but, like Daniel, I had been traumatized. My family was massacred and the remaining member—my great aunt Alice, whom I'm sure I loved—had sent me away. I must have been devastated and scared.

Will he be here? What if seeing me touches off the trauma related to the last time he was with me—when I opened the door, and he saw his mother in a bathtub of water, crimson with her own blood? What if my being here just causes Daniel more suffering?

The judge looks down at the paperwork before her.

"Daniel Pate."

"He's here, Your Honor." Tonya Melbourne, the same person who took him away, steps forward to stand before the judge. Daniel's hand is wrapped tightly around hers.

"V. Rose Brighton?" the judge says, consulting another piece of paper.

I take a breath and stand.

"Approach the bench, please."

I do. I have been in court a few times, but never on a personal matter when so much is at stake. I came out of the system okay, but what if Daniel falls in the wrong hands? What if no one wants him because of his disfigurement? Becca needs him. They need each other more than ever now. My heart is racing.

Someone has taken Daniel out of the courtroom.

"You have petitioned the court for custody of Daniel Pate," the judge says. She consults the paper before her. "I see you are single and live with a special-needs adult and her caretaker in Birmingham."

"Yes, Your Honor."

"And you're a police officer, a detective."

"I am."

"I have a character reference from a Detective Tracey Lohan and a Sergeant Dale Yonkin."

Good ole Sarge, my supervisor when I worked in the Patrol Division. He came through for me.

"You've not listed other family members." It was a statement, but with an implicit question.

"I'm an orphan, Your Honor. No siblings, but there is a full-time person at the house." I can't claim Alice as family since she is "dead."

"I see that, an employee named Irene Gideon." She puts down the papers she has scanned. "Why do you want custody of this child?"

I swallow. There is much I can't say. I'm burdened with guilt about what happened to him. He's suffered because of me. His mother died in our house. That lies on me too. He's my responsibility. I open my mouth to try to explain, but what comes out surprises me.

"I love him," I say.

The judge doesn't respond at first, just considers me. After a moment she says, "There are no other family members who have been located. I'm not going to go into depth questioning how you are prepared to take care of him at this time. I'm going to keep him in the state's custody pending a home evaluation. We'll review that report and Ms. Melbourne's recommendation before making a final decision. She will be in touch."

Her tone is dismissive, but I clear my throat and say, "Your Honor?"

She looks up over her reading glasses.

"May I speak to him? He's had a very traumatic experience, and I want him to know that we hope he's coming . . . home soon."

"Ms. Melbourne?"

"Your Honor?"

"Give the boy some time with Detective Brighton and make allowances for supervised visitation until the home report is done."

Melbourne instructs me to follow her to a room where Daniel is playing with some blocks and a plastic truck. Two other children, under the eye of another woman, are playing with other toys.

Daniel's hair is wet and combed. He looks thin, frail.

"Daniel?" I say.

He looks up and sees me. For a moment, his face is blank. Then he drops the truck he's holding and runs toward me, throwing his little arms around my legs.

"I want to see Becca and Gran-gran. I want to go home!"

I AM NOT READY TO GO BACK TO WORK. I call Alice and give her the report from the court.

"It sounds as if you did everything you could," she says.

"I don't know, but we have to prepare for the home inspection."

"What do we need to do?"

"I'll look it up on the Internet."

"Well, whatever it is, we will do it! Everything will work itself out."

Her words are the only comfort I'm going to get.

Normally, in a crisis where I need to think, I escape to the woods, but I don't want to trigger those memories. Instead, I drive to the center of downtown, parking under the railroad trestle. Above me the train track runs east-west, an iron river, splitting the city. Multicolored lights above brighten the dark of the viaduct.

Just south of the raised track bed, four blocks have been transformed into an award-winning park, Railroad Park, another pride of The Magic City. Across the street is Regions Park, where the historic Birmingham Barons baseball team plays. There's parking closer to the park, but I don't mind walking a block, and the trestle provides welcome shade.

I'm too agitated to sit anywhere. I begin walking the trails that wind around a small lake and stream. Retaining walls composed of stones excavated from the site during the park's development delineate the boundaries. Tall, graceful grasses and native plantings give the impression of marshland, a startling foreground to the northeastern skyline of downtown's cluster of high-rise buildings. To the south are the ever-expanding dark red brick of UAB's complex and the playful colors rippling down the wall of Children's Hospital. Rolling grassland hosts people walking their dogs and throwing Frisbees. Young children play on a small climbing hill. It's an urban paradise that has spawned the multi-storied residential growth around it.

How do you explain to a five year old that he can't go home until a report is done? And that he might never come home. Why is this tearing me up? Is it solely because Daniel is Becca's lifeline? I told the judge I loved Daniel. I didn't plan to say that. It just came out. I do love him. But I can love him without *raising* him, right? If we get Daniel back, Alice would happily take care of him, and I could be more of the aunt-person, but saving the Houses means having my own child, and that would be totally my responsibility.

As I start another lap, Becca insinuates herself into my thoughts. Her voice is so real, I feel as if she is walking beside me.

Why don't you want children, Rose? she asks.

I don't normally talk to myself, but talking to Becca is different, even if she's imaginary.

"Children," I mutter, "mean changing diapers—diapers are just plain terrifying."

You're being silly.

"I'm being real. Diapers are just the beginning. What about sticky fingers, throwing up, screaming?"

What about when they grab hold of your finger with a tiny, perfect hand—

"Then," I interrupt, "there's school, homework, piano lessons, interminable baseball games, dating, and don't forget paying for college."

You're just looking at the negative things. Why are you so negative? Children are wonderful.

A teenager on a skateboard passes me without a glance. I guess people assume a one-sided conversation means you're on the phone.

You're just scared, Becca accuses.

"Damned straight I am. And what if it was a girl?"

Oh, that would be fun! Think of all the adorable outfits, doing her hair in curls, teaching her about makeup. I've always wanted a little sister.

I guess even normal people worry about whether their child will grow up to be a serial killer, but what about raising a witch? Supposedly, abilities don't bloom until after puberty, but if it's a girl with the magic of more than one House, and the wait-until-puberty thing goes haywire?

Then we're talking about a tiny person with the potential for magical calamity. We're talking about mixing magics and killing people.

On top of everything else, we'd have to start with the whole pregnancy thing. I don't want to be pregnant. Who would want to carry a bowling ball around for nine months?

"Face it, Becca, I'm just not the 'mother type.'"

What is a mother type?

I don't answer out loud but I consider the question. My adoptive mother was kind and gentle, a dreamer. She hid her spark, the little flame that wanted to be an artist, but my father kept it extinguished with pickling criticism. It seemed to me she was trapped in a world that consisted solely of caring for me, cooking, cleaning, and trying to live up to his exacting expectations. I don't want to live to please another human being. In summary, I have never wanted to be . . . my mother.

Laying my hands over my belly, I include an imaginary fetus into the conversation. "And trust me, you wouldn't want me for a mother, either."

Walking in circles has done nothing more than send my thoughts into a descending spiral. I might as well return to work and try to solve a few homicides.

Chapter Thirty-Two

My steps are heavy when I mount the stairs of Alice's house that night. I always thought that was a silly figure of speech, but each step seems like a mountain and requires an effort of will. My feet know moving forward means facing what I will see when I open the door—Becca sitting on the couch staring at the space just above the TV. When I do enter the living room that is exactly what I see. And no Daniel.

My hand presses against my chest to try and ease the pain there, as if I swallowed something too large, and it has lodged in my esophagus. Because of me she is truly a living dead. I have to do something, but the only thing I can try is fraught with danger of making her worse.

I stop and watch her for a few moments. *How can anything be worse?*

Alice is not in the kitchen or her bedroom.

"Alice?" I call.

She doesn't seem to be in the house. I check the backyard and find her puttering in the garden in a big floppy sunhat tied with a scarf, protecting her fair skin, despite the fact that it's late afternoon and there is little threat from the sun. I guess she isn't worried that Becca will wander off. She stays wherever she is left.

Alice spots me. "Hello, dear." She is kneeling on the ground and sits back on her heels, amazingly limber for her age. The late afternoon sun is at her back, almost at the horizon, highlighting strands from the short red wig. She scratches her scalp.

"This thing itches. I think I'll do like the ancient Egyptians and shave my head underneath."

"They shaved their heads?"

"Yes, it kept down problems with lice." She pulls up a weed, inspecting the roots with apparent satisfaction before tossing it aside. "Not that I have lice."

"Why don't you just dye your hair?"

She blinks and gives a short laugh. "I never thought of that. Why not?"

I sit on the ground in front of her, which puts my face in the sun, but it's that time of day just before dusk when the sun is orange-red and easy on the eyes. Around us spring flowers and young vegetable plantings thrive under her green thumb.

I watch her for a while.

"I'm not going to get pregnant, Alice."

She doesn't say anything for a moment, patting the ground around a strawberry plant. Then, "It's your choice, dear."

"I've thought about it, but I'm really not mother material. You, of all people, should know that."

"Whatever you wish."

"That's it? All the Houses are going to die out because I'm selfish, and that's all you have to say?"

"I don't really have anything to say other than what I've told you. I didn't want to burden you with something like that, but it was my responsibility." She pats my knee and gives me the response I have come to expect in any crisis, in addition to a cup of tea. "Everything will work itself out."

"There's something else I want to tell you."

She waits, loosening dirt around a weed.

"I saw something while I was at the coast."

"A vision?" she asks.

"Yes. It was only for a moment, and it seemed to be an overlay of some kind."

"I don't understand."

I swat at a mosquito that lands on my arm. "Most of the time when I have a vision, it's been related to the place."

"A future that will happen in a certain place?"

"Yes, or the past that has happened in that place, the place where I am."

"Where were you?"

"At Barber Marina—it's on one of the bays near Orange Beach—or actually some property that's part of it. They have exhibits scattered around, dinosaurs mostly, but one is called Bama Henge. It's in the woods just off the road."

Her brows knit. "Bama Henge? I've never heard of it."

"It's supposedly an fairly accurate replication of Stonehenge in England, but it's not made of stone."

She is quiet for several heartbeats. "And your vision?"

"It seemed like additional stones superimposed on the replicas that were there."

"Stonehenge in England," Alice muses, "is a place of immense power in the earth."

"People have been saying that for a long time."

"The power lines are why it was built in that location, and the structure we see is actually built on top of earlier ones. It is said our people were buried there."

"Beneath Stonehenge?"

She nods.

"I was looking at the past then, but—. . . in England?"

"I don't know. It sounds like it. What else did you see?"

"A ceremony of some sort. A young girl kneeling before one of the smaller stones."

"A bluestone."

"Colors are difficult to distinguish in visions. Everything is black and gray and distorted, like little waves are running through it."

"The universe is full of unseen energy rippling through it. Our brains interpret only energy of limited wavelengths."

I can't help a passing smile. "I'm sure."

Her attention pulls away from whatever scientific jaunt it took and focuses back to me.

"Tell me everything you saw."

I close my eyes and try to remember. "A girl kneeling and . . . a semi-circle of people in hooded white robes." I snap my eyes open, realizing what that sounds like. "Not hoods like the Ku Klux Klan, more like Robin Hood hoods."

"Go on."

"One of the hooded people had her back to me."

"Her?"

"I'm not positive, but I think it was a woman from the way she moved. She approached the kneeling girl and put something around her neck."

Alice's hand rises to her mouth. "Oh my, the rose-stone!"

"I thought that too, though I couldn't see what it was."

"It must be. That sounds like stories I've heard of an ancient ceremony of the Houses, the passing of the rose-stone to the Y-Tair!"

I jump when my cell plays "Dances with Wolves," as if it has yanked me back through the centuries. It's Tracey.

"Hey," I answer. "What's up?"

"Looks like you have been right all along," he says.

"About what?"

"Benjamin Crompton."

"What do you mean?"

"Vestavia PD just reported a homicide."

"I don't understand."

"A woman found dead in her apartment."

I freeze.

"Rose, you there?"

"I'm here. Whose body is it?"

"It's Crompton's assistant, Laurie Stokes."

Chapter Thirty-Three

It's late by the time I meet Tracey at Laurie's apartment. There isn't much to see or maybe there is too much to see. We stand inside the front door looking down the narrow hall. Her body lies between the living room and the small dining area of her apartment. At this distance, I can't tell much except there's not a lot of blood, which means she died quickly.

The Vestavia detective handling the case, Sergeant Andy Young, a black man in his forties, badge clipped to his jeans, stands with us.

"Glad for your help," Young says. "Vestavia hasn't had a homicide in years."

I'm happy Tracey doesn't mention that his partner is a rookie. He, at least, has homicides under his belt and several more years as a detective.

"Can you give us the basics on this?" Tracey asks.

"Yeah. Young woman, a grad student at UAB. Shot at close range. We've got a light powder ring on her head."

I do know that means the gun was very close to her skull, close enough for gunpowder to leave a residue, which means the end of the gun was probably touching her head. This is often true in a suicide.

"Do you think it was a suicide?" I ask.

He shakes his head. "Not with the hole in the back of her head. It was definitely not a suicide, but we think the perpetrator may have used a suppressor, since the neighbor said he didn't hear anything, and the walls are pretty thin."

"Who found her?" Tracey asks.

"Same neighbor. He came over to borrow a spatula, and the door was unlocked. He said he knew she was home and opened it to call to her. That's when he saw her on the floor."

"Have you got a time of death?"

"Medical examiner put it roughly between 2 and 5 p.m. The body wasn't touched until the paramedics got to her, but she was obviously a goner, so they didn't move her."

"Any other evidence?"

"Nothing. Evidence tech made a thorough sweep. No signs of struggle. He tried to pick up some prints, but Miss—" He checks his report. "Miss Stokes kept a pretty clean house."

"Gloves?" I say.

Young nodded. "Could have."

"How did he get in?"

"That's the thing that makes us think she knew him or her. There were no signs of forced entry anywhere. She let him in."

"How many shots?" Tracey asks.

Young touches his forefinger to the back of his head, his thumb extended. "One shot."

Tracey frowns. "Doesn't sound personal."

"Professional job. Nothing taken that we can determine, though. Office said her name was flagged by Birmingham."

Tracey nods. "That's right. One of our cases."

"You think there's a connection?" Young asks.

"Might be," Tracey replies. "Or maybe just a coincidence."

"I don't believe too much in coincidences." Young scratches the side of his nose.

"Me either," Tracey says.

"What's the connection?"

"Two weeks ago Benjamin Crompton, a professor at UAB, was found dead in his office. We thought it was an accidental insulin overdose—" Tracey stops and looks at me. "At least I did. My partner had it pegged as a homicide from the beginning."

I feel my cheeks flush at the compliment, but I can't confess that I cheated because I "saw" what had happened in a vision.

Young gives me a curt nod.

"The puzzling thing," Tracey continues, "is that the person who gave him his dosage should be the prime suspect in Dr. Crompton's death too."

Young looks expectant. "There's a 'but' in there somewhere," he mutters.

"Yeah, there is," Tracey says, "That person is lying on the floor of this apartment along with parts of her brain."

As I follow Young and Tracey down the hallway, I can see part of her twisted torso on the floor. Only a few hours ago, she was alive, grieving Crompton's death, trying to figure out what her future would be. Now she is nothing but a cold corpse. *Why?*

When I'm in full view, I focus on the body and draw on the living-green, hoping for a vision of what happened. The energy comes with the familiar warm golden flush, but I see nothing. No visions, just a neat small pool of blood on the beige carpet.

"We need to talk," Tracey says as we leave the scene. "I'll meet you at your house."

"Not the best place for a private conversation."

"Just want to leave your car. I have somewhere else in mind for the conversation."

"Okay."

He follows me to Alice's house, and I leave my city-assigned car in the small driveway in the rear and slide into the passenger side of his car. We are cocooned in quiet while he drives. Fine by me. There's enough going on in my brain to kindle a small explosion.

To my surprise, he takes us down 20th Street and south on Highway 31, turns up the south side of Red Mountain and pulls into the parking lot of Vulcan Park. From his pedestal above us, the Big Man looks down over the valley that cups the city, while showing his bare backside to us and to the communities to his south.

This is where Team Rose—Becca and me—started the hike down the north side to the hidden old mine entrance. It was the beginning of the series of events that led to a hollowed out "room" in an old mine far below us, an iron chair, and a madman of House of Iron.

Speaking of mad men, Tracey suggests we climb the stairs to the statue's lookout. There is too much competition in my soul not to meet that little challenge. As the world's largest cast-iron statue, Vulcan, Roman god of fire and the forge, weighs in at 100,000 pounds of iron and stands fifty-six feet tall, but that neglects to mention the 122 feet of pedestal he stands on. The Big Man is lit from below. Against the dark sky, he does look like a god, a burly, bearded gray god in an iron leather apron, holding aloft a spear he is forging.

"Won't it be locked?" I ask. "It's well after open hours."

"Got that covered." He produces a flashlight and a key to the tower. Once inside, he flips the deadbolt on the beautiful old-wood door. "I promised I would keep all the doors locked."

"Fine by me. It's creepy enough to be in here."

Inside, the flashlight beam illuminates floor, walls, and stairs overlaid by the same prized white Alabama marble that graces the interiors of many older buildings, including the ceiling of the Lincoln Memorial and the U.S. Supreme court. A little fact I picked up on a tour to Washington D.C. with my father. The marble continues for the first few landings of the stairway. I run my fingers over the smooth, cool surface, wondering if there are any Houses that can call forth the magic from marble.

But by the time we climb the 159 steps and reach the viewing area, which is at least three quarters of the way up the pedestal, all thoughts about anything have left my mind, and I'm grateful to step out onto a metal grate walkway that wraps the pedestal. Temperatures have dropped and the wind is fierce.

Outside on the landing, Tracey leans against the beautiful wooden door. Despite his weight, he has to give it a hard shove to close it. The lock on this one is on the outside.

"No need to lock this one." Tracey says.

I look down at the grated floor. "It's a long way down if you dropped the key."

Heights are not one of my fears, and I love the breathtaking view. We move around the circular platform. Below, to our right, the lights of downtown glitter. To our left is the flat rooftop of the museum. The only structures higher than we are, besides the god himself, are the TV towers. Behind and above us, Vulcan looms. From our position, only a portion of his anvil is visible.

The palpable presence of a massive amount of iron, even though we are far above the ground, jacks me on alert. Until a crisis point during the Ordeal forced me to open a channel to the power of iron, I had been unaware of it, just as I had been unaware of the living-green all around and beneath me until Alice showed me how to reach it. But now that channel to iron is open, and that is dangerous. I can draw from either magic, but they don't mix without disastrous consequences. Tracey has no idea he is standing next to a potential ignition switch to a conflagration.

Except for us, the platform is deserted. Actually, the park is closed, and I'm not sure how or why Tracey had a key to the locked door, but it's exhilarating to be up here with the jeweled lights of the city sparkling below us. Wisps of clouds tease the pitted cream face of a full moon. No sound other than the constant whining of wind reaches us.

Tracey backs up to the outer sandstone wall of the pedestal that supports Vulcan and sits. I do the same, though the chiseled blocks of stone are hardly a comfortable backrest, and wait for him to say whatever it is he brought me here to say.

"This is a special thinking place for me."

"I have one of those." For me it's the woods or in front of my easel in the sunroom of my house.

"I haven't been honest with you, Rose." He is not looking at me, but at the city below. His face slips from moonlight to shadow with the passing clouds. His big hands clasp his knees.

I think he is maybe finally going to tell me why he lied about having a biochemistry class with Dr. Crompton, but I'm not prepared for what comes out of his mouth.

"I am House of Stone."

Chapter Thirty-Four

I am House of Stone.

The implications of what Tracey just told me reel in my head. I can't seem to get any of them to settle into a coherent thought. Wind whistles past the round stone column at my back. Vulcan stands silent above us, intent on the spearhead in his hand.

Tracey gives me time.

Finally, I say, "Then you know—"

"That you're House of Rose. Yes, of course."

Of course.

A section of my hair whips across my face. My spinning mind stops at an odd place.

"At Alice's graveside," I say, "you knew those people who came and put roses in her grave were from House of Iron."

"I never met any of them personally, but I'd seen a photo of Jason Blackwell. I recognized him and figured the others with him must be from his House."

"How long have you known . . . about me?"

"I knew you were in the city when you first touched the rose-stone. Everybody felt that."

Alice had told me the same thing. Somehow, when I found the rose-stone and touched it, vibrations spread out like an earthquake, alerting all members of the Houses. My hand starts to reach for the stone pendant where it rests against my chest, but I think better of it. Can I trust Tracey? He has lied to me. Theophalus Blackwell wanted the rose-stone badly enough to kill for it, presumably to stop the possibility of a *Y Tair* having it or using it. I know nothing about House of Stone or their motivations. They could feel the same way.

"Am I some kind of witch advertisement walking around?"

He snorts. "No. I would never have guessed who you were. After we were alerted that you were alive and close, we started searching for you. I wish we had been able to keep you out of Iron's hands, but we would have had to kidnap you ourselves to do that."

I stiffen. "Was that on the table?"

He looks directly at me. "Yes, to be frank. It was discussed. The stakes are that high."

"But—?"

"It was decided that would warp who we are as a people. It was not an easy decision."

My mouth is a tight line.

"Put yourself in our position. What would you be willing to do to save an entire race of people?"

That hits too close to home. "I don't know."

His look changes. "Sometimes personal decisions based on values are not . . . easy ones."

I change the subject. "How did you know a person from House of Rose had found the stone? What if someone from another House had touched it?"

"The stone doesn't 'react' like that unless the person touching it is a particular line of House of Rose."

"A line?"

"Yes." He puts a hand on my arm. In spite of the chill wind, it's warm. "I keep forgetting that you weren't brought up on House lore."

Jason had said much the same thing. And Alice—the only thing she'd said about a "line" was that the secrets of the rose-stone were only passed down through the eldest daughters and that she wasn't in that line. *I was. I am.*

"I didn't know anything about magic until I came to Birmingham. You're saying everyone—all the members of the Houses—knew when I touched the rose-stone, but not who I was?"

"Correct, but we soon did."

"How?"

"We set up observation on Alice," Tracey says. "She was the last living member of your House. Where else would you go?"

So simple. House of Iron had probably done the same thing.

"The only thing that raised doubts was that you had a legitimate police interest in Alice Rhodon. But you confirmed your identity when you showed up at Iron's Hallowed Eve celebration, bold as a she-lion with the rose-stone on your neck."

"How did you know about that?"

"Historically, the party is a celebration involving all the Houses, but ever since we realized Iron's intentions of wiping out House of Rose, Stone members don't attend. We have kept our identities secret for the past two hundred years. Our purpose is to protect House of Rose."

"For your own survival."

"That's fair. It's at least a major reason. If the cabal in Iron intent on killing off House of Rose realizes our intent to protect you and counter their purpose, they might decide we also need to go. In fact, they might decide that anyway, but are focusing on House of Rose for the moment. For the record, we also think eradicating a group of people, whoever they are, is immoral."

"How did you know I was at the party and wore the rose-stone?"

"We have an inside source."

"Who?" *Jason?*

He grins. "I don't know, detective. We have cell groups with different information and I'm not privy to that."

"Would you tell me if you did?"

"Probably not. Why do you ask?"

I want to say *because I don't trust you*, but instead I test his assertion that House of Stone wants to protect me. "I think it's important for my survival to know if anyone from House of Iron could be trusted."

"A point." He rubs his chin. "I can tell you that it is my impression that the source of inside information on Iron is not a warlock. Their loyalty to House is fanatic and beaten into them from an early age."

"A woman then. Or a servant?"

"Possibly.

"That would get complicated if someone from Iron used their power and asked them."

"Precisely why we have cells and hidden identities. The information source—"

"Spy."

"Yeah, the spy wouldn't be able to give enough information to hurt us. The contact goes through layers."

"Why didn't you tell me who you were, and why are you telling me now?"

He smiles. "Rose, you never saw a question you didn't like."

There are so many of them. And answering one seems to give birth to another, like bubbles in a boiling pot.

"You got any answers I might like, Lohan?" My reply comes out sharp. I'm not happy. I don't like being lied to or not being told things I need to know.

"Some answers, perhaps," he says.

"Give them a shot."

"You asked three questions at once. I'm going to start with the last—why I'm telling you who I am now."

I say nothing, my lips pressed together, my back tight against the bumpy stone wall. The wind has started to work cold fingers under my thin tee shirt. Seeing me shiver, Tracey takes off a light jacket he wears to hide his shoulder holster and offers it.

I start to refuse because I'm angry, but I take it and put it on. It's way too big, the sleeves would hang almost to my knees if I were standing, but it helps cut the bite of the growing wind.

"I'm telling you who I am now because of Laurie Stokes."

"Go on."

"If I had listened to you, she might be alive."

"What do you mean?"

"You tried to tell me Crompton's death was a homicide. I thought it was just because it was your first case."

I scowl.

"Or maybe," he says slowly, "I didn't listen because I didn't want it to be a homicide."

"Because you knew Crompton?"

"Yeah. Partly."

I look up at him and repeat what I have already confronted him with. "He was not your biochemistry professor. He never taught biochemistry."

"No, he wasn't."

I'm looking at his face, though I can't see his eyes. Dark clouds have moved in from nowhere and shut out the moonlight.

"Who was he, Lohan?"

"Why do you always call me by my last name?"

"Don't avoid the question."

He hesitates. "He's a relative, but it doesn't matter. He was Family. He was House of Stone. I didn't want to drag up anything that might expose us."

I let that settle. But I'm not ready to just swallow it. Was it truth or a way to cover another motivation?

"You said you knew Jason was House of Iron?"

"Yes."

"Does he know who you are?" I ask.

"That I don't know, but I doubt it. My House is very reticent about 'coming out,' and I stay out of politics as much as possible."

I take a breath. "House of Rose is pretty much extinct, except for me and—" I clamp my mouth shut, appalled at almost giving away Alice's secret. "I guess there is no 'and.' I'm it."

"That's why you're so important . . . or one reason, anyway."

I can't read his expression in the dark, but his last words seemed layered with meanings. He leans toward me and brushes the hair from my eyes.

"What about my last question?" I ask.

"Remind me?"

"Why did you keep this from me?"

"I don't know you well, but I know you well enough to know that you wouldn't tolerate 'being protected.'"

At least he has that right.

The wind now brings the tang of an approaching storm, loosening more of my hair from its clip. A flash of lightning and thunder crack close on its heels prompt us to our feet. I'm pretty sure a lightning rod exists somewhere on the statue, but I don't want to be near when it gets tested.

Before we can get to the door and the stairwell, I hear a definite *ping* off the metal railing and my first thought is hail.

"Get down!" Tracey shouts, sweeping his arm around my shoulders and pushing me down.

Chapter Thirty-Five

Tracey's body slamming into me like a truck sends me cheek-down onto the metal-grating floor of the tower platform just below the Vulcan statue. I gasp for breath at the impact.

"Damn it," Tracey says in my ear. "Get up. We have to move."

I want to protest that it's his fault I'm down and can't move, but I don't have breath for that either. With one arm, he snatches me up and moves us around the tower beside the door. Another *ping* follows us.

Setting me down, he scans the museum roof. "Get the door open and get in!"

I try to turn the knob. "I can't. It's stuck!"

A flash of light illuminates him. The sky opens and we are instantly drenched.

Another *ping* and a small puff of pulverized stone-dust rises near my head. I push as hard as I can against the stubborn door.

"Damn!" Tracey says, keeping his body between the museum and me.

An understatement.

I scrabble for the Glock in my purse, which I always wear with the strap across my chest. Too easy for a purse-snatcher to grab it off the shoulder.

"Did you see the shooter?" I shout over the wind.

"No, but the only place high enough to get a line on us in that direction is the roof of the TV station behind the museum."

Did he see a flash or is he taking a guess? We are looking directly down at the museum roof and there aren't many places there for a gunman to hide. He's right. Gotta be the woods or the TV station roof.

"Go beyond the door," Tracey orders.

I do. That puts a lot of thick stone between me and the shooter, provided we are right about where he is. But we're trapped up here. There's a grated walkway to another tower that houses the elevator, but I'm sure that's locked too, and the walkway would expose us.

Tracey slams his shoulder into the wooden door. It's solid wood.

On the second shove, the door flies inward with a sharp *crack*, wood splintered around the stuck latch.

Tracey shoves me inside, and I nearly fall down the stairs from the momentum of his push. Grabbing the railing, I straighten and turn. Tracey's back is to me. He takes a position with one foot forward, his gun braced against the wall, exposing only a tiny area, enough to look down his sights.

I grab his shoulder and pull. It's like pulling on Vulcan. Nothing moves.

"Lohan," I yell in his ear. "Get back. He's got to have a scope!"

It seems to take forever for him to acknowledge me before he steps away. Another bullet takes a piece out of the edge of the doorframe, right where his head had been.

We face each other in the narrow confines at the top of the stairwell, both dripping water, the guns in our hands pointing at the floor. I check out the busted door. A normal man, even one as big as Tracey, could not have done that. I peer down the curving stairwell. "Do you think he's going to wait until we exit at the bottom?"

"Likely. And he would have position on us."

"I think we better call in the troops," I say.

He is still staring at me. "Yeah, we should."

My heart still thundering, I replace my gun in my purse, exchanging it for my cell phone.

"NOW EXPLAIN TO ME AGAIN why you were up in Vulcan's statue after midnight," a scowling Lieutenant Faraday says, her arms crossed over her chest. She had come out to the scene, along with the cadre of patrol units and investigators called out whenever a police officer fires a weapon or is fired upon. No bodies were found, so things were not as messy as they could have been, but Faraday ordered us to the Admin building for a more private chewing out, despite the fact that it was 1 a.m.

There's not much room in her office, but Tracey and I stand, facing her desk. Behind it, she is also standing, glaring at us.

"It was my fault," Tracey says. "It's a place I go sometimes when I want to be alone. I have a cousin who works there. We needed privacy to talk about a case."

She snorts, obviously not believing a word. "Which case?"

"Dr. Benjamin Crompton."

"The accidental UAB death?" she asks.

"Yeah."

Her scowl deepens, something I hadn't thought possible. "Then what's to talk about?"

Tracey meets her glare calmly, and I'm happy to let him do the explaining. I wonder if she is going to kick me out of Homicide back to Burglary to get rid of me or if this is the last straw for the police department, and I will be waiting on tables somewhere.

"I was wrong about it being accidental," he says. "Rose had it right from the beginning."

Faraday gives me a look I can't read. "What did she have right, exactly?"

"That it was murder."

Her eyebrows lift. "Is that so? And what made you realize she was right?"

He takes a breath. "The only witness was killed tonight in Vestavia."

Laurie was the suspect, not a witness. But I'm not about to correct him. Nothing makes any sense.

"Coincidence?" Faraday asks.

"Not likely. It was a professional job."

"Hmm." She sits in her chair, swivels to her desk and picks up a report. "I hate it when I have to do paperwork. I hate it even more when two of my people get shot at."

"It wasn't exactly fun for us," Tracey says.

We're all silent for a few moments, and I'm hoping maybe we are going to escape with just the chewing out.

"You seem to attract bullets, Detective Brighton," Faraday says dryly without looking at me.

I don't know what to say to that, and I don't respond.

"But the real question is *why* someone was shooting at you."

On that point, I totally agree with her.

She tilts her head, which makes her look like an eagle considering its prey. "Any ideas?"

"Not yet," Tracey says. "We're working on it."

"Well, get busy. And get out of my office."

Chapter Thirty-Six

It's 2 a.m. by the time Tracey drops me off at Alice's. There's a lot more I want to ask him about House of Stone, but I'm exhausted and shaky. All I want is a hot shower and bed, but from the car window I can see Alice, in full disguise, of course, sitting in a porch chair waiting for me. The porch light glows a warm yellow that is supposed to lessen its attraction to mosquitos.

"Get some sleep," Tracey says.

"That's my plan."

I climb the concrete stairs to the porch.

"What are you doing up?" I ask Alice, trying to keep the weariness from my voice.

"I knew something was wrong," she says.

"Can we talk about it in the morning?"

"You'll be getting ready for work in the morning."

I plop into the chair across from her. Alice leans forward and pours hot water from a white porcelain teapot into the cup of leaves on the small table between us. I look at it doubtfully.

"Don't worry, it's chamomile. Will help you sleep."

"I wasn't thinking about the kind of leaves," I say, watching a curl of steam rise from the cup. If she'd been sitting out here any length of time, the water would have gone cold. "How did you know when to expect me?"

"I've told you I have a bit of premonition ability. Nothing like yours. It's a gift that bounces around in our House. That's how I knew you were coming that first day when you knocked on my door." Her forehead tightens, revealing wrinkles between her eyes that rarely show. "That's why I took the rose-stone out of hiding to polish it and how that young man who broke in found it and stole it."

She's talking about the man I shot in an alley. When he realized he was being chased, he had tossed away the rose-stone pendant, and I found it the next day.

"When I first picked the rose-stone up," I say, "it sent out some kind of vibration that alerted every member of every House in the city."

She nods. "I told you that was how I knew you were in Birmingham."

"You did, but what you didn't tell me was that it would only react like that for someone who was of a particular 'line' of House of Rose."

"Where did you hear that?"

"From a member of House of Stone." I don't tell her it's Tracey. That's his secret. I'm full of secrets, expanding like a ball of tightly wound wool with each added strand.

"I see," she says, leaning back. "They are finally coming out of hiding."

"Not 'they,' just one. What did he mean by 'a particular line'?"

"He meant someone with the potential to be the *Y Tair*, but my dear, please bear in mind that there is nothing to prove that the *Y Tair* ever really existed. She could be a conglomeration of stories. Myths and stories have a way of working into a culture so deeply, people believe them as truths. But," she adds, "I handled the rose-stone many times, and it never sung out for me. Your mother gave it to me to keep for you."

"What about my sister?"

"You were the eldest. That's tradition."

"When I first touched it," I say slowly, feeling my way with logic, "you felt the 'vibrations' or whatever happened, and now we know House of Stone felt it. That means House of Iron did too."

"I'm sure they did. That is why I decided to put 'Plan Death' in play as soon as I could."

"I'm not sure I understand the advantage of that."

"If those warlocks thought I was alive and protecting you, they would surely snuff me out. Then you would be alone."

"No offense, and I'm really glad you aren't 'snuffed out,' but just how are you 'protecting' me?"

"This is what worries me constantly, trying to figure out how to do that. Hiding you with a foster family gave you a chance to at least become an adult." She shakes her head. "And then you go and become a policewoman, which is dangerous in and of itself. Although, I suppose they taught you how to defend yourself, and you do carry a weapon, so it has a plus side."

I don't even try to respond to that.

"Your tea should be ready. I put the honey in the water while it was boiling." She keeps honey and sugar cubes on the table, but knows I prefer the honey.

I pick up the beautiful china cup. It triggers the memory of my first meeting with Alice. Stupefied that this small, elderly woman with a British accent had claimed to be my only living relative, I'd scalded my tongue with the first swallow. This tea tastes different from the usual mint. I can't decide if I like it or not.

"What happened tonight?" she asks. "I noticed your detective car was here earlier, but not you."

"Someone shot at me and my partner."

Her eyes widen and travel quickly over my body. "Are you hurt?"

"I'm fine and he is too."

"House of Iron." It's not a question.

"Not everything is related to that. You know I'm working a homicide, and a second person was killed tonight. I guess it's last night now." I can feel my lids drooping over my burning eyes.

"But why would they try to kill you?"

I shrug. "Because they don't want the case solved."

"Can't you just drop it?"

I see Laurie's body sprawled on her apartment carpet. She had worked hard to get into medical school. She wanted to be a researcher to find a cure for diseases that devastated lives. If she wasn't the person who killed Benjamin Crompton, who was? And who is next on the target list?

"No, I can't. And even if I could, I won't."

Chapter Thirty-Seven

The looks given to Tracey and me in the office the next day are speculative. News and rumor travel faster than a speeding bullet in the PD. What were we doing up on Vulcan in the middle of the night together? It was probably a more interesting topic of conversation than why somebody shot at us.

"Hey Tracey! You a member of the Mile-High Club now?" Finkman calls out to general laughter.

Tracey ignores him, but my cheeks and earlobes are aflame. Sexual innuendos are part of being a woman in a man's workplace, but I'm sure I don't have it anywhere near as bad as the first women to break the blue barrier. The least I can do is hold my head up.

I sink into my chair.

Tracey gets up and comes back with two cups of hot coffee.

"You look like a truck hit you," he says helpfully.

"It did." I keep my voice low. "You were the truck."

"Sorry about that."

"No need to apologize; it probably saved my life."

"Ditto to you for pulling me away from having a piece of my face chipped off. Don't know what I was thinking. Have you had breakfast?"

"Are you kidding? I just got to bed a couple of hours ago."

He stands. "Let's get out of here. We've got lots to talk about."

I'M LOST IN MY THOUGHTS when Tracey pulls up at a 24-hour diner I know only too well.

"What's wrong?" he asks, seeing my expression.

"What do you mean?"

"You look like you just bit into a horseradish. Are you sick?"

"No, it's this place. It has a lot of memories."

Putting the car in park, he turns to me, not commenting, just waiting.

"Paul and I used to come here during our shift," I admit, "and it's where I met Becca. She was a waitress here."

"Wanna go somewhere else?"

"No, it's fine." I open my door before he can say anything more.

We take the booth in the corner where the police eat. I always thought of it as "belonging" to Paul and me, but apparently in the daytime the detectives claim it too. Tracey orders the grand slam breakfast. I'm not a big breakfast person, although I make up for it at other meals. We order.

"Coffee?" the waitress asks.

"Hot tea for me," I say.

"Coffee," Tracey says, "high octane, black."

Paul always drank milk. Maybe he had an ulcer. I thought that old "remedy" had long ago been debunked, but Paul had been stubborn enough to ignore what he didn't want to hear. Or maybe he just liked milk.

We don't try to talk until the hot drinks arrive. Tracey doesn't even wait for his to cool.

"Does being Stone include a burn-proof tongue?" I ask.

He grins. "Never thought about it. Maybe."

"Just what does it include?"

He shrugs. "Muscle density mostly."

"Does it only work when you have a path to stone?"

"First, it's not any stone, it's limestone."

I nod. "Limestone. That's made from coral, right?"

"Yeah, basically calcium deposits."

"Bones are calcium. Could you draw on that?"

He takes another swig. "A little morbid, aren't we?"

"The living-green is carbon. Carbon exists in every living thing on earth and that includes people," I say. "I've thought a lot about this, about how easy it would be to kill everyone in this room, for instance, by drawing on the carbon in their bodies."

Tracey's gray eyes widen. "We're taught as soon as our ability manifests to only draw from the earth. It's a reflex."

"But if—?" I'm flashing back to the Ordeal, to darkness and desperation. I would have sucked the carbon out of Theophalus Blackwell without hesitation. But it wouldn't have worked, as all members of the Houses are immune to other House magic. The thing that did work was my instinctive combining of iron magic with the living-green. But what would happen to a "normal" person who suddenly lost the calcium in his bones and blood? Surely he would die . . . or want to. And isn't iron involved in how the blood transports oxygen in the body? All three of the Houses are deadly. If that was ever discovered—I shudder. The need to keep their—our—secrets sinks in deeper, along with the thought that maybe my ruminations on extinct horrors wasn't just wild conjecture, and I would be doing the world a favor to let witches and warlocks die out.

"Never mind," I say.

Breakfast arrives. Tracey attacks a stack of pancakes with knife and fork.

"You're big, but you don't look like that green guy in the comics."

He hesitates and looks up over my shoulder. The waitress has returned to see if we want anything else.

"We're good," Tracey says around a mouthful.

I load two packs of sugar, a scoop of butter, and some milk into my bowl of oatmeal.

When she leaves, he answers my question. "It's a little more complicated than that. When we hit puberty, we start putting on muscle. It's denser and heavier than a normal's."

A normal's. He says the word casually, but the message is clear. We are not "normals."

"Doesn't your doctor notice?" I ask.

He grins. "We try to stay off scales, but sometimes we get put on diets. There are also a couple of doctors in the House and that helps."

"It suddenly occurs to me why you almost drowned in the Gulf."

He spears a knot of scrambled eggs. "Water affects our ability to call on stone for energy to feed the muscles, but the muscles don't disappear. So, you're right, I sink like a rock. Which, as I said, makes me an idiot for jumping overboard. Thankfully, I had a little more buoyancy in the salt water. That just kept me up for a while, and then you had to pull me up."

I remember how hard that was to do. I thought it was because I was exhausted myself.

"What about you?" Tracey asks. "I always heard Rose folks were healers. That right?"

I give a quick snort of laughter. "I can't heal a splinter."

"Unfortunate. That would be handy."

"Yes, it would be nice. My Aunt Alice was very skillful. I have the power for it, but I'm sort of a nuclear option to an antibiotic. However," I add, swallowing a mouthful of overly sweet oatmeal, "I have other talents."

"Such as?"

I study him for a moment. *Trust or not trust?*

I make a decision. "I have a . . . relationship with time. Sometimes I can see pieces of the past or the future."

He leans back. "Whoa!" His gray eyes grow thoughtful. "I've heard of that in the old stories, but wasn't sure it was true."

"I can't control when it happens, but I 'saw' back in time in Dr. Crompton's office. Laurie Stokes said she filled the insulin syringes out of the refrigerator, but I saw her take a syringe *out of her pocket* and give it to Crompton."

He takes a moment to absorb this. "Then she was lying. That's why you kept trying to say it was a homicide. She killed him." He shakes his head. "But now she's dead. Why?"

"That is the million-dollar question, detective."

"I'm trying to sink my teeth into the whole idea of seeing the past and future."

"Scrying."

"Yeah. That's gotta be unusual."

"Alice, before she died, said it was an ability that skipped around generations. I think, like you said, it's pretty rare. My mother had a bit of it, and Alice had what she called premonitions."

"Too bad Alice isn't around to tell us more about it," he says.

I shift and concentrate on my oatmeal. I'm not a great liar or actor, as Alice has pointed out.

Chapter Thirty-Eight

"I have a theory," Tracey says, downing his third cup of diner coffee. "Rose?"

I jerk my attention from the dregs of my tea, which after three cups on the same bag is barely a shade darker than the water.

"Don't you want to hear my theory?" Tracey asks.

"About?"

"Benjamin Crompton's murder."

I take a deep breath and bring my exhausted head back to my job. "Yes, of course. What is it?"

"While I was being a stubborn pig-for-brains, you didn't back off the investigation, did you?"

My earlobes tingle, but I look him in the eyes. "What makes you say that?"

"I'm an ace detective, remember? Catch me up," he says, ignoring my play for innocence.

I take a mouthful of cold tea water, which I instantly regret, but have no choice other than to swallow and set the cup back on the table.

"Okay, I visited the victim's wife, Mrs. Crompton."

"A nutcase," Tracey says.

"Yeah, but she had a good reason to think her husband wasn't normal, didn't she?"

"True, but he wasn't an 'alien.'"

"How do you know?" I ask. "Alice had a theory about evolution, but do we really understand how the Houses originated?"

"That's ridiculous."

"Maybe, but not from Mrs. Crompton's point of view. Anyway, she wasn't helpful, except she knew or guessed that her husband was having an affair with Laurie Stokes. Apparently there was a series of women."

Tracey grimaces. "I know it sounds like he was a philanderer. Maybe he was, but I knew him, and I suspect there was more to it than that."

"What do you mean?"

Tapping his spoon, Tracey hesitates. "Maybe he was trying to find a woman he could have a child with, hoping for a son."

I sit up. "Laurie said he and his wife hadn't been able to have a child—" I suddenly realize what he means. *A son.* Not just to carry his personal lineage, but to keep his people alive.

"What else did you do?" Tracey asks.

"I interviewed Laurie Stokes again," I say, expecting an angry reaction.

"Thank goodness for that. What happened?"

"She didn't confess. I actually started believing that she didn't do it, even though I saw her do it."

He narrows his eyes. "How accurate is this 'vision'?"

"I've been over every instance. When it's a vision of the future, it can be changed, but when it's of the past, it's been true. Always."

"How many times is 'always'?"

"Um, twice."

"That's not a lot of data points."

I don't say anything. It feels strange to talk about it. I thought I couldn't tell anyone other than Alice, that I would be considered a nut case, for which I couldn't blame anyone. Finally, against all my better judgment, I had confided in Becca, who accepted it without question and thought it was wonderful that her best friend was a witch.

The thought I may have lost Becca forever constricts my chest anew.

"Can you tell me about them?" Tracey asks.

"The visions of the past?"

"Yeah."

"Once it was at a murder scene."

"Which one?"

"His name was Darren Jones. They called him 'Carrot Man.'"

"Yeah, that was Nix's case, wasn't it?"

"Yes."

I don't feel like sharing what had been between Paul Nix and me, although Carrot Man's murder was after our big fight, anyway.

"Rose, are you okay?"

"Yes, I'm just tired." I rub my gritty eyes.

"I get that. Do you want to talk later?"

"No, I'm fine." I want to tell him what I know about the visions. Maybe he will catch something I've missed. "I was talking to Paul, Detective Nix, that night and when he got a call on a homicide, I rode with him. I saw Carrot Man's body face down at the bottom of the stairs, and the world went into gray and black. Time ran backward. He lifted up and took a backward step up the steps and the bullet exited out of his forehead."

"Strange. What about the other instance of seeing the past?"

"That was when Becca and I were inside the mine entrance on Red Mountain." I wrinkle my forehead. "I knew I was looking at the past, because everything went backward. I saw a man—it was Theophalus Blackwell, but I didn't know who he was then. I was seeing him before he was crippled and confined to a wheelchair. Anyway, he was carrying a can of gasoline, and he stepped backward into the mine entrance through a hidden doorway."

My throat tightens with rage at what he was on his way to do. I had stuffed the childhood memories down, burying them, perhaps like Becca was buried in her own mind, only facing them when I returned to Birmingham as an adult, picked up the rose-stone and encountered my blood family, Aunt Alice. But facing the memories and grieving are two different things. I don't think I ever really grieved. Instead, a cesspool of anger and guilt lodges in my gut.

"This was from long ago?" Tracey asked, his voice gentle.

"Yeah, seventeen years ago." I realize my hands are clutching the table's edge.

"What were you seeing?"

"My family's murderer," I say hoarsely. "I was seeing him the night he came to shoot my parents and grandmother and sister and burn our house to the ground."

"I'm sorry," Tracey says.

I snatch a napkin and blow my nose. I'm not a crier. My adoptive mother said I was wrapped too tight. I think I was afraid that if I ever let go, if I ever started crying, I would never stop.

I guess I appear about to burst into tears now, however, because Tracey looks like someone put him in charge of an entire room of screaming infants.

"I don't know what to say," he manages.

I blow my nose again. "How about, 'What else did you learn, detective?'"

"What else did you learn, detective?"

With a firm swallow, I say, "I learned from Laurie that UAB has partnered with a private lab to develop a modified drug based on the research with zahablan and TXNIP."

He looks puzzled. "Why?"

"One of two reasons or a combination of them."

He raises an eyebrow.

"Reason number one: They might be able to come up with something better than zahablan."

"Okay, and reason number two?"

"Zahablan has been a generic for several years, which means the patent has run out. And the price of generics has been falling pretty drastically."

"Meaning," he says slowly, "even if they determine zahablan works, using it will not generate much profits."

"Yep."

"Who stands to gain from Crompton's death?"

I frown. "Crompton was one of many people monitoring the studies, but even he didn't know how the human trials would turn out. Remember it's a triple-blind study. The researchers don't know who got the drug and who got a placebo."

"But if the data flipped, he might be one to call foul and investigate," Tracey says. "He had the disease himself. He would be motivated to pursue it."

"Laurie said he volunteered to be involved the only way he ethically could. But there are lots of layers to the research and lots of people working on it."

"But he was the one killed."

"Yes."

"Why him?"

"I don't know, but I know who we need to talk to next."

Chapter Thirty-Nine

Parking at the Edge of Chaos is consistently impossible. We park in the back again and hope the municipal tag will stall any attempt to haul away our car. I eye the rooftops uncomfortably. On one rooftop above us, huge metal cylinders hum. Some kind of machinery—generators, air conditioners? I don't know, but they provide a great spot for a sniper. Call me paranoid. Getting shot at will do that to a person.

The alley we take as a shortcut was once a street, closed off to make the city center university more campus-like. Both sides are lined with cars. I'm not the only one with a touch of paranoia. Tracey also walks through the alley with frequent glances upward and between parked cars, even though it's broad daylight in the heart of the UAB campus.

Inside, we exit the elevator on the fourth floor. Enslen is nowhere in sight, only a scattering of people about, and no one challenges us. We make our own way to Segal's cubicle.

"Hey," he says. "What's up in the land of mayhem and murder?"

"Dr. Crompton's assistant was killed," I say.

He sobers instantly. "You're kidding me, I hope."

I frown. "No."

"Damn."

"We'd like to ask you a few more questions," Tracey says.

Segal's back stiffens. "I'm not a suspect, am I?"

"Should you be?" Tracey asks.

"You're kind of scaring me, man. Do I need a lawyer or anything?"

"Not unless you're involved," Tracey says. "We just want more information about what you're working on."

Visibly relaxing, he shrugs. "Sure, I mean, nobody sees the details of the clinical trials until the last results are in, and they aren't yet, but I can answer general questions."

"Does everyone get a look at the data right away?" I ask.

Segal shakes his head. "No, we lock the database, no more input, and do a data cleanup. Then the results are analyzed."

"What's involved in a 'data cleanup'?"

"We look for errors, missing data, that kind of thing. Make sure everyone entered everything."

I sit in the only chair and prop my chin on my hand, looking fascinated. "Who is 'we'?"

"Um, that would be me."

"Can you tell us about the trials?"

He rubs his palms on the sides of his thighs. "Yeah, I mean, the trials are pretty straightforward. The patients involved are split into three groups. Two are 'active.' That means they get the drug. One gets five milligrams and the other ten milligrams, or whatever dosage the researchers want tested."

"And the third group?" Tracey asks.

At the question, Segal jerks his head to Tracey as if he'd forgotten he was there.

"Uh, that's the placebo group. They get a pill that looks the same, but there's no active drug in it." He checks his computer screen. "Hey, like I gotta go. I promised to check on my little sister during my lunch break. She's in Children's Hospital."

I frown. "What's going on with her?"

His eyes flick down, and he hits a few keystrokes on his computer. "She's got cancer. They're doing chemo and radiation."

"That's tough," Tracey says.

Segal blinks. "She's a trooper, but, yeah . . . it's tough."

"Can we walk out with you?" I ask. "Got a couple more questions, but we don't want to cut into your time with your sister."

He shrugs. "Sure. Let me shut down." He taps the keyboard a couple more times and then leads us down the hall. In the elevator, I hold my questions when a young couple, eyes locked on their electronic devices, steps in with us.

We exit out the front of the library, and he turns down the same alley we came through. "I usually go this way," he says. "It's a straight shot, three blocks to Children's."

"We're parked this way, anyway," Tracey says.

As we start down the alley, the lighting shifts. What was daylight under a warm, cloudless sky is suddenly black and gray, and I can't move. My heart stills between beats. Ahead of us, a slender figure walks toward us in the alley, his single braid swinging with his slow-motion strides. There is no question of his identity. Segal is alone in the alley, coming toward us. But I'm not seeing the present.

And then he is not alone.

A dark shadow slips from behind a car, a gloved hand pushes Segal's arm across his chest. I can't see what he does next, but Segal bows low, knees crumpling. His attacker's face is covered in a black ski mask. Dropping to one knee, he plucks a wallet from Segal's back pocket and slips back between the cars and out of sight.

On the ground, Segal's body is twisted, but I can see something thick and dark pumping from his upper thigh. His femoral artery has been cut. He will bleed out in minutes.

Chapter Forty

When the vision releases me, I stumble and go to my knees. Tracey's reactions are fast. He grabs my upper arm as I'm going down and saves me anything worse than skinned knees.

"Rose!"

"You okay?" Segal says.

My head is throbbing, and my stomach is threatening to give my morning oatmeal back to the world.

"I'm okay, just give me a moment."

They do. I stay on my knees.

Segal shifts from foot to foot. "Do we need to call anyone? Paramedics get here pronto."

I shake my head.

"No," Tracey says. "Let's hold off a minute. May just be a dizzy spell. She had a blow to the head not long ago."

"I'm good," I say and hold my hand up for an assist.

Tracey pulls me to my feet with little effort, despite my awkward position. He catches my eye, and I give him a slight nod. I think he understands I had a vision. Something we obviously can't talk about in front of Segal.

"Let's get you to the car," Tracey says.

"No, I'm fine. I want to walk Segal to Children's."

Tracey hesitates before acquiescing. "Okay."

"Hey, that's not necessary," Segal says.

"I want to," I insist. "I want to meet your sister."

Nothing happens on the three-block walk to the hospital, except I try not to throw up from the pain in my head and focus on what Segal is saying about his situation. "My mom died. My dad works two jobs," he says. "But both are part time, and he has no health insurance. I have custody of Kaleshia so she can be under UAB insurance."

I don't do hospitals very well, or kids, for that matter, but Children's has made every effort to make it a cheerful environment. By the time we enter Kaleshia's room, which she shares with a sleeping child, she is sitting up waiting for her brother, and my pain has dissipated.

"Hey, Cheerios!" he says. "I brought a couple of visitors."

"Deon," she greets him, her mouth wide in a grin that shows both front teeth missing.

He glances at us and shrugs. "Everyone calls me Segal except Kaleshia."

"Because his name is Deon," Kaleshia says. She is about seven years old. Her head is devoid of hair, her eyes large, dark almonds with lashes as thick as Daniel's.

Segal takes her hand. "How ya doing today?"

"Good," she says. "But you missed them."

"Who?"

"The superheroes." She points to the window. "They were out there hanging in the air—Superman, Spider-man, Batman, and Captain America!"

"Wow!" Tracey walks over to the window and looks out. "I wish I could have seen them."

She beams. "You have to be special to see them, like me."

"You're special?" Segal teases.

She nods her head.

"Says who?"

"The nurses and doctors and blood people."

I flinch, realizing she is talking about the techs that draw her blood, probably on a regular basis, but she is matter-of-fact.

"Okay, Cheerios." Segal says. "I give up. If all those people say you're special, maybe you are."

"Why does he call you Cheerios?" I ask.

She purses her lips. "I don't know. Because I like them, I guess."

"That's all you would eat when you were little," Segal says.

She giggles. "I eat more things now. They help me be strong."

I'm feeling tightness in my throat and clear it.

Abruptly, Kaleshia yawns and her eyes close. She opens them again, but they are obviously heavy. "I'm tired," she says.

"Sleep, baby. It's okay. I'll come back to see you after work."

"Promise?"

"I promise."

The eyes close, giving up the burden of staying open, and we leave the room.

As we walk down the hall to the elevator, I'm trying to think of what to say to him. This is where he goes during his lunch hour. How do you tell someone you've seen his death in the future? How do you tell them not to walk down the alley they walk every day?

"Segal, when is the database going to be locked?" I ask.

"Soon as the last data is entered. Then I start combing through it for errors."

"And when do you think the last data will come in?"

"Not sure. Should just be a few days. If the last participants show and the info gets in, I'll start working on it. It'll take a couple of days to go through everything."

I hand him my card. "Can you call me when you know that the data is coming in for the last patient?"

He looks puzzled. "Why?"

"I can't explain right now, but it's important. Can you do that?"

He shrugs. "I guess. Sure."

Back in Tracey's car, he starts the engine but doesn't take it out of park.

"What is it?" he asks. "Did you see something in the alley?"

I tell him.

"A robbery?"

"No, it was too professional, too quick. Normal people don't think about slashing someone's femoral artery. I think he took the wallet to make it look like a robbery. Paramedics are quick downtown, but Segal would have bled out before they could have gotten to him."

He whistles through his teeth. "Crompton, Stokes, and Segal."

"And maybe others we don't know about."

"The only thing they have in common is this diabetes drug," he says. "That's all that makes sense."

I close my eyes. My body is screaming "lack of sleep."

"Lohan, we can't let Segal die."

"I know. That little girl needs him."

"Yes, she does. And no superhero window washer could fix that."

"We could watch the alley," he says. "Do you have any idea when it's going to happen?"

"Not from the vision, but I have an idea when."

He looks at me.

"I think this is about making sure that the study of zahablan fails. I'm not sure why Crompton was critical in that, but clearly Laurie Stokes was killed to cover up Crompton's murder."

"I'm with you."

"But the critical person is the one with access to the data. A few less positive results and/or a few more placebo positive results and that equal a failed drug. If I understood Segal right, he will be that person."

"You think Segal is going to screw up the data? He seemed pretty jazzed about the study."

"So was Laurie Stokes." My head is okay, but my stomach is still churning.

"Point, but it doesn't make sense."

"What if someone gets to Segal?" I glance toward Children's. "I'm betting, even with insurance, that Kaleshia's medical bills are way more than he can handle."

"You think someone will try to get to him to tweak the data?"

"I do. And then that someone will kill him."

Chapter Forty-One

By the time we walk into the office, my stomach has calmed. I stuff aside all the turmoil that doesn't have to do with our murder case. I don't have time for it.

And Finkman should not have time for anything other than his own homicide cases, a series of gang shootings on the city's West side. But he can't resist taking a shot at me. Maybe, if I hadn't been through everything I'd been through—the Ordeal, being a target for rifle practice, Nora's death, and the possibility of losing Daniel—I would have let it slide. But this time, when he cracks on me, insinuating Tracey and I have been out of the office screwing around instead of working, I've had enough.

As he walks by, returning to his desk with a cup of fresh coffee in his hand, I call on the martial arts training, especially the part Sensei Mark has been driving us about—that timing and creating off-balance are everything. I'm just a white belt, a beginner, but I've been training for two hours twice a week for the past month. As Finkman walks by, I extend my foot, just as he starts to move his left leg forward. Walking, I've learned is really a process of falling and catching yourself and propelling to the next cycle. And you need both legs to do it.

My foot in front of his ankle interferes with that process. I'm only retarding the reflexive forward movement of his leg . . . at just the right moment.

I may not be skilled enough to ever do this again, but Finkman does an ugly sprawl to the floor. I don't realize what happened to the hot coffee until he slowly gets to his feet, mumbling about tripping, and I see the wet stain on his groin.

Tracey looks up at me from the pile of assault cases he is going through. His face is expressionless, but I know he knows what I did. For a moment, I think he's going to chastise me for using my training outside of the bounds of defense, but he only says, "Let's get out of here."

He snatches up the pile of reports, and we escape to the nearby coffee shop.

Tracey orders a large coffee and an egg-bacon croissant, even though it's lunchtime. I'm drawn to a cinnamon and raisin bear claw. That should straighten out the too-little-sleep taste in my mouth. Despite my need for caffeine, I go with a lemon and ginger tea. The general buzz insulates our conversation.

Tracey opens his mouth.

"Don't," I say. "I know it was wrong."

"That isn't what I was going to say."

"What were you going to say?"

"How are you doing?" Concern deepens the fine lines around his clear gray eyes, and I realize despite the superficial words, he is really asking. He's a kind person, I decide. It's almost as if his size and strength have given him a responsibility to be careful with people. I, on the other hand, am prickly and defensive, guarding the territory of my personal privacy.

"I'm doing as well as can be expected. That is to say, like shit."

"Getting shot at is not fun, and neither is it easy to come home and find a dead woman in your bathtub."

"I'm more worried about how it affected Daniel and Becca. It was a double whammy to Becca—seeing that and having Daniel taken away from her."

"How is she handling it?"

"She's not. She's gone back to a zombie state. Won't speak, can't focus. It's a good thing we have some jars of baby food left over from after the Ordeal. That's all we can get her to eat when she's like that."

"I'm sorry."

I take a bite of the bear claw and lick the sugar flakes from my lips. Tracey shifts his gaze to the depths of his coffee, which he drinks black. Yuck.

"We should talk about the case," he says.

I nod.

"At this point," he says, "the things we know are: Dr. Crompton was killed by an overdose of insulin; his assistant administered it; said assistant was shot and killed by what appears to be an assassin; the young man in charge of managing the database for a diabetes human trial is also in danger of being killed; and the window for his time of death is unknown, but only days from now."

I take another bite and a tentative sip of the tea.

"Lohan, we have to solve this before Segal starts to edit the data. If we don't and he locks it down for analysis and messes with it, it will ruin any chance of having that drug available for the millions of people who need it."

Tracey rakes his fingers through the top of his head. "Not to mention that Segal will be a witness taken off the table."

"Yeah, not to mention that."

"I think we have to tell him his life is in danger."

"I'm not sure he knows he's going to mess with the data yet," I say.

Tracey gives me a sideways glance.

"You've talked to him as much as I have," I say. "Do you think he's *planning* to warp the data?"

"No, but I've learned that you can't always trust your instincts about what people will or won't do. If it's between adjusting some numbers and his little sister's well-being, he might not think twice about it."

"Point taken," I say.

"Give me his phone number," Tracey says. "I'll call him and warn him. I'll tell him that I can't share how I know he's in danger, just something we've uncovered in the investigation."

"Better than telling him I saw a vision of him getting stabbed. But—" I tap my pen against my teeth. "We can't count on it helping anything. I don't think he would stop walking down that alley."

Tracey makes the call and then lays his cell phone on the table. "Let's go back to recapping what we know," he says.

"What about physical evidence?"

"There's the syringe you found under Crompton's desk and not much more from that scene. I called the Vestavia detective and got an update on Laurie Stokes' case. Other than confirming a close contact wound by a .22 caliber weapon, they came up with zero. No prints, no disturbance in the apartment, no defense wounds on the victim. Nothing taken. Nobody saw him coming or going."

"Or her coming and going," I say. "We don't know if the killer is male or female."

"You're right. We can't assume anything without evidence. Unless you have details about the person you saw in your vision stabbing Segal?"

I think back to the blur of motion emerging from between parked cars. "I couldn't tell. He or she was powerful and quick and wearing dark clothes, including a ski mask, and the vision was at a distance and wavering, but my impression was a man."

"Not much, although it tends to confirm that whoever this is, he knows what he's doing and may have known his victims intimately. He knew, for example, that Crompton's assistant prepared his insulin. Who would know that?"

"Laurie Stokes, of course."

"Yes, but we know for a fact she didn't kill herself. There was no weapon in her house. We also know she isn't the person who will kill Segal."

"The future," I say, "is not set like the past. I've changed the future I saw."

"So you said. How do you know you can change it?"

"I wouldn't be sitting here now having this conversation otherwise." He waits.

I clear my throat. "It was the first time anything like that had happened to me. You know I was taken off the streets and put in Burglary as a detective because I shot a suspect in the back."

"Of course. You saved your partner's life is what I heard."

"What you don't know is that as I was chasing that suspect, I had a vision. Everything turned into a world of shadows, and I was stuck in it, stuck in time, I think. I couldn't move. I couldn't breathe. The man I was chasing split in two."

"What do you mean?"

I struggle to explain it. "A shadow duplicate of him just peeled off while the 'real' man seemed frozen in place, apparently stuck in time as I was."

"And?"

"Then Paul pulled the patrol car around the corner in front of him."

"Paul wasn't stuck like you were?"

"It wasn't the real Paul. It was the shadow-world Paul, a future Paul."

"Go on."

"The shadow-Paul bailed out of the patrol car, and the shadow-suspect shot him." The words are simple, but my breaths are shallow and rapid as I relive it. I make an effort to slow them, putting my knotting hands in my lap.

"The suspect shot your partner?" Tracey asks with a frown.

"Yes. In the vision, I saw Paul crumple. Then everything snapped back to reality. Paul, the my-time Paul, squealed around the corner, just as he had in my vision. He jumped out of the patrol car, and the suspect raised his arm. It was what I had just seen replaying itself in real time. It happened fast."

"You shot the suspect."

"Yes."

"You did save Paul's life."

I realize what a relief it is to tell the whole truth to a fellow police officer. Under the table, my hands are damp.

"I couldn't tell Internal Affairs the whole thing, of course."

He looks thoughtful. "Then the future can be changed. And we have a chance of saving Segal."

I nod, not trusting myself to speak.

"Who does that leave us as a suspect?" Tracey asks.

"Nobody yet. I think the only option we have is to follow the money."

"Who benefits from killing Crompton, Stokes, and Segal?"

"Actually, everyone who makes money off diabetes supplies or drugs."

"That is a lot of people."

"I know. Closer to home, I've checked the life insurance angle on Crompton." I say.

"I did too."

"Really, when?"

His mouth curves in a succinct smile. "The day you told me you thought it might be a homicide."

"But you disagreed. You closed the case."

He shrugged. "I checked it out anyway."

Somehow, it feels good that he took me seriously, even when he thought I was wrong.

"I think," I say, "we need a bigger picture of who gains from stopping zahablan from becoming a successful treatment."

"Agreed. The first place to look, as you say, is who stands to profit from the new research on a different drug."

"The private lab for one or any pharmaceutical company underwriting the research."

"Right." He polishes off the croissant. "Seems UAB would also gain if they have an agreement for profit sharing with the private lab, or if they've been promised a big donation."

"True."

He frowns. "If the private lab makes a 'better' drug, can they patent it regardless of what happens with the zahablan tests?"

"They could. They can continue to do research and patent anything new they come up with, whether zahablan proves to be effective or ineffective. But if these trials on zahablan are successful and the results are published, even if nobody tries to get it approved as a treatment for diabetes, doctors can write prescriptions off-label for zahablan, and that might significantly cut profits for anything new."

"How can they do that?"

"Doctors don't need permission from anyone to write a script for a drug for another purpose than what it's supposed to be for. Also, sometimes a drug company will buy out the right to sell a drug or its generic, but that would cost them, and it would be bad PR if they upped the price for zahablan."

"But PR or not, it's been done." He nods at the waitress who refills his coffee.

When she moves to the next table, he says, "I've read about pharmacies using other pressure tactics to push their products, like granting big discounts to middle men, and paying doctors, although I'm not sure how that works."

"They don't do it directly. They pay doctors' way to conferences or pay them for presenting at workshops."

"Where do you get all this?"

"There's a website that tracks it."

He downs the rest of his coffee. "You and that computer are pretty close, aren't you?"

"I haven't slept very well the past few nights."

"We need to find out who the drug company is that's supporting the alternative research and who their major players are." He leans back and his chair groans in protest. He's too big to be comfortable in booths, and he weighs a lot more than he appears to.

I pull out a couple of sheets of paper from my purse.

"These are the people and companies who own majority stock in the drug company ZQ Pharmaceuticals. ZQ is paying some of the bill on the new research."

"Where'd you get this?" he asks, sitting upright.

I shrug. "Yahoo.com."

This time his smile is wide and remains on his face while he looks at the list. "Good work, Rose."

Chapter Forty-Two

Tracey and I spend the rest of the morning doing background checks on the individuals listed as major stockholders of ZQ Pharmaceuticals, the drug company that has invested in finding an alternative to zahablan. Tracey is continuing to work on the individual owners through the national criminal databases, but I can check companies on my laptop. Once I have the name, a web search locates their home state. A call to the secretary of state's office yields info on the incorporators, which I learn may or may not be owners. To make it more complicated, a company can create subsidiary companies, thus hiding their ownership in layers. Frustrating.

Yesterday, I trained at the dojo, but today, instead of heading home, I go work out at the Y, taking out my frustration swimming laps or maybe just avoiding having to look at Becca. Sometimes I'm lucky enough to have the pool to myself, but today two men and a woman are swimming in the other lanes, their splashes echoing off the high ceiling. The sharp scent of chlorine and the smooth embrace of the water usually take my focus off myself, but I have a lot going on in my brain. I swim ten laps and push on, trying to reach a point of exhaustion where it won't feel like someone is playing a hot game of Ping-Pong inside my temples. When I finally stop, I half expect Angola to be standing at the shallow end of the pool's edge, or maybe Jason himself. But no one is there.

Tired, I go straight home, that being Alice's house, and eat dinner, a sad affair with just me and Alice and a non-responsive Becca. We break out the baby food for her. I concentrate on feeding her.

Segal has given me his mobile phone number and after dinner, I give him a call.

"How's Kaleshia?"

"She's doing good. A brave kid, my Cheerios," he says.

"Good. Any word on when the zahablan test results will be in?"

"Yeah, as a matter of fact. I asked about that, and the clinic said the last patient comes in Friday, three days from now."

Three days. We have three days to keep the killer from stealing an affordable diabetes treatment and taking little Kaleshia's brother away from her, permanently.

"Has anything unusual happened?" I ask. "Have you had any visitors?"

He laughs. "Nope. Nobody comes to see me, except Mr. Enslen or a couple of homicide detectives."

"Right. I'll check on you again."

"You are easy on the eyes, lady. Come see me anytime."

I click off. *Nobody comes to see me except Mr. Enslen.*

Have we overlooked something right in our faces? Enslen has been in the Army. He would know his way around guns and knives. Could he have been behind the ski mask? Yes, I decide, he could. He knows exactly who Segal is, his schedule, and the significance of what role Segal plays in the drug testing trials. What if Dr. Crompton had found out something fishy was going on and shown up at the Edge of Chaos asking questions? Enslen would have been in the perfect place to take notice. Did he have a financial interest in ZQ Pharmacological? Don't know at this point, but he certainly has interests in the University, which stands to make profits from a new drug patent. Could one arm of the massive institution be trying to track down how zahablan works for the good of humanity, while another is using that information for potential profit? And is that an unworthy goal? Turning research into successful business ventures is part of what a university does, isn't it? Where does right turn into wrong?

At murder.

Maybe we should pay Mr. Enslen another visit.

Tomorrow. Tonight, I help Alice get Becca ready for bed, undressing her, putting on a nightgown and adult diapers.

"I got her," I tell Alice. "You need a break."

I brush Becca's teeth, using a squirt water bottle to rinse and catching whatever she doesn't reflexively swallow into a plastic bowl. When she sits stiffly on the edge of her bed, I push her down gently and straighten her legs. Last night she lay on her back all night. I don't think she ever rolled over.

The same fears that haunted me after the Ordeal have returned. How do I get through to her scalded mind? How do I help her? Is she feeling anything, thinking anything? I touch her forehead. She doesn't even blink. Is she in there, trapped and sealed off as Jason implied?

After the Ordeal, her progress had been incremental, but when Daniel moved in, they made an instant connection, and she blossomed. Had she really been coming back before Nora killed herself or was that just her brain starting over, forming a new person, a child reborn with a fresh slate? She wasn't my Becca, but she wasn't this mockery of her. She was a human being trying to rediscover a world that was strange and new to her. What happened to that person?

In the confines of her room, I pace. It's Alice's only spare bedroom, not counting the one in the basement. We modified the study into a bedroom for Nora and Daniel, but most nights Daniel snuck into Becca's room and slept beside her. I would find them together in the morning. Daniel was a restless sleeper and often his foot would be on Becca's neck or his arm flung over her chest. She never seemed to mind.

The book I had been reading to her and Daniel sits on the bedside table. I guess Becca's situation was like the Glob's. She had to reform herself out of nothing. This is not the way the story is supposed to end—the Glob is not supposed to go backward, to return to the formless mass and float aimlessly.

I bite my lip and pick up the book on the bedside table, sitting beside her. She stares at the ceiling, but I recall hearing that people in comas can hear even when they can't respond. I open the book and start reading.

"Long ago there was a Glob. He was a shapeless thing and he floated to and fro in the tide of the early sea . . ."

Chapter Forty-Three

First thing in the morning, Tracey and I head to the Edge of Chaos to interview Max Enslen. It yields nothing. Dispirited, we return to the office. Enslen could have been lying, but neither of us could add anything other than he was in a position to know Segal's schedule and what he was doing. The night Laurie Stokes was killed, he was at an event with his wife and twenty people until midnight. We confirmed that with his wife and two of the other attendees. Dead end.

Back to the drawing board, or in this case, the computer and our lists.

Several hours later, I throw my pen on my desk and rub my eyes. "This is not fun." The growing list of corporations and their spinoffs has eaten two pages of a notebook. "I should be answering domestic disputes and writing speeding tickets."

"Stop grousing," Tracey says, glancing up from his terminal. "You know how many patrolmen would give their front teeth to work Homicide?"

"They can have it."

"A bit testy today, aren't we?"

"Not a morning person," I mutter.

He chuckles. "I have gotten that, but it's 10:00 a.m."

"What did you find on Mack Enslen's background?" I ask, changing the subject. "We've ruled him out as the person who pulled the trigger, but what if he hired someone to kill Stokes?"

"Nothing. He's clean as a whistle. No priors, honorable discharge from the Army. Married, no children. Graduated from Auburn."

"That last one alone should make him a suspect," I say.

He grins. "War Eagle."

"You didn't even go to Auburn."

"I know, but I find I enjoy riling you up."

The football rivalry between the two universities—Alabama and Auburn—divides the state in half. "War Eagle" is the rallying cry for Auburn University, and "Roll Tide" is the cheer for the University of Alabama—the one in Tuscaloosa, my alma mater, which is about sixty miles southwest of Birmingham.

I ignore his attempt to tease me out of my mood.

Lt. Faraday peers around the edge of our cubicle. "Good morning," she says. "Have some new cases for you."

Tracey and I exchange glances.

"Umm, anyone else you can assign them to, Lieutenant?" he asks. "We kinda got a clock ticking here."

She crosses her arms over her chest. "Nope." She eyes me. "That's why Brighton is here instead of in Burglary, to help with caseloads."

I suppress a groan. We can't explain to Faraday that our concerns for Deon Segal are based on a vision. We'll have to put our fingers in the dike on these cases and do what we need to. I suspect it will be another late night.

"IT'S 6 P.M.," FARADAY SAYS LATER. "It's okay for you guys to go home."

Tracey spreads his arms wide, an act that encompasses a lot of space. He stretches and yawns. "Just trying to get a few things done before you hand us more cases tomorrow, Lieutenant."

"It's not my fault people are violent," she says. "Although it does provide job security."

She turns to leave, stops, and looks at us over her shoulder, "I'm going home. Don't burn out. I don't know which homicide you're working on, but he's already dead."

When we are alone in the office, Tracey says, "It would help if we could tell her that Segal *will* be a dead man if we don't solve this soon."

"That would involve explaining how we know that." I lean back and stretch my neck from one side to the other. "And I don't think the explanation would fly."

"Probably not," he mutters, his attention back on his computer terminal. "The thing that's so frustrating is we're only halfway through this list, and we may have already looked at a suspect without knowing it. We're shooting in the dark."

"Is there anything else we should do?" I ask. "Follow Enslen?"

Tracey shakes his head. "I think that would be a waste of time, and we don't have that time. His alibi is tight."

He scowls. "If we don't get a lead, we're going to have to sit out on that alley while Segal works the data."

"And what if someone has already gotten to Segal, and he changes the data?"

Tracey's mouth flattens into a line. "Our first priority is to save his life. We may not be able to stop him from changing the data."

I think about Ferd Johnson, the man with diabetes who had his foot amputated. Maybe not the most heroic example of humanity, but he is just one of millions whose lives have been horribly affected by that disease. How can we not try to stop that? Researchers have toiled for years to find something that could. If we let all that work, all that hope be for nothing—

"We have to stop him," I say.

I ask myself a question I've been avoiding. Could I stop him with Iron's magic? Stand over Segal and keep him from changing the data? Putting aside that I have sworn not to do that, would I have any clue how to go about making sure the data was right? Segal said it took a couple of days to go over all the information. I wouldn't even understand what he was looking at.

But maybe there is a way at least to find out if someone is threatening him. My stomach roils thinking about using power to manipulate him. That is wrong. But so is doing nothing. It's an old question: Does the end justify the means?

I dig through my purse for my phone. My gun has a special place in a hidden Velcro enclosure, but the rest of my purse is chaos. It seems like things keep collecting there.

Segal answers the phone on the fifth ring. "Detective?"

"Hi. I need to talk to you. Where are you?"

"At the hospital."

"How long will you be there?"

"Just a few minutes. I was going to grab something to eat and go home."

"Where? I can meet you there."

"I was just going to get takeout."

"Can you eat it at the restaurant?"

"I guess. Sure. I have a hankering for Full Moon BBQ."

"Fine. The one near UAB?"

"Yeah."

"I know where it is." I also know they have cookies dipped in dark chocolate.

"I want to talk to Segal," I say, getting to my feet. "I want to feel out if someone is threatening him."

He nods. "If he can tell us who that person is, that would be a hell of a lot more productive than this." He jerks his head at pages of names. "Want me to come?"

"No, I think I can do better alone on this."

He meets my gaze. I have no way to know if he thinks I'm going to use my interview skills or feminine charms. What would he say if he knew I have Iron magic and plan to use it on Segal?

He sighs. "Just get the info. You're right. If there is any way we can stop sabotage on the research trials, we have to do it."

SEGAL IS ALREADY AT A TABLE when I get to the restaurant. I sit across from him in a booth.

"Hey, thanks for the ego boost," he says around a mouthful. "You just upped my reputation."

I smile. "My pleasure."

"Is this about the diabetes trial?" He sighs. "You sure are interested in that."

"We think it may have something to do with why Dr. Crompton was killed."

"Damn. I thought my good looks and charm finally got to you."

I "explore" the ground below us, searching for iron ore. It's not hard to find. At the same time, I touch Segal's arm, releasing a miniscule measure of Iron magic into him.

I don't want to do this, but I'm desperate. *Magic, I tell myself, even Iron magic is not evil. It is just a tool, like a gun. It's the wielder who decides whether to use it and how. I am using it for Segal, to save his life.*

"You will tell me the truth," I say with a smile. "Won't you?"

"Yes, of course."

His dark eyes are fixed on me, reminding me of the way Becca followed Theophalus Blackwell's every move as if she had no life outside of his will. A shudder serpents my spine, and I almost jerk away. But I clench my teeth. *I can't chicken out. I have to do this.* If Segal dies, a lot of people's hope will die with him."

"Do you have any intention of sabotaging the data on the trials?" I ask.

He blinks. "Of course not."

"Is anyone threatening you in any way to get you to do that?"

"No." He seems to pull back into himself a bit. "Should I worry about that?"

"Yes. And you should find a random hotel and go there. Call in sick. Don't tell anyone but Detective Lohan or me where you are. And if anyone threatens you in any way, I want you to call me immediately, no matter when or where or what is said to you. Will you do that?" I send an extra tiny push into him.

"Yes."

"And don't walk down any alleys. Go the long way."

Have I saved his life or just altered the future so that now we have no way to know how he will be stalked?

I sit back, trembling with the effort to restrict the magic to a pinhole trickle. It's different than holding the living-green. Iron is a cold, oily burn and a pressure that seeks relief. So much easier just to let it flow out and scald what it may.

Chapter Forty-Four

When I return from meeting Segal, Tracey is alone at the office. "Well, at least we don't have to climb Vulcan to have a private conversation."

He grunts. "I may have found something."

"What?"

"I was going through the data we collected on that pharmaceutical company involved in funding the new drug research at the private lab, and I discovered these parties." He slides a piece of paper toward me. On it is a long list of names, but one is circled.

"Fe, Inc.?"

"Yep."

"Strange name." Something about it is familiar. I try to recall high school chemistry. "Iron," I say. "'Fe' is the chemical symbol for iron."

"It is. I noticed that too and dug a little deeper into it. One of the incorporators was a Samuel Blackwell."

"Blackwell? That's House of Iron."

I recall the short, rotund man who had taken amusement in showing me the strange details of the basement of his house, a long corridor of rooms decorated to mirror different time periods. Becca and I had been imprisoned in one of those rooms.

"'Uncle Sam?'" I ask.

"Was he someone you met the night your aunt died?"

I grit my teeth. "Yes."

Misinterpreting my response, he puts a hand briefly on mine. "I'm really sorry. Your great aunt's death was a blow to all of us."

"It's okay."

"If House of Iron is connected to this thing with zahablan—" He leaves the rest of his sentence hanging.

"And if they know I'm working it, they may be trying to kill two birds with one stone. Stop the investigation and finish my House."

He looks at me, his gray eyes steel. "Rose, we're prepared to take you somewhere safe. Give you a new identity. Protect you. All the resources of House of Stone are committed to this."

I blink at him. "You mean 'run away'?"

"I mean give you a chance. That man on the roof at Vulcan Park meant business. If Iron is involved in this, solving the case is not going to stop them if they're intent on killing you."

"I hoped that was over when Theophalus Blackwell died. He was unbalanced. But that doesn't mean everyone else in House of Iron is."

"Maybe not, but I think others may have you in their sights."

"My mother mentioned a cabal in House of Iron committed to eradicating House of Rose."

He lifts an eyebrow. "I thought your mother died when you were young."

"She did, but she left a letter in my great aunt's custody, and Alice left it for me in a safety deposit box."

"If this cabal kills you, it's the end of House of Rose."

That is true, even though Alice is alive. At over a hundred, she's not going to have a child.

He looks up at the ceiling, avoiding my gaze. "It's none of my business, but have you ever . . . um . . . thought about having children?"

My head snaps up. "Why do you ask?"

He shifts. "My father is a geneticist. He's researched the House genes for a lot of years, and he believes House of Rose is important for all of us."

Could his father be the person Alice mentioned who sent her reports? He must be. What are the odds of there being another geneticist in House of Stone?

"That's why Stone is intent on protecting me? I'm a prize cow that's needed for the genetic line?"

I can feel my earlobes burning.

"Yeah, I'd be lying if I said differently."

I press my lips together and glare at Tracey. "I'm not running away."

Chapter Forty-Five

The next day is Thursday, day two of the three we have until the data is in. I wait in the most public place I could think of, an outside table at the Black Market Bar & Grill in the middle of Five Points South. The sidewalks buzz with an eclectic motley of people. Mirroring the diversity of the humans are the nearby statuaries. I can almost reach out and touch the kneeling statue of Brother Bryan praying for the sinful, lusty mining boomtown where bars and brothels outnumbered any other type of business. Just across the street, the whimsical "Story Teller" fountain features a bronze statue of "Bob" the ram, who reads to an audience of rabbits, turtles, frogs, and other creatures. Some people look at it askance, wondering if the ram (close enough to a goat, I guess) is a satanic image. Those folks would probably not be happy to know that a real witch sits nearby.

The leap of my pulse alerts me to Jason's presence before I actually see him. When he sits across from me, his hand on the table, magic zaps across the short distance between us like chemical transmitters leaping the synapse in the brain's circuitry. Okay, that metaphor is imaginary, but I believe Alice is right that what we label "magic" is science when you get down to the nitty-gritty. We just don't know enough to explain it yet, so it's "magic."

"I've missed you," Jason says.

I look away from the intensity of his gaze and remind myself why I asked him to meet me. Tracey and Alice would have been appalled that I am with him, but I don't care. Tomorrow, the last person in the research trials checks in. I have only a few hours to save Segal and zahablan.

"I need to know some things," I say.

"Yes, you do." He reaches over and lays two fingers lightly on my wrist. My breath catches.

"We should not fight what is between us," he says. "The magic pulls for a reason."

Ordinarily, I would have brushed off such a statement, but after my conversation with Alice, and now Tracey, I'm wondering if there is truth to that. Alice insists that the survival of our "species," if that's what we are, is dependent on genetic mixing of the Houses. Could the intense sexual attraction between Jason and me be about that? Nature designed hormonal surges to stimulate the sex drive, whose ultimate purpose is genetic, the survival of our genes. Perhaps this is the magical kin to that drive. I don't feel that pull with Tracey, but who knows why the hormones kick in "attraction vibes" for some people and not others? I make a mental note that the hormones' choices are not always wise ones.

I've never felt this kind of desire for anyone. Half of me resents the manipulation and the other half wants to mate with him right here and now on this table. That's just the truth. I close my eyes for a moment to find my self-control.

"That's not what I need to talk about," I say.

"But it is. Why are you fighting this? Rose, you are a beautiful person, inside as well as outside. I respect you, and I desire you more than I have desired any woman in my life."

I can easily imagine how hearing such words from someone like Jason Blackwell would spin any woman. My head is certainly spinning at full tilt. I pull my hand away and stow it along with the other one in my lap. He doesn't know I have House of Iron blood. Some instinct keeps me from telling him or Tracey.

"Listen," I force myself to say, "maybe later we can talk about desires, but there are things going on that have to be dealt with first."

He leans back. "Then I must console myself with being close to you . . . for now. What is so important, *il mio amore*?"

"Are you familiar with a company called Fe, Inc.?"

He shrugs. "It's one of many holdings of my Family, but it is local, in the U.S. I pay little attention to business acquisitions here. My focus is overseas."

"What do you do, anyway? Besides play the rich playboy?"

He smiles, "I enjoy that role, true, but I also travel for the Family, making connections."

"A little touch here and there to smooth business?" I ask.

His face hardens and he leans forward. "Rose, you must understand that our abilities are as natural as breathing to us. They have saved us countless times throughout history."

"And made you quite rich."

"Yes, that too. Money is part of security, is it not?"

I don't want to go down this road. "I'm sorry. I'm not here to criticize you or—" I start to say "your Family," but it's my House too. "Jason, I'm going to be blunt."

He throws his head back and laughs.

Annoyed, I wait for him to stop. "What's so damn funny?"

"Oh, *il mio amore*, when have you not been blunt? It is one of the things I adore about you."

I flush, not sure if it's from embarrassment or his freedom in speaking his heart . . . or his lust. I looked up *il mio amore*. It means "my love." He may think me blunt, but perhaps he is more honest than I, who cannot or will not speak of my own desire.

Desire is not love. I hold that between us like the early Christians used the symbol of the cross to ward off evil.

He smiles and lifts both hands skyward. "Ask me whatever you wish."

"I'm investigating a murder that revolves around the testing of a drug. The funding for that drug is coming through a company called ZQ Pharmaceuticals."

He shrugs, smiling. "This means nothing to me."

"One of the major stock holders in ZQ Pharmaceuticals is Fe, Inc."

The smile fades abruptly from his chiseled face. "Which my Family owns."

"Owns and controls," I say.

"You believe the Family had something to do with this murder?"

"Seems a distinct possibility, and we believe there are other people imminently at risk."

"I see. What do you want from me?"

"I want your help."

He cocks his head to the side, exposing it beyond the shadow of the umbrella. Sunlight plays in the gold of his hair. I pull my gaze from the glimmer back to his eyes, which doesn't help my concentration one bit.

"You also want to know if I am involved," he says.

"Yes."

"The answer to that is 'no.'"
I nod slowly, not sure I can believe him, but dead certain I want to.
"And how exactly do you want my help?"
"I want you to find out if anyone in your . . . Family is behind this."

Chapter Forty-Six

Ten minutes before my alarm goes off the next morning, I wake in a panic, bits of dream world clinging to my reality. All I can remember of it is that I was digging into the floor of Benjamin Crompton's house, uncovering pieces of debris and odd pieces of his past that were important, but I couldn't figure out why.

And I'm running out of time to figure things out. This is the day that the last patients in the zahablan trials check in. Segal is supposed to start checking the data. If he does, that is when the killer will strike. Theoretically, I've made sure he won't start doing that, but I have the feeling my efforts at using Iron magic is like a cheesecloth—full of holes. According to Jason, the effects wear off, but I have no idea how long that will take or if it is dependent on how I did it.

If House of Iron is involved, it means someone could have influenced Laurie Stokes, "suggesting" she give Crompton the insulin from her pocket and then forget about doing it. In order to ensure that memory never resurfaced, the real killer got rid of the only witness, Stokes, as he plans to do with Segal once Segal has tampered with the database. Then the zahablan trials will be a failure, and whatever the private lab produces will have a clear path to a new patent and profits. All the companies that make diabetes-related products will keep their profits, at least for several more years. And Deon Segal will be as dead as Laurie Stokes and Benjamin Crompton.

We have to find the killer before that happens. What have I overlooked? I go back over everything, unwilling to get out of bed until I have a plan. There must be something.

There is nothing besides calling Jason and hoping he has something.

A sudden wave of nausea convinces me I have to get up before I throw up all over my sheets. I stumble to the bathroom. Am I having psychological morning sickness? That's just great. Practice pregnancy. Just what I need. I'm allergic to even the idea of being a mother. Is this about getting Daniel back or the thing about being a mother to the race of witches and warlocks? Or something I ate?

"I've got Becca," Alice calls from upstairs. "You go on to work."

I close my eyes in gratitude that I don't have to face that today. *Coward.*

Suddenly, for no apparent reason, I know why I dreamed of digging in Mrs. Crompton's house. As soon as I determine I'm not really going to be sick and can safely exit the bathroom, I call Tracey.

"Morning," Tracey says with a yawn.

"Lohan, I have an idea. It might be nothing, but meet me at Benjamin Crompton's home. You got the address?"

"Yeah. What's up?"

"I'll tell you when you get there."

TRACEY IS WAITING WHEN I PULL up.

"You must have been up early," I say.

"Couldn't sleep."

"This is the last day we have."

"That's why I couldn't sleep. I keep going over everything, hoping something we missed will jump out."

"Me too."

"Why are we here?" he asks.

"I had a dream."

"A vision?"

"No just a dream, but I think it might have been my subconscious telling me what I missed."

"And that is?"

"I don't know."

"Rose, sometimes you are infuriating. I am the senior officer here, you know."

I give him a quick grin and stride up the sidewalk to the front door.

With a loud sigh, he follows me.

Mrs. Crompton answers the door in the same silk robe she wore the day I was there.

"You're back," she says and eyes Tracey suspiciously.

"Yes, ma'am. This is my partner, Detective Lohan."

"Did you find out who killed Ben?" she asks.

"We're working on that."

"It was the aliens," she says. "I'm sure it was them, but I don't know what he did to make them angry."

Tracey scratches his chin.

"You may be right," I say. "May we come in and talk about it?"

"Of course."

We follow her into the living room. She waves at the chairs, but I don't sit.

"Mrs. Crompton, we've hit a dead end in the investigation, and we need your help."

"What can I do?"

"When I was here before I asked you some questions, but what I didn't ask was whether your husband kept any notes or papers from the office here."

"He worked in his study. I haven't moved anything."

"May we take a look?" I ask.

"He was a private man," she says, staring at Tracey.

"It's important. Someone's life may depend on what we can find."

She turns back to face me. "Well, of course, if it is that critical. Go look."

She leads us to a study in the back of the house overlooking her well-manicured garden. I can't help thinking how different it is from Alice's chaotic mixture of herbs, vegetables, and flowers.

Tracey starts investigating the contents of the desk. I'm drawn to the bookshelves, giving them a quick scan. Most appear to be in the field of microbiology and biochemistry, along with a shelf of classic literature. I recognize a few of the titles.

A rosewood leather recliner faces the window. On a small table beside it lies a beautiful, wood-carved pipe with an ivory bowl, a leather tobacco pouch and a book, *The Tao of Pooh*. Curious, I open it at the bookmark. A line is highlighted in yellow marker.

. . . A Weakness of some sort can do you a big favor, if you acknowledge it's there.

I regret not knowing Benjamin Crompton. He must have been an interesting man. His weakness, I suppose, was trusting someone, specifically Laurie Stokes.

Tracey is shuffling through the papers he has found in the desk. I attack the filing cabinet.

"I have no idea what I'm looking for," Tracey says. "Can you give me a hint?"

"I would if I had a clue," I mumble. "Just keep looking."

An hour passes.

"This is ridiculous," Tracey says. "I've looked through every piece of paper in every drawer. I don't understand but five words. It's all technical papers."

"Zero here, too," I say, and plop down in the big chair next to the pipe.

"It was worth a shot. It's not like we have anything else to go on."

"Other than that connection with Iron and ZQ Pharmaceuticals," I say.

"A coincidence?"

"No. It explains too much."

"Like how Laurie Stokes was 'convinced' to kill a man she seemed to care about?"

"Yeah, like that."

"And how the killer expects to influence someone like Deon Segal."

I'm gratified our thoughts have traveled the same path, but I can't let go of the feeling that we're missing something.

"Something happened that made our suspect feel like he needed to off Crompton in the first place," I say.

"You think Crompton suspected something?"

"It's just a theory, but according to Laurie Stokes, a lot of people spread out over the UAB medical community were participating in this research in some way. Crompton and Stokes were the only ones targeted, other than Segal, who holds the key to the results." This is a repetition of what we already know, but I'm hoping by repeating it and bouncing it off Tracey, something new will emerge.

"Those are the only three that we know of," Tracey says.

"We know why Stokes was killed."

"We think we know. And only if a House was actually involved."

"Assume it was House of Iron. What made Crompton a particular target?"

Tracey shrugs. "He is . . . was House of Stone."

"Which means our killer couldn't influence him by means of magic."

"But why would he need to? Crompton wouldn't be privy to the data on the trials. That's why they call it a blind trial."

"Something made him a target, and we're missing it. Crompton was a smart man. If he figured out there was a possible scam going on, he would leave a clue if he could."

Tracey looks up at me. "But if he suspected House of Iron was involved, he couldn't make that known to outsiders."

"Yeah, like explaining to Lieutenant Faraday that we need surveillance on an alley because I saw a vision where a man gets killed there sometime in the future."

Tracey rubs his chin. "I agree that Crompton would let others in his House know about it, at the least."

"What if it didn't rise to that level? What if it was just something that didn't seem right to him? Or what if he did, but there wasn't enough info to do anything about it? What would he do?"

"Without real evidence, I don't know what he could do. Even my father wouldn't make a complaint against House of Iron under those circumstances."

"*Even* your father?"

"He's head of House of Stone."

"Oh." So the president of the City Council is a warlock of House of Stone. I wonder who other influential House members might be. I suspect they extend into places deep into the political structure of the country, perhaps the world, especially House of Iron.

"Stay focused, Lohan. What would Crompton do?"

"He'd want to leave a clue. It would have to be something subtle, meant for someone who knew he would hide it."

"A member of House of Stone."

"Probably. That's your area." I spread my arms. "See anything that would jump out at you?"

Tracey stands and slowly turns 360 degrees, twice. He steps to the bookshelf and examines two cut amethyst bookends, picking up each one and setting it back. Dropping his hands to his sides, he heaves a frustrated sigh. "I don't see anything unusual."

Unusual. Something is tickling my subconscious. Something about books. I again scan the heavy volumes lined up at attention along the bookshelves. Nothing. Then I do the same thing Tracey did, scrutinizing the whole room. My gaze falls to the copy of *The Tao of Pooh* beside the chair. It's amusingly different from the other books on his shelf. Why is it out? Is it just what he was reading? The bookmarked page said something about acknowledging your weakness and making it your strength. Maybe "weakness" in this case meant the "lesser" thing—perhaps like Winnie the Pooh in the company of technical and classical literary works? I move closer to the shelf that displays his highbrow taste, running my finger along each title.

A thin paper edge stuck between Dickens' *A Tale of Two Cities* and Dumas' *The Count of Monte Cristo* catches my attention. I pull it out—a paperback copy of *The Te of Piglet*, obviously the companion to the book by his chair. I ruffle the pages and a folded piece of paper flutters to the floor.

I bend to pick it up. Tracey moves behind me to look over my shoulder. It's hand written and dated a few weeks ago. In fact, it was two days before he died.

It reads:

Today, I saw a man I suspect might be interested in mineral commodities. He gave me a line, but I refused. Later saw him talking to a researcher involved in Z trials. Slim, dark, ponytail.

My heart dives. Slim, dark, ponytail. There is a man of House of Iron who fits that description—Jason Blackwell's driver, *Angola*.

Behind me Tracey says, "What the—?"

Then the unmistakable *crack* of close pistol fire and a grunt from Tracey. I whirl to face a gun and the woman wielding it.

Chapter Forty-Seven

Tracey is down on one knee. Crompton's wife holds a pistol in both trembling hands.

I step between her and Tracey, holding a palm out. My free hand dives into my purse, grasping the butt of my gun and lifting the muzzle so it points at her, but I don't draw it. "Mrs. Crompton."

She doesn't respond.

"Valinda," I say gently.

Slowly, her gaze moves from Tracey to me.

"He's one of them," she says in a loud whisper. "I can tell. One of the aliens."

"It's okay," I say. "Thank you for telling me. I'll make sure he is locked up."

"Really?"

"Yes. Just give me the gun so no one else gets hurt."

"It belonged to Benjamin," she says. "He told me I was to use it for my protection if one of 'them' came into the house."

Wrong group of aliens.

I take another step toward her and close my hand over hers, pushing her arm to the side across her body. "Give me the gun now," I say, my voice firmer.

She nods and releases her hold.

"Are there any more guns in the house?"

"No."

I spin back to Tracey.

He holds his upper arm, but blood is pulsing out, fast. I fumble for my phone and drop Crompton's gun into my purse. Aftershock of adrenaline is making my own hands shake, but I key in 911.

"Officer down," I say, giving the address. "It's 10-24. I have the suspect in custody. Need medics and ambulance. Fast."

Tracey shakes his head. "It's not that bad."

"Shut up and lie down, Lohan."

When he does, I put my hands on top of his and add pressure.

"Valinda, get me a towel or a long piece of cloth!" I twist to make sure she is responding, but can only see a heap of silk kimono billowed on the floor. She's fainted.

Great. No help there. I swallow. Blood still coming. Not good. He's bleeding out! I feel myself panicking. No time for panic. Think. I know direct pressure is number one. Next priority is slowing the bleeding.

"Do you carry a handkerchief?"

"Yes, back pocket."

"Roll toward the bookshelf."

As soon as his back pocket is accessible, I lift one hand from its position over his and grab the hanky with it, keeping pressure on the wound with my other hand. He rolls himself back, and I work the cloth beneath his hand. It quickly soaks through.

His face is growing pale. He's going to pass out soon. Damn. "I think we need a tourniquet."

What do I use?

His shirt is too difficult to remove without releasing pressure. My assessment ends up at his big feet.

"Take off a shoe," I say.

Tracey's eyes are unfocused.

I am not letting you die. I'm not.

"Your shoe, Lohan," I order, putting a sharp edge in my voice to get his attention. "Kick it off. The one closest to me."

He fumbles one foot to the other, wedges his toe in the back of his right heel and pushes down. The shoe hangs halfway off his foot.

"Can you raise your knee?" I ask.

He does, drawing the shoe closer.

Keeping one hand pressing on his arm, I reach over, knocking the shoe aside, and strip off his sock. Not sanitary, but it's not going on the wound. It wouldn't fit on the bulge of his triceps. I go for the area right above it. Fortunately the sock stretches. I have to release the wound to tie it, and blood spurts out between his fingers. A thick pool of red stains the carpet.

"Tracey, press down, damn it!"

No response. His hand drops away. Panting, I put my knee on the wound, using my weight to apply pressure. As quickly as I can tie a knot, I put both hands back on the blood-soaked handkerchief.

Valinda moans and sits up. "What have I done?"

"Get up," I snap at her. "Go to the front door and open it. Bring the paramedics here. Can you do that?"

"Yes," she says, sniffling. "I can."

"Then do it!"

The blood flow seems to have slowed, but Tracey's eyes are closed. I wish to God I remembered how often you're supposed to loosen a tourniquet. But stopping the bleeding is the priority. His life is more important than losing his arm, right? *Where are the damn paramedics?*

FROM HIS HOSPITAL BED, Tracey looks at me, his normally clear gray eyes dark, dilated, I assume, with opiates. How much would it take to affect a man from House of Stone? "Are you okay?"

"Fine," I say.

He turns his head to survey the fresh bandage on his arm.

"Is that it?" he asks sleepily.

"It nicked an artery," I say. "You almost bled to death. They had to stitch it and give you blood."

He gives me a weak smile. "I'm not easy to kill."

I've heard that claim before from Aunt Alice. Witches and warlocks apparently do heal faster than normal folk, but unfortunately not Wolverine-fast.

"And," he adds, "I'll be damned if I will exit because of a deranged woman who probably couldn't hit the side of a dinosaur."

"What's the last thing you remember?" I ask.

"You mean at Crompton's house?"

"Yeah."

"Umm. Gun. Woman in kimono. Getting my shoe off for some reason."

"Sock tourniquet," I say.

"Oh. Of course."

"I meant about the note in Crompton's office. Do you remember it?"

"Sort of. You got it?"

I check over my shoulder to make sure the door is closed. We lucked out that we got a private room. The semi-private ones were all full. Pulling the note from my purse, I read it aloud.

Today, I saw a man I suspect might be interested in mineral com-modities. He gave me a line, but I refused. Later saw him talking to a researcher involved in Z trials. Slim, dark, ponytail.

"Interested in mineral commodities," Tracey says, "has got to mean someone from a House."

"That's the way I read it. What about, 'He gave me a line, but I refused.'?"

Tracey reaches for a glass of juice by the bed on his right and winces.

I snatch it before he can try again, delivering it into his left hand. "Looks like men of Stone feel pain," I say.

"Most definitely, but I can't stay in here."

I hold up my hand. "Before we fight about that, what do you think Crompton meant by, 'He gave me a line, but I refused.'?"

"'A line' is something my Family says to refer to the power of Iron. It means someone from House of Iron tested him by giving a 'suggestion' he didn't take."

"Thereby learning that he was immune and therefore House of Stone."

"Right."

"Then that person, who I'm betting is Angola, 'made him'—he saw Crompton watching him. Angola may have been seeking information about who held the keys to the data base."

"And," Tracey says, "Angola planned to manipulate and then kill whoever that turned out to be. He might not have known it was Deon Segal at that point."

I sit back. "Angola knew no one would suspect magic at play, except someone from Stone, and when Angola stumbled on Crompton and discovered he was immune to House magic, he knew he had to be elim-inated before Crompton figured out what was going on."

"Makes sense," Tracey says. He shifts on the hospital bed, careful not to jostle his arm. "What we have is hardly evidence, though. Can't get an arrest warrant on brilliant logic, especially one that involves our 'Families.'"

He's right, of course, but I don't like it a bit.

Tracey rubs his chin and considers me. "It would be handy if we had a vision of Angola's next step." He makes it a question with lifted brows.

"Unfortunately, doesn't work that way," I say. "If I tried right now, assuming I got something, it would probably be what you're having for breakfast tomorrow."

"In that case, our first priority is to protect Segal."

"I told him to get a random hotel room and stay put."

"You think he did?"

I start to tell him I have House of Iron blood, and I used Iron magic to ensure that he did, but the words won't come out. They feel dirty, making me no different from Theophalus, Angola, or Jason.

Jason. Angola works for him. I can't pretend Jason's hands are not in this. Alice has been right all along.

Chapter Forty-Eight

The fact that Jason has his hands in the murder of two people and the planning of a third makes me nauseous. Maybe that is the real reason I woke up sick. Maybe my subconscious has known it all along. How could I have ever trusted him? And yet here I am meeting him again at the same place in Five Points.

A vertical line between his eyebrows mars the perfection of his face. This man requires no magic to lure women into his life or his bed, but no matter what he looks like, how simple to just touch someone and whisper in their ear.

I can do that too.

The thought startles me. It's the first time that the idea hasn't scared the bejesus out of me. What if I had been brought up believing I could use magic on others without ethical qualms? Did Jason believe that? Did he believe making suggestions to people was no different than using personal charm? Did he travel the world "sealing" deals for Iron with a clear conscience?

I don't even know what it would have been like to be part of House of Rose. Healers can't just run around . . . healing everything. I try to imagine what would happen if word got out about what Alice could do. Scientists would want to study her. Religious nuts would want to saint her, but worst would be all the desperate who would come, begging for healing for themselves or their loved one. How could anyone choose whom to help? How to bear the burden of all those you didn't? Could you have even a semblance of a life?

"Rose?" Jason says. "Are you okay?"

"Sorry. I was just thinking about something."

From his slightly surprised look, I imagine he's not used to someone being distracted around him. It's amazing that I could be, with the drumbeat of magic between us. Am I learning to push it aside or ignore it, like an overpowering smell or noise that saturates nerve endings to the point where they can no longer fire? I do have a lot on my mind.

I stuff all the questions into a mental box. I need to focus.

"Did you find out anything?" I ask.

"I did."

"And?"

"I confirmed we do have a major interest in Fe, Inc. and a piece of the pharmaceutical company you mentioned, ZQ."

My hands tighten around my cup. "Tell Angola to back off."

"Angola?"

"You remember him." My sarcasm makes him flinch. "Your chauffeur."

"What does he have to do with anything?"

"Is he a member of House of Iron?"

"Yes."

I study his face. Now *he* looks distracted. Is he lying?

"I have evidence Angola has killed a man and probably a woman too."

"What evidence?"

"A note describing him."

"Someone saw him killing a man and a woman?"

"Not exactly."

Suddenly my "evidence" seems weak. I have a note describing Angola—how many pony-tailed men in House of Iron can there be?—talking to someone at UAB. Outside the context of our theories, it sounds pretty lame.

"It's complicated," I say.

"Look, this is not amusing. I've acted against the interests of my House for you twice now. What else do you want of me?"

"I want the truth."

We are staring at each other. Maybe "glaring" is a better word.

"Angola is not a killer," Jason says. "Or is it *me* you believe is behind this?"

"I don't know what I believe, except that everything I have found points to Angola, and he works for you."

"Yes, he does."

My cell plays the intro to "A Space Odyssey." I glance down. It's a text from Alice, a reminder—*crap*. The home visit for custody of Daniel!

I PRACTICALLY RUN UP THE FRONT STEPS. I meant to come home early and help clean. I googled how to prepare for a home inspection visit, but didn't have a chance to tell Alice or help her prepare. Things have just been happening so fast.

Alice always locks the doors. I try it before getting out my keys. If the DHR social worker is already here, the door will be open. Alice wouldn't have locked it behind her. That would give the impression we didn't live in a safe neighborhood. If it's locked, I'm not late.

I take a deep breath and turn the handle. The door opens.

Heart sinking, I step quietly inside.

Tanya Melbourne sits on the sofa. The TV is off. Good. That was on the list. The living room is spotless. Bless her heart, Alice has her best china tea set out on the table with an empty cup waiting for me.

Bless her heart. That is something Becca would have said. My throat tightens.

"And there she is," Alice says lightly. "I told you she would be right along."

"I'm sorry I'm late," I say, trying to catch my breath.

"It's okay," Melbourne says. "I was just getting to know Ms. Gideon."

I swallow. "Um, yes, Irene's pretty much part of the family."

"So she was telling me."

"She's wonderful with Daniel," I say. "He loves her. He calls her 'Gran-gran.'"

"Yes, he's told me."

"Is he okay?" I ask. "Is he in a . . . good place? I mean, are they taking care of him?"

"Of course."

"Good. I was a foster child too." I catch Alice's eye. She twists her fingers together in her lap, evidence of her own nervousness, despite her airy tone.

"That is," I say, "until I was adopted. My foster family adopted me."

"I saw that in your file. You were raised in a military family."

"Yes."

"You traveled a lot?"

"Yeah, we were stationed in different places in the US, mostly in the South, and once in Germany."

"Must have been tough being bounced around like that. Hard to make friends."

I just nod.

"Can I get you some tea, dear?" Alice asks me.

"Um, no. No thanks."

"It's very good," Melbourne says. "I've never had tea with fresh mint before."

"Have you looked around the house?" I ask her.

"Yes. It's larger than it looks outside. Ms. Gideon—"

"Please, call me Irene," Alice says.

"Irene showed me the room that would be Daniel's room. She says she cooks for the family."

I give a weak smile. "Yes, but I can cook—"

Alice lifts one brow.

"Tuna casserole anyway, but Irene is way beyond me. We have vegetables at every meal. That is, except breakfast." I sound like an idiot.

I take a breath. "I'm sorry if I sound like an idiot. It's just because . . . well, I never thought I would be a mother, I mean, that I would want to be a mother, but Daniel—" I take another breath. "Daniel has come to mean a great deal to me, and I want, we want, to give him a home."

She studies me. "I understand that, but I'm hesitant to put him back in the house where such a horrible event occurred."

What can I say? Would he see his mother in a tub of blood every time he passes by that bathroom? What kind of nightmares would I have if my family's house had not burned down, and I had to live in it without them?

She stands. "I'll get back to you with the judge's decision."

Chapter Forty-Nine

After Tanya Melbourne leaves, Alice and I sit quietly in the living room. "I'm sorry I didn't tell you what I found out about how to prepare for a home visit."

"Do you think I don't know how to google? I'm not a complete antique."

"Uh, I mean, you never seem to spend any time doing that."

"Well, I don't, but it doesn't mean I don't know how."

I forget she is a scientist.

"Sorry," I say again, shifting in my seat. Something isn't right. "Where are the cats?" I ask.

She purses her lips. "I put them all downstairs in the unfinished part of the basement. I didn't want Ms. Melbourne to think I was some kind of eccentric old cat person."

"I don't know that it's going to make any difference."

"You don't know what her decision will be," Alice says, playing with her teacup.

"I think it's pretty obvious that Melbourne doesn't think Daniel should come back here."

"She's not the judge."

"But she's writing the report. The judge will be heavily influenced by it. And what if they find other family members?"

"That would be a good thing, wouldn't it?"

I think on that. "Maybe, but maybe not. What if they're alcoholics like Nora?"

"Nora was severely depressed."

"Is that supposed to be better? For all intents and purposes, she abandoned him."

"She brought him to a place where she knew he would be cared for by people who cared for him. She stopped drinking. She did her best."

"I could have done more to try and get through to her. I looked at her as a drunk, even when she wasn't drinking. I knew nothing about her or her life, really. I should have persuaded her to get help."

"I tried," Alice says. "She wouldn't go. You can't make a person get help who doesn't want it, and magic couldn't heal the kind of wounds she had."

"God, how is Daniel going to overcome this?"

"You did," she says. There are tears in her eyes. "Even after what happened to your family, even though I sent you away. You are that strong. Daniel is strong too."

"I had a family, a loving family, Alice. You gave me that opportunity. If . . . If I knew Daniel had that for sure, maybe that would be best for him."

"He should be here with us," Alice says. "I'm not sending another child away."

"Becca needs him," I say, "but is that fair to him? That shouldn't be a burden for a five-year-old to carry on his shoulders."

"He's almost six and he needs her too," Alice says.

"What do you mean?"

"He loves her just as she is. He's taken her on as his responsibility, and he needs that, especially right now. He should have a focus outside of himself."

My cell phone rings. Reluctantly, I pull it from my purse. I'd forgotten to turn it off as the web instructions recommended for a home evaluation.

The call is from Deon Segal.

"I have to take this," I say. "Segal, you okay?"

"No." Tension rattles his voice.

"What's wrong?"

"I got a call from Children's Hospital."

My heart dives.

"Kaleshia?"

"Yes."

"Did she—?" I can't stand the thought of that brave little spirit succumbing to her cancer.

"No, it's not the cancer. She's gone."

"What do you mean?"

"She's gone."

"I don't understand."

"She's not in the hospital."

"Did her father take her?"

"No, nobody took her. She's just gone. I'm going crazy. I didn't know who else to call."

"Segal, where are you?"

"I'm at the motel, but you gotta find her."

"We'll find her. Don't leave. Don't go anywhere. I'll call you as soon as I can."

Disconnecting, I turn to Alice. "I gotta run."

"Police business?"

"Yes."

On the way to my car, I call Tracey.

"Yeah?" he answers.

"You have any contacts at Children's Hospital security?"

"The head of security is Don Glass. He was in my rookie class at the Academy, but decided private security paid better. What's up?"

"Kaleshia is missing from Children's Hospital."

"Missing?"

"Yes. Just got a call from Segal."

"I'll meet you there."

"Have they released you—?" I'm talking to the dead line.

DON GLASS REACHES OUT to shake my hand. "Damnedest thing," he says. "The child—"

"Kaleshia Segal?"

"Yeah, a man walked out with her."

"Don't the discharge papers say who he was?" Tracey asks.

"No, they don't, because there aren't any discharge papers."

Tracey looks at me.

"What does the staff say?" I ask.

"They said they assumed he was family taking her out for some sunshine. She was smiling and holding his hand."

"You got video footage of the man?"

"Yeah."

"Can we take a look? We're working a case that might have connections."

"Sure."

He leads us into a room with camera displays and nods at a security guard sitting before it. "Run it again."

"Yes, sir."

"There are several tapes, but this is the best angle."

On the video clip, Kaleshia is dressed in street clothes and sitting in a wheelchair. The camera view is unfocused, and the face of the man beside her is turned as though he is aware of the camera as they walk past. It's very possible that the man has a short ponytail. I don't need a clear picture. I recognize his walk. There's no doubt about the man's identity.

"Freeze it," Glass says.

"Can we have a printout of that image?" Tracey asks.

"Of course. You recognize him? That's a pretty grainy photo, and you can't see the man's face."

"I think we know who he might be."

"Who is he?" Glass asks.

"His first name is Angola. That's all we know right now."

"Is the child safe with him?"

"No," I say. "She is not."

Glass's face is stiff. "What can we do?"

"You've already helped more than you know," Tracey says. "Did you file a report?"

"Of course, with UAB Police."

"You got a case number?"

"Sure. I'll get it for you."

Ice clogs my veins. Angola has Kaleshia.

When Glass hands Tracey a copy of the card left by the UAB officer who took the initial report, Tracey drops it in his shirt pocket. "Thanks. We'll let you know as soon as we find her."

Glass offers his hand. "I hope it's soon, and she's okay. This is on us. Anything I can do from my end, just holler."

"Will do," Tracey says.

On the sidewalk outside the security office, I turn to Tracey. His face is pinched.

"You know why Angola took her," I say.

He nods. "To get Segal to change the data."

"If he hurts Kaleshia—"

Tracey's fists clench. "If he hurts that child, he will wish he'd never met me."

Chapter Fifty

Tracey and I crowd into Lieutenant Faraday's office. She looks up over a stack of paperwork.

"You get released from the hospital that quick?" she asks Tracey.

"Um, yeah. I felt fine."

She narrows her eyes at him, but he jumps in before she can ask for more details.

"Lieutenant, we've got an active kidnapping going on."

"Really?" She eyes the papers before her. "I haven't seen a kidnapping come across my desk."

"University PD took the report at Children's Hospital about forty minutes ago."

"Someone took a child from the hospital?"

"She's a cancer patient."

"A family member?"

"No."

She sits up. "What else do you know?"

"Her name is Kaleshia Segal. UAB might have tagged it a missing person, but we're pretty sure the suspect is someone connected to one of our homicide cases," Tracey says.

"Which case?"

"Benjamin Crompton."

She raises an eyebrow. "The UAB insulin overdose? The one connected to the Vestavia homicide and someone shooting at you two?"

"We don't have enough evidence on him to charge the suspect with it, but we have reason to believe he wants to disrupt a drug trial research in progress at UAB, and the little girl he kidnapped is the sister of the guy who can do that."

"He's using the sister as leverage?"

"That's our theory."

"Any threats made?"

"Not yet."

"FBI?" she asks.

Tracey shakes his head. "No indication he intends to take her out of the state. It's our baby."

"Okay. Let UAB PD know we're on it. What can we do from here?"

"All we know is that his name is Angola. No last name or date of birth, but he's in his thirties, I'd guess. White male, but dark skinned or possibly a light-skinned black male. Dark eyes, no facial hair. Wears his hair in a ponytail."

"Possible military record," I add. "And he works for a Jason Blackwell."

Tracey's shoulders tense. We are pointing a finger at House of Iron and that puts everyone at risk, but I'm not willing to let them hurt Kaleshia.

"You guys want someone on the family?" Faraday asks.

"No," Tracey says quickly. "We'll handle that and ask for help as we need it."

"I want a report in my hands with all you know before you step foot out of the office," she says tightly.

"Yes, ma'am." Tracey leads me out her door.

"We need a location on Segal," Tracey says, "and any other family members. Since you have the rapport with Segal, get on that. I'll knock out a quick report for Faraday."

"Crap." I glance at my phone.

"What is it?"

It's Segal. He called, but I missed it and no voice message. I hit redial.

The phone rings several times and moves into voicemail. I hang up without leaving a message. "He's not answering."

Tracey pulls up a Supplemental Report form on his terminal and starts typing. "Keep trying."

I do, but he doesn't answer. My mouth goes dry. "Lohan, I can't get him to pick up. I just get his voice mail. He may be in trouble. How can we locate him through his phone GPS before his battery dies? Can the phone company do that as an emergency without a warrant?"

"Yep. Go talk to Faraday about it while I finish this."

Faraday makes the call to the phone company. They send an exigency request form by email, and she prints it. As quickly as I can, I fill out the form citing an emergency with a kidnapped child and scan it and send it back.

I'm grateful Faraday doesn't ask for details about the case. Knowing it's a kidnapping of a child is enough. She trusts her people. Lohan, anyway. If it were just me, she'd probably be grilling me to make sure we weren't violating someone's rights and privacy.

By the time Tracey finishes his report, I have GPS coordinates from the phone company. It's not exactly accurate. Only the military can access the precise coordinates that the satellites are capable of sending. But it will be close enough. I plug the coordinates into my own smart phone map app.

Tracey prints out his report and delivers it to Faraday, and we head full speed out of the office.

"Found him," I say, eyes on my phone as we move down the hall.

"Let me guess—the Edge of Chaos."

"If you knew, why did I go through all that with the phone company?"

"To confirm it before we busted our asses getting there, only to find he was somewhere else."

We use blue lights but no siren to clear the path.

To my relief, Segal is in his office at his computer, working. My House of Iron mojo must have worn off. I wonder if that process is hastened by stress. Learning his little sister was kidnapped would certainly fall into that category.

Stress is evident in Segal's hunched shoulders, pinched eyes and tight jaws. I think he's gritting his teeth.

"Segal." I say. He is intent on the numbers on his screen and jumps when I say his name.

"Damn. I didn't hear you come in."

"We were worried about you."

Tracey, standing behind me, is silent.

"Kaleshia?" Segal asks.

I shake my head. "But we know who took her."

"Where is she? Is she okay?"

"I'm sorry. We don't know that . . . yet." I pull up a chair and get eye level with him. "Tell me what happened."

His face tight with pain, he leans back, wrapping his arms around his chest as if to keep his heart from exploding. "A man called me. How did he get my number?"

"That's not important right now. What did he say?"

"He said that he had Kaleshia, and that if I didn't want her hurt, I had to adjust the zahablan trial data to ensure it was a failure without setting off any alarms. He said I wouldn't see my sister again until that made the news."

"The media would report something like that?" Tracey asks.

"Maybe not the big guys, but it would be reported on the UAB news sites as a follow-up for the other stories on those tests. A lot of people are watching that."

Segal takes a shaky breath. "Kaleshia's in the middle of a treatment. She needs to be in the hospital."

"We've got to have information to find her. "What else did he say?"

Segal swallows. "He said if I tell anyone, he'll kill her. You gotta find her before he . . . hurts her."

I take a breath. Segal called me as I instructed him to, but then his fear took over. Either everything wore off or he just followed my instructions rather than my intent. The command was to call me, not to make sure I answered or to tell me what happened. I clearly don't know what I'm doing with Iron magic.

My gaze drifts to the lines of data on his computer screen. "You know if zahablan really works, it could help millions of people."

"I don't care about millions of people right now. I care about my little sister."

"I do too," I say softly.

"We need the phone number the man called from," Tracey says.

Segal puts his hand over his cell phone where it sits on his desk. "I have to do what he says. If you call him, he'll know I told you."

"We're not going to call him," I say. "We're going to find him and Kaleshia."

"How?"

"Same way we found you," Tracey says. "We can get the phone company to ping his phone without alerting him."

"I can't risk it," Segal says. "No."

I lean forward. "Deon, look at me." I feel the pull of Iron magic, but I fight it. Deon deserves to make his own choices.

He does. The hand that covers the face of his phone is shaking, but not budging.

"This man is a ruthless killer," I say. "He's already murdered two people. After he gets what he wants, he will kill again. The only reason he is keeping Kaleshia alive is because it is leverage on you to do what he wants. As soon as you do what he wants, he has no reason to keep her alive."

"Why would he kill her if I do what he wants? Won't he just release her?"

"I'm being honest with you. I can't know for sure what he will do, but the best scenario is for us to find her while you stall him, so he has a reason not to hurt her."

"But if he thinks I'm stalling, he might hurt her to make me know he's for real."

My stomach clinches. "That's a possibility. You need to convince him you are really trying, but that you have to do it right to keep it from being obvious that you're manipulating the data. And that requires time. If you want any chance of saving her, you have to help us and give us time."

His hand tightens again on the phone, hovers there and drops away.

"Okay," he says, "but I'm doing what he says."

"You do what you have to." Tracey picks up Segal's phone. "Let us do what we have to."

"Trust us," I say. "Our primary goal is to protect you and your sister."

"What's your phone password?" Tracey asks.

Segal gives it to him.

"You got a charger for this thing?"

He nods.

"Good. Keep it charged. I have a feeling you may be here for a while."

"I'm not going anywhere until it's done," Segal says.

"Did you tell him how long it would take?"

"I said a couple of days, but I can do it faster."

"Don't or don't tell him you can. When he calls back, stall him."

"Every minute I stall is a risk for Kaleshia. You don't understand. She needs her medicine."

"Segal, listen to me. Kaleshia is only valuable to him as long as you are *not* finished." I said this before, but he is in such a state, it didn't seem to really register. I stare hard at him. "Get it?"

Slowly he nods. "Yeah, I get it."

"Phone company is going to call me back as soon as they have the GPS coordinates," Tracey says. "Let's let Segal work."

We step out into the hall.

"What if Angola used a burner phone?" I ask.

"Unless it has no GPS whatsoever, which is rare and hard to find, they can still give us a location. They could also use cell towers to triangulate his position, but that would only tell us he's somewhere in a 20 mile radius. Not much help."

"What if Angola calls back?" I ask. "We need somebody here to record the call and protect Segal."

"Yep and it can't be just anyone."

"I agree. Angola could touch anyone not Stone or Rose, and they would do or say whatever he wanted." Suddenly suspicious Tracey is going to give me guard duty, I add, "I'm not staying here."

He scowls. "I'm not letting you go after this guy alone."

"Exactly," I say.

We stare at each other.

Chapter Fifty-One

A plainclothes officer shows up in jeans and tee shirt, my kind of uniform. He introduces himself as Allen Self from the Technical Surveillance Unit and quickly plugs a device into the phone that allows it to continue charging. It has a split wire, one end going to a recorder and the other to a pair of headphones.

"This is going to be a long watch," Tracey says.

Self grins. "That's what I do. At least this is in air conditioning and not a surveillance in a van oven." He makes a gesture in a semicircle. "We got eyes on this place. If Ponytail sets a foot—" He glances at Segal's long dreadlock braid. "Uh—"

Segal is completely unaware, lost again in his data.

"I got another man coming up here," Tracey tells Self. "Councilman Hobart."

Self lifts thin eyebrows and shakes his head. "No good can come from a politician getting involved in an investigation."

"It's necessary," Tracey says. "Keep him informed."

Self shrugs. "Gonna be crowded."

"Can I speak to you in the hall?" I say to Tracey.

He steps out, and I lead him out of earshot. "What the hell are you doing?"

"We can't be stuck here if something breaks, and we need to move."

"But a city councilman?"

"He's tougher than you think, and I told him to come armed."

"Faraday will have a cow."

"We can worry about that later. Somebody from Stone has to be here in case Angola or Jason shows up. My father knows how to handle himself."

"There's no reason for Angola to 'show up.' He's holding all the cards and that would be taking a risk he didn't have to take."

"I know. It's a long shot, but we can't afford not to have someone here. Hobart can pretend it's connected in some way to City Hall. I briefed him."

Tracey's phone chimes. He glances at it. "It's the phone company."

I grab a pen and a scrap of paper out of my purse.

"Go," I say, ready to write.

Tracey recites the longitude and latitude the phone company retrieved from pinging Angola's cell phone. I write it down and plug it into my map app.

"Oh my God," I whisper hoarsely.

"What?" He steps to my side to look over my shoulder. "Where is he?"

I swallow, half turning to look up at him. "He's at Alice's, I mean, Alice's old house—"

Tracey burns the pavement to Southside. I call Alice while we are in route.

"Hello," she answers in her Southern lilt.

"Irene, are you—is everything okay?" She will know by me calling her Irene that someone else is with me.

"Becca's the same, if that's what you mean."

"No, I mean, are the doors locked?"

"Of course. Why?"

"We've located the position of the man who murdered Dr. Crompton and his assistant."

"Oh my! Be careful."

"You don't understand. He's there, at the house."

"Here?"

"Yes and he's dangerous. *Very* dangerous." I want to let her know he is House of Iron without saying that in front of Tracey.

"Whatever you do," I say, "don't let him touch you or Becca."

"I see."

"We're on our way."

"I'll check the house," she says.

"No, don't do that. If you aren't aware he's there, then he's hiding, and we need him to stay put."

"Should we leave?"

I start to say yes, but stop. "Hang on."

I put her on mute and turn to Tracey. "There's no sign of him. Shouldn't they get out?"

"Normally, I'd say yes, but I don't want to alert him, and I don't know what he would do. He might try to stop them. Maybe he's waiting for us, so no. Tell her to stay put."

When we pull up, I'm out the door before Tracey can put the car in park, taking the front steps two at a time, my gun in my hand. *If Angola has hurt Alice or Becca—*

I knock on the front door to keep from having to fumble with the key, standing to the side out of habit, in case Angola decides to shoot through it.

From inside, Alice peers out from behind the curtain covering the sidelight. A moment later, she opens the door. Her hand grasps a full-sized umbrella with a pointed end. In spite of my terror, I can't help a grin. "Is there a body anywhere we should know about?"

She sniffs. "Not yet." She peers over my shoulder. "I'm glad you brought that big partner of yours. I moved a chair over the trap door to your room. That's where I've been sitting in case he's down there and tries to come up." She shakes the umbrella.

"You and Becca stay in the living room. Until we know where he is, I want you behind us." Becca is sitting on the couch, staring at the blank TV, Angel curled beside her, one paw on her thigh.

Tracey and I move from room to room. While he covers me from the doorway, I check the closets and under the bed. We search everywhere. "One more place," I say.

He looks up. "Is there an attic?"

"No, a basement." I move the chair and push the rug aside with my foot.

Alice's forehead wrinkles with multiple lines.

"What is this?" Tracey says as I pull up the trap door. "Was this some kind of safe house during slavery days?"

"I had the same thought, but the house isn't that old," Alice says. "I guess some folks had secret places for other reasons."

"There's no indication from the outside of the house that there's much of a basement. It's sunk into the ground on one side and looks like an unfinished area on the other."

"There's not a light switch until you get down the stairs," I say, taking out my flashlight.

"Let me go first," he says. "I have a vest on."

"Be my guest." I wave him ahead.

He moves cautiously. We always keep the house locked tight, in case Becca wanders. Not to mention the little thing about House of Iron periodically trying to kill me. But someone could have gotten in by breaking the back window to the unfinished portion of the basement and then entering the connecting door to my room. It's solid wood with a deadbolt lock, but a crowbar can defeat almost any lock.

When Tracey reaches the bottom and I illuminate the light switch with the beam of my flashlight, he flicks it on and exposes just enough of his face around the corner to sweep the room, gun close to his body.

"There's just the one room and a bathroom," I whisper. "And a dirt basement on the other side of that door." From where we are, the door looks undisturbed.

"Whose room is this?" he asks.

"Mine."

"You need a housekeeper."

I peer over his shoulder. It looks okay to me. I put all the dirty clothes in a chair. Making up the bed is a waste of effort when you're just going to get back in it in a few hours. "The bathroom will impress you."

When Tracey is satisfied that everything is clear in my room and the unfinished portion of the basement, we go back upstairs. I take a deep breath. Tracey calls the phone company and has them ping the number again.

As he makes his request, Alice looks at me. "You have his phone number?"

I nod.

The same coordinates come back, indicating that Angola is in the house.

"He's not here," Tracey says, puzzled. "Unless maybe he's outside or in a car nearby."

"Or," I say, chewing lightly on my bottom lip, "the phone is here but he's not."

"Why don't you ring it up?" Alice asks.

Tracey and I exchange looks.

"Not sure we want to give away the fact that we know his location," Tracey says.

I nod. "It could put Kaleshia in danger."

"Who is Kaleshia?" Alice asks.

"A little girl who's been kidnapped," I say.

She clasps her hands in front of her. "But if he's here, or his phone is here, doesn't that mean he already knows you are involved?"

She has a point. "She's right. We should call the number." I start to dig for my cell.

"Wait." Tracey reaches out, grasping my arm. "Narcotics has an untraceable phone. I'll get them to call the number."

I nod. "Better."

Tracey gets on his cell phone. A few minutes later, we hear a phone ringing.

Chapter Fifty-Two

The ring of Angola's phone is muffled, but it's clearly in the house.
"Get Becca and stay in the kitchen," I instruct Alice.

She nods, snatches up the umbrella, guiding a compliant, but otherwise unresponsive, Becca to her feet and into the kitchen, where Alice takes up a stand between her and the living room. Gun still in hand, I am staggered behind and to Tracey's side. We spread out and pause at either side of the entrance to the living room, sweeping arcs before us, even though not ten minutes earlier we cleared the entire house.

"The couch," Tracey says, following the ring of the phone that belongs to Angola.

No way anyone could be under the couch. It sits only an inch or two above the floor. I lay my pistol on the coffee table and pull up one of the sofa seats to reveal the cell phone, still ringing. A chill chases my spine. *How did it get there?*

"Irene, you got a plastic baggie?" Tracey asks Alice when it finally stops.

She brings him one, and he works the phone into it without touching it.

"Fingerprints?" Alice asks, peering over his shoulder.

"I doubt it," I say. "He's much too careful for that."

"Well, he left his phone. I'd say he's not that careful." Alice's hands find her hips.

"It wasn't left here accidentally," Tracey says darkly.

"It's a message, isn't it?" I look up at him.

"Yes, but it didn't deposit itself here . . . magically."

I wince at the subtle reference and bite my lip. Have to tread carefully and not forget to act stupid about magic in front of Alice. Tracey might think that Angola just knocked on the door, touched Alice, waltzed in, dropped his phone under the cushion and told her to forget the whole thing. Plausible, but it wouldn't have worked on her. That means it didn't happen that way. But Alice has never seen Angola. Did he come in under some guise or sneak into the house?

"Angola called Segal on that phone today," I say aloud. "He had to get it in this house after that and before we pinged him."

"No man has been in this house today," Alice says.

"Has *anyone* been here today?" I ask.

"Well, yes," she says. "That lady from the court."

"Tanya Melbourne?"

"Yes."

"Why?" I press.

"She said she forgot to have you sign one of the forms. She left it here for you. It's on the kitchen counter. I completely forgot about it with all this about a killer in the house."

Her eyes widen and I know she suddenly understands, as I do, that Angola must have intercepted Melbourne and used Iron magic on her, telling her to hide the phone surreptitiously in the house. I turn to Tracey. "Melbourne is the social worker who—"

"I remember her," he says. "She took Daniel after his mother killed herself."

I don't need to explain it to him either.

"But why?" Alice says.

"That is the question." I press my hands over my chest, trying to hold in the blooming fear.

"It is a message," Tracey says. "Angola could have tossed that phone in a dumpster. He orchestrated this on purpose, letting you know that he knows we are on his trail and—"

I finish his sentence for him— "That neither I, nor the people I care about are safe."

THE THREE OF US SIT at the kitchen table sipping tea.

"I'm sorry I don't have any coffee," Alice says.

"No problem." Tracey waves his hand. "I've had enough caffeine for the day."

I'm staring through the stained water into the leaves at the bottom of my cup. "How can I even think about bringing Daniel here?"

Alice puts a hand on my arm. "It's the best place for him."

I look into her contact-brown eyes. "What do you mean? How can you say that?"

"This Angola person knows enough to have made a connection with Ms. Melbourne. It doesn't sound as if Daniel is safe from him anywhere. This might be the best place."

"My cousin in the personal security business, Jamal Henderson, is, um, out of work at the moment." Tracey clears his throat, and I assume Jamal was the security guard contact who gave Tracey the key to Vulcan, and that he lost his job because of it.

"I think I can convince him to stay here for a few days while we track Angola."

My gaze flicks to Alice. She gives a barely perceptible nod.

"That would be great," I say. I have no doubt Alice would take a bullet for Becca, but having House of Stone here would mean two people between her and Iron's magic, not to mention someone who could shoot back if necessary. At night there would be the three of us.

"Thank you," I say.

WHEN WE ARE BACK IN TRACEY'S CAR, he twists in his seat to look over his shoulder before pulling out onto the narrow street. "Her secret is safe with me."

I stiffen. "What do you mean?"

"'Irene' is your aunt, your Great Aunt Alice, isn't she?"

"What makes you say that?"

"Hey, I'm a detective, right?"

I give away nothing, waiting.

"I know the stories about Alice. Come on, Rose. She was the last of your House. Everybody knew who she was. She was a short feisty woman with intensely green eyes." He glances at me. "Like yours."

My ears tingle with a sudden infusion of blood. "Irene's eyes are not green."

"They haven't made contact lens that perfect yet. Up close, anyway."

"Lots of people wear contact lens."

"Granted, although not many her age. The wig is good though. Real hair."

I say nothing.

"But *you* actually confirmed it," he says.

"Me?" I'd been so careful. "How?"

"When I offered to have my cousin stay."

I frown. "I don't get it. What are you talking about?"

"The first thing you did, the instinctive thing, was to look at her. Not something an employer would do with an employee. It's her house, isn't it?"

"She willed it to me."

"Okay, but then it would be your house, and you wouldn't have looked at 'Irene' for permission."

"Irene's part of the family now. I didn't want to bring a man, a stranger, into the house without her being okay with it."

Tracey pulls into a driveway, stops the car and twists in his seat to look at me. "I get it that she wants to be 'dead.' That's actually normal for us. My father is on his third 'life.'"

I feel the line of my mouth flatten in stubbornness.

"I'm House of Stone. We're sworn to protect House of Rose."

"Sworn? That's the first I've heard that word."

"Yes."

"You haven't been doing much of a job of it," I say, unable or unwilling to keep the bitterness from my voice.

"No, you're right. We haven't. And I have made mistakes."

"Such as?"

"Such as refusing to . . . court you."

"*Court* me? You mean try to have babies with me?" The flush, this time from anger, has spread from my earlobes to my cheeks and neck.

"Calm down, Rose. There is a lot at stake."

I don't calm down easily. I count to ten silently. That always sounded like stupid advice, but it actually works. I can make a sentence.

"I know what's at stake, Lohan."

"You understand why House of Stone would pressure me to—?"

"Yes, I understand." I want to stay angry, but Tracey has never made a move on me. He has always treated me as an equal, even in my rookie status. There is no basis to be mad at him. But I am anyway.

"Well, why haven't you?" I ask.

He meets my eyes. "Are you angry because my House wants me to court you or angry because I haven't tried to?"

"Yes. I mean, no. I don't know. How can we talk about this right now?"

"You're right. I'm sorry. I don't know why I brought it up. Your family is in danger, and a young girl's life is in danger. We need to be partners, to work together, to . . . trust each other."

I glare at him, but he is right and that is exactly what I meant, which somehow just makes me angrier.

Chapter Fifty-Three

"Lieutenant Faraday got some information back from the military," Tracey says, leaning over my desk.

"How?"

"They have a pretty sophisticated data base. 'Angola' isn't a common name. She sent a photo." He shows me the photograph on his phone.

"That's him," I say, "minus the ponytail."

"Angola Simone. Served in Iraq, POW, Purple Heart. Honorably discharged."

I straighten when he gives me the last known address.

"That's the Swann/Simpson mansion."

He runs a hand through his hair. "Headquarters for House of Iron."

"What do we do?" I ask.

He shrugs. "Go knock on the door."

"You know someone there is trying to kill me," I remind him.

"Which is why I am going without you."

"No way."

I DON'T RELISH setting foot inside this house. Only a few months ago, Becca and I were prisoners in the basement. And deeper into the mountain is a room with a solid iron throne where Theophalus Blackwell wiped Becca's mind and tortured me, and where I killed two men and burned a child to escape him. I shudder and Tracey glances at me.

"You okay?"

"I'm fine."

I take a deep breath. Jason lives here when he's in the country. I'm still chewing on whether Jason wants to make me his lover or kill me. Maybe both.

It's a mansion with a multi-gabled roofline and more fireplace chimneys than I can count. According to the Internet, the owner designed it based on English castles. Only two levels are visible from the front, but there's a lower level in the back and an extensive basement, not to mention at least one secret tunnel into the mountain.

Our knock brings a man to the door. My first visit here at the annual All Hallows' Eve party, Angola answered the door. This man I don't know.

"May I help you?" His accent is crisp, and I wonder if he is a Family member or an employee who followed them from England.

Tracey opens his badge case. "Birmingham Police. We're investigating a homicide."

"You'll want Ms. Blackwell."

He escorts us into the living room. We don't sit. We're in the enemy's den. My skin crawls.

Stephanie Blackwell makes an entrance. Another person would have just walked in, but drama wraps her like a 1950s movie star. She's wearing black slacks and a white tailored shirt with a striking diamond pin. Her shoes are red, open-toed heels, more sensible than the stilettos she wore at the All Hallows Eve party, but fashionable. Becca would have approved.

Stephanie extends a slender hand with nails that match her shoes to Tracey and introduces herself. Then she turns to me. "Lovely to see you again, Veronica."

"Rose," I correct. I never use the "V" part of my name.

She gives a gracious nod. "Rose, of course."

"We're here on police business," I say.

"Won't you sit down? May I get you something to drink?"

I stay where I am, but Tracey sits and cocks his head at me. Stiffly, I sit opposite him.

"No, thank you," he says to the drink. "We're looking for information on someone—Angola Simone."

"Why here?" she asks.

"This was the address he gave when he was discharged from the military."

"That was several years ago, I believe."

"Is he here?" I ask.

"No, I'm afraid not."

"We understand he's employed by Jason Blackwell, who does live here, right?" Tracey says.

"Yes, my nephew."

At Tracey's reaction of surprise, she smiles. "Thank you for the unspoken compliment. I'm his step-aunt. I married at a young age to Jason's uncle."

"I see. If you don't know anything about Angola Simone, we'll need to speak to your nephew," Tracey says.

"I'm afraid he's not here either."

"But I *am* here, Aunt Stephanie," Jason says from the entranceway. "I am always here for Rose."

He strides in and my heart rate accelerates, as usual, but he steps back to keep a distance between us. Good move. We both need to concentrate without sexual fireworks.

Tracey stands and they shake hands, a custom that gives Iron the convenient opportunity to touch anyone they meet under the guise of civility and manners.

"Good to see you again," Jason says to Tracey, his voice the shell of politeness. He gives a slight bow in my direction, his face hidden from the others. "And you—detective." His lips silently add, "*mio amore*."

My earlobes burn, and I wish I had taken Stephanie's offer for water.

"I was just about to leave for the airport, and Angola is bringing the car around." Jason pulls out his phone, his fingers dancing out a text message. "I'll have him step inside."

"A little old fashioned to have a driver, isn't it?" Tracey asks.

"Business takes me into some uncomfortable situations," Jason returns smoothly. "My uncle prefers I have a driver and a bodyguard. Angola has been both for several years."

"We would prefer you don't leave town while we're investigating this case," Tracey says.

"Not possible. It's critical family business. I will be out of the country for several months." He shoots an apologetic glance at me.

Tracey's mouth is set. "We don't have any legal grounds to compel you—"

The object of our search steps into the room. Tracey stops mid sentence. I've had lots of opportunities to watch cats over the last several months. Angola moves like one. Tracey and I both instinctively stand.

Angola settles into a military "at ease" stance with his legs spread, but his hands are clasped together in front of him. I have the feeling he can explode into action given the slightest excuse.

"I will leave you to your business," Stephanie says.

Angola does not move. Stephanie has to take an extra step around him, which I read as arrogance on his part or perhaps a general disregard for women, or maybe he is just focused on us—me, in particular. For a moment, I meet the disturbing intensity of Angola's gaze. Why is he staring at me? He has always avoided looking at me, but whatever was behind that avoidance seems to have dissolved. I am the sole object of his attention, and it's disconcerting.

"Angola," Jason says, "These detectives from the Birmingham Police Department wish to speak with you."

"Of course." He is all servant-polite now. No more staring.

"They want to ask you some questions."

Angola shifts his gaze to Tracey, his expression passive.

Tracey remains standing. "I understand you served in the military."

"That's right."

"What branch?"

"First Battalion, 7th Marine Regiment, 2007–08."

"*Semper Fi.*"

Angola stares at him coldly.

"Second Battalion," Tracey says. "Rawah, 2008."

Angola nods in acknowledgement and responds with the location where he was stationed. "Anbar Province."

"Tough place. You were a POW, Purple Heart. ISIS doesn't take many prisoners. What happened?"

"I took a hit, Haji overran us. I was left for dead. Made the mistake of groaning at the wrong time."

"Lucky you made it out alive."

"Sometimes I didn't think so."

His comment jolts me. I've read about ISIS torture—throwing gasoline on a prisoner and threatening to set him afire or cutting off someone's head right in front of the prisoner. Those were some of the comparatively nicer things. Angola's gaze flicks to me. He knows what I endured in this house. Despite myself, a kindred spirit briefly unites us.

"You are a person of interest in a murder," Tracey says calmly.

"Am I?"

"Did you know Laurie Stokes?"

"Can't say that I do, or 'did,' I assume."

"Can you tell me your whereabouts the day of April 10?"

He shrugs. "If Jason was out, I was with him, otherwise at home."

"Let me check," Jason says, looking at the calendar on his phone. "We weren't anywhere that night other than home."

"And home is?" Tracey asks Angola, taking a step closer.

I ready myself to back him up if necessary, suddenly feeling like the dog that catches the bus he has chased. What do we do? If we arrest Angola, how do we find Kaleshia? Unless House of Stone guards him 24/7, he can just walk out of a normal officer's custody.

"Not your business," Angola says tightly. "Are you arresting me?"

"He lives here," Jason says. "I was with him all that day, and I imagine my aunt can testify to that as well."

"Are you arresting me?" Angola repeats.

A moment of silent tension thrums between them. "Not at the moment," Tracey says and turns to Jason. "There is a young girl missing."

He frowns. "What do you mean?"

"She was kidnapped. We have reason to believe Angola might have been involved."

"That's ridiculous."

Tracey takes the photograph taken with the hospital security camera from his shirt pocket and shows it to Jason.

"That could be anyone," he says.

"Then you wouldn't mind us searching the house for her?"

"My uncle is technically the owner, but I stand for him in his absence. Yes, of course, you may. Angola and I will escort you."

"Angola is a suspect," Tracey says. "We'll have to detain him while we search."

We call for a patrol car and put Angola, searched and handcuffed, in the back seat with instructions to the officer watching him under no circumstances to allow physical contact with him.

Then we search every inch of that house, including the secret tunnel, at least the one I know about, and the iron chair room where I was held captive. Tracey actually searches it. I can't bring myself to step inside.

Chapter Fifty-Four

It's a big house and we are stretching the limits of legitimate "detention," but how long we can keep Angola depends on the reasonability of the circumstances. It's a big house. An hour later, we have found no clue that connects him to Kaleshia. We stretch the rules further to take him to headquarters and question him.

Unruffled, he denies any connection with Crompton, Stokes, the unregistered phone we found in Alice's house, calling Segal, or knowing anything about Kaleshia. Jason was right that it's impossible to make any kind of ID with the photo from hospital camera. Our "evidence" is built on a dead man's statement that would make no sense to anyone not of a House. We can't hold him legally.

We are both more than frustrated when we release him.

"I never thought I'd say this," I tell Tracey when we are back in our car alone, "but I'd be willing to get him somewhere alone and get it out of him." I'm imagining Tracey's big hand around his neck.

"Maybe we should have. We could try to kidnap him and have Stone hold him, but if we do that and can't get him to reveal where Kaleshia is, we risk her dehydrating or starving to death or dying without her medications. And that man has seen some torture. I'm not sure we could break him."

My fist clenches. "I'm willing to risk it, rather than just let him go."

"Let's try it my way first."

"What way is that?" I lean back in the seat, mentally and physically worn thin.

"I put a magnetic tracker on Jason's car."

I sit up. "I didn't even see you do that."

"I'm good."

"But what if Angola has his own car?"

"Then we're shit out of luck."

I lean back again and close my eyes. I'm unsettled by more than having to confront the room where I was held captive and tortured, even though I didn't actually go in it. Standing outside was traumatic enough. And what had I seen in Angola's dark eyes? It wasn't just that he was a murderer. It was something else . . . something personal.

"What did Angola mean when he said 'Haji' attacked him?" I ask. "I thought Haji was a holy pilgrimage."

"It is, but for grunts in Iraq, it means Arabs or Persians."

"He didn't break a sweat about being questioned."

"I imagine it didn't compare to interrogation as an ISIS prisoner."

"I'm going to check on Segal," I say, fishing my phone from my purse.

Segal answers on the first ring. "Any news on my sister?"

I start to tell him we just talked to the suspect, but don't. He is vulnerable to Angola's touch. The less he knows, the less he can say. Besides, I don't know how to tell him we had him, but had to let him go. Instead I ask, "Has he contacted you?"

"No."

"If he does, tell him you need proof that Kaleshia is okay. Not just her voice, you want to see her, a video of her."

"Yeah." His voice is shaky. "I will, and I'll stall him as long as I can, but this guy knows what I do, and he knows how long it should take."

I hang up.

"Now what?" I ask Tracey.

"Now we turn it over to the tech guys."

"What do you mean?

"I have it set up for them to follow Jason's car."

"Why didn't you tell me you were going to do that?"

He shrugs. "Had no idea I would have the opportunity to do it, just came prepared."

I want to sulk about that, but I recall the stuff I did without him— checking on his story about taking a class from Crompton, interviewing Crompton's wife and Laurie Stokes.

"I guess you owe me that," I say. "What do we do meanwhile? Shouldn't we follow too?"

"No, they have a couple of cars with receivers and can stay far enough away not to spook them. They'll report everything to me. I don't want them trying to apprehend either of them."

"No. That would be a bad idea. We could end up with more bodies."

He shakes his head. "Never thought I'd have to deal with House of Iron like this. If we do put him in prison—"

"I don't see how any prison could hold him. I'm surprised he didn't just use Iron magic in Iraq and walk out. Why would he let them torture him?"

"There are awful stories. As for why he didn't just walk out, I'm guessing he hadn't hit 'magic puberty' yet and didn't have the ability to draw on his power."

"How old were you?"

"Twenty-five. That's about average."

"I wonder how he did escape."

Tracey's mouth is a grim line. I wonder if he is thinking about his own time in the Middle East.

"Doesn't matter now," he says.

"What do we do while we wait for a development from the surveillance or from Segal's end?"

"I'm going home and taking a shower. I suggest you find some way to relax and get some rest, 'cause at some point this is all going to blow up . . . or go to hell."

THE ONLY POSSIBILITY OF RELAXING for me is a workout and swim. I make quick circuit in the weight room, happy to have it to myself. In spite of the fact that I wear sloppy clothes and pull my hair into a tight ponytail, sometimes I have to deal with some steroid-happy male.

Mindful that I might have to run out should I get a call from Tracey or Segal, I take my gym bag to the pool. My clothes and purse are inside. I wrap my phone in a big towel and place it as far from the pool's edge as I can reach, but I'm not worried I will miss a call. My waterproof watch will vibrate to alert me. Technology can be handy.

The pool is also deserted, the crystal-clear water perfectly still. I like how every sound echoes beneath the high ceiling. This is my place. A quick flip, twist and clip of my ponytail fastens my hair on the top of my head. I adjust my eye goggles and slip in. Sometimes I dive, but today, I don't want to disturb the water. I just want to be part of it. Already warmed up from the weights, I just push off and ease into my stroke. Overhead crawl to start. *Reach; pull; breathe. Reach; pull; breathe.* The rhythm takes over, and I let my worries shed away like old skin.

After the fifth touch of the wall, I pause at the deep end, gripping the pool's edge. My head lifts to find a pair of shoes edging the water line between my hands. I recognize them.

Angola says calmly, "What good fortune on my part to find you in water."

I rip my goggles off and look up, straight into the muzzle of a semi-automatic handgun with an attached silencer.

The laps have me already taking quick breaths, but I manage to say, "I take it you're not here to bring me to a dinner date."

The slightest smile cracks his stoic face. "I admire your spirit."

In the movies, this is where the hero gets a confession because the bad guy figures he has nothing to lose. There is no way I can get out of the water, and I'm dead if I don't. I have to do something.

"You arranged Crompton's death and killed Stokes, didn't you?"

"I did," he says. "Spirited and clever. It's a shame to have to kill you."

He wouldn't tell me that unless he intends to kill me. Keep him talking!

"And you kidnapped a child. That's pretty low. Is money that important?"

His mouth tightens. "Not money."

"What then?" The knuckles of my fingers are white gripping the pool's edge.

"Honor."

"Honor?" I almost laugh, but it would be a hysterical sounding laugh and probably get me shot. I swallow it.

"Something perhaps you would not understand," he says, narrowing his dark eyes.

"But I want to. How could honor drive you to kill?"

"Perhaps your partner could explain it to you if he were around."

Something about being in the military, then. He and Tracey were both Marines. *Semper fi*—always faithful.

He is standing between my hands. His forefinger is already curled on the trigger. The first pull on a semi-automatic is harder than the rest. No time to think about what to do. *Just do something.*

I slap my right hand against the inside of his right knee, pushing out and down, while my left pushes in the opposite direction on his ankle. As his support collapses, I pull my legs under me, planting the balls of my feet against the pool wall and pushing off as hard as I can, hanging on to his ankle.

His weight hits me, forcing me under. A metallic *thump* of discharge from the gun feels like a punch to my chest. The bullet slices though the water in a white-churn trail at an angle from me. Angola is on his back, his feet near my head. He wraps his legs around my neck. I've lost track of the gun, but the chokehold on my neck is the priority. He's applying pressure on the carotid arteries. Only seconds before I lose consciousness. Jerking my head down, I push up on his ankles, which forces me down and out of his grasp.

I'm free. He is overhead, a dark shadow. I kick away, trying to put distance between us. The density of the water will slow a bullet, but not stop it. A shock vibrates my chest as another spinning bullet tunnels by. This one much closer.

Angola drops the gun and swims at me, a shark zeroing in on its prey. I raise my feet to push him off. This time he grabs a leg and pulls. As he drags me toward him, my other foot pops him hard in the face. Blood erupts in rising globules from his nose. I kick free and swim for my life. With every stroke I imagine his hand on my foot, dragging me toward him.

At the shallow end, I heave out of the pool, arms trembling with adrenaline and exhaustion, roll from the edge, snatch the towel with my phone, and run, grabbing my gym bag off the chair in front of the door. Soaking wet, I dart through the lobby and out the door. Let the guy at the desk wonder. No doubt Angola will erase his memories with a touch.

In my car, I start to tremble and fumble for my purse in the gym bag. The first thing I do is put my gun on my lap. There's no sign of Angola chasing me. Maybe I killed him with that kick, and he is floating in the pool. Or maybe he is going to show up in my rear-view mirror like a zombie that won't stay dead.

Chapter Fifty-Five

I hit Tracey's speed dial and pull my car out of the garage next to the gym, fumbling for the token I fortunately got before I worked out. It seems to take forever for Tracey to answer and for my fingers to get the damn token in the slot. The gate rises like it's stuck in molasses.

"What's up?" Tracey says.

I pull near the Y entrance and get out, gun in right hand, phone in my left, dripping water in a puddle on the street.

"Angola just tried to kill me."

"What? Where are you?"

"Outside the downtown YMCA. He tried to shoot me in the pool. I think he's still in there."

"Did you call 911?"

"No. No time and—" I leave it hanging. He knows the dangers of having armed officers mix with Iron magic.

"I'll do it and I'm on my way. Sit tight."

I sit at Alice's kitchen table late into the night, trying to think. This is not the first shooting incident I've been involved in, nor the first time someone has tried to kill me, but the boldness of it has unnerved me. After I called Tracey, police cars descended on the YMCA. Tracey was there almost as fast and insisted on leading them inside, only to find the pool deserted. No one recalled anything unusual except a wet woman running through the lobby and the fact that the alarm for the emergency exit went off. Angola, no doubt.

Any blood from our encounter had dispersed in the pool. Angola apparently recovered his gun before he fled, but bullets and shell casings were found.

Since I didn't fire my weapon, I'm not subjected to being on Administrative Leave pending an investigation, though Faraday has ordered me home, but I'm afraid she will send me back to the department shrink. And maybe I should go. . .

I'm not sure if the man sitting on our front porch helps or if he is just marked as another future victim. Jamal is House of Stone. He is African American—not as imposing as Tracey, a leopard to Tracey's bear, but I have no doubt of his competence. He's only come inside the house to use the bathroom. Tonight, he will sleep on the couch.

Alice walks into the kitchen and hands me an official-looking envelope. "This came earlier."

I open it and read it. "It's from the court. The judge has declined our request for custody of Daniel. He's to remain in foster care. We have visitation rights, but he's not to step foot in this house."

I hand her the paper.

She drops into the chair beside me, her shoulders slumping. All three of her cats—Alexander, Boo and Charlie—have followed her into the kitchen. Boo and Charlie are weaving under her chair legs. Alexander, the cat that hates me, inexplicably is sitting by mine, probably planning an ambush. Angel is not in sight, sulking somewhere. She is not terribly happy sharing a house and me with three other cats.

"I'm sorry," Alice says. "Poor Daniel." She wraps her arms around herself. "Maybe you were right. Maybe it's better for him to have a fresh start."

"Maybe, but what about Becca? Without Daniel, I don't know that she can come back, even as far as she had."

I pick up the cup of tea and put it down quickly to hide the shaking. I was not going to worry Alice about what happened, but I need her to know how serious this is.

"Angola tried to kill me today."

She looks up, startled. "Angola? The man you think left the cell phone here? The one who is holding that child with cancer hostage?"

I nod.

"What happened?"

I tell her. She sits silently throughout, then her eyes fill with tears. "I have failed."

"What do you mean?"

"I tried to protect you, but I can't."

"Alice," I say, "I'm not a child anymore."

"You're terribly young."

"That may be, but my safety isn't your responsibility, and you're not a failure. You protected me when I needed you to. If you hadn't faked my death and sent me away, I wouldn't be here."

"But I feel helpless."

I know the feeling.

"Dances with Wolves" interrupts us. It's Tracey.

"Tell me some good news," I say into my cell phone.

"I would if I had any. Got a district attorney and a judge out of bed and they gave me an arrest warrant for Angola for attempted murder of a police officer and a search warrant for him and any info related to the kidnapping, but he's not at the mansion. We turned the whole place upside down. No Angola and again, no Kaleshia. Confiscated a couple of computers and that was it. Angola probably gave them a heads up."

"That must have taken hours."

"It did, because I had to check every room myself even after officers swept it, in case someone got 'swayed.' Damn complicated."

"The tunnel too?"

"Yes, of course."

"I'm sorry about before."

"What do you mean?"

"When we were searching that . . . room in the tunnels for Kaleshia, and I chickened out."

"Rose, awful things happened in there. I can't imagine what it was like. Forget it. You would have come in if I'd needed you."

Would I?

"What about the tracker?" I ask.

"The tech guys found it in a dumpster."

"He's always a step ahead, isn't he?"

"Almost. He obviously wasn't counting on you surviving the swimming pool encounter. Now he is having to lay low."

"And no word from Segal?"

"Not yet. Angola hasn't made any attempt to get in contact with him. We have no idea where his sister is or . . . if she's even alive."

I close my eyes, my stomach twisting. If she is dead or like Becca, how would I ever live with the guilt of that?

I can't just wait around. I have to *do* something. But what?

Alexander puts two paws on my thigh, butting his head into my elbow. I pet him with my free hand, the one that bears a scar from his claws. Cats are complicated.

"I'm going back to see Segal and relieve Hobart," Tracey says.

"I'm coming with you."

"No, you sit tight and get some real rest. You can take a shift with Segal later. He refuses to leave until he's finished."

"How is he staying awake?"

"Lots of coffee and some stimulants. Hobart says Segal sleeps in snatches with his head on his arms at the desk."

"He loves his little sister."

"Yeah."

Tracey doesn't say anything more, but even with that one word I can hear the tightness in his throat.

We disconnect.

Alice is blotting the tears from her face.

"I want to tell you something else," I say.

"I'm afraid to ask."

"Tracey knows who you are."

"You told him?"

"No, he figured it out."

"How?" She's indignant now.

"He's House of Stone and a good detective."

"Oh, dear."

"He understands why it's important to keep you 'dead.' I think we can trust him."

"Think?"

"How do you ever know for certain you can trust anyone?" That is why I have kept my life simple. Or why I've tried to. It isn't working out.

"Do you think I should get a gun?" Alice asks.

"No."

"Oh, good. I don't know that I could shoot anyone."

"Just keep your umbrella handy."

She nods. I meant it as a joke, but she is dead serious.

"Meanwhile," I say, "there is something else I can do or at least try to do."

She lays a soft hand on my arm. "I hope not something by yourself."

"I'm afraid so." I don't tell her it's the scariest thing I have ever done in my life.

Chapter Fifty-Six

"What are you going to do?" Alice asks, her elbows propped on the kitchen table, hands on her cheeks and worry lines pleating her forehead.

"Heal Becca, or try to."

She looks confused. "I've tried."

"There are some things I haven't told you."

She picks up Boo and strokes him, waiting.

"When I was held captive by Theophalus Blackwell, I discovered how to channel the power of Iron. That's how I escaped." I swallow. "How I killed him. I mixed the powers of Iron and the living-green."

Her eyes widen. "And—?"

"And it killed Blackwell and Paul and nearly killed Daniel. That's how he got burned."

Her face softens. "It wasn't your fault. From the shape you were in, I imagine you had no choice."

"I try not to think about it."

"What would have happened to Daniel," Alice asks quietly, "if you had not done that?"

I shudder. "Theophalus would have killed Daniel. I would have died, and Becca would have died, although she is little better than dead now."

"Before Nora killed herself in that horrid way, Becca was improving daily."

"But it wasn't really Becca," I say. "Becca is locked away inside her mind."

"Becca laughed," Alice says stubbornly. "She enjoyed things. She learned. She will again."

"She did, but it wasn't *Becca*. And she's not doing any of those things now."

"We don't know that time won't bring her back again."

"It won't," I say. "She was never 'back.'" I search for a way to make Alice understand. "It was her mind rebuilding a personality from scratch."

"How do you know such a thing?"

"A friend looked it up for me."

She frowns. "That man from House of Iron?"

"He has a name, Alice. Jason Blackwell." I don't know why I keep trying to make her call him by his name.

She sniffs. "Iron is Iron."

"Maybe, but he went to a good bit of trouble to find this information."

She purses her lips. "What exactly did he 'find'?" Her tone says anything from him is suspect, and I agree, though I feel what he told me is true . . . or maybe I just want it to be true.

"What happened to Becca is not unknown. Jason had someone find mention of it in an ancient book. It's a condition brought on by a person highly skilled in the Iron arts, someone like Theophalus Blackwell, and it's called a *tabula rasa*."

"That's Latin for a blank slate," she says, her frown now more thoughtful than disapproving.

"He said a *tabula rasa* inhibits access to a part of the brain." I try to remember the exact phrase he used, knowing with Alice's medical background, she will grasp the significance better than I. "The fronto-parietal network."

She nods, as if to herself. "That is the lobe of the brain believed to compile the elements of personality."

I let her think about it. After a moment, she says, "If you are correct, if that region remains blocked, the brain's plasticity might try to work around not having access to her personality by—"

"By creating a new personality," I finish. "But Becca, the person I know, would be lost forever."

Our eyes meet for long heartbeats. I want her understanding. She is all the family I have left. My adoptive parents were good people, a kind mother, and a father who was demanding, but wanted the best for me. Until they died, I didn't even know I was adopted. I learned it at the reading of their will. I was eighteen. There was money for college. I thought it was from them, but I later learned it was a trust fund that Alice set up when she sent me into foster care. Strangely, I felt closer to my father than my mother, but it was her death that devastated me, though I could not find tears. Both their deaths were hard, storms shaking the tethers of my life. When I learned I was not their real child, the mooring broke. I was alone. For the next four years, while I attended college, I drifted emotionally. And then I found family again.

Alice is my home.

"Is there anything to be done?" she asks finally.

"Jason said there is a possibility of unlocking the sealed area, but it takes the power of Iron. That jives with what Theophalus Blackwell told me, that only he could 'give her back,' but at the time, I assumed he was lying to get the rose-stone from me."

"Yes, you mentioned that was the reason he tortured you." Her eyes gleam. "I am so very sorry you had to endure—I don't even know what you endured. Do you want to talk about it?"

"No, not now. But does this information help you in any way to heal Becca?"

"I can't imagine how. I hope you are not considering letting anyone from House of Iron touch her again?"

"Never. But . . . *I* am."

She stares at me. "Using the power of Iron?"

"Yes."

"You believe this is possible?"

I take a deep breath. "I'm choosing to believe it's possible."

Her gaze searches mine. "Iron magic is what did this to her. How can it fix it?"

"I'm not sure," I admit. "But I have to try."

"Why now?"

"When Angola pointed that gun at me, I realized how fragile life is and how quickly it can be taken away. If something happens to me, there will be no one to help her, and she'll be trapped forever."

Alice says nothing, as if she knows there is more.

"And I've realized that all this time I've been selfish."

"Selfish?"

"I was afraid—" I take a breath. "Afraid of losing her. Even when Jason told me there was a chance to bring her back, I couldn't do it, couldn't even think of doing it."

"It is dangerous."

She doesn't say what I am thinking—I don't know how to use Iron magic. And I could force her deeper into darkness or inadvertently create a *rasa* that wipes her mind forever.

"I know," I say. "That's why I wouldn't risk it."

"I don't understand how that is selfish."

"Because Becca would say, do it. She would want me to take that risk, but I wouldn't . . . I was afraid for me. I didn't want to lose her."

"Of course you didn't."

"I was wrong. I thought friendship and love were about protecting someone you cared about, but it's not just that. It's about trust and letting go of them."

Alice's mouth pinches and she looks down at her hands where they have grasped mine. Then she looks back at me with gleaming eyes. "I understand."

"I'm scared, Alice."

"The only thing I can think to offer is that healing, in essence, is love. Yes, the energy of the living-green is involved, but it is love that guides it. I don't know how to command cells to express chemical messages or produce proteins to heal. I simply nudge them with love. Maybe that will help you in some way."

I nod. "Maybe. But I can't mix the magics."

"I understand that, but perhaps, at the core, magic is magic. Energy is energy."

". . . And love is love?"

"Perhaps," she says.

I stand. "I think maybe Becca's room is best. She feels secure there."

Alice follows me into Becca's bedroom.

She is sitting in the rocking chair where Alice put her this morning, facing the window, but her gaze is far away, if anywhere. A glass of water sits on a small table beside her. It's exactly the same level as it was when I checked on her an hour earlier. She will swallow reflexively when water or baby food is in her mouth, and her body responds when we sit her on the toilet, but that is all the interaction she has with the world. Even when I try to read her favorite books—nothing.

What would it be like to have my personality, my memories, inaccessible? I can't imagine. Is "she" in there somewhere, unable to get to the sensory information that is feeding into her brain? Does she know she is cut off? *Is she screaming in the dark somewhere?*

I have asked these questions over and over with no answers.

Angel has followed us into Becca's room. I sit on the edge of the bed and pick her up. Stroking her calms me, as does her presence at night when I drift off to sleep or wake from a nightmare. The jujitsu classes are also helping. It's not about being a badass or thinking I can handle every situation that might arise, but the training has somehow restored some of the confidence I took for granted before the Ordeal. I think it's rewiring my brain to overwrite the role of victim, a role I "earned" and played for the months I hibernated in Alice's house.

I'm not a victim anymore. And neither is the Becca I know. Somehow, I will gather the courage to do this.

"I think I'd like to have Becca's head in my lap," I say, giving Angel to Alice, who puts her down outside the door and closes it. Since I don't know how long it will take, we determine it's best for me to sit with my back against the headboard and have Becca lie on the bed. Alice helps get her into position with her head in my lap.

Becca is compliant. She has no preferences.

Alice sits in the rocking chair. "I'll be right here if you need me."

"Just don't touch us," I say. "You might reach instinctively for the living-green and that could be disastrous."

"I understand."

"I don't know what kind of reaction to expect."

She nods. "I won't touch either of you."

I sit for a while, trying to settle my mind, my fingers stroking Becca's white hair from her face. She is calm, peaceful. What I'm about to do might take that from her. *Stop.* I'm working myself into a ball of tension. I need to be as calm as she is. I need to focus.

I take the rose-stone pendant from my neck and hold it before me. For what seems like a long time, I stare down at it, losing myself in the intricacies of the cut red diamond. Each time a fear rises, I face it and then put it aside and return my focus on the rose-stone, the layers on layers of prisms. Is there a gleam of another color deep in the facets, a hint of blue? Red diamonds are not supposed to have other elements besides carbon, but this is not just a diamond, it's a Family stone.

Finally, I reach down into the earth, rejecting the pockets of bright coal that wish to give up the sun's billion-year-old energy. I'm searching for an iron seam. It's plentiful, and I connect with a dark line and pull its power into myself.

My fingers now rest lightly on Becca's temples, and I close my eyes, guiding a tiny trickle of Iron magic into her, trying to find her.

Becca?

No answer.

I go deeper. I have no idea "where" the frontoparietal network is or how to unblock what was done.

Becca?

Nothing.

Is she there in the darkness? Trapped? How can I find her?

Becca!

Only darkness, a stillness that seems unnatural. Despite my desire to stay calm and detached, despair fills me. She is gone. I've failed. I may have even driven her deeper into that place of darkness.

I open my eyes and look in desperation at Alice. "I can't find her."

"Try again." Her response surprises me.

"How do I reach her?"

Alice's lips purse in thought. "How do you find the living-green or the seams of iron?"

The simple question stuns me. "I don't know."

She nods. "Not by conscious thought. You don't know *how* to do that any more than you know how to create the series of neurochemical signals sparking the muscle contractions that make you able to pick up a glass of water."

I stare at her.

"Trust your subconscious."

Although she has tried to tell me this before, her meaning crystalizes. Alice really doesn't know "how" to use the living-green to heal. She only knows how to love.

Closing my eyes, I reach back into the darkness. *Becca,* I whisper, riding the energy of Iron into her mind, come back. I say it with all the love I have for her. *You are my best friend. I need you. Come.*

Silence.

For a long moment, I'm certain nothing has changed, but something stirs. I don't know what, but somewhere distant I sense a sound, although it's more a vibration. I should know what it is, but I can't quite—

"Rose!"

I open my eyes.

"Look," Alice says.

I look down. Becca's head is in my lap, my fingers at her temples. She is crying, her shoulders shaking, her hand at her mouth.

And then I am crying too. I vaguely remember that I don't cry, but deep sobs wrench up from my chest and my tears fall on her upturned face, mixing with hers.

Chapter Fifty-Seven

Perhaps I wept as a young child, but I don't remember it. All my life, I've clutched everything tightly inside. But when Becca sits up and wraps her arms around me, we both cry convulsively. Tears stream down Alice's face too. I have shed a tear over Becca once before, but I've never known the agony, joy, and release of weeping like this. The strange mixture wrenches giant sobs from me.

Finally, Becca pulls back and looks at me. "You came for me. You found me."

I cradle her wet face in my hands. "I'm so sorry."

Her white brows furrow. "Why?"

"I was afraid to come. Afraid I would hurt you more or lose you forever."

"No. You came. You came. That's what's important. That's all that matters."

Alice hands us tissues. Becca wipes her eyes, and I blow my nose.

"This is indeed the bee's knees!" Alice says. "I didn't think it was possible, but you did it!"

I'm glad she didn't tell me she didn't think it was possible beforehand.

"How—?" I ask Becca. "What was it like?" I don't even know how to ask what I want to know, but she understands.

"It was like being in a dark room. Sometimes I could glimpse things," she says, "but they didn't mean anything. I couldn't touch, see, or hear anything. I wasn't afraid. I couldn't feel anything, not even emotions. I just knew I was . . . lost."

It's a great relief to me that she wasn't terrified.

She keeps looking at and touching things—my face, her face, the hand-stitched quilt on the bed, the water glass. "I just want to feed my eyes and skin with everything."

After a while, Alice moves us all to the kitchen table, and makes us tea, her response to all things, good or bad, while she fixes breakfast, even though it's 3 a.m.

"I can't believe you're really back," I say, one hand on the handle of my teacup, the fingers of the other on Becca's arm, wanting to touch her as much as she wants to touch the world, to assure myself she is real. Now that the tears have been unjammed, they keep threatening. "You sat here so many times, but you weren't here."

"I don't remember anything after that horrid tunnel and a cave with an iron throne thingee and a man in a wheelchair."

"Mr. Black," I say. "That was Theophalus Blackwell. He touched you right after that."

"I don't remember."

I fill her in on the basics of what has happened since then. By the time I'm up to date, we are eating eggs, ham, toast and juice. Becca eats everything but the ham. I take a plate out to Jamal, who insists on standing guard on the porch. He has kind eyes and a ready smile, though I'm sure there is steel behind both.

"Thanks," he says, taking the plate.

When I return, Becca says, "I can't decide what is more awful, you being tortured like that or the idea that I've been eating baby food." She makes a puke-face.

I laugh and wrap my arms around her. "It's good to have you back."

"And," she says, "it sounds like I'm just in time to help you with this kidnapping case."

Releasing her, I spin around to Alice. "What have you told her?"

Alice shrugs. "She wanted to know what was going on."

"Becca, there's nothing you can do."

"How do you know that?"

"I just—it's very dangerous. And you need to rest."

"Rest? I've been resting for months!"

I take a deep breath. "Angola will kill you or wipe your mind again in a heartbeat and if he does it, it will be permanent."

She rolls her lower lip over into her mouth. "We can't not do something just to keep me safe. We have to help that little girl, Kaleshia."

"I agree," Alice says.

"Not you too," I say, throwing my hands in the air.

My phone buzzes with a text. "It's Tracey. He's just pulled up outside."

"There's plenty of food," Alice says. "Tell him to come in and eat."

I get up and meet him at the door.

"Sorry for intruding at a crazy hour. Hey, something smells good," he says.

"Breakfast. I have a surprise."

He gives me an appraising look. "Something better than being shot at in a swimming pool, I hope?"

"Much."

I grab his hand and pull him into the kitchen. "I want you to meet my best friend, Becca. Becca, this is Tracey Lohan, my partner."

"I remember him," Becca says. "He came to the hospital after you got hit by that car, but I forgot he was such a hunk."

"Becca!" My earlobes burn in embarrassment.

"Sorry. I'm just sayin'." She smiles up at the stunned Tracey. "You wouldn't happen to have a brother, would you?"

It takes him a few moments to respond. "This is wonderful. You're so—"

"Normal?" she finishes brightly.

He turns to me. "What happened?"

Though he addressed me, Becca answers. "She rescued me, of course. That's what she does."

"How—?"

"I'm not sure," I say. "I used magic and just called her." My hand flies to my mouth.

Tracey looks at Becca and then Alice and then me, his brows raised in a question.

"Becca knows about the Houses," I say. "And Alice knows about you."

He shakes his head, apparently nonplussed that I revealed who he is to Alice. "You just called her? That's amazing."

"Damned straight," Becca says. "But what about Kaleshia?"

"Yes," Alice says, "is there any news about the little girl?"

Tracey shakes his head again. "Nothing. We haven't heard again from Angola. Segal is working on the database, but he says he's almost finished. Got someone watching the mansion driveway with orders to stay back and just report any movement, and someone watching the tunnel entrance, but there could be other tunnels and ways in and out."

"He's keeping her somewhere," I say. "We have to find out where."

Tracey pulls a chair up to the table and helps himself to a plate. "I think that encounter with you at the pool might have shaken Angola. Don't think that one is accustomed to having his ass kicked."

I smile. "That's hardly the way I would describe the encounter. I barely got out alive."

"Have I met this person?" Becca asks.

"Angola? Yes, but not that you would remember. He's House of Iron and a killer."

Tracey's phone buzzes and he glances at a text message. "That's Hobart, reporting in. He's got another . . . person taking over with Segal."

"I'm glad someone is getting a little sleep," I say.

Alice puts on a pair of oven mitts and reaches into the oven for what my nose announces is biscuits.

"With a little honey, they will be breakfast dessert," Alice says.

"Who's Hobart?" Becca asks. "Is that like the City Councilman Hobart?"

"Yes," I say, my gaze cutting to Tracey.

Tracey clears his throat. "I'm House of Stone, and Hobart is my father."

Her eyes widen. "Really? You're a warlock? That's so sexy!"

A twitch of amusement tugs one corner of his mouth.

"I am. A warlock, anyway."

"What magic can you do? I don't think anyone ever said."

He shrugs. "I just have a little extra muscle."

Becca, elbow on the table, chin cupped in her hand, stares dreamily at Tracey. "I noticed."

"Becca—" I start and give up.

Chapter Fifty-Eight

I turn to Tracey. "Since everyone here knows who everyone is now, there is something I want to talk about. But first I need to speak to Deon Segal."

I call Deon's cell. "Segal, where are you?"

"In the same place I've been for the last three days," he says. His voice is ragged. It's 6 a.m. now. I doubt he's had more than catnaps over those three days. If I feel run over by a truck, he must feel far worse.

"I'm finished with the database," he says. "What do I do now?"

"Hold on."

I put him on mute and address Tracey. "Segal's finished doctoring the database. How do we get something into the news so Angola knows it's done?"

"I got that covered," Tracey says. "Story is written. UAB will post it as soon as I pull the trigger."

Becca's eyes widen.

"Figuratively speaking," he adds at her expression.

"We'll handle that when we have to," I say into the phone to Segal. "Until you hear from him, we aren't doing anything."

"Right."

"Get some rest." I click off.

"I've been really stupid," I say.

This gets everyone's attention.

"Angola seems to know where I go too easily."

"I've been thinking the same thing," Tracey says. "I can usually make a tail, and I was paying attention when we left the scene at Laurie Stokes's apartment, but Angola—at least I assume it was him or someone on

Team Kill Rose—followed us and took pot shots at us at Vulcan."

"And he showed up at the Y pool once before when I was swimming," I say.

"Really? I don't think you mentioned that to me."

"Jason wanted to talk to me."

Tracey's mouth tightens.

"It was personal. Angola said Jason had information on how to help Becca."

"You could have been walking into a trap." Disapproval stains Tracey's voice.

"I took the chance," I say. "That's on me, but without that information Becca would not be here, and you're all sidestepping the point."

Tracey leans back in his chair, which creaks under the strain, and crosses his thick arms over his chest. "Which is?"

"That he knew exactly where I was again."

Tracey looks thoughtful. "And unless he was staking out the YMCA, Angola knew when you went there today—or, I guess, that's yesterday now."

"Yes, and that was just an hour or two after you and I confronted him at the mansion."

"He decided to take you out." Tracey says.

"That has always been on his agenda," I say, "but the point is, *how* did he know exactly where I went?"

"Maybe he put a tracker on your car," Tracey says, "like we did his."

"I thought about that," I say, "and we can look, but we were in your car when we went to Vulcan. Remember? You had me drop mine off here."

He nods.

"What about your purse?" Becca asks. "If I were looking to know where a girl went, that's where I would put something. And, unless this tracker thing is clunky or heavy, God knows, with all the stuff in there, I wouldn't notice something in mine unless it interfered with finding my lip gloss."

In the house, I now wear my gun in a holster, but my purse is in the living room.

I retrieve it, placing it on the cleared table, and start removing items—a set of plastic handcuffs; a slender wallet with a zipper compartment for money; a wide-toothed comb; a compact; under-eye cream; a business card holder; my badge case; a small notebook; two pens; an empty holster that fits in the hidden section where I carry my gun; and a couple of gem clips.

"That's it?" Becca asks.

I shrug. "That's plenty. It's heavy enough as it is."

I upend the purse and shake. A penny falls out.

"I want to double check your car," Tracey says, "and mine. You're right. He knows our moves."

Alice picks up my empty purse. I look over the items on the table, pluck up the compact and open it. Nothing but powder. I empty the wallet, spreading out twenty-four dollars and thirty-six cents on the table.

"Did he or Jason ever have access to your purse?" Becca asks.

"Maybe at the pool the first time when I was underwater."

"Or on Jason's yacht," Tracey says. "We were both in the water for a while."

"Or even before that," I add, somewhat guiltily. "I felt that drink Angola brought pretty hard, and I think I left my purse on Jason's bed when I went below to whiz."

"Whiz?" Alice asks with a puzzled look.

"Pee," Becca says.

"I wouldn't be surprised if he spiked your drink," Tracey says grimly, "or just doubled up on the alcohol."

"I think I've found something," Alice says. She has the purse's cloth liner pulled out, exposing the seam at the bottom.

"Someone has sewn this bit here," she says. The thread is different. Setting the purse on the counter, she pulls out a kitchen drawer and digs around, producing a seam ripper. I flinch when she rips the liner open, but after a moment she produces a small rectangular object from the bottom of my purse and lays it on the table.

"I can have the Tech Unit take a look," Tracey says, picking it up, "but I'm willing to bet it's a GPS transmitter."

I pick it up and march it off to the bathroom, setting it on the back of the toilet just in case it's a mic transmitter as well. Let him hear a toilet flushing. Then I return to the kitchen.

"That means it probably happened on the boat, and he was prepared to do it quickly."

After a few moments of silence, Becca says, "Now what?"

"Now," I say, "we stop waiting for that son-of-a-bitch."

Chapter Fifty-Nine

Becca sits up. "A trap. Nice."

"This doesn't involve you," Tracey says.

She lifts her chin. "I was her partner before you were, and just because you have a lot of muscles, and I've been in a . . . coma doesn't mean you get to boss me around."

If I had any doubts that Becca's back, they have melted.

"Lohan," I say, "I don't want anyone to get hurt, but we need everyone on board, or at least their thoughts. You know we can't involve the PD. They're vulnerable to Iron's touch, and they would never agree to this."

"What exactly is 'this'?" Tracey asks. "I'm not sure I'm agreeing to it."

"The trap," Becca says, hands on her hips.

Tracey narrows his eyes at me. "A trap has bait, and I suppose you are the bait?"

"What else do we have? What else does Angola want?"

"He wants Segal to mess up the database."

"And Segal is doing that, but Angola has Kaleshia. He has all the cards, except me, and he wants that too. I have to be the bait."

"No," Tracey says.

"Why?"

"It's too dangerous."

"I'm in constant danger not doing anything. Angola is just waiting for an opportunity. I can't live my whole life in fear, afraid to go to the store, afraid to go to the swimming pool. I won't let him do that to me."

Tracey is silent. At least he is thinking. I hit him with the rest of it.

"And doing it now gives us a shot at saving Kaleshia. Even if Segal does everything Angola wants, we don't know that Angola will release her. He knows we're involved now, and he can't just kill Segal and make it all go away."

"What if we're successful?" Tracey says slowly. "What if we arrest him?"

I know what he is saying. No jail is going to be able to hold him.

We search each other's eyes, looking for the resolve to do what we have to do, even though it goes against everything we are and believe we are as police officers. No one will be safe from him. This is now House business.

"And what if he's acting under someone else's orders?" Tracey asks softly.

He means Jason. *Am I willing to kill Jason?*

"We'll face that if and when we come to it," I say.

Alice wrings her hands. "But how are you going to find that little girl if you kill the only person who knows where she is?"

I look at Tracey. He demurred before about trying to get info out of Angola, but I've never seen this look in his eyes. They are stone. He knots his hands into fists. "Oh, he will tell us where she is."

To SAY I'M A NERVOUS WRECK would be an understatement—heart booming, head light, breath ragged. It's early Monday morning. None of us have had any sleep. We don't have time. Tracey and I have called in sick. I'm sure that set the gossip tongues flapping.

I fumble my keys out of my purse, making sure for the third time that the tracker is there, and open the front door to my house. I haven't been here since the trip down memory lane. Angola didn't show up that time, and he might not this time, but he seems to have upped his schedule for offing me. I'm counting on that and on my partners outside, primarily Tracey, who has the back door covered. The house's rear door opens to a wooded area at the base of Red Mountain.

The front door is harder to cover but a less likely entry point. Jamal has that. He, Alice, and Becca are in a car backed up into the driveway of a house for-sale-by-owner down the street. It would not have been a good option in daylight, but it's dusk now, and there are no house lights or working streetlights nearby, a common issue in this neighborhood.

I lock the front door behind me, flip on the porch light and check the back door and windows. All locked, as I left them. All curtains drawn.

There is no basement. Angola will have no option but to try to break in. As soon as he's spotted, Tracey will call for backup from Jamal, and I'll unlock the back door where my Glock and I will add our "invitation" for Angola to step inside for a "come to Jesus meeting."

"Testing," I say aloud for the fifth time, making sure my blue-tooth device is secure in my ear.

"Loud and clear," Tracey responds.

We argued about how to communicate. Tracey wanted to use the Vice-Narcotics radio-to-radio channel, which doesn't bounce off a repeater, but I was afraid somebody from the detail might be nearby and pick up the transmissions, or worse, be using the channel for an operation. I opted for buying some walkie-talkies, but Tracey said those weren't secure either, as they all worked in a limited range of bandwidth. So we are all on a conference call connection. Simple, but it never occurred to me. It was Becca who came up with the idea. She'd set up conference calls many times in her previous job as a receptionist at an attorney's office, before she lost her job for hitting her boss with a golf club. He deserved it.

Jamal echoes Tracey's confirmation, "I'm in place."

Alice and Becca are silent, although they are listening too. They're to keep the line free for the three of us.

Once more I check the entire house, including closets and bathtubs, the dryer, and under the beds. There is no way Angola would be here ahead of me unless he can read minds as well as manipulate them. God have mercy if there is a House somewhere that can do that! A nervous burst of laughter at that thought elicits a check from Tracey.

"You okay?"

"Ten-four, just a bizarre thought."

"Want to share it?"

He knows what I'm feeling. He's a Marine, ex-Marine. It's the waiting part that's hard.

"No, just nerves. I'm going to set up my paints and give him some time to show."

"Remember we're right here, and Rose, we have your six."

I can't think of anyone I'd rather have at my back. I take a deep breath. "I'm good."

At least half my anxiety comes from fretting about what we have to do when we catch him. I can handle whatever Tracey has in mind. A few bruises or broken bones are worth saving Kaleshia. But after that? Despite my resolve and knowing it's what we have to do, I don't know if I can kill an unarmed man. I once shot a man in the back, but that is apples to oranges—he was about to kill my partner. This is different. It's not what I signed up for. I'm supposed to be the good guy. But what is the good guy now—someone who follows rules and laws laid out for normal people or someone who protects the weak?

I try to quiet my tumbling thoughts. I've been over and over the same worn grooves of thought all day, a substitute for sleep. It only comes out one way—turning Angola over to armed police officers or jailers equals more deaths. He is House. He is our responsibility.

Nixing another urge to search the house, I step into the sunroom. Curtains are drawn here too, but I have good light overhead and a standing lamp. My easel is set up in the corner, ready. Two whole walls of windows. It's a perfect studio, though it gets chilly in the winter.

I start a new palette, taking my time to dab the colors. Brushes are lined up waiting. The incomplete painting before me is dry, ready for another layer. I eye the water. Too bright. It needs depth. I'll work on that and the sky, try to lose myself and the sense of time that makes waiting so difficult.

It works. I'm actually startled at the third ten-minute check-in from Tracey.

"All quiet," I say.

"Here too."

"Likewise," Jamal says.

That's when I notice something is wrong.

I was so focused on making sure there was nobody hiding in the house, I missed it. The last time I was here, when I started this part of the painting, I wanted more afternoon sun, and I angled the easel to catch that from the windows. But now it's a few inches over, more like it is when I want morning light. My heart lurches and I knock over a brush.

When I bend to pick it up, glass shatters. I drop to the floor.

"Rose!" Tracey shouts in my ear. "What's happening? We got a window broken at the rear of the house, your studio."

I look up at the wall opposite the broken window. Level to where I was standing, a hole has appeared in the far wall. I'm wearing a bullet-proof vest under my shirt, but that shot had been aimed for my head.

"Sniper," I say. "Due south in the woods."

"Are you okay?"

My hand is clenched around the paintbrush I retrieved. The brush that saved my life. It snaps in my fingers.

Chapter Sixty

"He set it up," I say in a voice I thought would be shaky but is flat of emotion. "We failed."

"How did he know where you were in the house?" Tracey asks, giving me a ride back to Alice's. I take a swig of water from the bottle he offers me, happy to have something to hold on to.

"He's been *inside* my house. He saw my studio and moved the easel. Not far, just enough, I guess, to judge exactly where I would be standing relative to the window and line me up in his sights. He marked the window. I didn't see it because the curtain covered it, but it's a flimsy curtain. With the lights on in the room, he saw my shadow. If I hadn't bent over to get a brush on the floor—"

"But how did he get in? There were no signs of forced entry. The windows were locked. You checked everything twice."

"Maybe lock picking is listed on his resume."

He leans back. "Maybe."

"I feel stupid thinking we were being smart. He's known every move I've made. I kept getting these panic attacks out of thin air. But I think he's been watching me and maybe, subconsciously, I felt it. He knew when I went home before." I shudder, imagining him watching me paint. "He would have known at some point I'd come back and finish my painting. All he had to do was get inside, move the easel, and then just watch the tracker and wait for me to go home and turn on the light in that room."

Tracey shakes his head. "It's my fault. I assumed he would come into the house to try and kill you, but I knew he had a rifle and scope. Those shots at Vulcan were too accurate."

I set the cup down without drinking from it. "It's not anybody's fault. I'm just lucky, and I guess this answers another question."

"Which is?"

"Would the living-green protect me? When I was checking out that old mine entrance last year, I had a vision, a bullet moving in slow motion right toward my head. Seeing that saved my life. This time my clumsiness and a paint brush saved me."

"I don't have an answer for you."

"I don't think anyone has. Alice said we make the magic."

"I don't want to go too far into conjecture here, but if it's something that *you* make happen, how would you know that you need to get a warning?"

"Over my pay grade, but Alice also said there might be multiple universes and timelines. If somehow I can sense that— I don't know. I'm stopping there. *Jesus*, Lohan, it was my idea to set a trap. I could've gotten everybody killed."

"Angola doesn't seem to particularly want everyone dead. Just you."

I look at him. "And not just because I'm working on this case."

"This guy has been more than one step ahead of us and that's on me."

"Stop beating yourself up. We tried. The question is, what do we do now?"

"It's Angola's play now since you threw that tracker into the woods."

"Maybe I shouldn't have done that."

"I should never have let you be bait."

"You didn't 'let me.' It was my idea."

"We have to get you out of here, Rose. Someplace far away where Iron won't find you." He reaches over to lay his fingers lightly on mine.

"Like where?"

"I don't know. New Zealand or something."

"That's ridiculous."

"Why? Why is it any more ridiculous than your aunt faking her death to save her life?"

"Stop it. I'm not going anywhere."

"Why not?"

"Because I have a job to do. Because there's a little girl's life at stake."

He stares at me. I give him the rest of the truth.

"Because I belong here. This is my city. It's why I came back. I don't understand it. Maybe it's about the magic. I don't know, but I'm not bailing out."

"That's nuts."

"Maybe." I feel my mouth thinning into what Becca calls its stubborn set.

"You are exasperating," Tracey says.

"I've been told that before."

"I'm not letting my House fail again. I'm calling in our people. Even if they're not trained, Iron can't manipulate them, and they can help protect you."

"For how long? Muscles don't stop bullets, Lohan. You can't protect me."

The set of his jaw says he will die trying, and that's exactly what I'm afraid of.

Chapter Sixty-One

We regroup at Alice's and try to grab a few hours rest. Even as deprived as I am, sleep is an erratic thing. I keep bouncing in and out of nightmares.

My phone dings and I answer.

"I heard from him," Segal says hoarsely.

I snap awake. "When? What did he say?"

"He sent an email with a photo of Kaleshia. It's got a time stamp. It's current, about ten minutes ago. She's alive!"

"Where is she?"

"I don't know." Segal's voice rises in desperation. "I can't tell. She's just standing on something in front of a window. I can't see anything but the top of a bush. How am I supposed to know where she is? He says time is up. He wants to know I've finished with the database and then he wants you and me to come to him. Just us. No weapons. In three hours. Any violation, and he will kill Kaleshia." His voice breaks.

"Where?"

"He didn't say, he just said if I wanted to see Kaleshia alive we need to come."

"What number did he call from?" I grab a pen and scratch pad.

"I wrote it down," Segal says. He reads out the number, and I scribble it on the paper.

"Segal, don't panic. Message me the photo, and I'll call you back in a few minutes."

"Okay. Okay, but we gotta find her!"

"We will. We will find her. I promise." I hang up. *Damn you, Angola Simone. I will find you.*

I call Tracey, who is sleeping upstairs in Nora's old room. He sounds like his mouth is full of cotton.

"Logan," he mutters. "I mean, hello."

"I'm coming upstairs."

"What's happened?"

"Angola sent Segal a photo of Kaleshia with an ultimatum. He forwarded it to me, and I'm sending it to you along with the number he called from. I think we're out of time. We need to publish the results with UAB, or I'm afraid things will get nasty."

"I'm on it."

I examine the photo Segal forwarded of Kaleshia. She looks okay, if bald and too thin and needing to be in the hospital having her treatment is "okay." She's standing on something, a chair, I presume, since a windowsill in the background is at the level of her hips. A normal window would have been higher on her. Only a small patch of the curtain is visible. It looks familiar. I zoom in. The wooden windowsill has long grooves in it, like a cat used it for a scratching post.

I throw on my clothes, gargle to wash the nasty taste from my mouth, splash water on my face and go upstairs. Tracey joins me in the living room. Alice and Becca, hearing us, do as well.

"UAB was on standby to publish the trial results," Tracy says, "and it's being pushed out now. The phone number Angola used belongs to a convenience store. I've got the Tech Unit checking the email address, but it looks like a dead-end one to me."

"Doesn't matter," I say.

"Why not?"

"I know where Kaleshia is."

I find myself the center of everyone's attention.

"She's standing on a chair in my kitchen."

A moment of silence greets this. No one misses the irony. We were just there a few hours ago.

"She wasn't there when I was," I say. "I know that house, and I searched every inch, twice. Wherever he had her hidden, he's moved her."

"You can't go there," Tracey says.

"I have to."

"You'll be walking right into his hands."

"He'll kill you," Alice says, tying the sash on her bathrobe. "Think of what you're risking. It's not just you. It's the future of our entire House, of all the Houses."

"I can't let him kill Kaleshia or wipe her mind. Segal will insist on going too."

Becca, the only one of us who looks as if she's not allergic to morning, plops down in a chair. "I guess calling in a SWAT team is not an option."

"They're called a TACT team in Birmingham," Tracey says. "And no, that's not an option, even though it's a hostage situation. Getting law enforcement engaged with House of Iron elevates the risks of a bloodbath. This is our responsibility."

"Well then," she says. "We have to outthink him."

Tracey turns to her. "You got any ideas?"

"Not yet," she says, "but we have to stop thinking like there're no other solutions than to just walk in and surrender to him."

"Becca's right," I say. "Thinking only along the lines that Angola has given is just a path to death. There has to be something else we can throw into the pot. But while we're trying to figure out what the heck that might be—Tracey, can we get someone to run Segal here?"

"Sure."

"We need everybody's thoughts," I say, as soon as Tracey disconnects with Hobart. "What advantages do we have?"

"Witches," Becca says immediately.

"Place and time are his choices," Tracey says. "I don't like anything about this."

"But I know the place." I don't mention that it didn't stop him from turning the trap I thought I was setting against me.

"If something goes wrong," Tracey asks, "and Angola wipes minds, could you 'fix' Kaleshia or Segal like you did Becca?"

I shake my head. "From what Jason has told me, I'm pretty sure Angola doesn't have the expertise to make it reversible. Even if he could do something as complex as a *tabula rasa*, why would he? He has everything to lose if Segal confesses to manipulating that database. Not to mention, if we deliver ourselves into his hands, Segal would be a witness that Angola murdered me. I'm pretty sure he would permanently burn out their personality and memories."

"I think his ultimate plan is to kill them," Tracey says, "at least Kaleshia."

My gut twists.

Alice puts both hands to her cheeks in horror. "Why would he murder a child?"

"My guess," Tracey says, "is once he's killed Rose and maybe Kaleshia, he will wipe Segal's mind and set up evidence that lays both murders on Segal. Then the man with the ponytail will vanish. Very convenient. Only survivor left will be a man who can't testify about anything. It's pretty brilliant, actually. The photo we have from the hospital is too grainy for an ID, and investigators looking at real evidence Segal killed his sister might assume he sent someone to the hospital to retrieve her. It's known we interviewed Segal on a murder case, which gives him a motive to kill Rose."

"We can't let him do that!" Becca says.

Tracey scowls. "I don't see we have any choices here. If we don't play according to his plan—if Segal doesn't show or Angola sees anyone else—"

I finish the sentence. "He can wipe Kaleshia's mind. He would still have her life to bargain with and no one could pin anything to him."

"We can't let that happen either," Becca says. "We have to keep him happy. Keep him thinking he holds all the cards."

Which he does. . . Except maybe one— "We can't forget Segal in the equation," I say.

"He's a liability." Tracey frowns. "Soon as Angola puts a finger on him, he's a slave."

"What if," I say slowly, "there was a way to protect Segal from Iron magic?"

Silence greets this question. Then Becca says, "then Segal would be a wildcard."

"How?" Tracey asks.

"I'm not sure, but I was able to give additional living-green to Alice once. Do we know that a normal person can't receive it and hang on to it for a while?"

"Yes, we do," Alice says. "That's been tried many times. It doesn't work, I'm afraid."

I chew my bottom lip. "There might be another possibility."

"What?" Alice asks.

"In my mother's letter, she said the rose-stone was able to 'contain' the powers of the Houses. And you mentioned it was possibly a receptacle for magic in some way."

She nods.

"What if I poured living-green into the rose-stone and put it on a person, a regular person?"

Alice sits straighter. "You mean would it protect the person in the same way being a member of a House is protected against other magic?"

"Yes. I think you told me once that we can't help taking in the living-green, just by the act of breathing; it's in our cells. I'm betting that's what protects us from other magics."

"Well," she says, knitting her fingers together, "that is just a hypothesis."

Tracey looks at Jamal, who shrugs. "Don't ask me. I got no idea how witch magic works."

"Even if you can store the energy in the rose-stone, how would we know it would work against Iron's magic?" Tracey asks.

I clear my throat. "There's House of Iron in my woodpile." Everyone looks at me. "So, I can do Iron magic."

Becca's golden arches rise. Tracey looks stunned. I'd already told Alice, of course.

"Then there's only one way to know," Becca says. "Let's test it."

She is the only possible person in the room we could test. We don't have enough time to wait for Segal.

"What if it doesn't work?" I say.

"It's just a test, Rose." Becca's hands go to her hips. "It's not like you haven't used that Iron magic on me. You just said that's how you brought me back."

"That was different. I would have to try to manipulate you to test it." I don't know how to explain how abhorrent the idea is to me. *You're a hypocrite. You've used Iron magic before on innocent people.*

"I trust you. You have my permission."

I trust you. Becca has always trusted me. She followed me into hell. She trusted me to come after her in her own hell.

Reluctantly, I pull the pendant off my neck and cradle the rose-stone in my palm. "I'm not sure how to do it."

Alice unlaces her fingers and sniffs. "You have poured living-green into me. However you did it, I'd start that way."

Chapter Sixty-Two

I stare down at the rose-stone in my lap. As always, the intricate chambers draw me in. Alice says a red diamond's atomic structure is an aberration. Can power reside in a crystal? I remember vaguely Alice once going off on a discussion about certain crystals being used in old radios. The crystals receive energy and release them in a controlled direction. She said diamonds generally conducted heat but not electricity, but the blue diamond was an exception due to the presence of an addition element. Sometimes I think I catch a secret gleam of blue in the rose diamond's depths.

"We know it can 'hold' some kind of energy or at least respond to it," Alice says. "Remember the first time you touched it?"

I do. I look up to Becca to explain. "It sent out some kind of signal that all the members of the Houses apparently felt. That makes it a transmitter of sorts, right?"

She nods.

"Worst case, you destroy it," she says.

"No, worst case, I hurt Becca."

"Let's do it," Becca says. She glances at a clock. "We have two and a half hours before you have to be there."

I take a deep breath, center myself and reach down, seeking the familiar golden pool of coal. How ironic that coal is black on the visual spectrum, but its essence is a bright warm glow to me. I make a mental note to ask Alice if she perceives it the same way. I've never thought to ask her.

Almost effortlessly, I find a rich seam and pull it in. For a brief moment, I simply bask in it. This is what I was born to do, my inheritance from generations past counting. For a moment, the world is right.

Then I lay a finger on the red diamond in my lap and channel the energy I have pulled into myself into the diamond. It has depths I never perceived before, chambers within chambers, like the spiral of a conch shell. I walk it over to where Becca sits on the sofa and place it around her neck.

"Put it under your blouse," I say, "next to your skin."

She does.

"Do you feel anything?" I ask.

She shakes her head and shrugs. "Nope, nothing except the weight of it around my neck."

"Okay." I dump every bit of the living-green residue inside me I can find. If Alice is right, then I can't really get rid of it, but the less there, the less chance of inadvertently mixing it with Iron magic. The only time I did that, it was extremely difficult. I had to rip carbon from its chemical bonds with another element. I fear it would be much easier to combine it the second time.

Finding iron is no problem in Birmingham, but especially this near the foothill of Red Mountain. Unlike the gold of the living-green, iron's energy feels dark and viscous. I pull it in.

Standing in front of Becca, I touch a finger to her temple, focusing hard on restricting the flow to a tiny narrow channel. I'm well aware that too much can push her mind into a *rasa*, eradicate her beyond reach of any healing, any magic.

After the smallest amount I can manage to give her, I whisper, "Stand."

She looks up at me and grins. "Nope."

"It works," Tracey says. "I'll be damned."

"Angola is not going to be as restrained," I say, and we have no idea how long it will last.

"Try more of the bad stuff," Becca says.

"No."

"Then how are you going to know?"

"I won't, but I'm not taking any chances with you."

"But that's dangerous," Alice says.

I shrug. "It works or it doesn't. If it doesn't, we are only back where we started."

We bounce around other ideas, but the facts are what they are. We can't risk Angola hurting Kaleshia. Segal and I will go alone and unarmed. I'm placing my life and this whole thing in his hands. If he gives away that he is not under Angola's influence, any advantage will be lost. This is obviously not police procedure, but we are way beyond that.

We go over a map of the house and grounds I had drawn for our previous unsuccessful attempt at setting Angola up. The last time, entry was going to be a matter of timing. This time, we need stealth. "Lohan, if you can get the back door clear, that would give us an escape route."

"I'll cover the front," Jamal says.

A knock at the door makes us all jump. Tracey, hand on his gun, pulls back a sliver of the sidelight curtain. I relax when he moves to open the door. Segal comes in, escorted by a patrolman.

Tracey thanks the officer and dismisses him. Segal is a mess. It's apparent he hasn't given any attention to himself. A three-day sprout spots his chin, and he smells rank.

"Segal, listen to me," I say. "If Kaleshia is to have any chance, you have to do exactly what I say from here on out, even if it sounds strange, okay?"

He nods, his bloodshot eyes desperate for something to hang on to.

I check the clock. An hour and twenty minutes. "Do you have other clothes?"

He holds up a gym bag.

"Get in the shower and change. Don't worry about shaving. Got it?"

He nods.

"I'll show you the bathroom," Alice says, leading him down the hall.

We return to the map. I give Tracey keys to both doors of my house. "This one is the back door. I think that's your best shot. There's an outside A/C unit just to the left of the door and thick bushes. I've been meaning to clear them out, but haven't gotten around to it. If there's a guard at the door, take him out quietly and stick him in the bushes.

"I can handle that."

"If you hear gunfire, everything has gone to hell," I say. "And I would appreciate backup."

He puts both hands on my shoulders, standing close. I can feel his breath on my forehead. "If I could do this for you, I would."

"I know."

"Rose."

"Don't say anything sweet, Lohan."

He smiles and pulls me to his chest in a brief, restrained-steel embrace. "Okay."

Chapter Sixty-Three

At the second knock on the door, Tracey and Jamal pull their weapons. Alice is closest to the window.

"It's that Iron man," she says.

Both Tracey and Jamal move to either side of the door. "Angola?" Tracey asks her.

"No, I don't know what he looks like. This is the man who was here before."

"Jason," I say with a sigh. "She means Jason Blackwell."

Jamal moves the curtain aside. "I don't see a weapon, but he's facing the door. Could be one at his back or on an ankle holster."

"Don't let him in." I don't want to risk Alice's death being discovered a ruse. It's the only thing protecting her from Iron.

Tracey's hand goes for the doorknob. "I'll see what he wants."

"He wants to talk to me." I bite my lip, conflicting emotions sparking in my brain.

Standing to one side, Tracey opens the door. I move to the window, peering over Alice's head.

"Back up," Tracey orders Jason, his gun drawn and level with Jason's chest.

Jason complies, lifting his hands.

"Turn around."

There's no gun in his belt, but Tracey isn't satisfied until Jamal has patted him down.

When the search for a weapon comes up empty, Tracey demands, "What do you want?"

"I need to speak with Rose."

"Not happening. Tell me and I'll tell her."

Anger ignites in my chest, and I step out onto the porch and grasp Tracey's arm, which feels like holding a steel pipe. "I can make my own decisions who I talk to."

Tracey scowls, not happy. He takes a moment to process this, obviously wanting to stand between danger and me.

"Give us the room . . . or the porch," I say, knowing whatever Jason wants to say, he isn't going to say it in front of Tracey or Jamal.

Tracey knows this too. He's also aware that however much he doesn't like it, we can't afford to reject any information that might tip the scales of the encounter with Angola. The odds are ridiculously against us. He glances at his watch. "You've got five minutes. Anything more will put . . . our subject . . . in danger.

"I'm leaving the door open," Tracey adds loudly.

I don't need to turn to know my partner is standing just inside the threshold. Jason may not know Tracey is House of Stone, but Tracey's physical presence alone is intimidating, not to mention the gun in his hand.

As soon as I move into the radius of Jason's orbit, magic crackles between us. I think our hearts must beat together. Perhaps our brain waves are synced. I don't understand it any more now than when I first experienced it, and I was wrong. It hasn't gotten easier to resist. My thighs are wet. My lips actually ache. Every hormone in my body is switched on.

I step back, breathing hard. A twitch on his perfect cheekbones and a catch of breath tells me he is as much under the magic's sway as I am, and that gives me all the satisfaction I'm going to get at the moment.

He swallows and points to the chairs at the end of the porch. They are far enough apart to give us a buffer and far enough from the doorway for a private conversation.

We keep our distance and sit.

"I only have five minutes. Say what you came to say."

"You are beautiful when you are angry, *il mio amore*." A crescent smile. "You are beautiful when you are sad. When you are happy. Do you have any idea what you do to me?"

"I have an idea. But that better not be what you came here to talk about because I don't have time for it." I focus on a mental picture of Kaleshia standing on my kitchen table, a bewildered look on her face, dark crescents below her eyes. She needs to be in a hospital. We can't wait.

"I will never give you up."

"Jason."

"Yes, I know. It's just worth a minute of my five to tell you."

"Only four left."

He leans forward and I lean back. "Rose, I changed my flight to tell you that, as difficult as it is for me to believe—" He hesitates. "You are perhaps correct about Angola."

"You lied for him."

He sits back and shrugs. "He is House. I believed him."

"Why are you telling me now?"

"I thought, I believed, that you were mistaken, that he was loyal to me, but I confronted him when you left our house."

"And?"

"He has disappeared."

"And?"

"I think he has been masterful in letting me believe that he was loyal to me all these years, but my eyes are opened. Everyone gives their loyalty and life to the head of House, beyond any other interest or pull. This is our universe. It is the heartbeat of our Family. Without this, we would tear apart, and we are already threatened with extinction."

"By the lack of children?"

Surprise lights the blue ice in his eyes. "Yes."

I wonder if he knows why that extinction is happening or if he just knows that children have become very rare in his House. Even if I told him, he might not believe it. He's been brought up with the "truth" that mixing the blood of Houses creates abominations.

"Three minutes."

"What I am trying to say is that I believe the head of House of Iron has interests he has not shared with me. Interests that involve Angola and perhaps others."

"Samuel Blackwell?"

"Yes."

I first met Samuel at an All Hallows' Eve gathering shortly after becoming a detective. It's difficult to reconcile the short, cheerful man with a silver cane who referred to himself as "Uncle Sam," as head of House of Iron.

"What interests?" I ask.

"I don't know."

"Then why are you wasting my time?"

"You are also beautiful when you are in haste."

"Jason."

"I do not know Samuel's agenda, but it is possible the fear you divulged to me has a basis of truth."

"Which fear?"

"The fear for your life. The eradication of House of Rose."

"I already know that truth. Angola tried to kill me. Face to face."

He pales and his hands clench. "When?"

"Recently. It doesn't matter."

"Rose, I can't protect you here. You must leave this country."

Strangely, the same thing Tracey said. "And go where?"

"I don't know yet, but I purchased an extra ticket to Rome. I must leave. Samuel has given direct orders. Come with me, *amore*. Once we are there, I will figure out what to do."

There is a part of me that wants to say yes and just walk away from what waits for me, fly away with him. Give in to the magic. A very strong part.

"That's sweet, but no can do."

He really does look devastated.

"Tell me then what to do," he says. "You have no conception of the power that is against you."

What would happen if I told Jason that Angola was a spider with a web spun at my house? And that he was demanding his prey come to him or he would kill an innocent child . . . or worse?

I don't know the answer to that. He's just told me that he is not the one who pulls Angola's strings. Even if he offered to go there himself and try to talk to Angola, it would be a useless effort and only put him in danger too, not to mention pissing off the spider. The stakes are too high to do that. I also can't risk him getting an attack of conscience and telling the head of his House what our plans are.

"Jason, I'm not going with you. I can't. Don't waste your breath trying to persuade me. All I can say is that I am . . . not easy to kill."

A wry smile. His mouth tightens in reluctant decision. "Then I must go alone." He consults his watch. "My plane departs in three hours. You have my number if you change that stubborn mind of yours. I will hold the ticket."

I nod.

"Take care, *amore*." He reaches across the gap between us and lightly brushes my lower lip with his fingertip. I don't try to stop him. I can't stop the spike of sexual electricity or the thought that I'm an idiot.

Chapter Sixty-Four

Inside, I lean against the door, trying to get my breathing under control, and glance at the clock. Segal is in the shower. We have a little over an hour before we need to leave.

Tracey stands at the window, watching, I'm sure, to make certain Jason is actually leaving.

"Lohan, we need to talk."

He glances at me. "Okay."

"Alone."

He follows me to the kitchen, but I don't sit. Instead, I pull back the chair and rug and lift the trap door below it.

His brows rise, but he says nothing, following me down the stairs to my bedroom.

"What is it?" he says, stopping at the threshold of my room. "Have you changed your mind? Rose, I'll back you on that. It's a crazy plan."

"No, I haven't changed my mind. At least, not about that." I look up at him. "I need to ask you something."

Worry furrows his brow. "What?"

"When you said your House—I assume your father—pressured you to 'court' me—" I clear my throat and lift my gaze above his chest to meet his eyes. "What I want to know is: Did you want to?"

"What?"

"Did you want to? I mean, would you have wanted to without being pushed into it or if we weren't partners—?"

He hesitates a moment, I assume processing what I'm asking. Then he takes a step toward me and cups my forearms in his hands, hands that could crush the bones there without much effort.

"I would have wanted to, Rose." His voice is low, though we are alone.

I can feel his breath on my forehead, the steel beneath his careful grip. "Is that the real reason you told me you were House of Stone?"

"What?"

"You told me who you were in spite of the fact that you were specifically told not to."

"Yeah?"

"You said you did it because of Laurie Stokes, and you didn't want someone else to die because I was hiding my abilities to see things."

"That's right."

"That's not all of the reason."

"You've never met a guy you didn't want to psychoanalyze, have you? So tell me why I told you I was Stone." He closes the distance between us. Our voices seem far away, like seagulls crying against the roar of waves.

"Because you wanted me to know. You knew I would fight against the 'plan,' and you wanted it to be my choice, an honest choice."

"You're a pretty good psychoanalyst." He hesitates. "Is it your choice?"

"I don't know what I want for the future but, I may die today and that means an entire race of people will disappear off the face of the earth."

His thick brows tug down in confusion. "I don't understand. If you die, that will still happen."

"If I live, if I come through this— I know that's a long shot. I know it's not logical, but I need to make a decision now."

His grip on my arms tightens incrementally, his breath stirring my hair. "Why now?"

"Because now is when I have the courage to decide."

Somehow I'm against his chest, as solid as a rock wall shaken by the thunder of his heartbeat. Or is it mine?

"I'm not making any promises about tomorrow, Lohan. I'm just asking for this one hour."

His fingers rest light as a whisper on my lips. "Stop," he says. "Stop talking."

Chapter Sixty-Five

I have no idea if that hour with Tracey will bear any fruit, but for a little while, I actually forgot to be afraid. Whatever happens, I don't regret it. It was hard to leave his arms, even though I knew they were a temporary haven.

But that is now the past. The present requires me to get out of the car and walk up the pathway and through the front door of my house.

Weeks ago, when I stalled at walking through Alice's door back to my job, I was afraid of the unknown. I know what waits for me on the other side of this door, and it calls for courage I don't have. Fear is front and center, banging away in my chest, but it's not a panic attack, just your run of the mill, scared-out-of-your-mind terror. That I'm willingly walking into the hands of House of Iron and almost certain death is beyond my rational comprehension.

It has not been a rational day.

In the end, I open the car door because Segal is here, willing to march into hell for his little sister. He's counting on me to get us out of this alive, and the odds are that I can't. It's that simple. We will both die. The Houses will die. Kaleshia will die. Or, if they're "lucky," their brains might just be wiped clean, as close to dying as you can get and still walk around. And if I live and they don't, I will suffocate from the guilt.

It's dusk. Too early in the year for the crickets, cicadas, and toads to chorus. Too early for the fireflies to swing their fairy lanterns. The two streetlights on the block that aren't out are on. A man in a tee shirt and sweatpants walking his neatly groomed sheltie passes us on the side-walk. The normalcy of that makes me want to scream.

Segal and I are alone. No guns, no communication devices. Angola will check for them. I quench the desire to look up the street to see if Becca is in position. She's not supposed to move until we're in the house, but the urge to check is as strong as an itch. Jamal is with her. Hobart is stationed halfway up the other side of the street.

"You good, Segal?" I ask as we slowly walk up the path to my front door.

"Not good," he says, a lot of breath in his wavering voice, "but I'm here."

Depending on an unraveled computer geek with no training is not my idea of the best plan, but it's what we have.

I suck in a breath, trying to keep it inaudible, and knock on the door before I can turn tail. It opens immediately. The person who opens it is not visible, but Angola is.

"Come in," he says. "Punctual. I appreciate that."

He's standing to the side of the door, a semiautomatic with an attached silencer in his hand. I wonder if it's the same one he used on Laurie Stokes or at the pool. He took the time to dive for it before climbing out, not worried about making up an explanation to anyone. All he had to do was get out of the building before the police arrived and things got complicated.

The man who actually opened my door closes it as we enter. I recognize the sun-bleached hair and dark tan—Lawrence, pilot of Jason's *Iron Fist*. He too is holding a gun, and it's aimed at my stomach. Half of me wants Jason to be here too, just to dissolve the tension of whether he is in on all this.

I lift my hands. Segal follows my lead.

The door closes behind us. It has always stuck a little, and Angola has to give it a push to close it. He flips the dead bolt.

"Where's Kaleshia?" I ask.

"First things first," Angola says. He puts a hand on Segal's arm. "You will be silent unless spoken to and not move unless I tell you to. Do you understand?"

"Yes," Segal says.

I have no way to know if the rose-stone is protecting him or if I've lost him.

"Stand against the far wall," Angola directs him.

Segal walks woodenly to the wall.

"Search her, Lawrence." Angola says, nodding at me.

Lawrence hands him his gun to hold and approaches me with a grin. "I've been looking forward to this."

"And I'm looking forward to kicking your teeth out your ass," I mutter.

"Hands higher." He moves behind me.

I lift my hands.

"Spread your legs."

Earlobes burning, I comply.

His hands travel slowly over my shoulders and chest, lingering on my breasts. "Just checking for wires," he says, brushing my nipples. I hold my breath when he slides his fingers around my waist. He takes his time as well on my hips and butt and the inside of my thighs. I try to concentrate on my breathing, reminding myself that anything I do will put Kaleshia and Segal at even more risk.

"That will do," Angola says tightly. "Cuff her." He tosses Lawrence a pair of steel handcuffs.

I put my hands behind me, not resisting but not helping him further either. If he doesn't know thumbs up is the best position, he can figure it out on his own. I tighten the muscles of my hands and arms while he fumbles with the cuffs. Theoretically, that will give me a little leeway when I relax. I doubt he will bother to double lock them or that he even knows how.

"What's taking so long?" Angola says sharply.

Lawrence gives the cuffs a cruel squeeze, biting them into the skin. When he is finally finished with me, Lawrence searches Segal, a much quicker process.

"In the kitchen," Angola orders. "That way."

I grit my teeth. "I know the way."

"Follow her," Angola tells Segal.

We proceed to the kitchen, which is adjacent to the living room. The smell of cinnamon and coffee wafts to my nose, a mixture that would be comforting under normal circumstances. But this is not a normal circumstance.

I want to grab Segal and shake him to remind him to follow orders. This is the first test. If he reacts verbally to seeing Kaleshia, we are up a creek without a paddle.

My story to Segal was that Angola is an accomplished hypnotist and an egomaniac who thinks he can hypnotize anyone quickly, and that it was critical for Segal to act as if he was completely under Angola's influence. It was a more difficult challenge to convince Segal that he needed to wear a piece of jewelry in his underwear. I was counting on the fact that a man, even a man searching for weapons, normally does not like to go feeling around another man's privates. Tracey told Segal the pendant had a microphone hidden in it.

In the kitchen, Kaleshia sits on one of the four wooden chairs, her back to the window where Angel has worn claw-sharpening grooves in the sill. When he sees his little sister, Segal stops dead. His face is momentarily out of Angola's view, but not mine. His mouth silently forms a word—*Cheerios.*

Joy lights the child's too-thin, too-pale face at the sight of her brother, but she doesn't speak. Angola has probably ordered her to be still and silent.

Relief cascades over me. Angola has not permanently wiped her mind . . . yet. If Tracey is right, he plans to kill her, wipe Segal's mind, and, oh yeah, kill me. I am the main target.

Angola puts a hand on Segal's shoulder and orders, "Sit in a chair, and be quiet." He turns to me. "You too."

Segal sits between Angola and Kaleshia. I choose the chair on Angola's other side where I can see Segal's face, the window, and down the hallway to the back door.

As soon as I sit, terror descends. *Chair. Handcuffs. Theophalus. A cattle prod.* I'm glad I went to the bathroom before we left Alice's because my body might betray me as a coward. Reflexively, I draw in the living-green, taking comfort in the warm rush.

But it doesn't prevent beads of sweat from moistening my hairline. My breath is jagged and shallow. *I can't give in to the terror. I can't. The little girl sitting at this table needs me to think.* I bite the inside of my lip, hard enough to taste blood, forcing my mind out of past terrors to the here and now, which is terrifying enough.

"Lawrence," Angola says, "check the back and then cover the front. You see any police or movement of any kind, let me know."

Is there is a third goon at the back? If so, Tracey is supposed to take him out quietly. Becca will signal as soon as he has and the back is cleared. But I don't know how long Angola wants to gloat or how long the rose-stone will protect Segal, if it is working at all. If I scream, Tracey will come in, but I'm not letting him barge in to certain death or put the hostages at risk and both of those look likely to happen.

"Who knows you're here?" Angola asks me.

I shrug and try to make my voice normal. "You said to come alone. We came alone."

"That is not what I asked." His cheek twitches. He is House of Iron. I don't think he's accustomed to not getting direct responses.

Stall him.

Tasting blood, I choke out a question. "Why should I answer your questions when you won't answer mine?"

His mouth curls in a tepid smile. "You continue to surprise me, Rose."

His attention is a physical pressure, not the magic-induced attraction of Jason's presence, but a connection that runs deep, a subtle accelerator on my already thudding heartbeat. I have no idea what it is or why I feel it, but I realize it has always been there in my subconscious, unacknowledged.

He takes a step closer. "What do you want to know?" His tone is light, almost playful.

His eyes are not playful. He is going to kill me.

Shouldn't he be distancing himself from me, making it easier to pull the trigger? Instead, I feel as if he is devouring me in some way and, despite my terror, or maybe because of it and the impending intimacy of death, something inside me is . . . responding.

"Who is behind this and why?" I ask, playing the outside game we are engaged in.

He snorts. "I think you know why."

"Then who do you work for?"

"The man who saved me."

Time. I need time.

Behind my back, I'm working my fingers under my untucked tee shirt. One key fits all cuffs. I wore a handcuff key on a necklace after I heard about a patrol officer handcuffing his rookie to the steering wheel as a practical joke. But the one time I truly needed it—during the Ordeal when I was cuffed to an iron chair deep underground—I couldn't get to it. I've rectified that by taping a key to the interior edge of both the front and back of my underpants. I wear briefs, and the waistband is not actually on my waist, but sits below it, not a place of interest for a weapons search or a pervert's fingers, and the thickness of the band hides it. Brilliant, if I do say so.

But if I drop that key, or they notice my movements, I'm in big trouble and not so smart. Working the key loose from the tape and into the lock is going to be extra tough since Lawrence gave the cuffs that sadistic squeeze. They're pressing on the nerves. My hands are already starting to tingle. Twisting them to try and get to the key is going to make it worse. I have to move fast, but fast is the enemy in this tricky maneuver.

My fingers find the slender key on the inner edge of my panties in the small of my back and start prying the tape. I'm counting on the key sticking to the tape until I can get it into position.

"The man who saved you," I repeat. "Saved you how?"

He ignores the question.

Slowly. If you fumble the key, it's all over.

Lawrence returns from the hallway that leads to the back door, and I freeze. My hands are covered by the tee shirt. Will he check them?

Without a second look at me, he passes through the kitchen into the living room, and I release the breath I was holding.

A moment later, in the window behind Angola, a car's headlights flash on and then off. Becca's signal. Tracey has cleared the back door.

Unworried about me or Segal, Angola sets his gun on the table and picks up the to-go coffee cup, taking a sip, his gaze locked on mine. Despite the other people in the house, we are alone.

Segal doesn't move. Is he with me or in Angola's power? Following a "suggestion" enforced by Iron magic doesn't strip you of your personality. Just because Segal mouthed "Cheerios" to Kaleshia doesn't mean he is not in Angola's thrall. He was told to be silent and not move unless told to, and he has obeyed that. I can't depend on him.

I keep my gaze on Angola. He said someone saved him. He's got to mean when he was in Iraq.

"Didn't the Marines come to get you when ISIS took you prisoner?" I ask.

I've obviously hit a button. This time the question seems to distract him, momentarily breaking that dark river coursing between us.

"No Marines came." Sarcasm slices the words. "*Semper Fi.* I was there two weeks. In the day, they tortured me for information. At night, they tortured me for fun."

I've peeled the handcuff key from the tape, pinching it between thumb and forefinger. I've practiced this, but it doesn't always work. In fact, most of the time I drop the key, something I failed to tell Tracey when I sold this stupid plan. I know by feel where the lock hole is supposed to be, but hitting it just right takes repetition and luck. My sweat-damp fingers aren't functioning well. *Damn Lawrence.* The tingling is moving into numbness. I'm losing feeling. If I don't get these cuffs off soon, having a key will be useless.

"You are not a stranger to torture," Angola says, and I hear a strand of respect in his voice.

I meet his gaze. A mistake. I may drown in the storm in those dark eyes.

"You have guts in this world of cowards. I don't like having to kill you."

I make my mouth move. "Then why do it?"

"Because he saved me—not my buddies, not the Marine Corp. *He* did. My House. He walked in and took me out."

"'He' is Samson Blackwell, isn't it?"

"I owe him everything for that."

"Even your conscience?"

"I have no conscience. It's a made-up word for a made-up society." He moves closer. We are locked together again, carried by the same current.

"I think you understand that," he says.

His acknowledgement of the undertow between us has given it strength, and I realize I do understand. I understand the darkness in him because it's my darkness too. I've known it all my life. I've just not been able to name it. I knew it when I saw the blood on my sister's blanket. I tasted it when the tall man threw a lit match into our bedroom window. Even as a five-year-old, I knew I would kill.

Doesn't every police officer have to come to this place—a place where you're ready to pull the trigger, to take a life? Maybe that is why friendship outside those in law enforcement or the military is difficult. We know we're different. We know inside, we are darkness. We wield death. It is recognition that thrums between Angola and me. At our cores, we are the same. Angola is a killer. His military training honed that in him, the torture released it. I am not who I thought I was. Being a police officer, helping people, is what I do to fight that darkness, to keep it at bay.

I have killed. I will again.

Slowly, Angola moves his hand toward the table, turning his head and his gaze from me.

I swallow, forcing back my distaste for what I am and what I am willing to do. I may be a killer too, but right now, Angola is the one with the gun. With my failure to get the handcuff key into the lock, panic builds. It's hard to breathe. Dizziness assaults me. All the progress I have made dissolves in an instant. I suck living-green.

Time freezes. The people in the room double into rippling shadow-figures. Helpless, I watch as a shadow-Angola sets down his coffee cup in slow motion and picks up the gun from the table, stepping toward me and holding the muzzle an inch from my forehead. His finger starts to squeeze the trigger.

From me erupts what looks like a corona burst of roiling hot gases. Angola screams, his face beginning to melt. The inferno widens, engulfing the room, including Segal and Kaleshia. And it keeps expanding—

No!

Reality snaps back and with it the realization that I've also drawn Iron magic. Without my conscious awareness, I'm already starting to swirl it with the living-green.

Angola's face tightens. "I do what I have to." He sets down his coffee cup and picks up the gun, stepping over to stand before me, the muzzle an inch from my forehead.

I fight for control of the forces inside me. The quantity of both magics that churn there feels unlimited. I have no idea the reach of such an inferno—the house, the block, farther?

My finger and thumb stab, searching for the handcuff keyhole.

"In front of a child?" I ask, desperate for seconds I don't have.

"She won't remember it."

Chapter Sixty-Six

It's the hardest thing I have ever done—to clamp down the compulsion to expel the black and gold magic burning inside me that edges toward conflagration. Perspiration weeps down my face, salting my tongue. My hands are cold, stiff. The bite of the steel on nerves has numbed them, especially my right one, the one bent to the limit allowed by the cuffs while I try to execute the delicate maneuvering to get a tiny key in a tiny lock hole. I have to be close, but the muzzle of Angola's gun at my forehead is even closer. *I'm going to die or the magic is going to erupt and kill Segal and Kaleshia and God knows who else.*

The key finds the hole. If it's not double locked, I just need one twist, but there's not enough time—

With a loud, wordless scream of rage and fear, Segal launches himself at Angola. Surprised, Angola turns toward him. They both crash to the floor.

Knocked off its course, the gun fires—a sharp bite into my right shoulder.

The handcuffs are unlocked, but still closed. I drop a knee in Angola's bladder. He groans, incapacitated for a moment.

"Get Kaleshia out!" I shout at Segal, scrambling to my feet and wrenching off one of the loosened cuffs.

Lawrence appears, his gun arcing from me to Segal, trying to ascertain the threat. I grab a kitchen chair with my left hand and throw it at him. My right, useless, hangs at my side, the cuff dangling from it.

The chair in Lawrence's face knocks him off balance, one hand tangling in the vertical back rungs and buying Segal seconds. Segal takes them, scooping Kaleshia into his arms and running with her down the hallway toward the rear door. Ahead of him, the back door flings open. Tracey's bulk fills the doorway. I've never been as glad to see anyone in my life. Lawrence disentangles himself from the chair and whirls to face Tracey.

Tracey meets Segal and Kaleshia. With a shove of his bearlike arm, he pushes them behind him, giving them a path to the back door.

I can't stop Lawrence and Angola at the same time. Angola is closest to me. He rolls to his side, his gun hand lifting—

I kick his wrist, knocking it aside, but he doesn't release the gun. Instead, he brings it back in a swing and smashes it against the side of my shin, taking my leg out from under me. I fall across him, trying to ignore the pain in my shin and grapple for his gun with my left hand. Without much effort, Angola throws me aside.

Another gunshot freezes me.

Lawrence's back is to us, but the view down the hallway is enough to see a hole in Tracey's shirt. Even with a bulletproof vest, a gunshot, especially at close range, will knock a man down.

But Tracey Lohan is not a normal man. He staggers back a step and then launches straight into a stunned Lawrence. That's all I have time to see, and I pay for the moment of distraction. A hand grabs my hair, yanking my head back. Still on his back, Angola presses his gun to my neck.

I have no idea if he intends to shoot me or hold me as a hostage, but I'm not waiting to find out. I slam my left elbow into his armpit. There are a lot of nerve endings in an armpit, I have learned.

Crying out, Angola rolls onto his side, his arm and gun cradled beneath him, out of my reach. Adrenaline courses through me. I scramble to my feet, this time stumbling down the now empty hall. I'm not sure where Tracey and Lawrence ended up, but I'm sure Angola is going to come after me. Killing me is priority one now.

Crouched low, I stagger toward the back door. Escape that way beckons, but I'm not leaving Tracey. Gunshots follow me, biting holes into the plaster walls on either side of the narrow hall.

Making a sharp left into my bedroom, I belly dive for the bed, reaching inside the pillowcase for the five-shot revolver I keep there. Pain stabs my shoulder for the first time since I realized I was hit. Orange spots dance into my visual field. I roll off the bed, putting it between the door and me. A trail of crimson blood stains the white cover.

Crouching, I grip the gun in my weaker hand, resting it on the mattress, and aim it toward the doorway. The throbbing right arm doesn't work. The left is shaking.

Breathe.

You can do this.

Breathe.

I'll get one shot, one chance. I lift the muzzle until the front sight is roughly between rear sights, though it won't stay put and dances like the spots in my vision.

Angola, no doubt thinking me trapped and unarmed, steps into view in the doorway. I fire twice. The first shot hits his collarbone, spinning him. Recoil jerks my weak hand off target. My second shot digs into the wooden doorframe beside him.

He disappears. By the time I get around the bed and peer out into the hall, it's empty. The back door is standing open.

Angola Simone is gone.

Tracey!

Hugging the wall, I stumble back toward the kitchen, trying to ignore the now excruciating pain in my shoulder. I talk to myself to keep focused. *Don't blunder into the room. Check it first. You can't help him if you dance out into plain view and get shot yourself. Use your head.*

At the entranceway to the living room, I position myself behind the right edge of the wooden frame, exposing just my gun barrel and only what I need to let my left eye peer down the sights and take in the situation.

Tracey turns to face me. Behind him, Lawrence lays on his stomach, hands cuffed behind him. He looks unconscious.

"I wanted to do that," I say, dropping my arm and panting out the words. "I hope you hit him hard."

"I did." He eyes the seeping blood on my arm. "You're shot!"

"I'll live. You okay?"

"Vest caught the bullet. Angola?"

I sink into my sofa, snatching a handful of tissues to slap on my shoulder. "Wounded, but he got away, unless Hobart snagged him."

"I told Hobart to intercept Segal and Kaleshia and get them to Becca and Jamal. I imagine Angola took off through the woods." We exchange a look of frustration and foreboding.

Police sirens sound in the distance.

"I better call it in." Tracey pulls out his radio and gives his individual call number and the address. "Shots fired. 10-24. Need paramedics and a supervisor."

"Crap," I say leaning back against the pillows. "We better get this story together before Lieutenant Faraday hears it."

Chapter Sixty-Seven

Tracey and I are working off a two-week suspension for failing to notify the dispatcher and call for the TACT team to handle a hostage situation. The days off are mild punishment compared to Faraday's scathing tongue-lashing. We survived that.

There are now two warrants out for Angola's arrest for Attempted Murder of a police officer as well as one for Kidnapping. Yet another search of House of Iron came up empty.

A handful of days into our suspension, I am sitting at Alice's kitchen table, one arm in a sling. Alice places her hand on my shoulder as she bends over to put a cup of tea before me.

"Oh, my!" she says.

"What's wrong?"

She hovers a hand over my belly. "May I?"

I nod, and she rests her hand on my abdomen, closing her eyes. After a few moments, she beams down at me.

"A girl."

"What are you talking about?"

"You are pregnant, dear."

"How is that possible to know—?" I catch myself. Magic, of course. Witch magic.

A tumble of confused emotions assault me. Primarily panic. *What have I done?*

"Don't tell anyone, please. I have to . . . think about it."

BECCA, ALICE, AND I KNOCK on the door of a one-story house on the eastern side of town. It's middle class, smaller than the older homes on Southside, but the yard is well kept with pink climbing roses along the fence.

Mrs. Bourdages waves us in. Her husband sits on the sofa, an acoustic guitar in his lap. Other than the spread of toys, the room is neat and perfused with the unmistakable smell of melting chocolate. I breathe in the intoxicating odor, but my attention is on the boy sitting on the floor, playing with toy action figures.

Daniel looks up and sees us. "Gran-gran! Becca, Rose!"

He runs to Becca first, grabbing her legs and pressing his face against her. She squats, getting eye level with him. Her memories of the time she was locked away in her own mind have only sporadically returned, but Alice and I have told her how Daniel appointed himself her caretaker.

"I missed you, Daniel," she says, hugging him.

My newfound tear ducts get into gear.

"I missed you too," Daniel says and looks over his shoulder at his foster parents.

"It's okay to love a lot of people, Daniel," Mrs. Bourdages says at his worried look. "The heart can make room as big as needed."

"Indeed," Alice says, approvingly.

Daniel turns to her for a hug and I'm next.

Mr. Bourdages is on his feet and extends his hand. "Welcome."

"Would you like some coffee?" his wife asks. "Or tea? I'm about to take some chocolate chip cookies from the oven."

Two hours later, Tracey joins Alice, Becca, and me at Children's Hospital. We ride the elevator to the cancer floor. I can feel Tracey's gaze on me. We have not spoken about what happened between us. I meant what I said about no promises, and he is giving me space. Alice has been true to her agreement to let me work out the pregnancy thing myself.

Segal sits on a reclining chair beside Kaleshia's bed, a book open in his lap.

Kaleshia starts when we walk in. I worry that the sight of me might trigger the terror she has lived through.

"Hi," I say. "You know the bad guys are gone, right?"

She nods.

"And your brother is a hero."

Her eyes widen.

"He risked his life to save me and you."

"Really?" she says, awe in her voice as she turns to Segal. "Deon, you're a superhero, just like Spiderman and Wonder Woman?"

Segal grins. "Sort of, I guess, but don't look for me to be swinging on a line outside your window."

"Young man, I think I have something of yours." Alice pulls a small object from her purse and offers it to Segal. "A finger drive, I believe."

"Thumb drive," he says with a grin. "Yeah."

I smile, not sure if this is part of Alice's fake persona or not.

"What's on it?" Tracey asks.

Segal smiles. "The original database before I started messing with it. I made a copy."

My mouth drops in surprise. "Then we get to see the real results of the zahablan trials?"

"That's right," he says. "Soon as I get back to work, but I'm not leaving this place until Kaleshia's treatment is over."

"And you have to finish the story," she says, pointing to the book.

It's the one I gave Segal for her, our copy of *The Glob*. I'll get another one for when Daniel visits.

Alice moves closer to the bed. "That's a very good story," she says, leaning over her to look at the pictures and putting a hand on Kaleshia's arm.

"Oh," Kaleshia says. "That's nice."

I step between them and Segal to distract him and give Alice time to do what she is doing.

"I think she's going to be fine," I tell him. "That is one strong little girl."

He grins. "Yeah, Cheerios is something else."

"When you get well," Alice says to Kaleshia, "we expect a visit. There's a young boy I think would like to meet you. He likes superheroes too."

WHILE WE WAIT FOR THE ELEVATOR in the hall of Children's Hospital, I stare out a large window at the western skyline stained with magenta and orange streaks. I want to hold that image and paint it later.

Lawrence and the man Tracey took out who was guarding the back door of my house are both in jail. Whether or not they stay there depends on whether they are House of Iron or just employees. I still don't know if Jason is involved in any of this, but no matter what he feels for me, his first priority is to protect his House.

Angola is out there. I don't believe he will mess with the drug trials again, not after the publicity, but it's open season on me.

I rest a hand on my belly. I fully expected to die when we marched into Angola's web and not to have to worry about actually having a child. Now that I haven't died, I have to decide what I'm going to do. For up to ten weeks into the pregnancy, there's a pill combo I can take to induce an abortion. I made a visit to a clinic shortly after Alice's pronouncement and have the pills in my purse. It's not fun and involves painful cramping, but my life would be back to being mine. I wouldn't have to worry about being a mother and a detective, or changing diapers, or that my child might hold the powers of a *Y Tair* and the potential to destroy city blocks. Not to mention worrying about keeping her alive and out of House of Iron's clutches.

I step back from the others who are taking in the beautiful view, dig in my purse and pull out the bottle, staring at it for a long moment, thinking about what Angola forced me to acknowledge in myself— what I am capable of. Then I take a deep breath and chuck the bottle in the trash dispenser by the elevator.

Looking back at the crimson city skyline, I keep the hand on my belly. I made a child for the sake of the Houses, to keep a unique people from dying out, but now it's not about them. It's about her. Silently, I make a promise to the child growing in me. I will do everything in my power to make sure she gets a chance at life and whatever it holds for her.

—END—

Photo by Robert Thorne

T.K. Thorne's childhood passion for storytelling deepened when she became a police officer in Birmingham, Alabama. "It was a crash course in life and what motivated and mattered to people." In her newest novels, *House of Rose* and *House of Stone*, murder and mayhem mix with a little magic when a police officer discovers she's a witch. Both her award-winning debut historical novels, *Noah's Wife* and *Angels at the Gate*, tell the stories of unknown women in famous biblical tales—the wife of Noah and the wife of Lot. Her first non-fiction book, *Last Chance for Justice*, the inside story of the investigation and trials of the 1963 Birmingham church bombing, was featured on the New York Post's "Books You Should Be Reading" list. Her newest nonfiction is *Behind the Magic Curtain: Secrets, Spies, and Unsung White Allies of Birmingham's Civil Rights Days*. T. K. loves traveling and speaking about her books and life lessons. She writes at her mountaintop home with a horse in the back yard and a cat and dog vying for her lap.